PRAISE FO  D0629033

"Hoskin's pessimistic narrative voice [is] bleakly transfixing, and his quickly paced plot will keep readers guessing until the very last page."
Publishers Weekly

"Irreverent, gritty, and poignant when it needs to be, Bystander 27 is a bloody blaze of a read that peels back the familiar trappings of a super-hero tale to explore loss, revenge, and the power imbalance when cape-wearing gods walk the Earth astride us mere mortals."
Pierce Brown, author of *Red Rising:*

"Rik Hoskin's Bystander 27 is a novel equal parts mystery and action that will appeal to fans of comic books and graphic novels."
Brandon Sanderson, author of *Mistborn* and *The Stormlight Archive*

"An epic and furious adventure!"
Alan Philipson, contributing author of the *Deathlands* series

"*Bystander 27* is a twisty page-turner that freaked me out and kept me guessing. Rik Hoskin, you are SuperScribe! Bring on the sequel!"
Nancy Holder, New York Times bestselling author of *The Wicked Saga*

"Wow! What a ride! Twisty, sneaky awesome book of superheroness with a dash of humor, mystery and thriller and completely different than anything you've ever read. Fun stuff! For comic book fans, for Marvel fans, for *Dr. Horrible Sing Along Blog* fans."
Patricia Briggs #1 New York Times author of the *Mercy Thompson* novels

Rik Hoskin

BYSTANDER 27

**ANGRY
ROBOT**

ANGRY ROBOT
An imprint of Watkins Media Ltd

Unit 11, Shepperton House
89 Shepperton Road
London N1 3DF
UK

angryrobotbooks.com
twitter.com/angryrobotbooks
No shoes, no shirt, no cape

An Angry Robot paperback original, 2020

Cover by Kieryn Tyler
Set in Meridien

ISBN 978 0 85766 859 2
Ebook ISBN 978 0 85766 860 8

Printed and bound in the United Kingdom by TJ International.

9 8 7 6 5 4 3 2 1

PART 1
Construction Lines

Everything changed when Hayes' wife died. He was waiting for her on the corner of Sixth and West 24th Street, close to Madison Square Park, and she was late. That was Melanie all over, late could have been her maiden name and marriage hadn't changed her one iota.

There was the other *late*, too, the one that had been good news for her and for Hayes and the reason they were meeting here today.

"Quo," she had said one night over dinner, "I'm late."

Hayes had looked up from the pasta he was working around the plate with his fork, a frown materializing on his forehead. "Late for–?"

"Late," Melanie had replied. "Late-late."

He looked at her, trying to make sense of the words she was saying, as her brown eyes the color of Turkish coffee looked hopefully into his. She looked beautiful then, more beautiful even than the day they had got married, eight weeks after he had got his discharge from the service. "You mean... we're going to be... a mommy?" he said, knowing the words were jumbled and wrong, knowing she would laugh.

Except Melanie didn't laugh, she smiled. She smiled a smile that engraved itself on his heart in that moment, and he realized that they were both going to be parents. "Yes, Quo," she said, nodding. "Isn't it... perfect?"

"It is," Hayes had replied, and he had reached across the table for her hand, leaned forward and kissed her. She had tasted of pre-packed pasta and sauce from a jar, and of their future.

That had been seven months ago, and now Melanie was in her third trimester, her belly distinctly ballooning, and they were meeting with her gynie in a clinic off Sixth Avenue to make sure everything was going okay. And she was late.

Melanie Hayes, nee Monroe, had graduated in social sciences from Columbia and had gone into advertising. Hayes had met her in her final year at an employers' fair, he there to represent the US Navy, she dressed for a party along with a gaggle of her friends, none of whom had any intention of signing up. But they had got talking somehow, an attraction flitting between them like a spark trying to catch fire, and when her friends sauntered off to check out the jobs in fashion and media and computers – shooting Warrant Officer Jon Hayes those judgmental looks that students have for "warmongers" as they went – Melanie had stayed.

"Do you swim?" she had asked, running a hand self-consciously through her long, dark hair.

"Yes, ma'am," Hayes had replied with the unambiguous abruptness of the Navy.

"I mean, privately," Melanie said. "You know – for fun."

Hayes had smiled, thinking of how he and his school friends used to sneak into McGinty's pool not so very long ago. "Yeah, whenever I can."

"My parents have a pool," Melanie said. "I mean, we do. I live with them." She had cursed then, a rising blush turning her pale cheeks pink.

"Where is that?" Hayes had asked.

"Jersey," Melanie replied, pulling a face that made Hayes laugh.

They had spoken more, exchanged numbers, and when he was on leave, they had met up and found that they enjoyed more than just swimming together.

Now, Jon Hayes was thirty-two and Melanie was twenty-nine, and they were about to have their first child. And Melanie was late.

Hayes checked his wristwatch. 11.07. They had arranged to meet here at 11, so that they could walk together to the clinic for the 11.15 appointment, and not have to rush.

Standing at the street corner, his back to a wall, away from the sidewalk traffic, Hayes withdrew the phone from his pocket and checked its suddenly illuminated screen. There were no messages. He could phone her, but he knew Melanie, knew it would not make her any faster.

Hayes had served in the Navy for eleven years before his honorable discharge. He had done two tours of Afghanistan and had chased all over South America in the name of Uncle Sam. The Navy had made sure he was always on time, and it was a habit that his civilian life was never going to break. Civilian life was paced differently, but he would always be that guy who turned up ten minutes early, shoes shined and pants pressed. He prided himself on it.

Melanie still approached life the way she had at uni, sleeping in at the weekends while Hayes was jogging the streets or on the treadmill in winter, arriving for the movie after the trailers had finished, catching the train as its doors played their closing serenade of beeps. In anyone else it would have driven Hayes mad, but Melanie was Melanie and he loved her for it.

He was still looking at his phone, its screen going dark, when he heard the explosion. He turned, along with everyone else on the block, and tried to locate the source of the noise.

For a moment there was nothing. And then, between towering skyscrapers two blocks away, a distant figure cut through the sky trailed by a familiar streak of light.

Excitement and fear ran through the crowd as they recognized the flying figure. Dressed in white with gold accents at the cuffs and matching boots, the flying man was Captain Light, hero and savior, protector of planet Earth. For a moment, Captain Light seemed to just hover in the air, forty stories above the street, while the trail of light he had left in his wake dissipated, stars fluttering away like smoke.

The crowd was jazzed.

"It's Captain Light!"

"I love him so much!"

"Go! Go!"

People adored Captain Light. Everyone knew his story. He had begun life as an ordinary scientist whose experiments with an energy reactor had ended in the freak accident that had granted him fantastic powers. Now he could utilize the properties of the spectrum in ingenious ways.

Captain Light hovered above the street for a few seconds, watching something that was hidden from Hayes' view by a skyscraper to the left. A news copter came lurching inelegantly into view in the distance, eating up the space to capture footage of the scene that would already be playing out live on rolling news channels.

Captain Light watched the unseen something for a moment. Then, with a spectrum trail of brilliance, the hero dipped down in a graceful arc like an Olympic high diver, trailed as ever by that brilliant streak of luminous propulsion. An instant later, he had disappeared behind the towering structure to the right, accompanied by the distant, muffled whoosh of displaced air.

"What do you think it is?" a woman in the crowd asked. She wore a headscarf and shades, like a fifties' movie star.

"Whatever it is," a heavyset, dark-skinned man with streaks of gray at his temples replied, "I hope Captain Light kicks its butt."

Hayes hoped so too. He had seen things overseas he wanted to forget, extremism fueled into hatred that had taken on a bloody and brutal physicality. But heroes like Captain Light dealt with something entirely different. They dealt with threats from the cosmos, or from other dimensions, or the kind of batty craziness that demented geniuses dreamed up in their lairs – which is to say they dealt with the kind of deranged bastards who had lairs to begin with.

Hayes had seen one of them before, a hero called the Hunter who worked under the cover of night and used a specially-adapted crossbow to topple his enemies. Hayes had been picking up drive-thru at the time, and as he pulled away, the Hunter had landed on the roof of his car with a sound like clashing cymbals, before leaping away into the night after his prey. Hayes hadn't even seen who the Hunter was chasing, it had been so quick.

Another time, he had emerged from the subway to find the office block he was supposed to visit had been totaled a quarter hour earlier by Doctor Decay. The building and its occupants had been reduced to dust that caught in the wind. People were coughing and choking on that dust, people's lives reduced to so much sand.

Hayes was a spectator now, watching the brilliant trail that Captain Light left in his wake, trying to figure where he was headed, when something else came around the edge of the far skyscraper. It was big and dark and moving, like an oil slick on the sky. The crowd watched as that dark cloud condensed into a figure, dressed in black with a dark green cloak swirling like mist around her supple form – the Jade Shade.

The news copter swayed overhead, lining up its shot as Captain Light reappeared from behind the far skyscraper, fists forward, speed up, powering towards the Jade Shade like a missile. From his mouth he emitted a beam of brilliance, gold but tinged with all the colors of the spectrum – his so-called spectral scream. From this far away, the scream was barely audible, its sound like the buzz of a fluorescent light bulb. Jade Shade seemed to shudder in the air as the scream burst struck her, and her demonic cloak lost integrity for an instant, its edges fraying outwards in wispy, powdery trails.

And that's when Hayes saw Melanie turn the corner. She was scared, head partway turned back to watch the incredible scene above her. She was just one member of a crowd of terrified civilians running for their lives from the battle playing out overhead. Seven months pregnant, she ran with all the grace of a water balloon, or like one of those stupid dachshund dogs whose legs are so short all they can do is waddle.

"Shit!" Hayes hissed, and he began to push his way through the crowd towards Melanie.

She was a block away, running scared. But she saw Hayes, raised her hand to wave, shouting something that was lost to a loud howl that suddenly ripped through the air. Hayes recognized that sound. It was the sound a helicopter engine made when it was in distress, a descending whine like a moping dog. Back in Afghanistan, Hayes had seen a friendly chopper get hit by an anti-aircraft missile, and it had made just that same moping dog whine before striking the ground in a fireball. Eight people had died.

What happened next, happened fast. People were panicking, running in all directions, scattering for cover. Melanie was caught up in a crowd, some of whom ran straight into traffic. Car horns blared, a truck's air brakes hissed loud as it fishtailed across the street.

Then the news copter appeared from behind a building. Its angle was all wrong, nose pointed almost directly towards the ground, but still fifty stories up. The chopper was surrounded by tendrils of Jade Shade's black mist.

Captain Light's indignant holler carried a whole block as he launched himself at Jade Shade, but his spectral scream dissipated as she threw up a shield of black mist that seemed to knock him from the sky.

Then, suddenly, the chopper began picking up speed as it was tossed straight towards Captain Light like a spear. He was knocked from the air as it struck him, and went hurtling away like a rag doll as the chopper continued its deadly descent.

"Run!" Hayes screamed, seeing the helicopter arrow down towards the crowds ahead of him. He was running towards the impact trajectory, towards Melanie. It was automatic for him. SEALs run towards danger, never away.

Melanie was still running when the chopper hit the street. Its starboard ski cut through her chest and abdomen in a sudden, gruesome explosion of blood and flesh and bone, before flattening a yellow cab like it was made of tapioca. The impact was so hard that it shook the street for a block in all directions. Hayes felt it, his legs still pumping, hours on the treadmill and pounding the streets around their house ultimately giving him no more time to reach her than if he had been standing still. Screaming came from everywhere at once, a chorus of shock rising to illustrate the scene.

Above, Captain Light and Jade Shade were exchanging blows, light against dark. One side of an office block shattered into glass shards as the villainess went caroming into it, but Light was at the scene in an instant, propping up the roof while the floor was swiftly evacuated. The Shade dove for the hero, bringing the full fury of her tesseract cloak to bear. Captain Light stood staunchly in place, holding the ceiling aloft as the Shade's demons screeched all around him, batting their pliable bodies uselessly against his chest and legs as they tried to unbalance him.

"Not today, Shade," Captain Light stated through gritted teeth. "Not even on your best day."

Ninety seconds later and it was all over. The Jade Shade was taken into custody, unconscious and with her supernatural cape removed and placed in a specially-designed crate.

The crowd cheered Captain Light, some freckled kid running over to ask for his autograph. There was a thirty-foot-wide crater on Sixth Avenue containing the flattened remains of a news helicopter that looked as though it had tried to merge with a taxi cab.

Hayes stood beside the crater and looked into its crumpled residue, a spider's web of cracks across the blacktop all around it. Emergency vehicles were on the scene, sirens wailing, and New York cops were hastily ushering everyone back behind the temporary barricades they had erected. Hayes found himself pushed back with the crowds, ushered behind those barricades with their candy cane stripes of red and white, as though someone was trying to prettify the scene of the deaths.

Just then, Hayes' phone burbled, trembling against his pants' pocket. Without thinking, he removed it from his pocket and looked at the illuminated screen. It was 11.15. Melanie's appointment.

2

Ginnie. That's what they were going to call her. Virginia. Virginia Hayes. But they had already shortened it to Ginnie by month five, when Melanie had felt the first kick.

Now Ginnie was dead before even being born, a thing that never was and never would be. A person, snuffed out before they had had a chance at life.

And Melanie…

Hayes waited outside the crematorium, shoulders back, chest out, in a suit with pants pressed and shoes shined the way he had been taught. He watched the middle distance, eyes unfocused, as a short line of cars arrived in the balmy air of early summer, heat that left Hayes cold. He had felt real heat in Afghanistan, and whatever they called summer in New York seemed chill by comparison, especially today.

Melanie's parents, Jack and Jodie, the ones with the pool, arrived and said things he did not hear. So did Hayes' supervisor from work, a ruddy-faced man called Jeff who was in his fifties with a hairstyle from the seventies. Hayes was thinking about the people he had lost in Afghanistan, the funeral services he had attended for colleagues, for brothers as they called them. And how with Melanie it was different. It was heartless, turned into ceremony by the very fact that it was not a ceremony. With the Navy it had been ordered, which made it somehow what the person had wanted and what everyone needed. Here it was sending a coffin to be burned.

Inside, the crematorium evoked the sense of a church without ever settling on any one denomination. Melanie had been raised Catholic, but she was at best lapsed and at worse couldn't care. Her parents didn't really attend church, not once she had left school and being a part of that community had not seemed as important anymore. So, the service was about nothing but a person who had died, and how they maybe might live on or go somewhere, but without any commitment to this that could offend anyone present.

The service was short, though it felt long. Thirty minutes summing up a life, thirty minutes that felt like a lifetime. Hayes stood and sat and stood again, paying respects in the ways the funeral director instructed along with the rest of the service's attendees. He could not feel anything, it was too raw. If he tried to think about Melanie, he just heard the whine of the helicopter going down, and then he would be back in Afghanistan with that Black Hawk spouting smoke as it spiraled down to earth before turning into a ball of flame.

Someone – Melanie's cousin, Hayes thought – came over and said that she was in a better place now, and Hayes just nodded, looking at the coffin as it was removed from the podium, like so much freight. Her remains were not in the coffin – there had not been enough of them left with the way the helicopter had crushed her – so it was really nothing more than an expensive box. An expensive box that would be set afire in memory of a woman he had loved, and a daughter who had never been born.

After the service, flowers were displayed in a room containing a book of condolences and a buffet. There was a framed picture of Melanie, recent but before the pregnancy. Hayes had not supplied it; he figured that her folks had.

"Jon? How are you feeling?" – that was Jodie Monroe, Melanie's mom. She was a caring woman, one of those women who seemed to have been born to be a mother and had that urge to mother everyone around her. She had been blonde when Hayes first met her, but now she wore her hair shorter and was letting the natural gray seep through in a gradual transition to retirement.

"I'm fine, ma'am," Hayes replied automatically.

Jodie reached forward and put a hand on Hayes' arm. She was dressed in black, a tailored jacket and skirt, court shoes and a delicate line of pearls that was unobtrusive and, hence, most probably expensive. "Jon, it's me," she said. "I know it must be hard. You saw... what happened." She was close to tears but she held onto them, squeezing them back into her eyes with a long, deliberate blink.

"I don't want to talk about it," Hayes said with a shake of his head.

"You should talk to someone," Jodie insisted.

"No, ma'am." Hayes corrected her assumption. "I mean I don't want to talk about it to you. I think it would only upset you. You loved her, and so did I, and what happened was... was not right. I'm sorry."

"You're a good man, Jon," Jodie told him. "You're family. You remember that if you need us. Whenever you need us. Just because Mel's... gone..." Her words trailed off mid-sentence, and the hot tears began to stream down her face without any effort on her part, no movement of her shoulders or chest, no wracking sobs. Even a blink could no longer hold them back. It was like watching a faulty faucet with a broken washer.

Hayes leaned forward and held Jodie, just letting her be sad.

Finally, Jodie Monroe pushed herself away, and she seemed a little unsteady and a little older than she had before. "I'm sorry," she said, looking away for a moment. "People bring such pretty flowers." And then she walked away, back to her husband who was reading the condolences, squinting through one lens of his glasses.

Jonathan "Jon" Hayes had grown up in Beaumont, Texas, the son of a locksmith and an elementary school teacher. His grades had been good, but he had been drawn to the military by 9/11 and what had happened after. He did not want to fight wars, he wanted to stop them.

Hayes had joined the US Navy at age nineteen, where he had gone into the SEALs program before his twenty-second birthday. Becoming a SEAL was a commitment. It took more than a year of training, almost half that time in BUD/S – Basic Underwater Demolition/School – which taught a man to push his body to its physical limits while keeping his mind razor sharp. Stamina and clear-thinking under pressure – these were the things that the Navy treasured. Leadership skills were assessed, too, but the real push was on extreme survival.

By the time Hayes came out of BUD/S twenty-four weeks later, more than half his class had washed out, submitting what was known as a "Drop on Request". Those who remained could fire a gun with astonishing accuracy, and were as comfortable in water as they were on land. They could perform stealth underwater work without leaving so much as a ripple on the surface, handle demolitions both above and below the water, and patch a buddy back together after a gunshot wound, all without breaking their stride. BUD/S taught a man to sharpen his body into a tool, and to put the mission before the individual.

Their superiors assured them that SEALs were the toughest fighting men in the world, deadly armed or unarmed. After enduring the final three weeks of BUD/S – where he and his colleagues were dropped into a remote location and tasked with survival – Hayes believed it.

As a SEAL he had seen action in Bolivia and Colombia, chasing down drug routes and their ties to the international web of terrorism. People got hurt sometimes, shot sometimes, killed sometimes; this was the life that it was. Afghanistan had been awful and unreal, each newly discovered atrocity challenging Hayes, by then a Chief Warrant Officer, to cling onto his faith in humanity.

When Hayes made Chief Warrant Officer, Melanie had taken

to calling him "CWO", and later just "Quo". She would write him while he was in Afghanistan, and every letter began "Dear Quo".

When he returned from Afghanistan that second time, Hayes had chosen to leave the service and concentrate on being a human again. He had seen a lot by then, allies tortured and then hung from trees like sides of meat where they were left to bleed dry, women raped, some of them barely more than kids, and life after life ruined. He had come back Stateside to forget all that, to make the life with Melanie that he had fought for, where they could raise kids and grow old and not worry about all the crazy that existed beyond the confines of their cozy little house, with its clanking water heater and the mold in its basement. For all its faults, it had been their home.

Hayes remembered the day they had moved in, that he had carried Melanie over the threshold like newlyweds, even though they had been wed for seven months by that point; how Melanie had laughed and called him soppy.

He stood in the hallway now, barely two years later, eyeing the frayed wallpaper that they had intended to strip, the aged wiring from which the chandelier hung. He had had two years to do all those things, to make it good for her, to make their tiny corner of the world perfect, but somehow life had kept getting in the way. And now it was too late, and the house was empty, its soul torn out when that falling news copter had cut through Melanie's body, Melanie's and Ginnie's, and now there was less life to get in the way.

Hayes closed the door behind him with a solid clunk. Then, the world sealed outside, he pulled at his tie to loosen it as he strode to the living room with its creaky old windows that howled when the wind got up, and its wall-mounted television screen that seemed incongruous to everything else about the house.

He sat on the sofa and, for the first time since Melanie had died, Hayes let his body sag down, and wept.

"Why were you always late?" Hayes muttered as the tears ran down his face. "Why couldn't you have been on time, just this once?"

Hayes remained there for a long time, until the tears had dried on his face and the side lamp came on via its timer circuit, eating away at the darkness that had taken the room to its breast.

Rising from the sofa, Hayes climbed the stairs and went to bed, sleeping on the right-hand side as though Melanie might come back to bed any minute.

Hayes dreamt of the chopper crash in New York. In his dream it was a Black Hawk helicopter. Melanie was there, but before he could reach her the whole mess was dragged into the earth by the tendrils of Jade Shade.

A week passed in darkness, like a storm. Hayes could not tell you what he did in those days. He ate, sure, and he slept a lot, but the sleep was restless and unrewarding, and his mind kept replaying things he did not want to revisit.

Six days into whatever it was he was feeling, he got a call from work – a packing company where he was a supervisor – but his boss was understanding about him needing more time.

"Take as long as you need, Jon," Jeff Puchenko said. "We got you covered."

The phone call tripped something in Hayes' head, and he went down into the basement for his toolbox, and got to work scraping that shitty wallpaper off the hallway wall. Manual work and the repetitive noise of the scraper soothed him, and the wall behind didn't much care whether he did a good job or just beat up on it.

The next morning, the hallway wall looked bad, but it was a different kind of bad, and there were shreds of aged wallpaper satisfyingly strewn all over the floor. Hayes looked at the mess from the bottommost stair and nodded. He had done something about that wall at last; Melanie would have liked that.

After that, he felt ready to look in on the nursery they had painted and furnished. The door had been closed since Melanie's death, and it had seemed to wait at the end of the upstairs hall like a beast poised to pounce. Hayes stood at the closed door, shutting his eyes and taking a breath, just like all those times he had tried a door in Afghanistan or Bolivia or any of those other anti-American hellholes he'd been posted to. In the SEALs they would have blown the door with a charge, or maybe just kicked it at the weak spot where the lock met the wood of the door. This time, Hayes just turned the doorknob and let out his breath as he opened his eyes, his body tensed for an explosion that never came.

Within, the room was the way they had left it. The child's crib, white with bars like a tiny cage, chubby lions and giraffes and monkeys painted across its end in an animal parade. A mobile hung over the crib, rotating with the rush of wind that the movement of the door had caused, spinning like the blades of a helicopter. Hayes tamped down the thought, reaching for the mobile and halting its twirling procession.

There was a chair in one corner of the room, a nursing chair with a plump cushion on it, upon which a crocheted blanket had been folded and stacked. Above and behind this, the drapes were partially drawn, pictures of those same stupid animals in their parade crisscrossing to and fro. Melanie had thought they were cute.

The bulb was bare, they still had not gotten around to choosing a lampshade, and there were tins of used paint stacked in one corner, along with a roller and a brush and a paint-streaked cloth.

Hayes took a deep breath, looking around the room, taking everything in. It was wasted effort now, a space that never was, the way their Ginnie would never be. But maybe he should take the paint tins down to the basement, just to clean it up and do something.

The paint tins were in the basement where they could form a community with the other empties that had once awaited application on living room and bedroom and banisters. They were different colors, sure, but they'd hopefully figure a way to get along.

Hayes felt an emptiness burning inside him, a space that he had carved there for Melanie and their daughter, an excavation that he did not know how to fill again. He sat on their bed, staring at the door to the en suite, wondering what he would do now Melanie wasn't here. Colleagues had died and he had attended their funerals at Arlington National Cemetery, but none of that felt like this. Then there had been a reason to carry on – a posting, an assignment, a mission; a Melanie. Now, he would go back to packing cases and forms to fill out, and rotas to juggle and irate customers wondering where their stuff was or why it got broke, and that was not enough. That was not a mission.

Hayes stood and opened the wardrobe, reaching up behind the rail for the box he kept on the shelf there. He pulled it down, and sat back on the bed before opening the lid. Inside was his Glock, sleek lines and a matte black finish, the barrel not much longer than his outstretched hand. Beside the Glock was an ammo magazine. He took the magazine in his hand and loaded it, slot by slot, before ramming it home in the pistol's grip. Then, Hayes looked at the pistol, wondering what came next.

He turned the pistol over until it faced him, and stared down the barrel. The soulless eye of the port stared back at him, waiting to unleash its deadly cargo.

Melanie would understand, wouldn't she? She'd know why. Why he had to let all this go. She always understood, that's why he loved her. Jodie, her mother, would be devastated, of course, and her father would be… well, who knew with Jack, he knew more about golf than he did about people. *But…*

The soulless eye stared at him, boring into his mind, not judging, not impatient, just waiting.

The trigger was ready, the weight of the gun familiar. An old friend in his hand, just waiting to do him one last solid. To fix this mess the way it had fixed things in Afghanistan and Bolivia and all those other hot zones.

But...

"No," Hayes murmured. This wasn't the answer. This wasn't what the SEALs had taught him. Giving up wasn't in his nature.

So, what then? *What now?*

3

Hayes located a multi-level parking garage opposite the Nexus
Range and did circuits until a space opened up that overlooked the
tower. The day rate for parking here was extortionate, of course,
because – well, *New York*. And Hayes did not really know why he
wanted to be here, but he had compassionate time away from
work and he couldn't mooch around the house forever.

Located on Fifth Avenue, the Nexus Range looked like any
other Manhattan skyscraper except for one thing: the top four
stories sported a halo of shimmering light which seemed to rotate
very slowly, hour by hour, day or night. It was a force field, Hayes
understood, erected to protect the celebrated occupants and their
many treasures, both self-created and incarcerated from their foes.
That light could be seen long into the night, like a lighthouse whose
illumination was the beam of justice – evil beware. No one got in
or out of those floors without a truck load of security clearance,
and even if they did, they still had to face the inquisition of the
likes of Astra and the Meld, who could read a man's mind the way
a normal man reads a news headline.

Hayes watched the tower through his windshield, engine
off, but with the keys still in the ignition. Nonsensically, he was
prepped for a quick getaway. He feared that one of those telepaths
would somehow sense him, even this far away, more than a block
distant and twenty stories lower, as if they were waiting for just

this eventuality. It was like passing a cop – even when you had nothing to hide, the guilt just set in.

He sat with his belt on, watching as that shimmering field of energy did its slow rotate, protecting the heroes and their secrets from the world outside their doors. If only Melanie had had that kind of protection.

The Nexus Rangers had banded together after Morgana Le Fey had drawn her faerie folk out of the woodwork of some nether dimension in a bid to take over the world. The Rangers – then just five heroes – had combined forces to drive her armies back, dispatching Le Fey to an other-dimensional prison from which she was unable to escape. Except when she did escape, but that was another story. After that first adventure, the heroes had opted to work together whenever the need arose, under the banner of the Nexus Rangers, later shortened to simply The Rangers.

The Rangers had been a hodgepodge back in those early days. They were led by an engineer calling himself Mechanist, who used his mechanical expertise to fight for justice. His allies included Captain Light, a super-strong savage known as the Missing Link, several inventors-turned-costumed heroes, and the mysterious woman called Astra, who could reach into a person's mindscape and turn their most spiteful desires against them.

The line-up had changed over time, with new members joining and old ones bowing out. Captain Light had been associated with the Rangers from their very start, though he had never taken up official membership.

It was speculated that the Rangers had saved the world at least fifteen times, though their spokeswoman would not be drawn on that.

Hayes watched the Nexus Range from his parking spot, waiting for something. He did not know what that something was, he just wanted to see what happened there. He opened his window a crack to let the air and noise in from outside, and waited, resting back in his seat.

For a long time, nothing happened. The constant hum of New York traffic droned like a distant beehive, and the whup-whup-whup of helicopters cut the air now and then, sometimes passing across the frame of the windshield, sometimes heard but not seen. There seemed to be a near-constant whine of sirens as emergency vehicles rushed to accident after accident, a fire, a heart attack, a car crash victim. But the heroes never emerged. They didn't do car crashes or heart attacks or any of that penny ante stuff that colored the day-to-day lives of ordinary people. No, the heroes waited in their fortress until something big came along that needed their might – a sentient world engine or a demonic attack or an alien landing on the White House lawn. *Bastards.*

It was 19.38 and Hayes was stretching his neck muscles when something actually happened. The distinct taint of boredom had begun to overwhelm him by then, having spent over ten hours sitting in the car just watching. His car – a 4WD with a soft-top roof – had always seemed comfortable until he spent those ten-and-a-half hours in it. Now it felt like he had spent his whole life trapped in this little box, but that if he left it, it would be game over and he would never be able to go back.

But at 19.38, something happened. There was a flash on the far side of the halo that orbited the Nexus Range, accompanied about a second later by the delayed sound of a jet engine being fired up. The sound was so loud that Hayes could feel it vibrate his insides, shaking his organs and his bones, making his chest tense.

Hayes watched as the Ranger Jet, a sleek shaft of metal with fins, lifted off from a hangar bay located to the far side of the roof of the Nexus Range.

"Damn it," Hayes cursed. He hadn't thought about which side of the building the hangar bay doors would open. Now he wished he had picked another parking lot so that he could see the launch more clearly.

The Ranger Jet took off with a rumble that shook the air, but the devastating effect of its exhaust was absorbed and negated by the force field. In a few seconds, once it was clear of the building and its protective halo, the rocket picked up speed in a sudden burst and shot high into the clouds, instantly disappearing from view.

Hayes looked for the sun, trying to figure which way he was facing in the maze of the parking garage. The jet was heading south west, to Washington maybe or Baltimore, maybe even Mexico. Although they seemed to be an American institution, the Rangers went all over, fighting the forces of evil wherever they were needed. They were kind of international that way, but locating themselves in New York made them feel like the "home team".

The rumble of the rocket engine grew fainter as it shot off on its transatmospheric circuit.

Hayes remained sitting there for a long time, just looking at the part of the sky where the Ranger Jet had disappeared and at the corner of the building where it had initially emerged. The edges of the sky were very slowly changing from blue to pink as the summer sun began its lazy descent.

"What are you doing, Quo?" the voice asked. It came from behind Hayes.

Hayes jumped. His eyes flicked automatically to the mirror and he saw Melanie there in the back seat, pretty as ever, her dark eyes as transfixing as he remembered.

"Do you think this will bring me back?" Melanie asked.

"I–"

"I died, Quo," Melanie told him. "I died. There's no coming back from that."

"Heroes come back all the time," Hayes argued, his voice fiercer than he had intended. "What about Eternal Flame? What about Kid Ocean? They came back from the dead."

"I'm not one of them, Quo," Melanie told him, meeting

his eyes in the mirror. "They were heroes. I'm just a person, a normal person."

"But if you–"

Suddenly someone tapped on the glass of the driver's window, the sound loud and unexpected.

Hayes turned to see who it was, and came face to face with a heavy-jowled woman leaning sideways to talk to him through the gap between window and frame. "Hey, you see a kid come running through here?" she asked. She looked sweaty and harassed, and she did not wear her weight well.

"What?" Hayes asked, confused.

"My kid," the woman said with that broad NY drawl. "You seen my kid? The little shit's ran off while I was loading the groceries. You seen him or not?"

Hayes rubbed at the side of his face, as if to wake himself up. "I'm sorry, no. I didn't see anyone."

"Yeah, thanks for nothing, pal," the woman snarled, edging away from Hayes' car. "Sorry to disturb your masturbating..." – the rest was lost to the winds as she walked away in search of her kid.

Hayes turned back to the mirror, saw the back seat was empty. He turned in his seat, reaching behind the passenger's headrest automatically as though he was going to reverse. There was no one there, Melanie was gone.

Hayes' breath came heavy, powering down his nostrils with what seemed the same force as the Ranger Jet taking off. "Shit."

It was time to go home.

Hayes returned to an empty house. Melanie had not appeared again on his back seat during the drive home through New York's evening traffic, an experience in patience, tolerance and quick-thinking.

Even with the lights on, the house felt unoccupied. Melanie had been the heart of the place, Hayes realized. Without her, no amount of illumination or decoration or music could turn the building into anything more than an empty husk. He sat in the lounge, with the TV on, eyes glazing over as his thoughts slipped away, one by one.

They lived in a world of incredible people like the Rangers. There were heroes and there were villains. It was clear cut, except when it wasn't – those days when heroes fought heroes or heroes turned out to be villains in disguise, some lousy alien with shape changing tech or a magic whamma-jamma. Hayes had not paid much attention to all of that. The heroes lived their lives, full of color and excitement and lightning flashes of derring-do, while people like him cleaned up crap holes like Afghanistan, crap holes that could never really be cleaned up, that just festered with new forms of hatred passed down from one generation to the next, adapted by each one into something even more destructive and cruel. Places like Afghanistan were a world away from these things that happened in New York City, these things that people like the Hunter and Eternal Flame and Captain Light tackled. Kid Ocean had turned back a sentient tsunami once – that kind of thing never happened in the Middle East.

So what the hell is behind these people? Hayes wondered. *What's motivating them?*

He glanced up at the television screen as a news report started up.

"… where reports are coming in that the Bride has taken control of the Pentagon."

The footage showed a shaky aerial shot of the Pentagon, taken from a helicopter. The camera tightened focus on a section of tinted windows as the reporter continued to talk.

"The Bride's demands are currently unclear, but it's understood that the Rangers are on site and–"

The reporter halted mid-sentence as something exploded from a wall a little way up from where the camera focused. Shaky footage followed as the camera operator tried to capture the action. Dressed in brown leather and a trailing head wrap, the Bride bounced across the parking lot followed by a humanoid figure in a glowing metal suit.

"The Mechanist has just emerged through a wall of the Pentagon," the reporter burbled redundantly as the metallic figure strode towards the Bride.

"Stay down!" the Mechanist's electronically enhanced voice commanded, though it was unclear whether he was talking to the Bride or any innocent bystanders who might be close to the scene.

The Bride raised her hand as the Mechanist approached, saying something which the camera's mic could not pick up. She claimed to be the immortal bride of Genghis Khan, Hayes remembered, and was hell bent on completing her husband's mission to take control of the whole of the world. It sounded kind of crazy, but a lot of these bad guys' intentions did.

The Bride had the ability to – how did they phrase it? – turn men's minds. Which was another way of saying, she filled up her victims' brain centers with dopamine until they could not help but feel happy in her company. Happy, lusty and obedient as a hungry dog.

On screen, the two combatants clashed in a swiftly played-out bout. The Mechanist had been susceptible to the Bride's powers once, but it seemed he was utilizing some device – likely of his own creation – to block her uncanny mesmeric abilities.

Hayes watched, removed from the whole thing. The television rendered it as distant and unimportant, it meant no more to him than a sports game. Probably, the Bride had gained access to nuclear codes or military secrets just ten minutes earlier – she had done that before, one time taking control of a Polaris sub and threatening to nuke Cape Canaveral, until Captain Light had intervened. But the threat seemed unreal and commonplace; another mad villain, another world-threatening scheme.

A cheer went up from the reporter and her camera operator as, on screen, the Mechanist fired some kind of power beam at the Bride, knocking her clean through a parked automobile.

"The Bride is down," the reporter stated with a sense of relief coming through in her voice. "I repeat, Mechanist has taken down the Bride."

Other members of the Rangers were emerging from the busted side of the Pentagon, some of them rubbing their heads where the Bride's powers had momentarily held them in thrall. They descended on the Bride as she struggled to recover from her forced meeting with the auto, surrounding her and targeting her with their own abilities or weapons – supernatural or artificial – to hold her at bay.

Hayes watched, his mind wandering as the live footage played out. *Where did these people come from?* he wondered. Where did they get their abilities? Some of those details were out there in public, but most of it was kept secret. Were they heroes full time? Were the bad guys always being bad? And what was driving these people to keep fighting, to keep clashing and causing mayhem and righting wrongs?

How do these heroes and villains do what they do?

4

Friday passed effortlessly into Saturday, and the weekend merged into one for Hayes. Without Melanie – and without a job to hurry back to – he found no reason to keep track of the days. Instead, he started to research the colorful heroes and villains who populated the news reports. He was not sure yet what he was looking for; he was just looking.

Hayes brought up a web search on Captain Light that resulted in four million pages.

"Four million?" Hayes muttered, astonished. "Is there anyone on the 'net not talking about this guy?"

He started at the wiki entry for Captain Light, which combined information from news reports and interviews along with some educated speculation. It didn't tell him much that he did not already know – that Captain Light had first appeared seven years ago during the infamous "Space Flight Disaster" and was presumed to be about thirty years old now. Under the heading of "allies and group affiliations", it listed the Mighty Rangers, but offered no further information about his role with the team.

Although he had divulged his origin, Captain Light rarely gave interviews, and certainly offered no information up about his personal life. A few women had come forward to say that they had slept with him, but no proof had ever been offered and so they were considered either delusional or groupies who were trying to make a fast buck out of their stories. Most of them didn't sell, although there was one in the early days of Light's career – a woman called Sheila Shannon – who had turned her moment of fame into genuine celebrity, doing the interview circuit and appearing on game shows as well as launching a perfume called "Light Power" which had failed to capture the public's imagination.

Light had his own webpage, which Hayes dutifully clicked on after getting a firmer sense of the man's background from other sites. He did not want to be sold the PR line, that didn't interest him. But he was intrigued by how Captain Light saw himself, and how he chose to portray himself to the public. The site was in English and Spanish, and gave very little information. There was certainly no mention of Sheila Shannon or any of the women like her who had come forward claiming to have had relations with the man.

After three hours of web surfing, Hayes felt he was no closer to finding whatever the hell it was he was looking for. He tapped in another search on the computer keyboard:

The Hunter

Millions of hits came back, the term was so vague. He was offered alternatives:

The Hunter hero
The Hunter Blondie
– and others.

He clicked on "The Hunter hero" and the results changed, bringing the page numbers down, but only fractionally. So that wasn't helping, though it did bring up some blurry news photos of the night-stalking vigilante, along with illustrations of his full-face mask and an exploded diagram of how his crossbow likely worked. It was a crossbow, the fact someone had felt the need to explain its workings struck Hayes as kind of redundant.

"*The Hunter official*" Hayes tried next, but that search only brought up a ream of quite obviously unofficial pages dedicated to the hero. When Hayes clicked on one, he was asked if he was interested in Russian women who wanted a husband who could fulfill their insatiable appetites for sex in return, presumably, for a Green Card. Their inflated bodies looked curved and swollen, and their eyes looked vacant.

"Sure, guys like the Hunter don't have official websites," Hayes muttered as he trawled back through a handful of other options.

He found himself on ViewTube and watched several clips of the Hunter in action. They were mostly blurry phone footage where the light balance was a crapshoot, smudging the night streets with grain and turning the street lamps into brilliant stars of sodium yellow, with thick vertical bars of black to either side cropping the picture. Several used the same footage, sometimes in compilation, sometimes just lifted wholesale until the original uploader could no longer be traced. None showed Hayes much; the Hunter was an enigma, and his dark outfit coupled with his fast movements ensured he blended with the shadows.

So, "Captain Light" then. That brought up more footage, a lot of it clear, some of it professionally shot for news channels. There were scenes of devastation, bad guys getting walloped, great mechanical devices crashing to the street in the wake of various battles. There was a lot of footage from the aftermath of events, a lot of talking heads and shocked faces covered in dust who were just grateful to be alive.

Hayes watched the footage for a while, getting nothing from it but a mild sense of déjà vu. He had seen so much of this during his tours, the results of one atrocity after another and what was left in their wake. The reality was that this was getting him nowhere.

He tapped his fingers on the desk, turning his head away from the computer monitor, trying to clear his thoughts. What was it that he was looking for?

The why of it.

– That's what he was after. He could not phrase it better than that, not yet at least. But he was circling on an idea, a plan maybe.

Hayes reached for the desk's drawer and found a notepad and a pencil. The pad had been partially filled by Melanie's flattened and rounded scrawl, notes on ad campaigns and fashion trends, along with more mundane things like email addresses and shopping lists.

One page was devoted to the things she intended to organize for the nursery, most of them crossed through where they had now been completed. Hayes tapped the pencil against the pad and read through the words that had been crossed through. *Crib. Drapes. Lamp.*

"Damn," Hayes muttered, then turned over the page.

He came to a blank sheet and began to write out a list: *The why of it.*

> *Why do they do this?*
> *Heroes?*
> *Villains?*
> *How do they do it?*
> *How do they get into it?*
> *Where do they get their hardware?*
> *What do they hope to gain?*

Yeah, he thought. That would do for now. Those were some of the questions that needed to be answered if he was going to find that elusive thing he was actually looking for.

"You already know what you're looking for, Quo," Melanie chastised from the doorway behind him.

Hayes wanted to turn, but he didn't. Instead he looked at the computer screen where it had switched over to a darkened screen saver. Melanie's reflection was there, hair down, wearing the same clothes she had worn that day she had told him that they were going to have a child.

"Do I?" Hayes asked.

"You're looking for a way to bring me back," she said, "but I've already told you that it can't be done. I'm dead, Quo."

"You're here," Hayes insisted. "Why can't it be done if you're here?"

Melanie was silent for a few seconds before she finally answered. "You know why," she said.

"No, I..." Hayes turned to face her, but she was already gone.

Hayes had done some ops work with the SEALs. Mostly that stuff was handled by the CIA, but he had seen them in action and had been briefed by guys who did this shit for a living. He knew how they did it, and a lot of it was simple logic.

He started by amassing as much information on the costumed types as he could, writing out notes in longhand. He wasn't looking for specific things yet, just putting the puzzle down in one place so he could start to piece it all together.

Fifteen pages of notes turned into tables that showed who used what power, and where, and how. Then he needed a map, and realized what he wanted to know was who was operating locally – in New York – whereabouts and when. The why wasn't so important, there was always a reason that Damocles or the Hunter were chasing down somebody, he could chart those reasons if he needed to, but that detail began to feel extraneous.

Two days later and he had begun to find the patterns. Heroes fought villains, but they didn't do it by lottery and chance; there was a hierarchy of good guys and a hierarchy of bad guys. So while really powerful heroes like Captain Light and Eternal Flame took on the big threats – Morgana Le Fey, the Wild Riders and the Jade Shade levels of craziness, whose battles crossed dimensional planes or stretched beyond the boundaries of the Solar System – there were street guys like the Hunter and Damocles who took on what Hayes labeled lower-level threats.

Those lower level threats were interesting – they tended to be normal guys wearing augmentation suits or wielding high-tech weapons. They were kind of just jumped up mobsters and second story men who got access to tech either through their smarts, their conniving or sheer damn luck.

It was these lower level guys who fascinated Hayes. He figured it was fucking unlikely he was going to turn out to be the ruler of the fae or command an army of resurrected legionaries anytime soon; but there was a believable chance he could get his hands on some tech that could do real damage to these people, these *costumes*.

And that was another thing. At first, he had thought of them as heroes and villains, two distinct categories of people. But he had realized early on that if you were going to study these people, you needed to take on the lot of them; that was the only way to find the patterns and maybe figure a way to—

"What? Defeat them? Is that your plan, Quo?"

– It was Melanie's voice, speaking to him from the toilet stall as he took a shower. The bathroom was misted up from the hot water, a fog enveloping the tub where the shower curtain hemmed it in. He hated it when she talked to him from the john, there was some boundary there that shouldn't be crossed but she crossed it anyway.

"Well?" Melanie asked, impatient for his answer.

Hayes reached for the shower control and shut off the water. "Well what?" he asked. There was an edge of irritation in his voice that he could hear and he knew Melanie would hear too, but it was there now and he couldn't take it back.

He waited.

No answer. Nothing.

Irked, he drew back the shower curtain and glared at the toilet. But Melanie wasn't there. The stall, and the bathroom, was empty.

However, Melanie's question remained, hanging there amongst the hot mist that danced across the ceiling. What was he going to do with all this knowledge?

Hayes dried himself off, grabbed his gun from the bedroom, and took a ride out to the firing range.

The firing range was off Fifth Avenue, past Washington Square Park. From outside it looked like a city hotel, the kind of place you'd stay for a night so you could do some shopping or maybe attend a friend's wedding.

Inside, the staff treated you nice. They were friendly without being intrusive. You came to shoot, and so they figured that's what you wanted to do, not shoot the breeze.

Ear defenders on, Hayes took up a spot at one end of the range and triggered the session to begin. A target dropped into place, a man's silhouette, head and torso, with concentric rings to illustrate the various merits of targeting each area. Those concentric white rings on black looked like a costume to Hayes as he raised his Glock-19.

Bang!

His first bullet went through the chest, cutting a hole an inch right of center where the heart would be.

Bang!

His second bullet drilled right between the eyes, obliterating the bridge of the nose on the silhouette and leaving a scorched hole in its place.

Hayes' time in the SEALs had taught him how to handle a weapon, taught him where to aim – head and center mass – to efficiently drop a man. It was automatic to him, and despite everything else he had lost that day on Sixth, when Melanie had been taken from him, Hayes had not lost this. No, he could never lose this.

The mistake would be to take this ability and use it for hatred. He knew that, felt it deep in his core. So whatever costume he could envisage from those concentric circles on black, he pushed it out of his mind and squeezed the trigger again, shooting nobody but a paper man who had no life outside of the single page on which he had been printed.

Bang!

Each shot was a beat, clearing his mess of thoughts, drilling down to the truth.

Bang!

And he could feel it forming at the back of his mind, that sense that there was an answer to all this mess.

Bang!

Something was going to give. Sooner or later something was going to give and it would sweep Hayes up and take him to where he needed to be, to the ultimate truth of what he was searching for in all those hours of footage –

Bang!

– all those pages of notes –

Bang!

– those marked maps, charts and tables.

Bang!

Something was coming, he knew. Something that would change everything.

Bang!

5

What kind of a bullet would stop Captain Light? That was the question that was rattling around Hayes' mind as he drove north on Lafayette, on his way home.

It was late. The sun was sinking below the horizon, the last of its rays probing through the gaps between the skyscrapers like grasping, yellow fingers. Above it, the sky had turned a perfectly clear blue, darkening minute by minute as the cerulean gave way to indigo, and the indigo to black. Stars like pinpricks were showing their whites, brighter with every moment as the sky went dark.

What do you use to drop a man who can hold back a runaway train and blast someone into another dimension with a scream?

"A Magnum .44," Hayes muttered to himself with a self-deprecating laugh. Because even the stopping power of a Magnum .44, or a submachine gun, or even a missile, had proven no match for the Beacon of Light.

And more to the point, did Hayes actually want to drop Captain Light? Was it a revenge kick he was on?

The Jade Shade had been the one who had thrown that news helicopter, launching it at Captain Light like a javelin. If Hayes was going to take revenge on anyone, shouldn't it be her?

Captain Light had powers, he knew. He could tap something he called the Morphic Spectrum, which provided the source of all of his incredible abilities. He could fly, had super strength, invulnerability, could blast his celebrated light beam from his mouth in the form of his spectral scream, plus he had some kind of weird warning sense that allowed him to foresee certain kinds of danger before it happened. Captain Light had explained that in a rare interview clip that Hayes had found in his research, wherein he described it as:

"I see shadows sometimes, but they're from the future. Just a few seconds, enough that I know where I'm needed."

Really, Hayes wondered as he pulled up at a stop light, what did that actually mean? That Captain Light could see into the future, or that he could see what was going on around him maybe two or three seconds ahead of the reality. And, honestly, how much benefit would being able to see three seconds into the future actually be? Wouldn't be much use in avoiding that traffic light turning red.

The light changed, and at the same moment there came a sound like a lightning strike.

"What the hell...?" Hayes muttered, looking to either side of the intersection. He wound down his window, trying to locate the source of the noise. Down the street to his left he saw something glow momentarily, colored an eerie blue.

Behind him, someone began tootling their horn as though they were trying out the tune for Broadway. Before they hit the chorus, they pulled around Hayes' stationary vehicle with a roar of the accelerator. "The light's green, idiot!" the impatient driver shouted through their open window before tearing past Hayes' jeep and across the intersection.

There were more cars behind that exuded that same sense of impatience. Hayes checked his mirror, flicked the arm of his indicator and pulled across traffic to the left, heading for where he had seen that momentary flash of light. A cab driver sat on his horn as Hayes' crossed his path, shouting obscenities in a language Hayes didn't recognize.

Hayes found he was on West *Something* Street, somewhere in Lower Manhattan. He didn't know the street, but he knew he was

headed roughly in the direction of Washington Square Park and
the Village.

The noise came again and this time Hayes caught the flash of
blue light over to his right. He wrenched the steering wheel in that
direction, taking the next turn at speed, pumping the accelerator
as his 4WD arrowed down a narrow side street barely wider than
the car.

Washington Square Park was up ahead now, a green smear of
trees peering up over the road.

A door opened ahead to his left, and out walked a man dressed
in an apron and carrying a black trash bag, white ear buds in,
oblivious. With barely any wiggle room in the alley, Hayes nudged
the wheel to the right, scraping paint off his side door as he glanced
momentarily against the wall before hurtling past the oblivious
kitchen hand.

Then he was out in the street, joining the traffic on Washington
Square South, almost clipping a FedEx truck as he spun the wheel.

And then Hayes saw it. A flow of people traipsing across the
park, in a huge mass. Except they weren't people, they were just
clothes – business suits and skirts and sweaters, all of them brought
to uncanny life by some force on the far side of the park. People
were running for cover, freaked out by the relentless parade
of living clothes. Students from the nearby uni were huddled
together, taking photos on their phones.

Over at the far side, where the marble arch stood sentinel close
to the north gate, another flash of that eerie, brilliant blue sparked
into existence for just a few seconds.

Hayes looked for a parking spot – impossible, of course, in this
district – then cut across a lane of traffic and bumped up the curb
in a screeching halt of brakes.

He tore the keys from the ignition, and shoved his door open
amid a cacophony of complaints from the pedestrians he had
almost mown down.

"Hey, what gives, man?" a jogger with what could only be
considered an ironic afro shouted right in his face.

"You lose your assistance dog, asshole?" a guy in a business suit added, holding his brown leather briefcase to his chest defensively.

"Sorry," Hayes said, pushing his way through the throng.

There were people all around him, some gawking at the weird activity in the park, others come to see whether Hayes had somehow lost control of his car during the ruckus. It would be slow-going reaching the stone arch at this rate, and so Hayes reverted to the way he had been in Afghanistan and in Bolivia, when the locals had massed around him and his unit in gratitude when the situation itself was still dangerous. "Everybody get back," Hayes said with authority, raising his voice. "Official business, coming through."

He had pulled this same stunt once when he and Melanie got caught up leaving a food hall at some soulless shopping mall, the name of which had been entirely obliterated from his memory. Then he had said it to a bunch of shocked teens who were massed around the escalator like bees around lavender. They had been so shocked that they had parted to let the couple through, like the parting of the Red Sea. Melanie had given Hayes a stern look, but then she had burst out laughing while they were traveling down the escalator.

"They thought you were James Bond," she told him, watching the kids milling around on the level above in bewilderment.

"Shaken, not shtirred, Mish Moneypenny," Hayes had replied with his best Scottish accent.

Melanie had kissed him on the cheek as they neared the bottom of the escalator. "You sound like Daffy Duck," she whispered in his ear.

"Suffering succotash!" Hayes had replied.

Hayes pushed his way through the crowd, wondering if he should have brought his Glock. In the park, the eerie unworn clothes were massing around Washington Square Arch. Standing atop the arch was a figure dressed in a dark, ragged jump suit with a helmet that entirely masked the top half of his features, leaving only his mouth exposed. The helmet looked like something out of World War II, bug eyes like a gas mask and with stylized ears like a rodent. His name was Rattenfanger and in his hand he held his infamous weapon – the Rat Pipe. It was the pipe which was expelling those random flashes of blue brilliance as it played its mysterious melody.

Rattenfanger was, according to the stories, following in the great tradition of mind control that had begun with his namesake, who was known in English as the Pied Piper of Hamlyn. Rattenfanger was a criminal – a "bag guy" – whose schemes revolved around influencing politicians or the wealthy into giving him money, power or both. One time he had kidnapped the wealthy heiress to the Tendr shoe empire and, by her account, used the Rat Pipe to make her his willing slave for over four months. A lot of people suggested she just became infatuated with the bad boy behind the mask and had hoped to foster some kind of modern-day *Bonnie and Clyde* jam, only to lose her nerve when faced with a real life hero who was more than willing to pound her into next week.

Rattenfanger was strictly at the low end of the bad guy chart, according to Hayes' recollection. He could give the Hunter or Beanbag a decent work out, but he didn't have the power set – or the ambition – to take on Tankman or Captain Light.

Hayes reached the park's central fountain at a run, heading in the opposite direction from almost everyone else except for the bodiless suits of clothes.

"I'm here to repopulate this stink hole!" Rattenfanger rasped from atop Washington Square Arch. "Unless the city gives me a million dollars in cold, hard cash!" He drew his Rat Pipe to his lips and tootled off another refrain, which seemed to instill urgency into the bodiless figures hurrying mindlessly through the park. As he did, the pipe glowed brighter, a crackle of blue lightning splitting the air. "Think on that, Mayor Castlebridge! Soon the only people left in this city will be empty clothes, and you'll be *darned* if you can figure a way to get their votes come next spring!"

Hayes grimaced at the pun. Why these lethal human weapons had to make bad jokes was beyond him, but it seemed to almost be a compulsion with a lot of them.

Suddenly, the air was rent by a sound like a fighter jet passing by, accompanied by a momentary gust of wind. Rattenfanger turned in surprise at the second figure who was now perched at the edge of the marble archway.

"Tell me I'm not too late for the party, chuckles," the figure said, drawing his rapier blade from its sheath on his back.

"Damocles!" Rattenfanger hissed in evident irritation.

Damocles was, according to Hayes' calculations, one of the street-level heroes. Armed with an intelligent sword, Damocles was primarily a loner who stuck closely to the five boroughs, and was mostly sighted in Manhattan and Brooklyn. He wore a brightly colored suit of red and yellow, that seemed to be made from some kind of armored lycra hybrid, along with a red mask over his eyes. When it wasn't in use, his sword was sheathed in its diagonal red sleeve across his back, the design of which was mirrored across his chest and, in miniaturized form, as accents on his boots and cuffs. Quite how his intelligent sword worked no one seemed to know, but it was often described as having a life of its own, and was able to operate away from its master's hand.

"Why don't we *sew* this up before someone gets hurt," Damocles taunted, holding his sword in ready position as Rattenfanger stalked towards him. "And by someone, I mean you."

"Cursed hindrance!" Rattenfanger growled, launching himself at Damocles with a sweep of his Rat Pipe.

Damocles leapt high – impossibly so to Hayes' eyes – back flipping in mid-air over the swinging length of pipe before landing on almost the exact same spot. The move wrong-footed Rattenfanger, who took several steps to right himself, treading perilously close to the edge of the marble archway.

"Gotta watch that first step, Whistles," Damocles taunted, and he reached out to grab the back of Rattenfanger's ragged costume from between the shoulder blades, yanking him away.

Damocles was fast, that was for sure – Hayes had not even thought about that when he was watching all those clips on the 'net. Seen through the removed nature of a lens, Damocles' fights had seemed uncoordinated and chaotic to Hayes, showing none of the discipline he had had instilled into him in the service. But seeing it this close, the whole thing played out incredibly fast, blows traded as rapidly as puns as Damocles ran circles around his grim-visaged opponent.

But Rattenfänger was not going to make this easy. As Damocles knocked him down against the surface of the archway, the villain rattled off a further refrain on his pipe. From all around the park, bodiless sets of clothes moved towards the archway, climbing its sides in spider fashion, empty sleeves grasping for Damocles as he approached his fallen foe.

Damocles performed another of those impossible leaps as the open cuff of a business suit tried to trip him. "This is why I always buy off the peg!" he quipped, landing squarely on the grasping sleeve and forcing the "life" – if that's what it was – out of it.

All around, more clothes were converging as if they contained soldiers charging into battle. Damocles ducked left and right, avoiding one unliving attacker only to find himself backed against two more.

In an instant, the gaudily-dressed hero disappeared beneath a swarm of grays and blues and blacks, power suits and women's summer dresses and jackets and ties descending upon him like a football dog pile.

From the ground below, Hayes watched with bated breath. He had been drawn here not knowing what to expect, just seen the unearthly lightning and knew he needed to be part of whatever was happening. He had figured he would see a hero doing something, but he didn't expect to witness a hero's death. He had to help, somehow.

"Shit!" Hayes cursed, remembering the Glock sitting in his glove box. That would have made things easy. He could have shot Rattenfanger from down here, taken the creep out with one shot. Instead, Hayes would have to scale the arch somehow. He looked around, trying to find a way up the archway's smooth sides, when suddenly figures started to drop from above. No, not figures – it was clothes. Lifeless, limp clothes.

"Sorry to break it to ya, but this one's not my color!" – that was Damocles' voice, coming from above. "And nor's this, and this is a definite no-no!"

Hayes took several steps back, striving to find a better viewpoint. Damocles was still atop the structure of the marble arch along with Rattenfanger, but now Damocles' sword was cutting through the animated clothing, flying in a looping, roller-coaster path under its own power with a whistle of fast-moving air. Each item of clothing that the sword touched fell away, its momentary life extinguished, becoming no more alive than a rag.

"No!" Rattenfanger shouted. He brought his Rat Pipe to his lips once more and his fingers began to dance across its holes.

But Damocles was free now, and with a pointed instruction he sent his sentient sword striking out towards the dark-clad villain. The sword halted over Rattenfanger's head, poised to drop in the signature move that Damocles had used on his opponents, time and again.

"I may not know much about fashion," Damocles admitted with bravado, "but I have to tell ya – you're not on trend!"

Rattenfanger knew he was beaten, but still he played a few notes from the pipe before the sword of Damocles dropped down in a lightning-fast swipe. The Rat Pipe was instantly sheared in two, and fell away from Rattenfanger's hands.

"My pipe," Rattenfanger gasped, falling to his knees. "My beautiful pipe."

By then the blue-and-whites had arrived, and the whole park seemed to be lit by their beacons. Cops and the media surrounded the Washington Square Arch, guns and cameras aimed as Rattenfanger realized his scheme was doomed. Damocles nodded to the cops from where he stood astride the arch, offering a casual salute as he grabbed his sword out of the air.

"I'll leave this loser to you guys," Damocles said with a broad smile, then turned and leapt from the arch.

Hayes watched as Damocles vaulted towards the closest entrance of the park. The gathered crowd parted for him, a woman in a headscarf and shades smiling as he paid her some compliment that only she could hear.

Hayes watched for a moment longer until the hero was lost behind the massing crowd. Around him, ties and jackets were just ties and jackets once more, their freakish animation departed as though it had never been. At the marble monument, a fire truck was positioning its ladder in such a way that someone could ascend and grab Rattenfanger from the top.

Hayes stood back, watching the bustle of activity play out as policemen retrieved the sheared halves of Rattenfanger's supernatural Rat Pipe. Rattenfanger himself was brought down the ladder in cuffs – not an easy thing to do at the best of times – and led to a paddy wagon. The crowd began to dissipate, realizing that there was nothing more to see here, while a few people picked up items of clothing as souvenirs, and a homeless guy with a tobacco-stained beard tried on a jacket with a great rent across its back from its tangle with Damocles' sword.

Was that it then? Not even a crime scene to be locked off and examined?

Hayes paused, wondering if he should go back to his car, or if it had already been towed. Two people were passing, a well-dressed woman and a man, obviously a couple.

"Did you hear what Damocles said to her?" the man was saying. "I couldn't catch it."

"He said he liked her scarf," the woman explained, "and I swear to you, like, six women in the crowd all ran off to try to find a scarf like it in the debris."

The man laughed at that, and then they had passed Hayes.

The woman in the scarf, Hayes thought. *A headscarf. And sunglasses.*

Hayes realized that he had seen her before – *she was on the street when Melanie died.*

6

"Excuse me. Excuse me – ma'am," Hayes called, reaching out for the woman in the headscarf. He had tracked her across Washington Square Park and over the street, jaywalking between traffic to catch up with her as she turned away down Fifth Avenue.

The woman was oblivious to him until Hayes touched her arm. When he did, she turned, sudden and angry, typical New York reaction.

Hayes stepped back, holding his hands up in the surrender position. "Ma'am... ma'am... I'm not going to hurt you," he explained.

She glared at him from behind her dark glasses, her brows knitted. "Why did you grab me, you pervert?" she said. She had a local accent, a nasal twang to her words making each one an accusation.

People on the street were looking now, wondering what was going on, excited and fearful that they might be witnesses to a lovers' quarrel, or to something bad.

"It's okay, I didn't mean to scare you," Hayes began.

"It's not okay," the woman snarled. "Don't tell me what's okay. I'll tell you what's okay, you fucking creep."

Hayes lowered his hands just slightly, gesturing for calm. "Ma'am, please," he said, "just let me explain."

"Yeah, you better," a guy blurted from a pace behind the

woman in the headscarf. He had olive skin and wore a T-shirt with a logo Hayes didn't recognize.

Hayes assessed T-shirt with a professional up and down, knowing he could take him if he had to. He had the front of a tough guy, but the gut pressing against the T-shirt told its own story, one of too many TV dinners, too much fast food. "It's okay," Hayes said. "I know this woman."

"Nuh-uh," the woman in the headscarf corrected. "I'm gonna call a cop unless you give me a reason not to right this instant." She was rooting in her purse for her phone as she said it, her glossy lips permanently pulled back in a sneer.

"I saw what happened in the Park," Hayes said, speaking quickly. "Saw that Damocles said something to you."

She looked up from her bag, while Olive Skin T-shirt looked at the woman with newly discovered surprise.

"You a reporter?" the woman asked, that challenging note still in her voice, but lessening a little.

"I'm not..." Hayes began to say he wasn't, but then he realized that maybe that was his way to get her to talk, "– one of those tabloid paps, if that's what you're worried about. If I can just get five minutes of your time, just to clarify what happened. Anonymously."

The woman smiled tentatively and nodded. "Okay," she said. "But you better make it worth my while."

Hayes' mind raced. Was he going to have to pay this woman for information? It didn't matter right now, what mattered was what she had seen those weeks ago, back on Sixth.

They found a street café serving overpriced lattes that came accompanied by a tiny cookie the size of a fingernail.

"Well, you got five minutes," the woman told him as they took a table on the sidewalk, breathing in the fumes and noise of the street.

"My name is Jon Hayes," Hayes explained. "I saw you."

"Yeah," the woman said, blowing on her latte, not giving him her name. "I got that much."

"No, I mean," Hayes continued, trying to frame his words into something coherent, "three weeks ago, Wednesday the twentieth, there was a... altercation off Sixth Avenue."

Eyes hidden behind her shades, the woman looked at Hayes with suspicion. "This some kind of gag?"

"No, ma'am," Hayes said, hurrying on with his story. "This... altercation involved Captain Light and a villainess called Jade Shade. I don't know how it started."

The woman shook her head just slightly as she sipped at her coffee.

"You'd remember it," Hayes continued. "There was some damage to an office building, and Jade Shade tossed a news helicopter down onto the street."

"I don't remember that," the woman said. "You'd think I would, from the way you describe it."

"You have to," Hayes said, insistent. "It was a little after eleven in the morning. The news copter was white with a kind of red band –" he drew a squiggle in the air with his fingers to illustrate.

"I'm sorry, you must have me mistaken with someone else," the woman told him. "I didn't see what you're describing."

"Think back," Hayes pressed. "My wife died that day. She was under the helicopter when it... when it..." he trailed off.

The woman in the headscarf looked at Hayes through the dark lenses of her glasses, pity on her features. "I'm sorry to hear that," she said gently. "It must be hard. But I really wasn't there."

"I saw you," Hayes insisted. "You said... shit, what was it...? You said something when they first appeared. You asked what it was."

The woman reached into her bag and withdrew her cell phone, swiping the screen. Then she looked up and smiled forlornly. "Wednesday the twentieth... I had an appointment in Crown Heights then. I model sometimes, skin stuff, nothing glamorous."

"But I saw you on Sixth," Hayes stated, feeling uncertain now. "Are you sure you were in... Brooklyn?"

"Yeah," the sometimes model told him. "I remember it clearly. Guy wanted to show me his tats before we started and, well, he was no looker, you get me? Not like you, huh? I'm sorry, I shouldn't have said that. You just lost your wife an' all. I just… I'm sorry, okay?"

The woman got up to leave the table, her latte only half drunk. Hayes watched her walk away until she had merged with the rest of the evening's pedestrian traffic and disappeared from view. He remained at the table for a few minutes, fidgeting with his paper napkin, folding and refolding the same crease between his fingers, wondering if maybe he was losing his mind.

After a while, he left. His latte had gone stone cold and his car had five parking tickets on the windshield and a tow truck poised menacingly before it like some mythological beast. He paid off the driver and figured he would pay the fines first thing in the morning.

"I'm losing my mind," Hayes told himself as he washed his hands. He was home, standing at the basin in the bathroom, the night sky turned into a mosaic by the frosted glass in the window.

Approaching women – strangers – on the street. Making accusations. I need help, that's what I need. He had seen people lose it in the service, PTSD from the shit they'd seen and the horror. The service had people who could help with that, talk people down, bring them back to some kind of normal. But some never found their way back to normality, some just stayed out there at the fringes of objective reality, making hats out of tinfoil and talking about the coded instructions that the television people were giving them. And some were pretty well okay until they went to sleep, and then their mind would go wacko on them and they'd wake up screaming. He'd known a couple of guys who went that way, after they'd helped dismantle a sports stadium in Raqqa that had been turned into a slaughter house by Daesh.

Hayes twisted the faucet off and wiped his hands on the towel that hung over the rail by the heater. *Losing it*. That wasn't good.

Hayes toggled the light off as he left the bathroom, and when he did, he heard Melanie calling to him from the dark.

"You're not giving up, are you, Quo?" she said, a hint of sarcasm in her tone.

"Just fuck off," Hayes spat without turning back, striding away from the ghost in the bathroom.

He made his way downstairs to the kitchen and filled the kettle, his body quivering with anger. He should not have said that to Melanie. He had never once sworn at her, never in all their years together. Just because she was dead – and he knew that for a fact, that she was dead – didn't mean he could start cussing at her.

Her words rattled around his head as the kettle boiled: "*You're not giving up…*"

He had got a mug from the mug tree, was standing with it clutched in his hand, wondering what he was doing.

"Coffee," he said aloud, putting the mug down on the counter.

"*You're not giving up, are you, Quo?*"

"No," he told the empty darkness behind him as he spooned instant coffee into his mug and added water. "SEALs don't quit. They don't rush either. They just do the job before them."

Then do the job, Melanie would have said, if she was still here.

Hayes turned, looking through the kitchen doorway that led into the corridor and the lounge, looking for Melanie. "Tell me then," he said to the empty house. "Tell me to do the job."

No one answered. The house was empty. If Melanie had ever been there in some manner, in some second spirit life, she had taken his advice to heart and fucked off.

"Shit," Hayes muttered, shaking his head. He flicked off the light and moved down the corridor in a daze, one foot after the other like the last mile of a twenty-mile route march, when all you thought about was nothing because thinking about something meant remembering how much you wanted to stop and lie down.

He felt like the ghost now, moving through the empty house

like he wasn't really there, his passage barely noticed by even the smallest particle of dust.

He trudged past the lounge and its big screen TV, up the stairs without any real direction in mind, mug of piping hot coffee in hand. He stopped at the top of the landing and looked at the bathroom, feeling a flash of anger at how he had behaved just a few minutes before.

Bathroom. Bedroom. Nursery. The doors waited with nothing behind them, waited for his presence to bring them life.

Melanie's words played through his mind again: *"You're not giving up, are you, Quo?"*

"No, I just don't know what it is I'm trying to do," Hayes admitted loudly to the empty hallway. "I don't know what it is I'm looking for."

He moved into the bedroom, not knowing where else to go, and switched on the television for company. Some tedious sitcom was playing in rerun, when it hadn't been funny the first time around. Hayes slumped down on the bed and poked at the remote control, flicking past a docu-drama which featured familiar actors in costumes and false beards, past something that looked like an archeology dig in the blazing sun, clipped through a sports program, weather, news, more news, a game show, sitcom, this, that, that.

After a while he tossed the remote down on the bed and slurped his coffee, ignoring the noise from the TV speakers.

The woman in the scarf and dark glasses had been familiar. He had a way with faces, he had learnt that trick in the Middle East, so that he could even figure who was behind the masking veils and beards the locals wore. And that woman, in that scarf, in those glasses – that was the same woman who had been on Sixth the day that Melanie had died. And she had said…

"What do you think it is?"

He remembered her, she had stuck out in his mind because she looked like a fifties movie star.

"Whatever it is," a heavyset, dark-skinned man with streaks of gray at his temples had replied, "I hope Captain Light kicks its butt."

Yeah, that was the exchange they had had; strictly call and response.

Hayes opened his eyes, lids he had not realized he had closed, and looked once more at the television screen on the wall at the foot of the bed. Working the remote, he skipped through channels until he hit the News. A gray-haired man in a gray suit with a gray voice was discussing the state of the trade deficit. Hayes waited, guzzling coffee in big, warm gulps.

The story changed, a typhoon overseas, and then it went back to something that had been reported earlier, and Hayes smiled.

"Here in New York's Washington Square Park, it seems one lady caught the eye of a certain hero," the reporter said archly with a knowing wink in her voice. "Damocles had just wrapped up a tussle with Rattenfanger, whose latest scheme involved animating – get this, Paul – *clothing*, in an attempt to threaten the city."

The scene changed to pre-recorded footage of the evening's events as the reporter carried on her giddy narration. Damocles could just about be seen bursting free from a mass of rags before lunging towards Rattenfanger, his sword a streak in the air beside him.

"With the Rattenfanger case all sewn up, Damocles exited for parts unknown," the reporter continued, "but not before saying something to one of the bystanders."

A crash zoom focused on Damocles as he landed spryly amongst the watching crowd, capturing the moment he spoke with the woman in scarf and shades. Hayes watched, observing carefully, as the woman smiled and blushed, before the hero sprang away into the night.

Then we were back with the blond-haired reporter standing with the Washington Square Arch perfectly framed behind her, lit up for the night.

"Whatever Damocles said, it sure put a smile on one lady's face," she said, as if intimating she knew more but could not say. "This is Bethany Mackenzie in New York."

"Thanks, Bethany," the newscaster said with an air of authority as they cut back to the studio.

Hayes muted the sound as the news agenda moved on to stock prices and the Dow Jones.

It was her. He was sure of it. The same woman he had seen on Sixth Avenue the day Melanie had been killed.

So why had she lied?

7

Hayes had no way of tracing her. He didn't have her number. Hell, he didn't even have her name. She was just some woman he had followed out of the park, and taking *that* story to the police was likely to get him branded as a stalker.

So, what then? What could he do?

Hayes lay there and stared at the flickering television screen with the sound turned down, unfocused his eyes and just let the whole cascade of colors wash over him, setting his mind adrift.

There was footage of her. That was something. If he could find the footage, isolate her image, maybe speak to that reporter, Bethany Mackenzie...? But Mackenzie had not interviewed the woman, she wasn't a celebrity, her fifteen minutes of fame had lasted just four seconds in the hastily focused lens of a news report.

Maybe there were more news cameras there. Maybe there were other angles. But even that wouldn't get him far, would it? Not unless the woman got interviewed by someone, and he knew that hadn't happened because he had followed her right out of the park.

Social media would be abuzz with the incident, wouldn't it? That's what happened with these things, no one had privacy anymore, not really.

Hayes went to the little office in back of the house and fired up the computer.

There was nothing. Well, there was talk, but no one knew who the woman was, or if they did, they weren't saying.

Damocles didn't put out press statements – strictly speaking he was an outlaw, albeit a *cause célèbre* – so that was a dead end. So, where to look?

Hayes clicked on the tab at the top of his internet browser, bringing up his surfing history. He had spent days on ViewTube, looking at clips of various costumes in action, trying to find any pattern to their actions. He went back to one of those clips, one with Damocles tackling the intelligent gorilla that had adopted the name Professor Freakside and had declared himself the ruler of a revolutionary new cause based on Zoonomics. The news report was scathing of Professor Freakside, but questioned whether Damocles himself was somehow to blame in attracting all these freaks to New York – or perhaps even creating them the way he had presumably created his smart sword.

Hayes shook his head bitterly. Maybe having all these so-called heroes around New York did attract the menaces. After all, you never heard anything about an alien fleet attacking Boise, Idaho or a new death ray blasting out from a shed in suburban Detroit.

Then he saw her on the screen, just before the report ended and the clip cycled on to whatever followed. It was the woman – the woman in the headscarf and the shades, there at the zoo, standing by the Reptile House with a few other people, watching as Professor Freakside was led away in handcuffs. Seeing a hyper-intelligent gorilla being led away in handcuffs by the police was about as ridiculous as it sounded, incidentally, but Hayes paid it no mind.

Hayes tapped at the cursor, replaying the clip and forwarding to the point near the end where he thought that he had spotted the woman. He paused it, and enlarged the image until he could focus in on the figures in the background. The definition was not crystal clear – in fact, it became worse the larger he made it – but he felt certain it was her.

Who was this woman? Why did she keep turning up at hero/

villain smack-downs? Was she somehow connected to them?

Hayes leaned back in his seat, the screen frozen on that image of the woman and a handful of others watching from the shade of the Reptile House as the reporter spoke to camera. The date of the report was sixteen months ago.

"You're up to something," Hayes told the screen. "Whoever you are, you're a part of all of this."

All of what? Some grand conspiracy to get his wife murdered?

"It was an accident, Quo," Melanie said from over his shoulder.

Hayes' heart thudded hard in his chest, a feeling of elation sweeping over him. "You came back," he said, hardly believing it.

"The helicopter, Jade Shade, Captain Light – it was all just an accident," Melanie said with utter conviction. "No conspiracy, no grand scheme. Just bad timing. It shouldn't have happened. I was late."

"You were always late," Hayes told her. "Someone could have known that. Anyone with half a brain could have known that."

He turned then, annoyed that she didn't realize that she had been targeted. But Melanie wasn't there, all that was there was her perfectly-ordered notice board beside the wall calendar that hadn't been turned over in a month, not since she had died.

Hayes brought up another clip, then another, and another. News report followed news report, phone footage and homemade video cam films where some poor unsuspecting schmo's vacation footage had suddenly been interrupted by a battle between Kid Ocean and Neutron Solstice, or the Missing Link throwing Retention through the side of a fast food joint.

"Come on, Matilda, why don't you give Daddy a big smile for the–"

Crash!

"What the fu–?!"

It was three in the morning by the time Hayes finally found the woman again. This time she was at the forefront of a police barricade in the aftermath of a truly titanic clash between the

Rangers and a group of evildoers called Hell's Teeth that had lasted for hours. He paused the footage as the camera dwelled for a moment on where she stood amidst a group of gawkers. She had the same shades on, and a headscarf over her hair, this time in different colors but still the same pattern in the weave.

What did it mean? Judging by her accent, the woman was clearly from New York, so it was not beyond the realms of possibility that she had happened upon these cataclysmic battles each time. New York was a city with a population of over eight-and-a-half-million, plus commuters, tourists and others. So, the woman in the headscarf was the proverbial needle in the haystack, but that did not preclude her attending these crazy fights and their aftermath. Dumb luck could put her at the scene more than once, Hayes knew – he himself had witnessed three costume incidents in the city, going back to that first time with the Hunter bouncing off his car roof. The Hunter, Captain Light, Damocles – he had seen three of them, all NY based. Hayes was nothing special; except for that final time, he had not gone out of his way looking for one of these costumed battles, and even that time it had been luck as much as anything, following his own curiosity when he saw the blue lightning. The woman in the headscarf could be just the same, no one special, having no more effect on proceedings than she did on whether it rained that day – just because she went out in a downpour, wouldn't mean she had made it happen.

Hayes rubbed his eyes with the heels of his hands, pressed his cheeks and forehead to try to bring some life back into his face. It was 3am and he was still looking at his needle in the vastness of the haystack.

But when he opened his eyes again, blinking back the blur of tiredness, he noticed something on the frozen screen that he hadn't seen before. Across from the woman, two people to her left, was a man dressed in a sleeveless T-shirt and sporting the type of afro that had gone out of fashion with *Shaft*. Hayes knew this guy. It was the jogger, the same man who had shouted at him when he had parked up on the sidewalk before chasing off to observe the fight between Damocles and Rattenfanger.

Hayes leaned closer to the computer monitor, not quite comprehending what he was looking at. Finding the woman in the footage was a coincidence, but he had been looking for her. But the jogger? Was that just coincidence, too? He scanned the faces of the crowd more carefully, a half dozen people visible in the first ranks behind the police barricade, with more behind them. He did not recognize anyone in the first row, but when he peered at the faces in the second rank, forwarding the footage at quarter speed, he thought that maybe he had seen another of the men before. This man was dark-skinned and heavyset, with streaks of gray at his temples. Hadn't he been with the headscarf woman on Sixth Avenue when Melanie had been struck down?

They weren't standing together. The man with the gray temples was way over to the right of the frame, while the woman in the scarf was just off center. If they knew each other then they had become split up in the crowd. Or, if they didn't know each other, then it was just one glorious damned coincidence.

Hayes continued to watch as the footage proceeded to its slow-motion conclusion. Then the upload ended, and options flashed up on screen – to view the clip again, or to watch something similar selected by the algorithmic alchemy of ViewTube based on his prior viewing choices.

Hayes awoke to the warbling of his telephone landline. He had been dreaming about film clips being projected on the Washington Square Arch. In his dream, the New York traffic had halted to view them at each end of the park, like a drive-in movie.

Ring-ring!

The phone shrilled again, reminding him of its urgency.

He was still at the desk in the little office Melanie had used when she worked from home. The computer was still warm, but the screen had powered down through non-usage, switching to sleep mode. He must have fallen asleep in the chair. When he moved, he felt a stiffness in his lower back and across his shoulders like someone had secretly caked him in cement during the night.

Ring-ring!

"I'm coming," Hayes groused as he staggered from the office and into the hallway.

The cordless phone sat in its cradle under the stairwell, its rectangular screen lit up as it awoke into life. Hayes plucked it from the cradle as it excitedly concluded its fourth ring.

"Yeah, hello?" Hayes said, his voice sounding hoarse.

"Jon boy? That you?" the cheerful male voice at the other end began. "You sound awful. Did I catch you in the middle of something?"

"What?" Hayes asked. "No. I was just… What time is it?"

"Ten-Oh-Seven," the voice on the phone announced, delivering the time check as if it was a man's name. It was Hayes' boss from the packing unit, Jeff Puchenko, a good guy who had five kids by three different women and worked all the hours sent him to try to put two of those kids through college. "Why, you weren't having a lie-in, were you?"

"Me?" Hayes said. "No. I wasn't in bed."

"Course not," Jeff said. "They make you get up at the crack of dawn in the Navy, I heard, and I guess that's a habit that's hard to break. Bet you already done a ten-mile run before I was even eating my morning waffles, right?"

"Something like that," Hayes agreed. He was walking down the hallway to the kitchen where he tipped the kettle to check if it had water in it. "How are things there, Jeff?"

"Was about to ask you the exact same question, Jon," his supervisor said. "Look, friend, nobody wants to rush you and we all know you went through a hell of a thing with… well, with Melanie, rest her soul. But I'm figuring out the rota and was just trying to, you know, work out whether I need to put you back on there or…" Jeff left the end of the sentence hanging, a question implicit therein.

"I think I need a little more time," Hayes said as he flicked the kettle on.

There was a long pause, and then Jeff spoke from the other end of the line. "That's fine, pal, just fine. You take as long as you need. You figure – what? – a week maybe? I'm just trying to get my ducks all in a line here, you understand, doesn't need to be a week, could be longer."

"A week sounds good," Hayes said as the kettle began to quietly rumble to itself as the element heated the water. "That's good of you to offer that."

"Won't be paid, Jon," Jeff said. "I can't swing that for you, I'm afraid."

"No, I understand," Hayes assured him.

They spoke a little more, Jeff offering some words of sympathy as well as passing on an anecdote about one of his kids getting busted by the cops for what sounded an awful lot like carjacking. Hayes grunted his way through the conversation, making himself a coffee while he held the phone between shoulder and neck. Eventually, Jeff rang off.

Afterwards, the house went back to silence again, and Hayes just stood in the kitchen, leaning against the counter and drinking coffee. It was 10.21, and outside the world was awake and hurrying about its day, cars passing on the street with the swish of tires on blacktop, dogs barking for their missing owners who had departed for their daytime jobs hours before, kids shouting in schoolyards as morning recess arrived.

Hayes' head was full of cobwebs, so he changed into sweats and went for a run.

Back home, Hayes sat down before the computer once again in the little room that Melanie had called her office.

He had run four miles and hit the shower after, putting all his thoughts into some kind of semblance of order. Back in his BUD/S training, he had frequently been expected to run five or six miles without slowing; he had found it was an ideal way to clear one's mind and find method to any madness revolving around him.

Now, dressed in clean clothes, having shaved and run a comb through his hair, Hayes began an internet search for more footage, this time working to a specific agenda he had jotted down on the little notepad. He was looking at a particular period, eighteen months to today, and focusing on certain parts of New York to try to find if the same people turned up in the crowds.

The first two hours yielded nothing of note. He caught a possible glimpse of the heavyset man with the gray temples wading in the aftermath of an invasion by minions of the devil god Angra Mainyu, but the man in question was covered in dust and Hayes could not be sure it was him. Then came a possible sighting of the woman with the headscarf watching as the Mechanist helped contain a fire in Brooklyn, but again Hayes was uncertain, the camera passing over the woman too fast to be sure.

Hayes stuck at it. He figured it was like fishing – you threw out a lot of bait in those first few hours, but, if you were lucky, you would eventually get a bite.

When the bite came it was big.

The woman with the headscarf was easy to spot. That headscarf marked her out, along with her shades. The scarf would change colors sometimes, but it was always the same design. Hayes figured she must have a whole wardrobe of them.

The shades too, fifties style with slight points at the outside edge of their elliptic. Maybe she had a wardrobe full of those too, Hayes thought, or perhaps a drawer at least.

He began to speculate on what she looked like without the shades, without the headscarves. She was young and pretty, with full lips that she often accentuated with a dark shade of lipstick. He froze an image of her on screen and masked the top of her face with the notepad until he could look just at her lips.

Could it be that she was in other footage too, but without the sunglasses and the scarf? Could it be that he had dismissed a multitude of shots of the woman because she wasn't wearing her "disguise", her "costume"?

Hayes set the notepad back on the desk and began writing notes in pencil. This woman was appearing at maybe one-in-twenty of these super incidents, maybe a little more frequently than that.

Hayes wrote down: *1/20? 1/12?*

So, who was she? Who would be most likely to appear at these super-powered throw downs?

Hayes wrote: *Another super costume? Secret identity.* Then added: *Heroine?*

He thought about the super-powered heroines who populated New York. There was Astra, one of the Rangers, but her body type didn't seem right. There was Swan – her escapades had made the papers for a while, but he hadn't heard much about her in the past few months. She had the ability to fly and to move real fast, he knew, which kind of tied with his headscarf woman's ability to materialize at all these incidents, but it was, admittedly, a pretty thin line of reasoning. The incidents were spread apart by days, sometimes weeks, and the Swan had not been involved in them.

Even so, he wrote down: *The Swan?* before entering a new search into the computer.

"Swan, heroine"

A line of entries appeared, and Hayes spent a little time studying photos that had been captured of the heroine. Her white costume had a low neck line and a kind of spread of feathers beneath her butt that trailed out behind her when she was in flight. Her hair, like her costume, was pure white; very distinctive. That distinctive hair was something that could be easily hidden beneath a headscarf, Hayes realized.

He brought up footage of the Swan in action. She was a loner mostly, apart from a single adventure she had shared with Damocles. She was probably mid-range in power, not quite up there with Eternal Flame or Captain Light, but easily out-powering the more street-level costumes like the Hunter. Her rogues' gallery consisted mostly of robots and alien threats, which implied there might be some alien connection to her origins.

A little later, Hayes was watching a short clip showing the aftermath of the Swan's battle with something called the Prime Intelligence, a kind of beefed-up suit of armor with an insectoid helmet who wielded a glowing ax made of some kind of indestructible, alien glass. The battle had destroyed a tenement block that had thankfully been scheduled for destruction anyhow.

A reporter called Trent Nedergaard had his microphone shoved under the Swan's chin as he asked about the tussle she had just survived. The sweat was visible under her silver headband but she looked exhilarated.

"What do you say to rumors that this so-called Prime Intelligence is merely the first volley in an intergalactic war?" Trent Nedergaard asked.

The Swan looked straight into the camera, all blue eyes and a girl-next-door smile that practically shouted sincerity. "There's no war," she said levelly. "The Earth is safe, and it always will be so long as I have any say in the matter."

It was the kind of soundbite the news loved and the costumes were happy to give. No one knew the future, no one could guess where the next threat would come from.

Then the Swan lifted off, effortlessly taking to the skies in a graceful twirl. The camera artfully lingered for a few seconds on the crowd as they watched her ascent. Hayes saw the woman in the headscarf there, along with the heavyset man with gray at his temples, and, next to him, Afro jogger. He was beginning to recognize other faces too, or so he thought. There was an elderly woman wearing a hat with a ribbon, and a bald man with a mustache. A freckled kid was there too, looking like the same one who had asked for Captain Light's autograph back when Melanie had been killed.

And there was someone else who he hadn't noticed before.

A family – young parents and their daughter, who looked to be maybe four or five years old. The daughter had long dark hair and dark eyes that matched the mother's, and her smile matched too. The smile was Melanie's and the kid's parents – the two people standing beside her – were Melanie and Hayes himself.

PART 2
Breakdown

8

It felt as though the floor had dropped away from under his feet.

Hayes sat there, staring at the screen as the ViewTube footage played through to the end of the report, feeling totally unreal.

In a few seconds, the uploaded footage cut to black, and then began the cycling of ViewTube sequencing to line up whatever selection it had automatically proposed to play next. Hayes tapped on the screen, halting the selection process.

His breath was coming hard, his heart thundering inside his chest, the blood pounding in his ears. It felt like when his squad had been caught in an ambush in Afghanistan.

What had he just seen? What the hell was happening?

He reloaded the footage, skipped forward to that same lingering shot of the crowd, and paused the image when it reached the young couple and their daughter. The woman was Melanie all right, he had no doubt about that. Her or some uncanny double who not only looked like her and smiled like her but did those other things, those unconscious things that people do, the way she stood, the subtle tilt of her head. Which meant the man who looked like Hayes *was* Hayes. And the four year-old whose shoulder his hand was resting lovingly upon…?

"Ginnie," Hayes whispered.

It was utterly unreal.

He pinched himself, the way they tell you to do in a dream, but all it did was make the nerves of his arm sing for a moment, and he did not wake up.

Hayes pushed himself away from the screen, leaving the static image on hold, people frozen in time. He got to his feet, paced the tiny length of the room, stopped at the window and looked outside. It was afternoon. There were kids playing on the street as they made their dawdling way home, and soccer moms shuttling their progeny to this or that activity, cocooned in their people carriers that were colored like battleships and driven with the same determination.

"Ginnie," Hayes said, louder this time, turning back to look at the screen where it lurked across the room like some monster of myth. His daughter's name, the daughter he and Melanie had never had, *would* never have, because of that damn helicopter and the deranged bitch who threw it out of the sky.

Hayes needed a drink. Nothing was making sense. He had gone searching for the woman in the headscarf and had found she kept popping up in the crowds, witness to the chaos wrought by New York's heroes and villains. But then he had found other faces he recognized, and that was strange. But *this?* It was too much.

In the lounge, Hayes opened up the drinks cabinet that he had not touched since Melanie died. He knew how easy it was to lose yourself in a bottle, had seen colleagues go that way, even his father for a while after his mother was diagnosed with cancer and he didn't know how to process it. Dad bounced back, but some of Hayes' friends never had.

Hayes poured himself a half inch of whisky, sat and held it in his hand, feeling the coolness of the glass against his skin. "It's impossible," he informed the empty room.

The empty room offered no reply, so Hayes drank his whisky, its taste like fire on his tongue and throat.

* * *

Afterwards, his mind felt clearer. The shock had passed, and now he was thinking straighter again.

If he and Melanie had seen the Swan that day, he would remember it. But he had never seen the Swan. Never.

So how was it that he and Melanie had been there? "Take Ginnie out of the equation," he instructed himself as he sat back at the computer and brought up the footage once more. She was a random factor he had no ability to track yet, not until he knew more.

There was a date on the news report – fourteen months ago – and a location somewhere in the Bronx, somewhere called Belmont Avenue. Hayes had been to the Bronx, passing through it often, but he could not recall ever visiting any Belmont Avenue, not fourteen months ago, nor any time before or since.

He brought up a calendar on screen and worked his way back to the day of the report. It was a Saturday in April. The incident had occurred at around 4 pm. Hayes cursed – had it been a weekday he could have very easily confirmed that he was at work, but weekends could be trickier to account for. However, Melanie kept a diary for her appointments, he knew, something she had done since university. He rifled through the desk's drawers until he found the one from last year, thankful that she had kept it. It was pink and its edges had rounded where it had lived in her purse for a year, and there were sticky notes protruding from its pages.

He turned to Saturday's entry and saw a handwritten note which read: *Mom & Dad, 3 pm.*

Three o'clock. An hour before the Swan's battle in the Bronx.

Hayes made a phone call to his in-laws, waited while the phone trilled at the other end. He was relieved when it was Jodie who picked up, suddenly safe in the distant embrace of her mothering ways.

"Jodie, I need a favor," Hayes said after they had exchanged pleasantries.

"Anything we can do, Jon," Jodie replied, "you know that."

"You keep a diary, right?"

Jodie laughed dismissively. "It's not really a diary. It's an appointment book, just so we know when to go to the dentist or when the heater's due for servicing."

"Do you still have last year's?" Hayes asked, feeling a twinge of hope. "I'm trying to check something." He gave her the date.

"It's filed away in my bedside podium," Jodie told him. "It might be a few minutes before I can locate it."

"That's fine," Hayes said. "You want I should wait, or do you want to call me back?"

"I can call you," Jodie assured him, a rising note of confusion in her voice. "Jon, what is this all about?"

"It's about… Virginia," Hayes said. He and Melanie had not told her parents that they were planning to call their daughter that. Melanie had insisted that it was their secret and it would be bad luck to tell. Turns out, bad luck was gunning for Ginnie anyhow.

At the other end of the phone line, Jodie sounded even more confused, but she agreed to go look and promised to call Hayes back.

Hayes hung up, wondering what Jodie would find.

The phone rang thirty-five minutes later. It was Jodie, and she started out with an apology at taking so long.

"Doesn't matter," Hayes said. He was tense, more tense than he had been opening those terror cell doors in Afghanistan, the ones where they'd had to use explosives and throw flash-bangs into the ensuing fog to confuse and overwhelm anybody waiting inside.

Jodie read off the date, confirming it with Hayes. "We had you over for dinner. Duck a l'orange, and a raspberry coulis for dessert. I didn't write down the starter."

"That doesn't matter," Hayes said. "I remember the duck. You remember what time we got there?"

"Diary says three," Jodie said.

"Yeah."

"Jon?" Jodie began, her tone a question. "Is everything okay?

Because, I mean to say, this was a very odd request."

"I'm just trying to get something straight," Hayes told her. "That's all. You've been a big help."

Jodie sounded uncertain as she replied, "Well, okay then, if I've been some help."

"You have," Hayes assured her before hanging up.

Hayes remembered the dinner. He paced around the lounge, putting the day's events together in his mind's eye. The duck had been greasy but good, the dessert irrelevant – Hayes did not have a sweet tooth. But what he recalled was that they had arrived early, because Jodie had wanted to have a discussion about what they were doing for Jack's sixtieth birthday, and she didn't want Jack to know. That's why they had arrived at three, because Jodie's husband would still be at the golf course until four-thirty, and if he asked, they could say they had just got there.

"Damn," Hayes muttered, deflated with the sense of when the right answer isn't the answer you want. He went back to the computer.

9

Hayes searched obsessively through the clips he could find online, first of the Swan, then of other costume events and their aftermaths, scanning the bystanders for himself and for Melanie and for Ginnie.

He found Melanie again, just once – and just a maybe, he couldn't be sure. The report came from four months before when she had apparently witnessed a bank robbery in Manhattan perpetrated by a costumed gang called the Imps.

The Imps had ghost tech that allowed them to adopt the guise of anyone they saw, and they had taken on the appearance of the bank's security guard, manager and several of the tellers to get access to the vault. They had been rumbled by an armored truck driver who was brother-in-law to the security guard and knew his wife had been rushed to hospital that morning and that he had gone with her.

A hero called the Skater had chased down the Imp gang, sliding through the downtown streets as they tried to make their getaway, after shooting the observant armored truck driver.

On screen, Melanie was standing among a crowd behind some vox pops-type who gave his excited reaction to what he had witnessed to a somber news reporter. Melanie had a two year-old girl who looked like Ginnie in her arms.

"We heard gunshots and then that bank truck mounted the

sidewalk, followed by the Skater," the interviewee said. He had a goatee beard and a trilby hat he probably wore ironically. "He got in front of the truck and shot something from his hand that made the truck stop like it had been crazy-glued to the asphalt."

The story was picked up by another bystander, a man with long hair and a mustache, his eyes fixed in a permanent squint. "The gang barreled outta that truck like they had the last tickets for Woodstock, man…"

Hayes stopped the clip, feeling the wetness on his face, where tears were leaking unbidden from his eyes.

Hayes left the computer with its hidden memories of himself and Melanie and the child they had never had. He went to the lounge and drew out their wedding album from the bookcase. Melanie had often looked at it, but he hadn't really, only with her.

Now, huddled on the sofa, Hayes looked at the pictures. *Smiles* – that was the word that described all of those pictures. Smiles and smiles and smiles. So much happiness. They were right together, fitted like parts of a child's construction kit.

Hayes picked up his cell phone and sent a text to Peter Dunn, an old friend from the Navy. Pete was a chopper pilot who had been stationed with Hayes in Bolivia and again in Colombia. They were close the way service guys were, a lot of trust, some pranking, but mostly professional. Pete had left the service four years ago with a bum knee after he had taken a bullet. He lived in Queens, close to Hayes. They would meet up now and then to talk over old times, but not that often. Pete was one of those guys who was a friend because of proximity, but he was also a good guy.

You free for a drink?

Pete's reply came back a minute later:

At Skinny's, 20.00. Okay?

Okay.

* * *

Skinny Jake's was a bar in Queens that featured live acoustic music and hot food. The place was sprawling and featured plenty of underlit corners like a rabbit's warren. A man could get lost in Skinny's trying to find the restroom. No one knew who Skinny Jake was, if indeed he was anyone at all, but he sure didn't get skinny from eating the establishment's food, which was deep fried and rich in salt.

Pete Dunn was at the bar when Hayes got there, placing an order for food. He was wearing a beat-up camo jacket with frayed seams, and had his crutch leaned against a bar stool beside him.

"Ten-hut," Hayes said as he joined Pete at the bar.

Pete turned to him and smiled. "Hayes, you look like you need another promotion," he said. He always said this to Hayes, every time they met. Maybe he thought it was funny. Maybe it was.

"I don't know about a promotion," Hayes said, "but I could use some advice."

Pete's brows furrowed. "What's on your mind, brother?"

They found a table, in sight of the bar and away from the musicians, and talked over a couple of beers.

"What do you know about the Imps?" Hayes asked.

"Probably about the same as you do," Pete said after a few seconds of consideration. "They're a gang of criminals, four of them – three guys and a chick – who use some kinda stealth tech to change their appearances. I heard they got banged up two months ago after hitting a bank downtown."

"Four months ago," Hayes corrected him.

"'Z'at so?" Pete said. "Seems more recent. Why the interest?"

Hayes surreptitiously checked their surroundings before speaking in a quieter voice. "You're familiar with stealth tech," he said. "Your choppers had it, right?"

"Yeah," Pete confirmed, "but it ain't the same thing if that's where you're going. The stuff that Imp gang uses, it's holographic static. That's what I read anyhow."

"Me too," Hayes said. "I just wonder – you think they could use that to impersonate my wife."

"I guess they could," Pete said, and a crafty smile crossed his face. "Why? You thinking about some kinky threesome thing?"

"Melanie's dead," Hayes said, cutting Pete's jocular tone in an instant.

"Shit, man," Pete said. "I'm sorry. I hadn't heard..."

"That's okay," Hayes assured him.

"She was young, man," Pete said, with a weary shake of his head. "What happened?"

"She got caught up in a costume fight," Hayes told him. "The Jade Shade dropped a helicopter on her."

Pete swore and looked away, watching the bar for a few moments as he took those words in.

"Well?" Hayes prompted. "You think the Imps could impersonate her?"

Pete leaned in, his face deadly serious. "What have you got in mind, buddy? You don't want to... to replace her, right? Because that would be all kinds of messed-up."

"No. I found some clips of Melanie online," Hayes said. "Nothing weird, just some news reports. I was in one of them too. Except, I wasn't there. I'd remember if we had been there, and I wasn't there. So I figure maybe the Imps...?"

"Used you and Mel as a disguise?" Pete said, but his tone was skeptical. "It's possible, I guess. Good way to evade the cops, and the costumes, too."

"You said there were four of them, right?" Hayes confirmed.

"Yeah, three guys, one woman," Peter said, drawing his cell phone from his pocket. He brought up the internet connection and tapped in a query before flashing the screen to Hayes. "There they are. And you were right about them getting arrested four months ago. Still awaiting trial by the looks of it."

"It say how they copy other people?" Hayes asked, though he had already read up on the gang.

Pete scanned his screen for a few seconds. "Some kind of hologram projection, like I said. They need to see the victim, presumably take some kind of photograph from which they can replicate the image."

"You ever hear of them impersonating a child, Pete?"

"No. They can't do that. Too much body mass to hide behind a projection."

"That's what I thought," Hayes said, perplexed.

Pete saw the frown on Hayes' face. "What is it, man? You think the Imps used you and Melanie's faces somehow?"

"I don't know," Hayes admitted. "There's another factor, an unknown. A kid. In the footage I saw, we had a kid."

"You don't have a kid?" Pete asked. Things could change when you didn't see people in a while, so he asked to be certain.

"No, but Melanie was pregnant when she… when it happened," Hayes said.

"That's rough, man," Pete said. "How far was she gone?"

"Seven months," Hayes said, feeling a sudden rush of sadness.

A bowl of fries and dip arrived, brought to the table by a perky waitress with a smile that seemed just slightly too wide for her face. Pete thanked her and ordered another round of drinks. Once she had gone, he spoke solemnly to Hayes.

"What are you thinking here, man?" Pete asked.

"I don't know," Hayes admitted. "Something happened with my wife on Sixth Avenue, when the Shade dropped that helicopter on her. I think maybe it was planned."

"What? That the Shade wanted to kill your wife?" Pete asked, incredulity in his tone.

"Not the Shade, no," Hayes said. "Someone else. Behind Jade Shade."

"Why? Why would someone do that?"

"Because they'd replaced her already," Hayes said. "They'd replaced her and me and our daughter."

"You said you didn't have a daughter," Pete reminded him. "That she hadn't been born yet."

"Someone wanted us out of the picture," Hayes said.

"You're still here," Pete pointed out.

"Then either they missed or they just wanted Melanie,"

Hayes insisted.

"Why?" Pete asked levelly. "What would they gain? Your wife was… nobody, man. I mean, she was great and you loved her, and I remember her cooking a mean BBQ that one time, but she didn't matter to these costumed types. She was just collateral damage."

Hayes reached for his second beer but his hand was trembling with adrenalin and anger and he could not pick it up. He took a slow, deep breath to steady himself and Pete spoke again.

"I'm sorry," Pete said.

"If she was collateral damage, what was she doing at the bank that day with the Imps?" Hayes asked. "What were we doing together at that demolition site in the Bronx when the Swan fought the Prime Intelligence? When we were not there."

Pete looked momentarily confused before realization dawned. "The other footage. Maybe it's just coincidence. People look different on film. You ever see a Hollywood actor in the flesh? They look real different. Short runts, most of them."

"This was her," Hayes said with certainty.

Pete locked his eyes with Hayes. "Then what are you going to do?"

"I'm going to… talk to these costumes, find out what they know. Find out why they killed my wife," Hayes said.

Pete smiled, shaking his head. "You'll get killed. Their world isn't ours. They fight against impossible odds to save the planet while we stand on the sidelines and applaud. You go up against them, and they'll turn you into paste with a look or a heat ray or a robot powered by thought-waves."

"They killed Melanie," Hayes said, "and replaced her, replaced her in the past, and someone knows why."

Pete fixed Hayes with a look. "And what if they don't? What then?"

"Then I guess I'll have been turned to paste for nothing," Hayes said grimly.

10

Hayes started checking news photos, theorizing that the quality of the pictures would be better than the blurry nature of the moving footage on ViewTube. By the end of the first day, he had noticed that there was one particular photographer who snagged a lot of pics of a costumed hero called Eternal Flame. The photographer's name was Benjamin Jermain. Eternal Flame had incarcerated the Imps early in his career, and sure enough there was a photo of the Imps bound and dumped on the steps of a precinct house by him. The photo was credited to Benjamin Jermain.

Hayes looked into Jermain's background, doing a profile search on the internet, and accessed a fee-paying site to do a full background check. Jermain lived in Harlem and freelanced. Like most freelances, he sold his work to the same clients over and over, most frequently to the *New York Echo*. He appeared in a few photos relating to the *Echo*, but mostly kept out of the limelight. In the photos he seemed unremarkable, just some millennial with an unruly mop of dark hair who favored baggy clothes.

The next morning, Hayes took the subway to Rockefeller Center and made his way to the offices of the *Echo*. It was a breezy summer morning, still feeling cold in the shade. Hayes had dressed in a dark hoodie and jeans, the kind of unmemorable things that he figured would help him blend into a crowd.

Hayes had done a little stake-out work with the SEALs, but that was really just waiting around a place for a go-signal rather than trying to actually follow someone. He had seen it done on cop shows, though, and figured that either he'd succeed and it would be fine, or he'd get spotted and run – it wasn't as though he had a rigid plan for what was going to happen next. He had a vague idea that he might corner Jermain and ask what he knew about the Imps, based on his taking their photo four years ago. As plans went, it was hardly intricate.

The *Echo* was situated in a grand monument of steel and glass whose tinted windows snared the reflection of similar buildings located all around it, drawing them into its embrace. The entrance consisted of three sets of double doors, one next to the other, with a wider single door adjacent to these for access by wheelchairs, buggies and the trolleys that were used for deliveries. Some work was being done to the building façade that stretched along West 46th Street. The scaffolding reached up five stories with a plastic chute snaking down to a skip parked at the curbside.

Hayes walked past the set of doors twice, first one way and then the other, wondering what to do now. When he passed the second time, he was conscious of how it might seem conspicuous, so he glanced up at the skyscraper on the opposite side of the street, as though lost and looking for a landmark. As if anyone cared who he was, some insignificant face in the crowd.

Otherwise known as the Avenue of the Americas to people outside of New York, Sixth Avenue was a long road. This was where Melanie had died, but a little way further downtown, further south.

Hayes passed by a newsstand on Sixth, close to the main entrance to the *Echo*'s office building, and he strolled over to it. There were newspapers and magazines, the latter with gaudy covers of celebrities, glorying in their improprieties and their peccadilloes. Among the beaming celebrities was a cover showing

Ghost Bot, one of the newer costumed "heroes" whose loyalties were still unclear. Hayes flicked through the magazine, keeping an eye on the entrance to the *Echo* offices. Ghost Bot walked through walls to catch perpetrators, much to their bewilderment.

"Hey, hey, this ain't no library, pal," the stall holder shouted from his post behind the counter.

Hayes looked up.

"Yeah, you," the newsstand guy said, glaring at Hayes. He was sixty if he was a day, wearing a flat cap out of the forties and with the steely, accusing stare of a man who no longer had patience for anyone he hadn't known for at least fifty years. He probably fished at the weekend.

"I was just looking," Hayes said noncommittally.

"Well, it ain't a looking stand," the stall holder said, "it's a newsstand. And if it's had your paws all over it, the news ain't gonna look so new, is it? So, either you buy it or you park it back where you found it. Capeesh?"

Hayes put the magazine down on the counter on top of a newspaper which touted the breakdown of trade talks with the Far East. "Sure, sure." So that was his perfect cover blown, and it had taken a full two minutes.

Then, as he was walking away from the newsstand, his mind racing for new options, Hayes spotted Ben Jermain walking out of the *Echo* offices with a blond-haired woman. Jermain was skinny and looked underfed, hair messy as though it had last seen a comb sometime in the spring. He walked with a loping stride, snacking on a high-protein bar straight from the wrapper. Despite being an adult, the woman beside him was dressed hipster smart, like she was thirteen and going off to band camp for the summer.

Hayes checked his watch – 09.22 – and increased his pace to follow Jermain and his friend as they hurried away in the opposite direction, deep in discussion.

Hayes picked up his pace, weaving through the crowd in pursuit. He figured he could question the photographer, explain what had happened to his wife and hopefully get some insight into the Imps and how these costumes operated. There was a slim chance, but it might be his "in". He could figure what to do with "Band Camp" if she objected.

Jermain kept looking behind him as though suspicious of something – like he knew he was being followed. Hayes pulled up his hoodie, trusting its shadow to mask his features.

Jermain and the blonde were at the curbside, looking back again. Hayes faltered – should he accost this guy right here in the middle of the street? The last time he had done that – when he'd approached the woman in the headscarf and shades – he'd almost got into a punch up with a public-spirited passerby, and then the whole thing had descended into a mess anyhow because he had not prepared what to ask. He waited a moment, composing his thoughts. It was unlikely that the photographer would know about Melanie, so he wanted to keep that in reserve. He just wanted to know about the costumes, about Eternal Flame whom this Jermain guy photographed so frequently, and find a way to talk to the people themselves. Jermain probably didn't know much about the Imps, but Flame would.

I'll sound like a groupie, Hayes realized. Another Sheila Shannon, grafting himself onto a hero's rep in a hungry bid for fame.

Jermain seemed to be looking at Hayes, and Hayes turned his head, sidestepping into the pedestrian traffic. Then he saw what was happening – the photographer was not looking at him, he was looking at the cab his partner had just called over. A hurried discussion through the side window and then Jermain and the blonde slipped in back. The cab peeled away from the sidewalk and into the traffic flow.

So that was it all along. Jermain had not been looking at Hayes. He had been trying to get the attention of a cab.

Hayes headed back towards the newsstand, feeling deflated.

Hayes bummed around for most of the morning, circling back to the *Echo* offices every twenty minutes or so, trying to remain

inconspicuous. The first time a cop car came by, he turned away
and made as if to take a side street. But by the time the third cop
car passed by, oblivious to his presence, he realized that the only
person who thought he was guilty of anything was himself, and if
he was questioned, he could legitimately claim he really was doing
nothing more than wasting a sick day.

His cell phone rang at 11.06 and again at 12.04. He let it go to
voice mail both times after checking the number. It was work;
probably Jeff Puchenko again, asking if Hayes was thinking about
coming back to work anytime soon. He wasn't.

At 12.34, a car came speeding into Sixth from a cross road. It
took the corner on two wheels with a roar of acceleration. Hayes
heard the sound and was instantly alert, tensing as the car sped
away with a blare of its horn. The driver – a woman with streaked
blond hair and a startled poodle in the passenger seat beside her
– looked terrified, like she was trying to outrace the grim reaper
himself.

Hayes turned back to study the cross street, realizing it wasn't
the car that was the worry. From the side, something that looked
like a train engine came chuntering into view. It was constructed
of a patchwork of metal, but it was not a road vehicle. It had long
spindly legs which it rode on at their widest extension, so that
its belly almost hugged the ground. A head extended from the
front like a tortoise's, peering left and right as it trudged over the
intersection, trailing its long, mismatched body behind it. It was
at least thirty feet long, and almost half that in height. Within the
body were parts of cars – doors and fenders and a whole line of
exhaust pipes sticking up in a row at the thing's midsection.

Around Hayes, people were reacting with horror
and astonishment.

"What is that thing?" a guy in a letterman jacket asked, pulling
out his ear buds.

"It's hideous!" a woman to Hayes' right commented, her

already punky, hairspray-rich hair seeming to stand up even more in her shock.

People screamed as the metal creature – if that's what it was – collided with a bus in a cough of spluttering airbrakes. The bus was swallowed up by the metal monster, literally absorbed into the monster's make-up as the two touched. Chunks of bus paneling and grill rippled down the mechanical thing's sides as it continued to cross the intersection, accompanied by the strained howls of the bus passengers and driver as they disappeared from view. In an instant, the people inside the bus were lost within the uncanny body of the snaking metal monstrosity.

The owner of the newsstand facing the offices of the *Echo* vaulted over his counter as the creature's massive tail swished into the side of his stand, collapsing the wood to splinters in an instant. The surface of the tail was characterized by car tires and manhole covers, a fire hydrant sticking out momentarily like a boil before disappearing beneath the surface once more.

People were running in every direction to get away from the mechanical beast. Hayes made a snap decision then – instead of running away, he followed, chasing westwards after the mech as it scuttled further away along West 46th Street.

Hayes could run. He had trained to peak physical condition when he had joined the SEALs, and he still kept in shape two years after leaving. What slowed him down were the people – and there were a lot of them – running in the opposite direction as he tried to give chase.

The serpentine monstrosity was still moving ahead, crashing through the scaffolding that ran along the edge of the *Echo* building and absorbing the metal poles holding it aloft. In an instant, the scaffolding lost integrity and came tumbling down, spilling workmen to the street care of the unforgiving drag of gravity.

A whole line of road works, including a steam roller and jack hammer, disappeared as the oblivious mechanism continued on its path, scampering over them like an insect, adding them to its growing mass. All around, the sounds of screaming were echoing through the glass canyons of midtown, a great wave of fear as this freakish metal giant ploughed on without halt or hindrance.

Hayes diverted off the sidewalk, where the terrified crowds were blocking his path, and hit the pavement of the street instead. Cars had pulled up, some now missing their front ends or their sides where the creature had touched and hence absorbed them into its bulk. Hayes admittedly had no idea what it was, but with people getting caught up in its mass, he felt compelled to do something.

He was at its tail now, and this close he could see the way the surface of its patchwork skin constantly rippled, each part moving and adjusting to a new position. It was like looking at the surface of a rushing river. The base of a streetlamp hurtled past high overhead, protruding from the thing's tail, three stories up.

"Hey!" Hayes shouted.

The creature did not slow. It carried on slithering down the street, pulling in more cars and debris to add to its growing mass, paying Hayes' cry no attention.

"Hey!" Hayes tried again. "Hey! Metal head! I'm talking to you!"

If the thing had intelligence, and Hayes suspected that it did, it either didn't hear him or it didn't care.

Hayes ran faster, picking up from a fast jog to a sprint as he reached for the creature. He had been watching how it absorbed its – nutrition? Prey? – and figured it was only taking things in from the front end, kind of like a worm.

As the tail shimmied before him, Hayes leapt, vaulting over the swaying mass of metal, and keeping pace with the side of the creature. On the sidewalk, people were cowering in doorways, terrified by what they saw. *You'd think they'd be used to it by now*, Hayes thought uncharitably. *This is New York. If it ain't Alien Invasion Day, it's show-and-tell at the mad scientists' convention.*

Hayes was close to the thing's head now, as it barreled on towards Times Square. He unzipped his hoodie, reaching for his Glock in its shoulder rig – another reason he had worn the hoodie, it was loose and could hide the gun easily.

The Glock slipped into his hand comfortably, its familiar weight like a natural extension of himself. Hayes had used various small arms in the military, as well as bigger fare right through to anti-tank artillery. The Glock-19 was a compact piece of hardware and one the US Navy favored. Its barrel was less than seven-and-a-half inches long, while the Glock's magazine held fifteen shots which equated to a whole lot of 147 grain parabellum stopping power. If you came across something that took more than fifteen bullets to drop, chances were, it wasn't going to drop at all.

Up at its head end, the metal train-beast was thundering into a parked mail truck, swallowing the back end of the vehicle into its mass with a sound like metal through a wood chipper. The driver leapt from the open door as the back of his truck disappeared, rolling against the blacktop of the street and into the beast's path.

"Hey!" Hayes shouted as the monster bore down on the mailman. "Metal lips! Eat this!"

Bang! The Glock shuddered in Hayes' hand, discharging its first bullet into the side of the metal behemoth, close to its swaying head. The head dipped for a moment, hovering above the fallen mailman. Then, halted in its path, the beast turned towards Hayes, acknowledging him for the very first time.

"Yeah," Hayes shouted squeezing the trigger again. "That's it! Come on!"

Two further shots spat from the Glock, one drilling into the center of the thing's head, the other ricocheting from the extended metal neck. Neither had any discernable effect.

Hayes lined up another shot, conscious that the mailman was running for cover behind him now.

Bang!

Another shot from the Glock hit the metal beast's head, striking with a shower of white sparks.

There came a creaking sound as the beast turned to face Hayes. Head on, its face was an extended cone that narrowed to a point like a bird's beak. Two "eyes" loomed above the beak, rectangular slits that glowed red with menace. And then it spoke in a voice that sounded like the contents of a cutlery drawer being tipped out:

"I am Dread-0!" it said, pronouncing the 0 as "naught". *Dread-naught.* "I must repair all!"

"Hayes," Hayes snarled back. "Remember it!" As he spoke, Hayes fired again, then leapt aside as the beast's head jabbed forward like a chicken pecking for grain. As he did so he felt the pistol pluck from his hand – not by a hand but as if it was being snatched away by a powerful magnet. Hayes rolled on the pavement as his gun was sucked whole into the face of the metal thing, disappearing into its mass.

Then the metal creature turned away, leaving Hayes sprawling on the asphalt between the half-consumed remains of the mail truck and a skip. Its long body – longer now than it had been when Hayes had first seen it just a few minutes before – trailed past Hayes like a freight train backing into a siding, heading towards Times Square.

Hayes lay between the lurching remains of the mail truck and the skip, feeling his heart pounding against his chest, and tried to bring his breathing back to normal. Dread-0. Dread-0? He had never heard of this one, was not even sure what the hell it was. And he had just lost his Glock to the thing, without its even trying. He knew he was lucky to be alive, and maybe his actions had saved that mailman from a similar fate to that which the bus passengers had suffered.

In Times Square, the sentient machine known as Dread-0 was painted by the illuminated displays as cars screeched out of its path, and another cab disappeared into its guts. At the same moment, something came streaking across the sky like a comet, trailed by a slash of red fire. It was Eternal Flame, on the scene at last to protect the citizens of New York City.

"Meal time's over, Dread-0!" he announced as he landed directly in the path of the incredible metal construct.

"I am Dread-0," Dread-0 said. "I must repair!"

"Then repair this!" Eternal Flame shouted, joining his hands together and aiming them at the approaching mechanical monster.

There followed a blast of brilliant red laser light, bursting from Eternal Flame's entwined hands in a perfectly straight beam, its color matching the one-piece uniform the hero wore. The beam struck Dread-0 dead center of its head and it reared back. But the beam continued to track it, delivering a single strand of heat and light into its pointed head. In a few seconds the silver head began to smoke as the metal started to glow, first red, then orange, then, finally, white.

Eternal Flame stood his ground, legs placed wide. The color of his metabolic costume changed from red to orange to white, too, as he channeled the incredible forces that roiled within his super-charged body into the machine intelligence that threatened to consume Times Square.

Crowds of onlookers watched, some cheering for Eternal Flame – the hero who had once died for them only to be reborn in the heart of the sun – to whup that beast.

The brilliance sparking off the two combatants put the illuminated hoardings of Times Square in the shade; that advertising had as much effect now as shining a flashlight at the surface of a star. The crowd shielded their eyes, turning away as the whole of Dread-0's body glowed brighter and brighter as it began to melt.

11

The Glock was useless

– Hayes wrote the words on Melanie's notepad. He was sitting in front of the flat screen TV in his lounge in Queens, watching a news report about Eternal Flame's battle with the thinking machine known as Dread-0.

Not that that should have come as a surprise to Hayes, that his Glock-19 with its quick loading action and its impressive stopping power was out of its league when faced with a demented, sentient machine. What the hell were you supposed to use against an AI set on "repairing" the city?

According to the news report, Dread-0 had escaped from TomorrowTech Labs, a cutting-edge industrial plant located next to the East River close to the Midtown Tunnel. A spokesman for the company – a bald man with glasses that seemed comically too large for his face – explained in dry tones that the *Digital Repair Enabling and Access Device, Number Naught* – or *Dread-0* – had been developed by the company as an intelligent, self-repair system for satellites. However, they were now investigating whether its artificial intelligence programming had been faulty, or if there was something more sinister behind the thing's autonomous rampage downtown.

Hayes mulled those words over in his mind, eyeing the notebook that rested on the arm of the sofa. *Everything has an origin*, he realized. These costumes and the insanity they deal with on a daily basis – they all have stories to tell, full of malfunctions and lightning strikes and industrial sabotage.

"And Glocks don't work," Hayes muttered as he jabbed at a button on the remote to shut off the TV.

Exhausted, Hayes fell asleep early. He dreamt of a line of cars moving in convoy through the street outside his house. The cars were joined at the fenders, and the lead one had a face made of metal.

Hayes woke in the middle of the night, and wondered if what he had done in saving that mailman had made him a hero. In the eyes of that guy, maybe, but not to anyone else. Not even to Hayes himself.

The next morning, Hayes showered and shaved, got dressed and did a five-mile run before breakfast. His head was full of ideas – about Dread-0 and about the wider context of battling costumes.

By 7am he was sitting at the scarred table in the kitchen eating oatmeal. He left the bowl in the sink and hopped a train into town.

Hayes was in Times Square before nine. It was busy with morning traffic, commuters making their way to work, early tourists already marveling at the bright lights through jet-lagged eyes.

There was no indication that an incredible battle had been fought here less than twenty-four hours ago. Hayes looked at the street, eyeballing the ground for some evidence of where Dread-0 had been turned to slag. Apart from a few tire marks, which may

or may not have been caused by drivers veering out the way
of Dread-0's approach, there was nothing. Someone must have
come in and cleaned up all the damage overnight, Elves-and-
the-Shoemaker style.

Eternal Flame had helped the authorities remove the melted
remains of Dread-0 itself. The people who had been absorbed
within had popped free while it was heating up under Eternal
Flame's power blast, firing from holes in the thing's carapace like
bread from a toaster. There were a few broken bones, but the
people were relieved simply to be alive.

No evidence. That was the conclusion Hayes reached after
scouting the area for the best part of an hour, working around the
foot and road traffic. *No evidence at all. As if it had never been.*

Hayes found a reasonably priced café close by, bought himself a
cappuccino and snagged a table looking out on the street.

He could buy another Glock. But that wouldn't do much against
things like Dread-0, which meant it was useless against people
like Captain Light. It was Captain Light he needed to get to, or
someone of that level; someone who was in on the conspiracy
that had killed Melanie and replaced him and her with clones or
impersonators or robots or whatever the hell those things were
who appeared on old news reports where they had never been.

The heroes only turned up when villains pulled their schemes,
and they weren't easy to approach otherwise. There was the
Nexus Range uptown, of course, the headquarters of the Rangers,
but they didn't simply let any Joe Schmo in off the street with a
sob story.

Which left the bad guys.

Hayes could buy another Glock and go after the lower tier of
costumes then, those street-level bad guys he had identified, the
jumped-up mobsters who had somehow accessed some tech.

But if he did that, how would he find them? The heroes never
got the villains before they committed their crimes, they always

happened upon them during or after, once something had been snatched or wrecked or had its molecules rearranged. Was that a justice thing? A legal thing? Would it be setting a bad precedent to go after these bad guys before they committed their atrocities? Because, that was odd – if you're a half-lion monster like the Devourer and you hung with Hell's Teeth, it was a sure bet you were there to commit some illegal act or other.

Unless these bad guys had hiding places where they weren't dressed up like freaks all the time. Hiding places and aliases, assumed names… hell, maybe *real names*. That was possible.

Hayes drank the last of his cappuccino and realized he had begun to form a plan. What he needed to do was go after the small fries, the part-time players who were low on the power rankings and didn't have anyone to fall back on. He could rule out the heroes. They were a fraternity, a club that looked out for each other. Even when loners like the Hunter got into trouble there were reports of someone like Eternal Flame or Damocles coming to his aid.

So, bad guys first. If he shook enough of them, maybe he would find an in on the bigger story.

Hayes went back to the firing range just off Fifth, showed some ID and purchased a new Glock along with a box of ammo. The woman behind the counter recognized him, although she didn't know his name.

"You come in here a lot, right?" she asked.

Hayes brushed back his short hair and looked non-committal. "I wouldn't say 'a lot'…"

The counter assistant smiled. She had jet black dyed hair and a piercing in her lip, and wore mascara like she had applied it in the dark. Her clothes were black, too, and she had webbing tattooed over the back of her left hand and all the way up her arm. "So, what is this? An upgrade?"

"Replacement," Hayes told her. "I lost my old one."

The assistant's brows rose along with a line of studs embedded at the outside edge of one of them, her interest piqued. "Did you report it?"

"It wasn't stolen," Hayes said. "It got taken from me by that Dread-0 thing."

The counter assistant looked blankly.

"Big articulated robot," Hayes elaborated. "Came crashing through midtown yesterday, absorbed metal objects as it went. My gun included."

Counter girl shook her head. "I don't see much news. What happened?"

"Eternal Flame settled its hash when it reached Times Square," Hayes told her while she rang the ammo through the till. "Reduced it to slag. I was just there twenty minutes ago, but there's nothing there now."

"Madness," the woman concluded as Hayes ran his card across the sensor to pay.

As he was leaving, something dawned on Hayes. He stopped at the end of the aisle by the exit and turned back, returning to the counter. The mascara-loving assistant smiled hopefully as he approached.

"You forget something?" she asked.

"No," Hayes told her, "I was just wondering – you didn't hear about Eternal Flame and Dread-0? None of it?"

"Like I said, I don't really see the news," shop girl told him.

"And no one said anything?" Hayes asked.

The counter assistant took a half-step away from the counter, a look of suspicion on her face. "No, why?"

Seeing that look on the woman's face, Hayes realized that asking odd questions in a gun store was a pretty dumb ass thing to do. "No reason," Hayes said, trying to sound reassuring. "Just surprised. It probably seemed a bigger deal to me because I saw it happening."

"Uh-huh," the counter girl said. She sounded uncertain, like she was worried about what Hayes was going to do. Her eyes flicked down to where Hayes guessed she had a hidden stud that triggered an alarm.

"Have a good day," Hayes told her and made his way back through the store towards the exit. He was aware that the girl was watching him with a wary suspicion. *It isn't me you have to worry about, ma'am*, Hayes thought. *It's crazies like Dread-0 and the Imps.*

Out on the street, it had started raining hard. People were ducking for shelter, umbrellas thrust upright like Excalibur emerging from the lake, newspapers and bags over the heads of those who had come out unprepared.

Hayes let the rain hit him, enjoying its coolness in the summer heat. He replayed the conversation with the counter assistant in his mind as he ambled towards the metro at Prince Street. Her words had surprised him, but maybe they were not so strange. The things that happened in this city, the constant stream of costumed criminals, of tech gone bad and of beings from other dimensions or time zones or galaxies wreaking havoc – it was normal. It was a kind of impossible normal that New Yorkers had grown to live with. They didn't even notice when a hyper-intelligent coral reef emerged from the Hudson River and got beaten back by Kid Ocean, or when yet another mayoral candidate turned out not only to have links to the costume community, but was actually some costumed mobster himself. New Yorkers had got to a stage of ignoring it all, brushing it aside like none of it mattered.

And maybe none of it did. Maybe whatever ravages befell the city care of the Bride of Genghis Khan or the Tyrant or Psychant, everyone knew, in their hearts, that it would ultimately reset and that everything would go back to normal, that everything would be all right again tomorrow.

Even the Imps, with their stolen faces and their trick camouflage – even the lives they stole just came back, as if nothing had changed, as if they had not been victims of the most violating identity theft one could imagine. Hayes had never once seen or heard or read a report where someone complained about their life being ruined by one of the Imps impersonating them. It always got resolved.

And all those bad guys and all those bad things just disappeared, waiting for another day in another month or another year to start the whole grim cycle again.

Hayes waited on the metro platform, thinking about the whole set up, how the costumes' lives seemed to be separate from those of people like him and the gun store clerk and the mystery woman in the headscarf and shades. Separate lives to those lived by people like Melanie.

He wondered: *Do you have to wear a costume to be a part of that world?*

12

The subway car hurtled into darkness with the clackety-clack of wheels on rails, shuttling its human cargo beneath the New York streets.

Hayes offered his seat to an older woman balancing a bright red hat box on top of three large bags of clothes shopping. "Thank you, young man," she said, taking the seat as he helped her with the box. She looked rich.

Hayes stood with his Glock in its bag, feeling the jostle of the subway car like lapping waves on a beach. Did he need a costume? Was that the thing that brought you into this weird community of heroes and evildoers? Without that, would his gun be snatched away by another Dread-0, or whatever else it was he came up against?

The car stopped and people disembarked while others got on, a change of anonymous faces from one group to another. The seats filled and emptied and filled again, the subway car galloping along the underground maze of tracks.

Hayes was lost in his own thoughts when they stopped at Lexington Avenue, and so he wasn't immediately aware of the strange-looking man who got on there. The man was dressed in a long duster coat too warm for the season, like he was going to a costume party, and sported an elaborately waxed mustache.

Hayes finally looked up at the sound of embarrassed muttering, some sixth sense alerting him that something was wrong. He peered along the car, trying to locate the source of the noise.

The man in the duster was leaning close to the woman he had boarded with. She looked to be about nineteen, frail as a bird, and more than a little spaced out. Waxed 'stache was sitting with her, leaning right in her face as she tried to rear away.

"Come on, doll," the man pleaded. "You an' me can take this town."

Hayes excused me'd his way through the bumping subway car, trying to get closer. He thought he recognized the man in the coat from the news, one of the low tier costumed bad guys who trotted out now and again, only to get the living daylights beaten out of them by novice heroes on their first assignment.

"I don't know, Rhett," the woman was saying. "I don't like the idea of, y'know..." *shooting anyone* – she mouthed these last words.

"So, we'll just fire a warning shot, doll," the man called Rhett said in a voice like Bogart. "I've done this stuff before, see? People hand over the cash, and then we can twenty-three skidoo off to Mexico for a long vacation. Spend a couple of years drinking tequilas."

Retro, Hayes recalled. That was this palooka's name. Or *codename*, or whatever you called them. Retro was his *costumed name*. Not that he was in-costume now, not really – the duster looked more thrift store cowboy than super bad guy, and when he was in action, he wore tinted goggles over his eyes. But the 'stache gave him away, that and the 1920s idiom.

Hayes knew who Retro was – a stick-up man who favored a kind of historical flourish to his crimes – but he had not done any particular research on the guy. If Retro worked with a female partner, he couldn't say that he recalled her. Maybe she was new.

But something ran through Hayes' mind: Retro had done a job with the Imps once. A stick-up job at a power plant to steal uranium or something like it. They had got busted by Damocles.

Hayes hung back, standing close to the doors of the car, nominally minding his own business while Retro and his acquaintance continued their discussion. The way the woman lolled in her seat, while Retro's physical gestures were a little too grand, made it clear they were wired – on alcohol or poppers or something.

The couple got off at Elmhurst Avenue, Queens. Hayes followed, using another door on the car and hanging back while he tailed them out of the station.

The rain had stopped. The afternoon sun painted everything in its orange glow, making the streets feel warmer. The puddles glistened under its brilliance, turned momentarily to pools of molten gold.

They were in the middle of Queens, just a few miles away from Hayes' house. Here it was mostly apartments, people crammed together, piled one on top of the other like poultry in a battery farm.

Retro and his friend staggered across the street and down a side turning, and Hayes followed. They walked like they were out of it, and her voice echoed back shrilly as Retro said something disagreeable.

"Don't be like that, doll face," Hayes heard him say as he stumbled back from the woman, doing a little two-step by the curb. "Let's go inside."

Hayes waited close to the street corner as the couple continued down the street away from him and turned. He watched from the end of the street as they ascended the stone steps of an apartment block. There was chipped paint on the railing by the steps, and a metal fire escape running zigzag across the side of the building.

Once they had disappeared inside, Hayes waited a little longer before following. He went into a convenience store on the corner and bought gum, just to kill some time. The proprietor did not speak English but he understood the universal language of dollar bills.

Hayes paced the street towards the building with the chipped railings. He did not know what he was going to do, not yet, but he was conscious that he was carrying a bag within which was a semi-automatic and ammo. Wouldn't be much use where it was, he thought, and it could only get him in trouble if he got caught.

Hayes reached the strip of sidewalk before the apartment block and assessed it. It looked cheap and tired, but there were some expensive automobiles outside. That didn't mean a thing these days – people treasured their cars more than the rat holes they lived in, Hayes knew.

He climbed the steps, eight thick stone slabs up to the double door frontage. The building was old, dating way back to around nineteen-hundred, but the doors were newer. They had been replaced sympathetically, but not very sympathetically, wood frames and glass windows with a gold edge that had mostly peeled off. Up close they looked nineteen-eighties, with scratches around their edges and a bad crack in the wood where they met from where someone had tried to force the lock. Hayes tried the doors, felt them shudder in their frame, but they held. He waited.

It took eleven minutes. Hayes walked up and down the block a couple of times, scoping out the building and a side alley around it, finding a discarded pizza delivery box in a dumpster just around back below the zigzag fire escape. He returned with the box balanced in one hand, watching the doors until a car pulled up and its passenger – a teen girl dressed like she'd had a fight with a rainbow – hopped out with a shrill "Thank you!" to the driver. As she climbed the steps, Hayes followed, pizza box in hand.

"Can you hold the door, please?" he called.

The teen looked back at him, fifteen years old and teeth wired in place with braces, and smiled. "You okay?"

"Yeah, just don't have enough hands," Hayes said.

"That's okay," the girl assured him with a chuckle as she worked the lock.

"Thanks," Hayes said as they walked through into the communal lobby together. There was a line of mail slots to the right as a part of the wall, made from walnut and scarred from many decades of use.

The girl hurried towards the stairs while Hayes hung back.

He waited a moment until she had disappeared, then looked at the names on the mail slots.

Hayes did not know what he was expecting to find. It wasn't like there would be a slot that read "Retro, professional bank robber", was it? Except...

... It kind of *did*. The mail poking from one of the slots read: *Rhett Rowe.*

"Rhett Rowe," Hayes muttered. "Rhett-Ro... Ret-ro! Son of a gun! You can't be serious!"

It was apartment ten, up on the third floor. Rowe must have been too drunk or too horny to bother to collect his mail.

Hayes discarded the empty pizza box in a trash receptacle that looked like it had been in need of emptying since sometime around when the doors were replaced, took the envelope addressed to Rhett Rowe, and climbed the stairs to the third floor.

The floor was like an ageing screen beauty who had seen better days. There was a 1930s glamour to the wallpaper and the fixtures, but bulbs had not been replaced and the walls had a grime to them that had been there for so long that it wouldn't ever go away now. The grime was as much a part of the hallway as the doorframes or the ceiling.

Hayes paced past several closed apartment doors, the sounds of boisterous televisions and loud, one-sided phone conversations reverberating from within, until he reached number ten. It was an old wooden door with a new brass lock that caught the flickering light of an on-again-off-again bulb that was committing a very protracted suicide a few feet away. There was no name on the door, just the number and a spy hole. Hayes stood there for a moment, wondering what to do now.

"You think I'm in there, Quo?" Melanie asked from where she waited under that flicking lamp. She was there in the darkness, gone in the light.

Hayes shook his head and gestured for her to hush. Now was not the time for talking.

"Or maybe they have one of those doubles of me that you

keep finding," Melanie suggested as the light buzzed and went out, "when you look at the news reports." The light returned, extinguishing her presence.

Hayes leaned close to the door, listening, ignoring Melanie's presence, non-presence, presence. A quiz show playing too loud in the apartment next door obscured any real chance he had of hearing anything. So he knocked.

He waited. Five seconds, ten, it seemed like a lifetime, the same way waiting for those doors to open up in Afghanistan and Bolivia had, wondering if someone was going to shoot you clean through the door itself.

"You think I'll be inside, Quo?" Melanie teased as the light flickered out again.

Then the man opened the door. He was no longer in his duster, just an undershirt and pants, and his face looked flushed. He was smiling, kind of giddy. It was Retro. "Yes, what is it?" he snapped. Behind him, the apartment was dingy and cluttered, with a back window that looked out on the side alley.

Hayes remembered the mail in his hand. "I... er... picked this up by mistake," he said, handing the envelope over. "Didn't want to go all the way back to the lobby with it. Apartment ten, right?"

Retro took the envelope without even looking at it, at the same time as a woman's voice drawled from somewhere behind the door. "Rhett? Who is it?"

"Just some idiot," Retro said, smiling a kind of vacant, patronizing smile at Hayes. "Thanking you," he added, before shutting the door in Hayes' face.

Hayes walked back down the corridor and headed for the stairs. If Melanie was by the flickering light, he left her there, figuring she could make her own way home.

When he got back home, Hayes went straight to the computer and brought up everything he could about the criminal dubbed Retro.

He still could not quite believe that the guy's real name was Rhett Rowe. That was dumb and kind of hilarious.

According to what he could find, Retro was strictly a stick-up man. He held up banks, armored cars and jewelry stores mostly, employing out-of-date weaponry with modern twists – muskets which fired heat rays, electrified rapiers, that kind of thing. He had scuffled with three heroes – Skater, Black Nova (who had later renamed himself Star Nova) and Damocles in that ill-fated power plant heist which had involved the Imps. None of the bouts was notable, his tussle with Damocles had lasted just seventeen seconds.

Retro had done a couple of stretches in the pen. By Hayes' reckoning he had been out six months now, and hadn't reappeared on the news radar in that time.

Hayes studied the guy's modus operandi. He acted like one of those stuffed shirts who populated Marx Brothers films, the kinds Groucho would mock straight to their faces. He always dressed smart when he was on a job, suit, tie, cufflinks and a walking cane. The cane was one of several gadgets he utilized, and it hid a powerful jet which could knock a man off his feet with a sudden blast of air.

His other weapons were all just weapons, guns and swords, only they were adapted, upscaled in power, and laden with hidden gimmicks. When Retro had produced a knife in a bank, the blade had been superheated to cut through the bulletproof glass of the teller's window.

"I can take this guy," Hayes told himself as he looked at bank footage of Retro pulling a stick-up. He was strictly small scale.

13

One night later, Hayes made his way back to the apartment building off Elmhurst Avenue. He parked a block away, and ducked out into the chill night air. Hayes was dressed in dark clothes, a hooded sweatshirt with a zip up the front, and under this he wore the new Glock in a shoulder rig. The Glock should be fine so long as he didn't encounter another Dread-0 or whatever.

The streets were quieter than in the daytime, but there were still people around, and the constant buzz of traffic. Hayes pulled up the hood of his sweatshirt against the cold night air.

It was after midnight when he reached the building. He had spent the day studying a map of the area, committing the streets to memory so that he could get away quickly. This is how they had done things in the SEALs, it was all *preparation, preparation, preparation* before an op.

Hayes passed by the side of the building and into a service alleyway that led behind it. The fire escape was located here, metal rungs locked a story above street level and leading up to a stairwell that ran outside the building. Hayes began to run, picking up speed before tic-tacking up the walls, left foot bounding against the building wall, right on the wall opposite, rising ten feet until he could grab the bottom of that fire escape ladder. It creaked as it took his weight, threatening to counterbalance and drop to the street. He did not want it to do that.

Hayes adjusted his weight to make sure that the ladder did not drop, aware that the noise it would make if it did so would attract attention. Then, he pulled himself up, reaching for the bottom landing.

A moment later, he was ascending the metal stairs, putting his feet down gently to lessen the noise that his movements made. He looked across to Rowe's apartment, checking for a light. The windows were dark, and there were drapes over the farthest – most probably the bedroom.

Hayes reached the closest window and stopped, holding his breath and listening. No noise came from inside. He risked a peek in the window, the swiftest motion of his head before drawing himself back to the cover of the wall. It was the living room, crammed full of scrappy furniture and papers, an old-fashioned, boxy TV set in one corner. There was no one there.

Hayes moved forward, more confident this time. Somewhere below, a dog was barking, setting off others in the neighborhood.

Hayes crouched down and reached for the sash window, applying a little pressure. It rose about an inch before being jammed by the lock. He reached up and under, working the inside lock from outside. It took a few tries before the catch slipped free.

A moment later and Hayes had climbed through the window. He was in the living room, and there was crap everywhere. One table had been pushed up against a wall, high like a store counter, with a high wooden stool beside it. The table contained what looked like the parts to a motorcycle engine or maybe a lawnmower, along with several car batteries, circuit boards and a desk fan with its guard missing. It was a workshop, Hayes realized. Retro must make his own gadgets right here.

Hayes reached over and picked up something that looked like either a gun or a hairdryer, its aperture wide like the latter, examining it in the faint street illumination from the window. As he did so, something rolled from the table and struck the floor with a loud, metal clang.

Shit!

From within the apartment, there was a murmur of confusion, and the sounds of movement. Hayes replaced the hairdryer and drew the Glock from its shoulder rig, moving away from the window in a crouch walk. He had the Glock up in the ready position, steadied by a two-handed grip. As he moved across the room, he knocked over an empty bottle in the darkness – tall like a wine or spirits bottle – where it had been left beside the couch. He had located the door to the bedroom the moment he entered, situated behind a couch that smelled of cigarettes and sagged in the center.

The bedroom door opened, bringing a flash of illumination from a bedside lamp. A figure stood there, a woman, silhouetted by the lamp behind her. It was Retro's girl.

"I tell you, I heard... shit!" she said, leaping back and slamming the door. "There's a man in there!" Hayes heard her shriek from behind the door.

A shouted conversation followed, muffled only by the flimsy bedroom door, as Hayes crossed the room:

"What?"

"Some guy! A stinking... I don't know!"

"What do you mean?"

"I don't know!!!"

Bare feet struck the floor heavily as a man exited the bed and crossed the room. Hayes waited, Glock covering the door. He positioned for cover now, close to the apartment's short hallway.

There came a strange sound then, a rapidly rising hum like a guitar chord. And then the door was reduced to sharp splinters that burst across the room, embedding in the sagging couch and the wall beyond. Hayes ducked, bringing his gun arm up reflexively so that his bicep protected his face.

"Stay here!" Retro ordered.

He emerged from the bedroom in his underwear, but wearing the trademark goggles he had worn in every photograph that Hayes had found of him on a heist. In his hand was something that looked like a dueling pistol in the darkness, curved like a bone.

"Who's there?" Retro snarled, looking around. An instant later, he swung the dueling pistol up to target Hayes and fired. The guitar chord wailed again:

Eeeee-owwwww!

Hayes leapt as a blast of invisible force drilled into the cabinet that had been behind him a moment before, smashing through its wooden front like it was made of rice paper. From the bedroom, the woman was screaming.

"I can see you, sir," Retro hissed, tracking Hayes with the pistol.

The goggles, Hayes realized. Those old-fashioned, train engineer goggles, were some kind of night lenses, plus who knew what else. Hayes had used night vision goggles in the service, but it was not something he had at home, not something he'd even considered bringing along today. Maybe he should change that – if he survived.

The Jimi Hendrix guitar lick strummed again, and Hayes rolled behind an overstuffed armchair, wondering just what the hell he had run into. This Retro guy was a low-tier bad guy, a jumped-up stick-up man with a little quirky tech. Suddenly, Hayes was developing newfound admiration for that tech – this was serious.

Beside Hayes, the armchair rocked sideways on its treads and toppled over, spilling stuffing everywhere. Two more empty bottles tipped over where they had stood by the armchair, one of them shattering as it struck the floor where carpet had worn down to the floorboards.

Retro's gun fired some kind of intense blast of air, a pressure wave like the Long Range Acoustic Devices used by the Navy. LRADs employed intense sound waves to literally knock pirates and other boats back, and the results could vary from temporary hearing loss to permanent deafness, as well as the more obvious physical effect the blast had.

Hayes scrambled, coming up from the floor like a leaping panther. Retro was quick, and he had the weird gun pointed at Hayes in a fraction of a second. But Hayes had his own pistol ready, firing a shot at Retro, center mass.

The shot missed its target in the darkness, but not by much. There was a scream, and Retro went down as his left shoulder erupted in an explosion of blood.

Hayes was on the man in an instant, bringing his Glock up towards Retro's face as he landed on him to hold him down. "Okay, Retro, you and I are going to–"

He did not have the chance to finish that sentence. From out of the gloom to his right, something struck him across the side of his head with a resounding clang.

Hayes grunted and found himself tumbling over, his vision suddenly blurring. Something was coming at him again from the right, he realized, and instinctively he blocked it with his arm. It struck hard, accompanied by a hollow clang, and Hayes' gun arm went numb.

Still on his back, Hayes kicked out with a leg sweep, tripping the second attacker. He watched them drop to the floor, a blurred shape against the dull illumination from the open bedroom, landing with a hard thump and a moan. It was the woman, Hayes realized; she must have used a vase or jug to strike him. He was wet too; either water or blood, it was too dark to tell.

Beside Hayes, Retro was rising to his feet in a swaying, uncertain manner. Still holding the strange pistol, Retro pressed the heel of his right hand to his left shoulder and hissed in agony. "That cad shot me," he said.

There came hammering from below, a neighbor banging on their ceiling in response to being awoken. There was a strong chance that someone had called a cop, Hayes realized. He had to do this fast. *Slow is smooth; smooth is fast* – that's what they'd said in the SEALs. You rushed an op and you lost it, but doing it right was doing it fast.

Hayes was up on his feet a moment later. Retro was woozy with blood loss and shock, standing in a slump against the bedroom doorframe. The woman was on the floor moaning, semiconscious.

Hayes stepped forward and reached out for Retro's gun hand, shoving it and the man himself back against the frame. Retro screeched in pain as the pressure on his shoulder intensified.

"I need information," Hayes said.

"Go to hell," Retro snarled.

Hayes looked down and fired, drilling a bullet into Retro's foot. Retro screamed in agony, tried to slump forward but Hayes was holding him so that he could not move.

"I need information," Hayes said again.

"Go... to... hell," Retro repeated, only this time each word came out as a gasp.

"Really?" Hayes said. "You got two feet – do the math."

"What... is this?" Retro asked after a pause. "A... shake down?"

"Places, names," Hayes said. He could feel liquid on the side of his face now, suspected it was his own blood from where Retro's partner had cold-cocked him. "What do you know about the Imps?"

"What...?" Retro was slipping out of consciousness from his own blood loss. He sagged against Hayes, feeling heavier.

"The Imps," Hayes repeated. "How do they copy people? How do they go back in time?"

In the distance, from the broken window, Hayes could hear sirens. Someone had called the police, one of the neighbors understandably panicked by the noise of the ruckus. He had not thought any of this through, he realized; he had somehow thought it would be easy, or maybe he just hadn't thought about anything other than Melanie being dead and how he wanted to do something to make that make sense.

"How do they go back in time?" Hayes repeated through gritted teeth.

Retro whispered something in response, his voice fading like an old photograph in sunlight: "They don't." Then he had slumped entirely against Hayes' grip, and drifted away into unconsciousness.

"Damn," Hayes muttered.

The sirens were getting louder. In the service they would call this a total SNAFU.

He let go of Retro and sneered as the man dropped to the floor as a dead weight, his goggles catching the light from the bedroom for a single, dazzling moment. The woman was still lying there, moaning as she tried to get back to her feet.

Outside, the sirens shut down. Brilliant red and white lights were playing across the ceiling of the room like ripples on the surface of a pond.

Hayes leaned down and plucked the weird duelling pistol from Retro's hand, shoving it in the pocket at the front of his hoodie. He hoped it had some kind of safety feature, or he ran a genuine risk of blowing his ribs out through his spine if he moved wrong.

Then, slipping the Glock back into its shoulder rig, Hayes made his way to the window he had forced. There was a cop car out there at the street end of the alleyway, its emergency lights illuminating the whole alleyway in a continuous whir of red and white. From this position, Hayes could just see the edge of the police car, and spotted a cop coming out of the side door.

"Shit," Hayes hissed. He only had two escape routes – the fire escape, which was tantamount to walking into at least one police car, or the front door, which ultimately meant going through the lobby which was exactly the route the cops would be taking to get here.

"The devil or the deep," Hayes told himself, clambering out of the window. You could not have indecision in the SEALs. Indecision resulted in your buddy getting shot in the back, or you lying on the roadside in Kandahar with your guts hanging out the front of your shirt.

He chose the fire escape because it was outside. Better that than being penned in by the walls of the building's hallways like a rat in a maze. The cop car was waiting below him so instead he went up, ascending the fire escape swift as he could, not worrying now about how much noise he made, just getting it done quick.

Hayes' boots thundered against the metal of the fire escape as he raced up two flights. As he turned onto the third, he heard the sounds of shouting coming from down below at street level and suddenly the beam of a flashlight started playing up the side of the apartment building.

He swung around the turn in the exterior stairwell, reaching the top. His feet pounded hard against the metal weave of the topmost level as he scrambled for a ladder there that led up to the roof. The head of flashlight beam was a story below, searching back and forth like a hungry snake.

Hayes grabbed the bottom rung of the ladder and pulled himself up, bending at his waist to bring his feet up a few rungs and then powering himself up the last few steps in a leap. He emerged on the roof an instant later, springing over the top of the fire escape ladder like a bottle rocket.

His feet struck the roof hard, and he slipped, skidding down to one knee where he had struck some loose gravel. He got back to his feet and ran, passing the roof access and onwards, heading for the far edge of the roof. He brought the map of the area to the forefront of his mind, working out which direction he was facing: *West*.

There would be a four-lane street there, too wide for him to jump. He spun in place on the rooftop, as hollering shouts came from down below along with the squawk of police radios. Hayes was running north now, towards a back road that provided access only to a parking bay. The road was narrow, barely wide enough to get a fire truck down.

Behind him, someone was jangling the door of the roof access, working the lock. The door opened a moment later, and a policeman came warily out, the nose of his .38 preceding him.

Hayes took the edge of the roof at a sprint, stepping up onto the raised lip and leaping. He could not recall how tall the opposite building was and, suddenly, it was like his stomach was in his mouth as he left solid ground. His arms and legs pin-wheeled in the air, searching for something solid.

With a crash, Hayes landed on the far roof, the jolt through his ankles reverberating up his body and expelling the breath from his lungs. He rolled, dropping on his side the way he had been taught in parachute training. Behind him, on the roof he had just left, someone was shouting for him to stop, but they could not make their voice loud enough to be heard clearly over the blood rushing in his ears.

Hayes rose and ran, a muscle in his left leg firing with a burst of pain, head wet on one side where he had been struck. He kept his head down, a loping, graceless run, as he scrambled across the rooftop, turning east. East was the service alley, the same one he had used to reach the fire escape of Retro's building. Without slowing, Hayes ran towards the roof's edge and sprang, crossing the gap – far narrower than the first he had leapt – and onto another roof that loomed in the darkness one story below.

He cursed as another blast of pain shot through his legs; kept running. There was a fire escape at the far end – Hayes spied its metal glint in the moonlight. He hurried towards it, slowing as he reached the roof's edge. Behind him, two rooftops away, a cop was reporting in on his radio, calling for aerial assistance. Hayes knew he had to get out of here right away.

Down the ladder, then, and onto another fire escape, and from there down to a passageway that ran in the rear of a twenty-four-hour grocery.

When Hayes reached terra firma, he was buzzing with adrenalin. He checked his pocket with a pat, feeling for Retro's gun. It was still there, its curved handle feeling like an elephant's tusk through the sweatshirt material.

Where had he parked? Hayes recalled the street, brought up that mental map again and tried to figure out where he was. The grocery store was three blocks over from his car, he remembered. Three blocks, two of which could be crossed via service alleys that would keep him out of sight. His head had been bleeding where that woman had struck him with the vase or whatever it was, and though the cut had dried, he probably looked like something out of an old Universal horror pic right now. Best to keep to the back alleys then, at least until he could get cleaned up.

Hayes turned east and headed back to his car, cautiously avoiding the cops and anyone else.

14

Hayes' heart was pumping when he pulled up outside his house. There were no cops on his tail, and he had got out of Retro's neighborhood without even being stopped, although he had passed another cop car on his way to Forest Hills.

He shut off the engine and just leaned back in his seat, concentrating on his breath. The side of his head hurt where the woman had clobbered him, but when he felt there the blood had dried. Under the hood, his hair was matted.

Taking another deep breath, Hayes reached for the door handle and got out of the 4WD. It was almost 2am, and the street was quiet. A few porch lights were on and, a little way down the block, one lone light could be seen in an upstairs window, but there were no signs of life anywhere.

Hayes fumbled momentarily with his door key, before letting himself in and flicking the lights on. The light seemed bright after the darkness, and the scraped wall of the lobby looked like up-chuck under its relentless glare.

Hayes moved through the house like a specter, reached the kitchen and poured himself a glass of water. Then he took some ice from the Frigidaire which he wrapped in the cloth from the basin. Pushing back the hood, he put the ice on his head where it had taken the blow, and made his way to the basement.

The bare bulb came on with a noise like a fingernail tapping against glass, revealing the wooden slat stairs and the patch of mold clinging to one wall like a distraught Jackson Pollock. Hayes trudged heavily down the stairs until he was standing before the little community of paint cans which were evidence of his decorating. He grabbed a screwdriver from his toolkit and opened up the largest of the cans. It was empty, just a dried smudge of the brilliant white he had used on the ceilings in the hallways and bedrooms back when they had first moved in. Then Hayes removed Retro's gun from his pocket, wrapped it in a rag, and placed it in the empty paint can. The barrel of the gun was fifteen inches long, but with a little tilt it fit snugly inside the can. Once it was within, Hayes resealed the lid.

Then he went upstairs and took a look at the head wound in his shaving mirror. There was blood in his hair, but it was dried and brown now, and the wound itself had scabbed over nicely. The wound was small, just an inch or so, where the hairline ended a little way above his right eye. It stung when he touched it, stung even more when he cleaned it with ammonia from the bathroom cabinet, but it looked okay.

After that, Hayes undressed and went to bed. His mind was racing, but sleep wanted his companionship anyway.

Hayes awoke in a room that felt too bright, with a pain in his side and a throbbing headache. He had not pulled the drapes last night. He rolled himself up and out of bed, and when he sat up, he felt a stab of pain run up his left leg when the foot touched the floor. He'd have to be careful with it for a couple of days.

He went into the en suite and grabbed some over-the-counter painkillers, downing two with some water. Then he went downstairs.

Retro had told him that the Imps never traveled through time, and he believed him. He had never heard of the Imps traveling through time. Time travel was rare, and usually one way –

jumped up dictators hopping back from the future to try to take over the world. And the Imps were no future dictators, they were just thieves. Which put Hayes back at square one.

It was 10.58 am, later than Hayes could ever remember getting up. He had always been an early bird, even when he was a kid in school. Often he would make models or play video games before school, because he liked being up early with the house to himself; the house and the quiet.

The answer phone was flashing: *two messages*.

Hayes played them as he went into the kitchen to make coffee. They were both from Jeff Puchenko asking when he would be coming back to work. Hayes pushed that to the back of his mind – something to deal with later. Then, steaming hot coffee in hand, he went into the lounge, switched on the TV and brought up a news channel.

He watched, wondering if last night's incident with Retro would make the news, wondering if he was on an APB, wanted for breaking and entering, and for assault. Twenty-five minutes later, with a summary of the headlines and the scrolling bar of additional news beneath the presenters – the bar of news they couldn't fit into the actual broadcast – Hayes was relieved to find what had happened in Queens didn't even warrant a mention. Relieved and something else too; a sense of almost disappointment, maybe.

"So you wanted to be a celebrity, Quo?" Melanie asked.

Hayes shook his head. "Not me."

"But you're disappointed, I can tell," Melanie said. She was standing just out of his eye line, in the lounge doorway, the place she always stood when dinner needed another couple of minutes or she was washing a glass when something interesting came on the tube. "Were you hoping that by fighting with a costume you'd become one of them?"

"No," Hayes insisted. "That's not why I fought Retro, and you know it."

"Then why did you do it?"

"For you," Hayes said.

"Beating up some guy and stealing his gun is not going to bring me back, Quo," Melanie told him. "Did you really think it would?"

"No," Hayes said. "But the costumes are in on this. They know why you were killed."

"They don't."

"They all know each other and one of them knows," Hayes insisted. "You follow the strands, and every one of these dress-up bastards are linked up somehow. The Hunter fights Compound who fights Damocles who fights someone else. It's a huge game of *Six Degrees*."

"And what?" Melanie asked him. "You want to be part of their world?"

"No," Hayes told her, his eyes still on the television screen. "I want to find out who's behind it."

Melanie did not say anything else, and when Hayes looked over to the doorway she wasn't there.

He shut off the TV and made his way to the basement, to go check on the gun.

Hayes studied Retro's gun under the basement's single, 60-watt light bulb. To his eye, it looked like an eighteenth-century dueling pistol, the kind that came in a paired set, with a barrel that curved gracefully around into the handle, and a flintlock action as the firing mechanism. It was nothing of the sort, of course, and on closer inspection Hayes could see a digital display hidden by a sliding flap on the inside of the handle, where it could be checked with a simple flick of the thumb. There was a blob of solder there, but it was neatly done. The display showed a power-bar-style column, descending from green through yellow to red. When Hayes pulled the trigger in one notch, unlocking the safety, the bar came to life and showed the gun to be about two-thirds full.

Hayes turned the pistol over and found a hinged flap on the

bottom of the grip. When he pulled it loose, it revealed a charging point – two holes rimmed with metal connectors, of a type he did not specifically recognize. Hayes speculated that it took a strong electrical charge which it converted into the powerful force blasts which had shattered Retro's door and chair and had almost knocked Hayes through a wall.

Assuming the gun had been at full strength when Retro had first shot at him, that equated to three bursts being one third of the charge. That left him with six shots still in the gun.

"A gun like this could do a lot of damage," Hayes muttered. "A whole hell of a lot of damage."

"To who?" Melanie asked. She was sitting on the third step, where the diameter of 60-watt light failed to penetrate. Hayes ignored her.

After a moment, Hayes replaced the flap and wrapped the gun back in its cloth before popping it back into the empty paint tin and sealing the lid. The police might not be after him, but that did not mean he could just go out and use this thing in public.

Then, another thought occurred to him. The police might not be his main worry. He had taken on a costume last night – a low-level one, true, but still a costume. And as he had told Melanie in the lounge, they were all connected to each other, the strands of their lives interwoven, each battle informing the next. By tackling Retro, Hayes had made himself a part of that web too, far more so than when he had shot at Dread-0. Dread-0 had been a machine intelligence, a jumped-up vacuum cleaner. But guys like Retro – they were a part of the tapestry, the close New York scene of heroes and villains.

Shoot Retro and you could get Crassh or Rhinoserious or some maniac like the Spin after you.

Hayes headed up the wooden slat stairs, and shut off the light. He needed more information, a whole lot more. And weapons.

Retro utilized a vast selection of quirky weaponry. There was no record on the 'net of the force gun being used, so Hayes figured it was something new. From that work bench in his apartment, Retro was most probably a weaponsmith and he might also be a supplier for these things, because they sure as hell didn't just pop out of thin air.

So where did they pop out from? Was there some guy, a back-street workshop right here in Queens, that pumped out these weird gadgets and weapons that the bad guys used? Or did they each develop their own, sharing designs maybe when they found something that was effective against a particular hero like Captain Light.

Hayes wondered what the force gun, as he had taken to calling it, would do to Captain Light. It could maybe knock him out of the sky with a clear shot, if Hayes had the element of surprise. But Light was pretty near invulnerable by all accounts, so even being knocked out of the sky, assuming the gun could do that, wouldn't do much more than momentarily inconvenience him. And make him mad.

Hayes began thinking about other bad guys – because it was inevitably bad guys in this case – and the weapons they used. Characters like Fade and Doctor Interzone seemed to have a never-ending supply of weaponry, weird stuff that had almost incomprehensible effects, like turning a security man into a statue for twenty-four hours, or stripping away a single ability that a hero had so that they were forced to fight the rest of the battle without the power of flight or strength or animal communication, say.

But all those guys got captured, at least most of the time, which led to two obvious questions: Where did they go next, and where did all that hardware end up?

The first question was easy to answer. There were cells, some specially designed, over on Rikers Island in the East River. Super criminals like the Jade Shade got stuffed there with all kinds of security measures designed to stop them from busting out and from anyone sneaking in. No way he could get inside there.

Which left that other question, about the hardware. Where did it go?

Hayes thought back to the battle he had witnessed in Washington Square Park between Damocles and Rattenfanger. Rattenfanger used something called the Rat Pipe. It was not his first, Hayes knew – in fact Rattenfanger had gone through at least six different iterations of his mesmerizing musical instrument. In Washington Square, Rattenfanger had been defeated and his pipe had been cut in two by the sentient sword of Damocles, the two ends dropping from the marble arch onto the paths below. Hayes had seen cops collect those pieces, presumably to store safely away under lock and key.

But these hero battles were fast and often chaotic. There was a chance that some of that discarded tech had found its way into the hands of the general public, wasn't there?

Hayes looked at the flickering computer screen, wondering what he needed to type into the search engine.

"*I own costume tech*" – he tried.

Hundreds of sites came up, along with sponsored ads for Halloween costume shops.

"*I collect costume tech*" – Hayes tried.

This time the results were more focused. A few weird choices were followed by a link to an article that had appeared in the *New York Echo*'s Sunday supplement about a man called Jonas Culper, who lived in upstate New York and collected what he termed "discarded super tech".

Hayes read the article. Culper was a dot com business owner who had sold his company at age forty-one for several million dollars and a lucrative consultancy position. He lived alone in the Catskills with a collection of classic cars along with what was described as his private museum of discarded super tech. This included two of Rattenfanger's Rat Pipes still in working order, a book that had once been wielded by Doctor Answer, a gun from Aquarius and some preserved leaves from the body of Treeman.

The article was accompanied by photographs showing several of these items, as well as a shot of Culper sitting in his lounge, all cherry wood fittings and leather chairs, whose large windows overlooked the mountains.

The article came from nine months ago.

Hayes opened a new tab on screen and ran a search on Jonas Culper, seeing what else he could find out about the man. As the article had stated, Culper had been the brains behind a successful travel app which he had sold for an unimaginable amount two years ago, while retaining a well-paid consultancy position with the company. He lived alone but had a young son from a marriage that had broken up when he was thirty-seven. Hayes worked out that the son would be coming up to nine years-old by now.

There was a company website, but Culper himself had no social media presence. He probably did not want to be bothered by would-be millionaires after tips for their own start-ups, or who might hope Culper would bank roll them; Hayes figured there were likely quite a few of those.

After a little searching, Hayes brought up a street address for Culper. It did not give the house number, but he had the road. He ran a search on a real estate website that gave values and prices at the time of last sale. He figured that, since Culper was forty-three now, he likely bought the property when his marriage had dissolved roughly six or seven years ago. And like that –

Bingo!

– Hayes had an address.

Right or wrong, he was going to check it out.

15

Hayes drove up to the Catskills. It was a three hour drive. It gave him time to think.

The mountain road felt open, a far cry from the city and its artificial canyons of concrete, metal and glass.

He had been lucky to catch Retro. Pure luck, nothing else but. Recognizing him on that subway car, even without the goggles that usually masked his face, had been lottery ticket good fortune. Hayes was good with faces; that and sensing when people were acting weird had kept him alive in Afghanistan and Bolivia and a check-box list of other hot zones where US SEALs weren't wanted but were definitely needed. Retro – Rhett Rowe – had been acting oddly, drunk maybe, and had been speaking in that faux oldie worldy language he favored. Anyone else would have dismissed him and his girl as drunks or high on meth, which they probably had been. But Hayes had recognized him.

Hayes wondered if maybe he should have informed the police of where Retro – a known criminal, after all – lived. They knew now. Or maybe they didn't. Maybe Retro and guys like him had become masters at covering their tracks, at blending in when they weren't on a job. Heroes like Captain Light and Eternal Flame made the news daily, but bad guys like Retro only poked their head out every once in a while, when they hit a bank or a jeweler's or kidnapped a socialite heiress from her Sweet Sixteen and demanded a six-figure ransom.

A bend in the road and Hayes recognized Culper's house up ahead, having done a street view of it on his computer. It looked like a potato chip resting on a glass podium, two stories that gave breathtaking views from every window. Hayes slowed down, pulling to a halt across the end of the drive.

The driveway leading up to the house had been paved with red bricks, and ended in a covered area under which were parked an SUV and a little sports number, silver and red, alongside a Harley whose chrome had been polished until it gleamed like mercury. Hayes admired the sports car as he passed it, alert to everything around him. Out here the air seemed fresher, its coolness replenishing Hayes' lungs like a drowning man dragged from the ocean.

Hayes reached the front door and thumbed the doorbell. He heard chimes from inside; he waited.

Nothing happened. No one came. He had half expected an old-fashioned butler to arrive at the door – penguin suit and all – or maybe some pretty model dressed like a maid, paid more for how she looked than whether she could dust. Hayes pushed the bell again, resting the heel of his hand against it for a good long stretch. From inside he heard the first chime sound a long, mournful note, until he took his hand from the bell and the rest of the chime clanged.

Eventually Jonas Culper arrived at the door, visible through the glass to the side, looking flustered. He looked older than he had in the article, his hair more untidy. He peered through the side window, frowned, and spoke unhappily to Hayes through an intercom that buzzed like a poorly tuned radio.

"May I help you?" he asked. There was aggression there, a challenge for his visitor to justify his presence, perhaps even his very existence.

"Mister Culper?" Hayes checked. "My name is Hayes. I came to speak to you about some artifacts."

"Not interested," Culper said, and he made a brushing motion with his hand as though to sweep Hayes away. The intercom buzz ceased. Then Culper turned and started to make his way back into the house.

Hayes thought fast. He wanted to see this guy's collection, learn how he had acquired these objects, maybe even borrow one or two. He rapped his knuckles on the side window's glass, watched Culper stop and turn with irritation on his face.

"You heard of a guy called Retro?" Hayes shouted through the glass.

Culper took a step closer to the front door, eyes narrowed.

"I know his real name," Hayes said, "and where he lives. I got his gun."

At this last, Culper was visibly intrigued, and he strode back to the front door. He stopped on the far side, speaking again through the hiss of the intercom. "You have it on you?" he asked.

"No," Hayes told him. "It's in my car. Figured you might think I was going to shoot you if I came to the door with it."

There was a pause, and then the buzzing sound of an electronic lock being drawn back and the door opened. Culper looked shorter than Hayes had expected, and there was a stain on his sport shirt that looked like engine oil. "Can I see it?" Culper asked.

Hayes nodded. "I'll go get it," he said, returning to his car.

"Bring your car up," Culper told him, pointing to a spot behind the SUV. "Park it over there."

Hayes did.

"Where did you get it?" Culper asked as he looked at the gun.

They were in the spacious lounge section of the open plan first floor. It was set over the garage area, and served as a living space. Hayes recognized it from the *Echo*'s article. He had to admit that the view through the windows was even more impressive in person.

Hayes shook his head as he answered Culper's question. "You don't want to know," he said.

Culper pointed at his face. "Is that how you got the cut?"

"Something like that," Hayes said, keeping his answer vague.

"And you said you know his real name?" Culper pressed.

"Yeah," Hayes said, feeling suddenly stupid. "Retro is actually, don't laugh, Rhett Rowe." He spelled it out while Culper just nodded.

"A lot of these guys, the bad ones anyway, have names like that," Culper explained. "Calandrome is really called Julius August, the Leaper is really Maurice Springwell."

Hayes didn't know whether to laugh or not. Both villains were in custody, which is likely why Culper knew their real names. "Rowe lives in a place in Queens," Hayes said.

"And this is genuine?" Culper asked as he turned the gun over in his hands, then corrected himself before Hayes could answer. "No, I can see that it is. This is Retro's work all right. I have one of his muskets downstairs. He's a craftsman.

"Well – how much do you want for it?"

"Me? No, it's not for sale," Hayes told him.

Culper looked Hayes up and down from the leather armchair he sat in. It was the kind of look the locals had given his troop when they arrived in town anywhere in the Middle East, that look of mistrust that something here was too good to be true. "Then why did you come here?" he asked. "I'm not an easy man to find."

"It wasn't that hard," Hayes told him. "I wanted to talk to you about your collection, maybe take a look if I may."

"Do you think you would sell this gun to me," Culper asked, "if you ever did sell it?"

"When that day comes, I'll give it to you," Hayes told him. "Free. Gratis."

Culper took one last look at Retro's pistol before handing it back to Hayes, who slipped it into the pocket of his indigo hoodie.

"Come with me," Culper said, rising from his chair. "Let me show you what I've amassed."

* * *

Limping slightly on his left foot, Hayes followed Culper downstairs to a large room populated by display cabinets and podiums. It was simple, elegant and felt kind of empty, but Hayes estimated that the stuff on show here had probably cost Jonas Culper millions of dollars.

As they reached the bottom of the staircase, something occurred to Hayes, and he asked if Culper had ever heard of a photographer called Benjamin Jermain.

Culper shook his head. "Should I have?"

"He works for the *Echo*," Hayes said. "Snags a lot of pictures of Eternal Flame and a few others. I wondered if maybe he did the photos for your article last year."

"No," Culper said absently. "That was a woman – a graduate, fresh out of college. Dressed like she'd just come from a mosh pit."

Hayes nodded. "Sure."

Then, smiling like a spoilt child, Culper pointed out some of the items in his collection.

"Compound's centrifuge…" he indicated a large item the size of a medieval shield, on which was mounted an elaborate rotating device.

"Fade's war hammer." A hammer with a length of chain attached.

"This musket belonged to Retro, along with his laser monocle. Same workmanship, see?"

Hayes looked and nodded, not really sure whether he saw or not.

"Two of Flakeout's gas canisters – one's empty, I'm afraid."

Hayes was drawn to an ordinary-looking pistol in a display stand. From what he could tell it was just a stubby Colt, the kind they used to call a *Saturday Night Special*. "What's this?"

"That's the gun that shot Holly Belle," Culper said, puffing out his chest with pride.

Hayes frowned. "Who?"

"Holly Belle," Culper repeated. "She was the first costumed hero to die. Or at least, the first to die that we know of. That gun cost me twenty-thousand dollars nine years ago, and it still has a bullet in the chamber."

"Yeah, maybe I heard of her," Hayes said, thinking back.

"1961," Culper told him. "Shot and killed. She clung on for two days in hospital."

"She ever come back?" Hayes asked. Back to life, he meant. It was an occupational hazard with costumes, death was temporary.

"Not so far," Culper said, pulling a framed photograph down from a support pillar. He handed it to Hayes. It was a black and white showing a striking woman with dark eyes and dark hair, a beauty mark on her left cheek. It had been posed for a studio. "She was a doll. She was really an actress called Yvonne Alister. Not her real name, that was Leibowitz but, well – Hollywood in the forties. She was pretty good. Played opposite Reagan once."

"And no one recognized that she was this costume – Holly Belle?" Hayes asked.

"They were simpler times, I guess," Culper speculated. "She didn't even wear a mask."

Hayes was still looking at the photograph of Alister. "What was special about the gun?" he asked.

"Nothing," Culper told him. "It's a standard Colt Detective Special, there are thousands of them out there. It was just a lucky shot."

"Or unlucky," Hayes said as he handed the framed photograph back to Culper.

"So," Culper asked, "what is it I can do for you, Mister...?"

"Hayes," Hayes said. "I was wondering what it would take to bring down Captain Light."

Culper's eyes bugged. "To... bring him down? You mean, kill him?"

"No," Hayes said. "I need to speak to him. Some way he can't run off. Or fly off."

"Have you thought of simply asking him?" Culper suggested.

"I'm imagining it won't be that kind of discussion," Hayes said bluntly.

Culper had replaced the photograph of Yvonne Alister on the pillar. He turned to face Hayes, folding his arms across his chest. "What is this, that you have in mind?"

Hayes' eyes wandered over the treasures in the room, guns and blades and weirdly shaped sticks that had once shot out death rays. "My wife was killed last month, Mister Culper," he said. "The Jade Shade threw a news copter at Captain Light and it missed him and hit my wife instead. Flattened her."

Culper cursed, shaking his head.

"I just need to know why," Hayes told him.

"I'm sorry for your loss, Mister Hayes," Culper said with genuine sincerity. "I lost my brother last year in an auto accident. DUI. Death is not an easy thing, not when it's sudden like that."

"Thank you, I appreciate you saying that," Hayes said. "I'm sorry about your brother."

Culper looked thoughtful for a few seconds. "From what you've told me this was just a random accident," he said. "No intent, or at least not to target your wife. To be blunt, it sounds to me like you want to go after the Jade Shade if you go after anyone at all. And she's... well, imprisoned in a cell that can survive a direct hit from a nuclear warhead, if I remember correctly. For our safety."

"I don't want revenge," Hayes told him. "I want to know why."

"You've already told me why, unless I misunderstood," Culper said. "Jade Shade intended to drop a helicopter on Captain Light. It missed and, tragically, your wife was in the wrong place at the wrong time."

Hayes scratched his head, feeling the sting of the scab where he had been clobbered the night before. "I think there's more to it than that," Hayes said. "There's news footage of me and my wife in the Bronx a year ago, along with our little girl, Ginnie."

"That doesn't sound so unusual," Culper said. "I've been on news programs both with and without my consent more times than I can count."

"Except, we weren't in the Bronx, I can prove that," Hayes told him. "And Melanie never had time to give birth to our daughter."

Culper's brow furrowed.

"I'll be blunt with you, Mister Culper," Hayes said, "I was in the Navy, toured overseas. I saw people who couldn't take it, I saw what it did to them. If I was you and I heard me telling this story, I'd wonder if I'd joined the tin-foil hat brigade."

"And have you?" Culper asked.

"I don't think so," Hayes replied. "It sounds crazy, but I think someone's behind this. All of it. The heroes, the villains, the clashes on Broadway and over Central Park and the Hudson. I think someone is manipulating all of it, all the costumes."

Culper laughed. "Why? Why would they do that?"

"I don't know," Hayes admitted. "That's why I need to get to Captain Light. 'Cause he's high on the food chain and he was there. He'll know something. He has to."

"So, let me get this straight," Culper outlined with the voice of a man who knew he was entertaining something ridiculous. "You think that the costumes are some kind of – what? – New World Order. That they are involved in a conspiracy that somehow manipulates all of these clashes, making them happen?"

Hayes nodded. "You're a smart guy, or so your bank balance tells me," he told Culper, "so coming from you it sounds kind of out there."

"It does," Culper agreed. "And not just from me. You're grieving, I understand that. But this crusade that you're on is not going to make that pain just go away. Trust me, I still go to call my brother sometimes before I remember. And I'm pissed as hell at the asshole who hit him that night."

Hayes looked at the cabinets of treasures, recognizing two of Rattenfanger's Rat Pipes standing side by side in a display. "If I'm wrong, then tell me this," he said. "Why do they fight? What's the end game?"

"Because the bad guys commit crimes and need to be stopped," Culper told him.

"But why is that?" Hayes pressed. "Why do these bad guys have these gadgets, these incredible powers? Why do monarchs keep invading us from other worlds – Silver Senator and the Tyrant and Bridgemaker? Why? What's so special about New York?"

Culper snorted and shook his head. "I don't know," he admitted.

Hayes looked at him, a smile emerging on the corners of his lips. "You wanna know?"

Culper was still shaking his head. "You really think that there's some big fight card somewhere and everyone puts their name down and agrees to be a part of it?"

"I don't even know if most of them know they're a part of it," Hayes admitted. "I haven't figured that much out yet."

"How much have you figured out?" Culper asked him.

Hayes sucked at his teeth in thought. "Not enough," he said.

"You'd need a gun," Culper said.

"What?"

"To drop Captain Light," Culper explained. "You'd need a gun."

"What kind of gun?" Hayes asked. "Given that he's invulnerable."

"Holly Belle fought Nazis in World War II," Culper said. "She fought Commies in the fifties. And she did it all with some martial arts training and a lot of moxy, what they'd call Girl Power these days. But all it took to bring her down, the woman who had fought Hitler and saved the world – at a conservative estimate – a dozen times, was a single bullet."

"But *she* wasn't invulnerable," Hayes pointed out.

"She was until somebody shot her," Culper told him. "You need a lucky shot. One helluva lucky shot. That's the way you'll bring Captain Light down to Earth."

Hayes gestured around at the trophy cabinets. "What about this stuff? Where do I get things like this?"

Culper smiled, and began to explain.

16

It transpired that there existed a thriving secondary market for costume tech. Some of it turned up in other crimes, discarded by the costumes and subsequently wielded by some stick-up kid at a gas station in Harlem. Weapons changed hands, sometimes the same device would be used in multiple robberies by multiple criminals until the police finally seized it or someone like Jonas Culper acquired it for their collection and it was taken off the streets.

Culper was not the only collector either. There were a lot of them, some specializing in particular characters or a particular hero's rogues gallery, others chasing a certain subset of device – swords or electronics or whatever they were drawn to. Culper called this the gray market, and when Hayes had asked where that stuff came from, the multimillionaire had explained that there were two sources.

"Oftentimes people pick up a souvenir from a costume battle. Could be a bit of rubble or a bent up street sign. Sometimes they walk away with something a bad guy's dropped, like a fear grenade. They're usually small things, items that people can stuff in a bag or their pocket without anyone noticing. Those things regularly come up on the market – auction sites or classified listings. You have to be careful that they're genuine, though; there are a lot of fakers out there."

"What's the second source?" Hayes asked.

"Police lock-ups," Culper told him without so much as batting an eye. "Stuff's put away, but sometimes it finds its way into the secondary market."

"You mean they sell it?"

"Not legally," Culper said. "But there are always people who want to make a little money on the side. Some gangs will steal to order."

Hayes was uncomfortable with where this discussion was going. "You ever get involved in that?"

"No," Culper said. "I work through intermediaries. By the time these objects reach me, it's one hundred percent legal. I wouldn't be on the cover of the Sunday supplement with this stuff if it wasn't, would I?"

"I guess not," Hayes acknowledged. "Anywhere else you can get this tech?"

"People retire now and then," Culper said. "I only know of two who did that and sold off their belongings. There was a third – the Dark-keeper – whose ex-wife sold his props after she got them in the divorce settlement."

Hayes laughed at that.

"It's not that funny," Culper said. "Dark-keeper tried to strangle her when he found out. He's serving a six-year term in Clinton right now for attempted murder."

They talked some more about the so-called secondary market, about the sources for these props, as Culper called them, and the kinds of sums they were commanding. You could pick up rubble or a dented fender from a Doc Solid fight for twenty or thirty bucks, but any kind of weapon or gadget would set you back at least four-hundred dollars. If you wanted one that was still in working order, the price practically tripled. To get anything that could knock Captain Light out of the sky was likely going to cost in the region of five figures, which put it well out of Hayes' range. He would have to think of something else.

* * *

The sky was turning dark when Hayes began the long drive home, dosed up on painkillers for his foot. It was the kind of darkness that you only got out in the mountains, so absolute that it was almost a physical thing, like a bag being pulled over your face.

Hayes' headlights were twin lances of white painted across the ink black of the road.

The stars dozed in the night sky above the mountain peaks, settling into their cozy hammocks for the night, lazily drifting westwards across the heavens.

"You'd need a gun," Culper had told him. The kind of gun that, coupled with a lucky shot, could yank Captain Light out of the sky. But getting hold of the kind of tech the costumes used, the kind of tech that would ground Captain Light, was tricky, and financially ambitious, to say the least.

Hayes had simply stolen Retro's gun. But he had found Retro by luck. He could not rely on that luck again. Or could he? Was there a way to weight the odds in his favor, to rip these costumed bastards off and take their tech out from under them?

When he was fourteen or fifteen, Hayes' father had told him that you made your own luck. "The luckiest man is the one who keeps trying and trying and trying, Jonny," he had said over the blare of the television set. "Forget the odds. Those only mean something to the guys who gave up too soon."

Hayes traced a bend in the road, feeding the wheel slowly through his hands. *How do you weight the odds to win?* he wondered. How had he found Retro? Luck, yes, but not just luck. He had had to be on that train at that time on that day.

Serendipity?

Coincidence?

Both true, but there was something else, wasn't there? To catch a mouse, you laid your trap by the mouse hole.

Hayes remembered the map he had made when he had first started looking into the costumes. It was a map showing the location of "costume incidents" and it had showed that they gravitated to New York. Manhattan, in fact. Not always, but often. Like that was where all these costumed loons went to work, clocking in for the day, holding up a jeweler's or reanimating corpses in a graveyard, and where the so-called good guys would go to right wrongs.

Washington Square Park was in Manhattan. And so was Times Square. And so too was Fifth Avenue and that spot of real estate where Jade Shade had dropped a helicopter on Melanie's fragile body. All these things, with Damocles and Rattenfanger, Eternal Flame and Dread-0, Captain Light and the Jade Shade – they all occurred in Manhattan, an area less than twenty-three square miles. More than that, Hayes realized, most of them actually occurred within a tiny strip of that space, perhaps five or six square miles. The place where the Nexus Range was located, with its security force field.

"Manhattan," Hayes muttered as he joined the interstate. Maybe there was a way to get the jump on these costumes after all. He just needed to wait around the mouse hole – those few square miles – long enough for something to happen, some nutty inventor to unleash his lethal artificial intelligence, or some no-hoper like Flip-out to rob a Broadway show of its takings. Then he could do the same thing he had done to Retro – follow the guy home and take him for all he was worth.

It was a plan.

The thing about plans, however, is they rely on things going right.

When Hayes emerged from the Lincoln Tunnel it was 11pm and dark. In the sky above, a bed of black clouds was being lit infrequently by flashes of lightning that crossed the heavens without rain to accompany them, white streaks coursing over the surface of those clouds like skimming stones. The lightning seemed to be fighting a losing battle with Manhattan's light pollution to get itself noticed, which is why no one gave a damn about it.

Night life was the way it always was in this most twenty-four-hour-city of all cities, people eating out, getting drunk, taking in a show and enjoying themselves. The roads were populated by the usual parade of cars and bikes and late-night buses going about their business, a proliferation of yellow cabs appearing like a rash as Hayes reached the wide intersections on Tenth Avenue.

After a couple of blocks, the street started to sound different under Hayes' wheels. It got bumpier too, as if New York's notorious potholes had started multiplying in the few hours that he had been away. Hayes cursed, figuring he had got a flat somewhere between here and the Catskills, a slow puncture that was only now making itself known. He would be lucky to get home before midnight as it was – a flat was the last thing he needed.

Hayes followed familiar streets, heading in the direction of Queens. He should probably pull over, but maybe he could ride it out.

The noise of the road became louder and more disconcerting as he crossed midtown, and he could feel the undulating of his jeep's chassis now, even through the suspension. Something was wrong. He was going to have to take a look at the puncture before he found himself driving on his rims, and he sure as hell did not relish the thought of calling out a tow truck at this time of night.

Hayes turned at the next junction with the light, into a cross street with less traffic. He spotted a space – illegal, at the end of a bay – flicked his signal and pulled in to a discordant blare of car horns behind him.

"Yeah, yeah, yeah," Hayes replied, waving the drivers on. It wasn't like he wanted the flat.

He switched off the engine and waited a moment, watching his side mirror with his hand gripped on the handle of the driver's door. When the lights changed, he opened the door a couple of feet while the street was empty, and stepped out to check the tires. The tires looked fine on this side, but as his foot touched the road's surface, he felt something weird.

Hayes peered down with surprise. There were cobblestones underfoot where there should be asphalt. It was strange; unreal even. No wonder his suspension had been jostling him about in his seat the past block. It wasn't a flat, it was the road. The road had changed.

Twenty feet away, the lights at the intersection turned back to green and the race track that was New York traffic started up once more, thundering towards him.

Amid another chorus of disgruntled car horns, Hayes slipped back into the driver's seat of his 4WD and tried to figure what was happening. Where was he? Some cross street linking Amsterdam Avenue to Broadway. This street had not always been cobbled, had it? Maybe once, a hundred or so years ago, but not in living memory, not once they got rid of those guys who walked in front of a car holding a red flag.

Overhead, the dark clouds were lit by more lightning cascading across the sky. It seemed to be coalescing over Central Park, just a couple of blocks away.

Drivers were pulling over now too, suspecting like Hayes that they had got themselves a flat or shot their suspension somehow. Pedestrians were looking around, confused, as if there was something in the air that they sensed.

To Hayes' left, a little Pekinese walked by a slim blonde on a cell phone began howling and straining at its leash, much to the blonde's surprise.

"Choochie, stop that!" the blonde yelped. "Choochie!"

The dog continued to yip, showing its vicious little teeth.

Hayes flicked on his signal and pulled back out into the traffic flow, glancing in his mirror. He saw something cross the street behind him in the mirror, cutting high between the buildings like a comet. It was trailed by a glistening tail of light, a tail rendered all the more brilliant by the darkness. It was Captain Light, his star trail marking his path as he flew through the air in the direction of Central Park.

Hayes wrestled with the wheel, making a U-turn amidst a chorus of honking horns and complaining brakes, following Captain Light as the hero soared across Columbus Avenue about five stories above the street. People were running away from where the hero was heading, fleeing in terror, on the sidewalks and in the center of the street itself, dodging between the traffic. For a moment, Hayes thought he saw Afro Jogger again, cutting across the traffic as he ran from whatever was going on up ahead.

Then, without warning, a blast of blood red lightning shot out from beyond the trees of Central Park ahead of Hayes. The blast struck Captain Light in the center of his chest, hitting him hard. Hayes craned his neck to see, watching as Captain Light hurtled erratically earthwards, out of control, plummeting down towards the Sheep Meadow area of Central Park. Behind him, the streak of star-like brilliance that always followed the hero in flight seemed to splutter and fade, scattered bursts of it marking his trail in the air like Morse Code.

Morgana Le Fey was rising from the center of Sheep Meadow as Captain Light crashed to the dirt at her feet, his body smoldering and trailed by a smear of broken stars. Le Fey was a few feet above the ground, walking on air, her wand poised in her hand. The wand looked like a stick that had been torn from a tree, all twisted and knotted, and a tracery of scarlet lightning ran up and down its length. In her other hand was an ancient, leather-bound book, large and heavy as a toddler, and clutched to her breast like one, too. Morgana Le Fey was dressed in layers of black, silks and lace and leather, her cape like a bat's wings as it billowed out behind her on the breeze. She was laughing – an ugly cackle that seemed to carry across Central Park and out into the surrounding Manhattan streets.

Hayes gunned his engine, speeding towards the park as innocent bystanders ran for cover, weaving between the other vehicles as drivers skidded to a halt or tried to turn back from the madness they could see ahead of them. All around Hayes, in some weird, ripple effect, the buildings were altering. They shimmered in place, their façades becoming impossibly older, their windows narrower, until each was no longer a tower of concrete and glass but was constructed of huge blocks of stone like a medieval castle.

In the park, Morgana Le Fey loomed over Captain Light's smoking form where he lay sprawled in the dirt, literally standing over him, hovering as she was a few feet above the ground. Around her, emerging from the dark corners in space that lurked forever unseen, came her army of faerie folk, their features neither male nor female, each one beautiful and hideous, angular and wrong.

The engine of Hayes' 4WD roared as he overtook a stalled cab and crossed the wide boulevard of Central Park West. And then –

Bang!

– Hayes hit something hard. He slammed on his brakes as it went crashing over his hood and bounced off his windshield. It was a man, some terrified passer-by who was running away from the whole whatever-it-was in Central Park; running right across the center of the street.

"Damn it, damn it," Hayes hissed. Hayes was stopped mid-lane, leapt out of his car, leaving the engine running. He scrambled around the front of the car to the far side, to check on the person he had struck, pushing to the back of his mind what was occurring in the park. Behind him, high above Sheep Meadow, lightning was coruscating across the coal black clouds.

"I'm sorry, man," Hayes babbled as he rushed to where the accident victim had landed. "I didn't see you. I was–"

Hayes stopped, his heart pounding against his chest as he saw the man lying there, eyes staring bewildered up at the lightning-streaked sky.

The man's face looked exactly like his own.

PART 3
Framed

17

Hayes looked incredulously at the figure lying flat on his back on the roadway of Central Park West. Behind and all around, the world was rippling as it adopted the new reality enforced upon it by Morgana Le Fey's spell, asphalt roads switching to cobbled streets, reinforced glass windows replaced by crude, rectangular holes in stone, towers replaced by turrets.

Above, the night sky was lit by a crisscrossing of lightning, streaks of blood red firing through the clouds. While, in Central Park itself, Morgana Le Fey was cackling with cruel humor as her armies emerged from Faerieland and her spell of change took effect.

Despite all of that, despite the madness that seemed to be escalating all around him, Hayes was transfixed by the face of the man whom he had struck. Because it was *his* face.

"Are you okay–?" Hayes began. What did you say? What did you say to yourself in the aftermath of running *you* down with a four-wheel-drive?

The man with Hayes' face groaned, and his eyes fluttered open. They were eyes that matched Hayes' eyes, in a face that matched Hayes' face. "Wha–?" he muttered, this man who was and was not Hayes. He was dressed in casual clothes, a short-sleeved shirt and sweat pants with sneakers. "Wha'… happened?"

"You were hit by a car," Hayes explained. "My car. You ran

out and I didn't see you until it was too late." The words seemed surreal, like he was trying to explain his actions to the mirror.

"Ohhh hell," the man with his face said, speaking to himself. "I gotta check on Bobbi." He sat up woozily, swaying in place and reaching for his head, and then his side.

"Okay, man," Hayes told him, helping him to sit. "Just take it slow."

Across the intersection, a set of traffic lights had warped into a flaming sconce, and the street lamps were turning into pillars topped by flames. Everything was changing. *Everything,* Hayes realized.

"You got a name?" Hayes asked, realizing as he said it that it was a stupid question. Everyone had a name. "I'm Jon."

"Jon," the man with Hayes' face said. Hayes was not sure if he was repeating the name or giving his own. "You hit me pretty hard, huh? Side hurts like something's broke in there."

Hayes held up his hands in admission of guilt. "I clipped you, for sure," he admitted. "You came right across my path. I couldn't stop in time. I'm... I'm sorry." This was weird. He wanted to ask the man the obvious question, whether he recognized him, whether it was as disconcerting for him to see his own face staring back.

Then Hayes realized that maybe that fact had not dawned on the man in the road. He had the hood of his sweatshirt up, pulled close in defense against that cold mountain air he had stepped out into when he had left Culper's earlier that evening. Maybe it hid so much of his face that the man, in his bewilderment, had not realized their similarity.

"You need me to drive you to a hospital?" Hayes asked, looking around at the street. The street signs had all been replaced by what appeared to be heraldic shields, with words written in Latin below them in an elaborate script.

The other Hayes stood up – woozy and trembling, leaning over where he had bruised his side. "Hospital?!" he asked, outraged. "Look around you, man. The world's ending. The whole damn spitball is going up in smoke."

Hayes watched, uncertain, as the man with his face staggered away to the curb. The mysterious man called back to Hayes as he reached the sidewalk: "Go be with your loved ones, man. Go tell 'em you love 'em before it's too late."

Hayes stood by his car, feeling confused and wrong-footed and nauseous. He felt as though he had just taken a punch to the gut, and his breath just wouldn't come back.

Who was that man and why did he have his face? Hayes wondered if he should chase after him, but the man was already starting to lose himself amongst the masses of terrified locals, all of them trying to get away from the reality-changing altercation in Central Park, moving down sidewalks that were now dirt tracks, past buildings whose concrete and steel had been replaced by granite and iron.

Reality-changing – that was the key, maybe. That could explain why a man he had struck with his fender looked just like him, couldn't it?

Hayes looked around, searching the faces of the terrified crowds, looking to see if there was perhaps another him, maybe a dozen. There had to be a hundred people on the street, maybe even more than that, and all of them were running away from the costume throw down in Central Park. Which in itself was madness, because whatever Le Fey was doing was affecting New York in a radial pattern which centered on the Sheep Meadow area where she was grandstanding. How far could you run when, like Hayes' counterpart had said, the world was ending? Or, if not ending, then certainly changing – changing beyond comprehension. Hayes could not see anyone he recognized, and certainly no one who looked like him; but everything was moving fast and frantic, everyone panicking. Suddenly a car mounted the sidewalk as the driver lost control, knocking into a mailbox before slamming into the wall of what looked now like a medieval castle but had been a designer boutique just a few minutes before.

"Come on, pal!" a cabbie shouted from out of his wound-down window behind Hayes. "Move outta the way a'ready!"

Hayes looked up, meeting the gaze of the cabbie. The driver did not look angry so much as weary, like he had driven through the apocalypse so many times he was more put out with the traffic than the end of the world.

"Sorry," Hayes shouted back, waving his arms. "I'll move." He trotted around the back of his car and leapt back in the driver's seat while, all around, cars and trucks and buses tried to squirm through tight gaps in the cobblestone gridlock.

So that was "Hayes Number Two" lost, Hayes realized. Lost to the crowd, with just the possibility of a fractured rib to show for meeting him. And who the hell was this "Bobbi" he had mentioned? Hayes did not know anyone called Bobbi; no Roberta, no Barbara, no Bobbi.

Hayes whipped the wheel around and pulled through a gap in the snarl of traffic heading into Central Park, bumping the curb as he snaked past an abandoned delivery truck. He was on the 65th Street Transverse that went through Central Park at a lowered level, right past the area known as Sheep Meadow. Traffic was coming out from under the pedestrian bridge up ahead at a high speed, drivers desperate to get away from what was going on here. But the same was true of people heading into the park, driving through and hoping to escape on the far side. Two fast lanes of traffic in opposing directions, and everyone in a heightened state of panic except for that world-weary cab driver. It felt like a recipe for disaster.

Hayes made a decision as he reached the point where the two lines of traffic met, made a hard left and bumped onto the grassy verge there that divided the opposing flows of vehicles. Then he braked, stopping on the narrow verge amid a chorus of tooting horns. He shut off his car and shoved the driver's door open, jumping out. The car would survive or it wouldn't. He needed to know what was happening in the park, and how it related to the man who looked just like him.

A blare of car horns sounded as Hayes crossed the street towards a wall that abutted Sheep Meadow. The wall was too high to ascend where the road dropped, and Hayes considered turning back for a moment and finding a pedestrian route. Behind him, an angry driver in a hatchback sat on his horn, glaring in annoyance and fear through the thick lenses of his spectacles.

Hayes took a step towards the hatchback, climbing up onto the hood as the surprised driver hammered on his windshield. Hayes ignored him, stepping up onto the car's roof. Then, in a running jump, he picked up speed and leapt for the Central Park wall, grabbing its flat top with his right hand and pulling himself up.

A moment later, Hayes was atop the wall. He dropped down on the far side.

Sheep Meadow was ahead of him, a great, flat expanse of grass which was open to the public and frequently hosted events like runs and yoga classes. However, it had never hosted an event quite like the one Hayes was witnessing now.

Crossing the grassy plains, a stone wall had been erected, twenty-five feet high by twenty feet across. The wall looked ancient, like it had been here for centuries, and yet in actuality it had only materialized within the last hour.

On the wall, chained with glowing manacles, were the seven current members of the Rangers – the Mechanist in his armor, the super-speedster known as Chase, Skater, the Phase, the telepath Astra, wearing a hood that looked like a fishbowl to prevent her from employing her mindcraft abilities, Ray Cathode, and a wimpy-looking man in manacles who could assume the guise of Missing Link but had been rendered unconscious. Morgana Le Fey strode up and down before her prisoners as her faerie minions added Captain Light's listless form to the wall, chaining him up at a spot in the bottom right below Cathode. His head hung limply as he struggled in semi-consciousness.

Le Fey held her wand loosely in her hand, twirling it like a majorette's baton as she gloated. In the sky above, the dark clouds seemed to be turning like a whirlpool seen from below, with constant flashes of lightning darting through their ominous depths.

There were people cowering amongst the vegetation of the park, stragglers who were too afraid or too infirm to run. They hid in bushes or just watched from a distance, some capturing the incident on their cell phone cameras. Figures moved among those stragglers, creatures from the Faerieworld which Morgana Le Fey ruled. They were shadow things, their faces beautiful and genderless, their bodies smooth, their motions as graceful as pouring fluid. They were accompanied by the giddy sounds of syrinx pipe music, rolling gleefully up and down the scale at odds to the danger that was in the air.

It was unnerving to watch those faerie folk, the way they slipped through the park like wraiths, emerging and dematerializing amidst the shadows, walking out of impossible angles in the world that should not – could not – exist. They were a child's nightmares brought to life, haunting and unknowable and somehow ever-present.

Hayes made his way towards the wall, a twinge of pain playing down his left leg where he had landed hard on it – again – climbing up to get here.

"… arrogant fleas," Le Fey was saying. "You dared to cast me away, unable to recognize my superiority! The way that all of man's world has failed to recognize me as their superior!"

"Slow your yap, sister," Chase said from where she was chained to the towering wall under the swirling, uncanny lightning storm. "We've got equal rights now, men and women get treated the same. Sure, it may not be perfect, but at least we're trying to make a better world."

"Silence," Morgana Le Fey snarled, turning to face Chase and pressing the glowing tip of her wand under the super-speedster's chin. "This world *will* be better – and I shall make it so! Already my spells are turning your debauched streets into the new Camelot, and the people of this city shall be my loyal subjects!"

Hoo boy, Hayes thought. He might not have followed Morgana Le Fey's career, but remembered when she had first fought with the Rangers. That had been big news, marking as it did the first appearance of a costume-team since World War II. Le Fey was nutty as a fruitcake, and right now she was presiding over eight of the most powerful costumed heroes to call New York their home. This was big. Huge. This was one of those events that could change everything.

"You'll never get your way, Morgana," Captain Light spat from the bottom row of trapped heroes, raising his head heavily to look at her. "The people will never accept you, no matter what you do."

"You're wrong," Le Fey snarled, turning on Captain Light. She whipped her wand up and away from Chase, so swiftly that it sounded as though a bone had snapped in the speed-woman's neck. Hayes watched, horrified, as Chase's head slumped down against her chest. "The people will love me, admire me, *worship* me. They will serve me in any way I choose, just as you shall. Just as all of you so-called heroes shall."

Le Fey was standing before Captain Light now, her unsettling fae folk huddled around her, shadows with amorphous faces. "Will you love me, Captain Light?" she asked in a mock-solicitous tone.

Despite the way the shackles held his arms above and behind him, forcing him to hang uncomfortably forward, Captain Light met Morgana Le Fey's gaze with a proud jut to his jaw. "Never."

Hayes was closer now – roughly fifty yards – using the tree cover the way they had trained him in the SEALs, so that he could see and hear everything that was occurring at the imprisonment wall.

"Sometimes my subjects need tough love," Le Fey explained, as she brought her wand towards Captain Light. She traced the knotted wand slowly up Light's body until it was under his chin. Then, there came a spark like a socket shorting out, and the wand dispatched a blast of crimson lightning full into Captain Light's face with an accompanying clap of thunder. The lightning played across the good Captain's head, and for a fraction of a second Hayes could see the man's skull as if in an x-ray image. At the same time, the book clenched in Le Fey's other arm seemed to throb and bulge, as if it contained something alive within it.

The hero unleashed a chilling scream at the torture he was undergoing. It was a scream like his famous spectral scream, and materialized as a physical blast of energy from his open jaws, a swirling beam of whiteness shaded with multicolors, like a gasoline sheen on water. Le Fey stepped back, laughing wickedly as the spectral scream scorched the grass of Central Park, leaving a blazing, gaping hole that seemed to open a rift in reality itself. The rift showed stars and distant planets in its depths, before sealing again as if it had never been there.

"Love hurts," Le Fey told Captain Light as he sagged in his bonds, a sheen of sweat on his face. "And that pain you felt is only the beginning. Before I am done here, you and your foolish colleagues shall know pain the likes of which you cannot imagine. For pain is love."

This is serious, Hayes thought. Dropping eight of the most powerful costumes in one hit was pretty much unheard of. Sure, strictly speaking, the Rangers were a mishmash of abilities, many with their own rogues galleries who didn't stand a chance against someone in the weight class of Captain Light or even the Mechanist; but despite that, when they were all together they compensated for one another's limitations, the whole proving to be more than the sum of its parts. But now they were down, defeated, chained up against a wall as all of Manhattan began to change under the faerie warp of Morgana Le Fey's spellcrafting.

And what could Hayes do? A trained SEAL, and he was nothing more now than a victim, a bystander, to powers far beyond his comprehension. Some nameless bystander, a face in the crowd who may as well be assigned a number for all the effect he would have here today.

Hayes looked to the skies as Le Fey prattled on, seeing that upturned whirlpool of lightning-flecked clouds as it loomed above the city of New York. He hoped he might see something else up there too – the brilliant, fiery streak that heralded the appearance of Eternal Flame, the last of the power-heavyweights who populated the costumed fraternity. Because there had to be someone to save the day, there just had to be.

Only there wasn't. No Eternal Flame. No Swan stepping out of retirement for one last brouhaha against the forces of evil. No Doc Solid or even the secretive team known only as the Number Men, whose adventures seemed to be more rumor than fact. No one was coming.

Which left... him? Could he stand idly by?

18

Maybe it won't be so bad getting killed, Hayes told himself. Maybe that other guy who had his face, the one he had run over, could take over his life and get that wall in the lobby finally stripped back properly and figure out what to do about all those empty paint cans that were congregating in the basement.

It was two hundred yards straight to the wall, but straight wasn't going to cut it. Hayes sprinted across the grassed plain of Sheep Meadow, arms pumping, legs whipping out in long strides, heading in the direction of Morgana Le Fey and her trophy wall of heroes. He knew he would need the heroes' help if he was actually going to stand any chance against Le Fey and her faerie army, which meant he would have to go through her.

He ran in a long loop, whipping across the grass so that he would come at the wall from the reverse side, and remain unseen as long as possible. It was hardly a sneak attack, but at least this way he might get close before having to dodge lightning blasts from her magic wand.

Morgana Le Fey was still occupied with her bragging right now, lording it over the costumed heroes as they hung from their manacles. Her warp spell was filtering farther outwards, altering all of Manhattan Island, building by building, street by street, block by block. Across the park, Hayes could see the skyline had changed. Where once there had been up-and-down structures, all

straight lines and slim towers, now there were jagged turrets and
fortifications, built to a height unseen ever before.

Speed and stealth was all Hayes had, just like the old days
breaking some drug supply chain out in Colombia. The night
shadows in Central Park were thick enough to hide his approach,
and with the continued sounds of panic from the streets close by,
Hayes could get away with making noise.

However, there were fae moving through the park in packs.
Hayes guessed they were soldiers, or whatever passed for soldiers
in Faerieland, having traveled here with, and hence answerable
to, Morgana Le Fey. Hayes baulked for a moment when he saw
one figure drop down from the swirling clouds above the park
astride what looked like an honest-to-goodness dragon.

The dragon was large as a private jet, with a webbing of leather
straps across its scaly body. Hayes spotted the small, humanoid
figure riding on a saddle atop the beast's back, sitting between its
flapping wings, with a lance balanced in his hands. The dragon's
scales flashed silver as they reflected the coruscating lightning in
the clouds above.

"Shit," Hayes muttered when he saw the dragon begin to circle
the edges of the park, patrolling the perimeter like a helicopter.
They sure as hell hadn't covered dealing with dragons in BUD/S.
No, this was some heavy stuff, and it was going to take something
really special to fix. Hayes had no damn idea what that would be
just yet.

Hayes continued running, feeling the sharp jab of pain in his
left foot where he had landed badly the night before. That blasted
ankle was going to slow him down, he knew. He would have to
ride out the pain and hope he could free one of those hero types
in time to stop this whole faerie takeover.

Hayes had circled and made it fifty yards from the wall of heroes
when a soldier from the fae army spotted his approach. The fae –
a slim and elegant figure in glistening armor forged from dragon
scale – said something to alert its colleagues. The fae's words were
like a susurration of the wind through leaves – whispered, whistled

things as ephemeral as the soldier itself, words that barely seemed to be words at all. Several of the soldier's colleagues turned to where it was pointing to indicate the approaching form of Hayes.

Hayes did not slow, he just kept running, meeting the three of them as they were still drawing their otherworldly blades. They were beautiful, ethereal creatures. Their features were asexual, with narrow faces and pale hair with the quality of feathers.

Hayes met the first warrior with a vicious pump of his right fist, knuckles slamming into the beautiful thing's jaw with a loud clap. The fae – surprised as all get out – dropped like so much dead weight, striking the grass with a muffled thud. Hayes kicked it hard in the gut as he moved on, and was rewarded with the pained sounds of the fae's breath being forced from its lungs in a splutter.

The next warrior had his knife unsheathed. It lunged at Hayes, blade slicing through the air with a sound like birdsong, eyes glistening black like a spider's.

Hayes' training came back automatically. Hayes had been a Navy SEAL, and it was said that the SEALs were the most formidable unarmed fighting men in the world. *Time to prove it*, he thought, *and remind this fucker that I earned my trident.*

Hayes sidestepped the arc of his opponent's swing, struck the soldier's wrist and deflected the knife attack, all in one swift move. The fae reacted immediately, bringing the birdsong blade back in an instant reverse. But Hayes ducked easily, and the blade swept overhead, twittering as it went.

Hayes continued his movements, one into the next, using his momentum to lunge at the fae warrior, piling into it with his left shoulder like he was sacking a quarterback. The fae was knocked back, feet leaving the ground and tumbling over itself before crashing to the grass. But Hayes was still moving, barreling forward almost out of control so that he nearly lost his balance. Hayes realized that the fae were lighter than he expected, as if their bones were hollow like a bird's. Perhaps that was his advantage here then – his weight, his solid mass.

There was no time to stop and think, however. The third soldier – the one who had first sounded the weird, whisper-breeze alert – came at Hayes from the shadows, moving fast to get behind him, where it had not been a fraction of a second before. *These damned things can walk through shadows*, Hayes realized, *using them like hidden doors.*

Hayes' body responded without conscious thought, driving the sharp corner of his bent elbow into the fae's beautiful face with such force that its nose caved in with a spray of watery, blue-gray blood. The fae stumbled back, holding its face and moaning.

Hayes spun and kicked out, delivering a powerful boot to the fae's abdomen, forcing it to double over. The fae hissed an expression of pain, and Hayes moved in for the kill – bringing both his arms up and driving the elbows together hard into the fae warrior's back. The fae sagged forward with a splutter of strained breath, collapsing on the ground.

Three down, Hayes thought grimly as he moved away from the fallen bodies.

Hayes gathered his bearings, sighting the wall of heroes up ahead, blank on this side. He was thirty yards from it now, and still hidden from Morgana Le Fey. Above, the clouds seemed to be swirling faster, forming a kind of funnel that began to drop from the heavens as lightning fluttered and spat through its depths. It reminded Hayes of the twister that had taken Dorothy's house in *The Wizard of Oz.*

Hayes was conscious that he was moving slower now. His foot felt tender, and there was only so much that adrenalin could carry him through. Fighting one on one he had a chance; taking on an army from otherworld – that was asking a lot.

There were more fae warriors moving towards Hayes now. He looked around, assessing the situation in a single glance, realizing that there had to be twenty or more of the beautiful, unsettling creatures closing towards him. Some had swords, some had daggers, a few carried what looked like a cross between an ax and some kind of nunchucku, linked by a chain – Hayes had no idea what those were but he did not relish fighting against some expert at using one. Twenty against one. Bad odds. Real bad.

Thirty yards to cover, with thick shadows that hid him but also hid the faerie creatures who formed Morgana Le Fey's army. Thirty yards and not a chance. Not a chance unless… Hayes felt the weight in his pocket, striking against his belly as he closed in on the next group of warriors. It was Retro's gun – he had stashed it there when he had left Jonas Culper's place in the mountains.

Two fae soldiers were charging towards Hayes from the direction of the wall – the direction he needed to go. One had one of those weird ax devices which it was swinging around to his side like a bolas. The ax whined like a mournful dog as it cut the air.

Running, Hayes pulled Retro's gun from his sweatshirt and clicked the trigger in one notch, releasing the safety as he raised it to eye level. The ax-wielder was sweeping the blade out towards Hayes' head on the length of chain even as Hayes fired the gun, and –

Eeeee-owwwww!

Retro's gun blasted with that weird electric guitar chord. The butt kicked against Hayes' hand but the recoil was negligible; the device had been beautifully crafted to minimize its effect on the shooter.

Before Hayes, both fae warriors were knocked off their feet, and the side of the one to the right tore apart in a shower of tiny bones that looked like the remains of a family roast.

Hayes smiled grimly.

Six shots, he remembered. *Now five.* Six had been the estimate he had made based on when he had seen the gun in action. He had no way of knowing if it was right, there were so many variables, too many unknowns. Just like all these freaks in their masks, there were too many unknowns.

Hayes detected something moving across his vision from the corner of his eye. It was one of the fae, stepping out of those impossible, unseen corners, the hiding spaces in the world, stepping out into the light.

Without hesitation, Hayes turned the gun on his would-be attacker and squeezed the trigger.

Eeeee-owwwww!

The force blast struck the beautiful, ethereal fae creature so hard that its chest seemed to cave inwards. Hayes watched as the faerie creature fell away from him. In the stuttering light cast by the lightning above, in the in-between places that the faerie traversed, the beautiful face looked like –

"Melanie," Hayes whispered.

The fae flopped to the ground, seizures running through its ruined body like a beached fish. Its face – that asexual, impossibly beautiful face – looked just like Melanie's in that instant.

"Is this where it's leading, Quo?" Melanie asked him from the shadows in the face of the dying fae thing as she clutched at her ruined chest cavity. "Is this what you want to happen?"

Hayes had stopped. He stood over the body as it flipped and flopped, straining in its death throes, with Melanie's words echoing in his skull. It was not Melanie. He knew that, looking again, watching closely as the thing died in sheer agony, its body ripped through by the hammer blow of force from Retro's gun. It had just been a trick of the light, the way these supernatural creatures could look like everyone and no one all at the same time. The way they challenged the very concept of appearance.

Yet, still, it felt like Hayes had killed Melanie. That shock of seeing her here, just momentarily, the same way he had seen her ever since she had died on Sixth Avenue. It hurt.

"I'm sorry," Hayes said. Hayes had killed before, in the line of duty, and never once had he felt the need to apologize.

Around Hayes, there were fae warriors amassing, crossing the grass field towards him, the dragon circling overhead. Hayes did nothing. He was conscious of their approach, conscious that this would be it, this would be the end; but then maybe the end is what he had really wanted all along, maybe that was what he craved. Maybe in killing this thing that, just for a moment, had had Melanie's face, maybe he had finally reached whatever it was that he was destined to reach. Maybe he died here and now, as the world he knew ended at the hands of Morgana Le Fey. Maybe that was closure.

"What's going on here?" a man's voice said from nearby. There was a mocking tone to his words.

Hayes looked up at the voice, saw the figure silhouetted atop the stone wall which held the imprisoned heroes, his back to Hayes. The figure was addressing Morgana Le Fey where she stood on the far side of the wall, Hayes realized. Then, there was another flash of lightning from the swirling, unnatural sky, though Hayes had not needed it to tell him who the man atop the wall was – he had recognized him instantly from the casual way he held that sword in his right hand. It was Damocles.

"You're having a party," Damocles continued, "and you didn't invite lil' ol' me? Is it my aftershave?"

As he said this last, Damocles leapt from where he had been standing atop the wall, executing a double somersault that took him out of Hayes' eye line and down to the ground. Hayes saw movement to the right-hand edge of the wall where Damocles faced off against Morgana Le Fey, her cape swirling about her like the spreading wings of a bat taking flight. In the same moment, Hayes was conscious that Le Fey's loyal army had ceased in their attempts to reach him, hurrying instead across Sheep Meadow to defend their mistress.

Hayes assessed the situation with a weary smile. *Stop Damocles the costumed hero, or stop the guy with four shots left in a gun he stole?* He reasoned that in their faerie shoes he would have made the same faerie choice.

"Insignificant vermin!" Morgana Le Fey hissed as Damocles landed gracefully a few feet before her. "What chance do think you stand against me when your most powerful allies have already fallen?" As she said this, she indicated the wall where the Rangers and Captain Light remained chained.

"Well, they tell me I was dropped on my head a lot as a kid," Damocles mocked, springing towards the faerie sorceress and jabbing at her with his sentient sword.

"Babbling idiot!" Le Fey snarled. With a flick of her wand, she hooked Damocles' sword from his hand and sent it flying off towards the distant trees.

Damocles ducked as Le Fey's counter swing targeted his head. "Hey, I don't mind being called an idiot," he taunted, "but I work on this babble for several hours every day. It doesn't –"

Damocles leapt a bolt of blood red lightning from Le Fey's wand.

"– just –"

Damocles ducked another blast, this one a sickly yellow like pus.

"– write itself!"

With this last, Damocles did a handspring and kicked both feet into Le Fey's face with a loud crack.

Morgana Le Fey stumbled back with a howl of irritation as much as pain, wiping a hand across her face.

Behind her, the army of faerie folk were massing, lining Sheep Meadow and bearing down on the disarmed Damocles as he crouched in combat readiness. A second dragon had joined the first, landing on the grass as another crack of thunder shook the swirling skies.

Morgana Le Fey spat before fixing Damocles with a stare so cruel it felt as though it might stop his heart. "What chance do you, an insignificant little human being, honestly think you stand alone against me?"

"Well," Damocles said, loosening the red-and-yellow tunic of his collar with one finger, "since you put it that way, I think I don't stand any chance at all –"

Morgana Le Fey grinned, her smile like a shark's.

"– *alone*," Damocles finished. "Which is why I invited a play date!"

"What?!" Morgana Le Fey hissed, both confused and outraged.

From his position behind the wall, Hayes could not quite see what was happening for a moment. Then he spotted a familiar armored boot emerge at the edge of the wall. It was the Mechanist's foot, and an instant later his armored form stepped out from behind where the wall had obscured him from Hayes' sight. He had somehow got free from his shackles on the wall in a way that Hayes could not discern.

As the Mechanist strode into view at the edge of the wall, his shiny, metallic form was accompanied by Chase, her limbs a blur, then the Skater, whose skates glinted as they reflected the lightning from the skies, Ray Cathode, sweeping his long coat of ever-changing color behind him, and Captain Light, who tossed aside the last, glowing chain link of his own shackles. Out in the park, one of the dragon riders found itself suddenly under attack from the multi-fractal wraith forms of the Phase, popping in and out of the time flow in an infinite number of "nows", all somehow occurring in the same fraction of a second.

At the wall, Astra was removing the fishbowl-like hood which had dampened her mind powers. Once she had done so, she would trigger the metamorphosis in the disheveled and distressingly human figure who stood catching his breath beside her, so that he could once more change form and become the powerhouse known as the Missing Link.

"How can this be?" Le Fey raged as she saw the heroes striding across the grass towards her.

"You see," Damocles said as he rose once more from the grass to join his fellow costumed heroes, "you should never, ever take your eye off the sentient sword!"

Morgana Le Fey fired a blast of magic energy from her wand as nine heroes went into battle against her and her army.

19

The rest of the battle with Le Fey played out the way that these battles always played out. Hayes watched from close by, the pain in his left foot nagging at him enough that he knew he would need to take painkillers again shortly. He was outclassed and out of the fight.

Morgana Le Fey and her army put up a passable resistance, but once the dragons were knocked out of the battle – initially when the Phase knocked one rider unconscious, then with the combined strength of Captain Light and the Missing Link tossing both dragons into one another – things finally seemed to turn. Le Fey's army of faerie folk was devious and well-armed, but they were dealt with in short measure in a variety of ways by the combined forces of the Rangers, Damocles and Captain Light.

Hayes could not see everything – some of it he pieced together later by watching various news reports – but he saw the Missing Link knock over a whole platoon of fae warriors as if they were bowling pins, watched Astra draw forth the greatest fears of a group of fae who foolishly endeavored to surround her, and saw the Skater and Chase double tag an army of mounted soldiers who emerged from the reality breach as last-minute reinforcements riding armored horses.

Finally, it all came down to Morgana Le Fey herself facing nine heroes en masse. Bolts of magic lit the air, shaking Hayes down to the core. Damocles was thrown across Central Park only to be rescued by Chase who ran at super-high speed to catch him before he struck the ground, a sonic boom left in her wake.

The Mechanist was stripped of his armor by a cascade of brilliant magic that looked like he was being attacked by a waterfall, retaining only the neural web headpiece atop his skull with which he presumably controlled his suit. Even then, using only the neural web, the Mechanist manipulated the functioning parts of his armor to protect himself from a thundering blast of fae magic.

Somehow Le Fey managed to split her own form momentarily when the Phase launched his multi-chronal assault, snatching several versions of the synthetic man and leaving the whole multitude stunned. Hayes watched that with his own eyes, and baulked when he saw the Phase regather with a plethora of images of himself falling together, like some weird slow-motion film effect. The effort knocked Phase out of the battle, but that still left the heavy hitters.

The Missing Link was momentarily blinded by one of Le Fey's dazzle spells, but it left a space for Captain Light and the Skater to attack her physical form. At the same moment Ray Cathode flicked something at Morgana Le Fey and her spell book suddenly went up in a burst of flames in her hand, forcing her to drop it. The flames were moss green and the deep purple of a plum, reminding Hayes of a bruise.

As Le Fey dropped the spell book, its pages shot up into the air like fireworks, popping in the sky.

The faerie witch queen was not finished yet. She knocked back the Skater with an incredible burst of force from her wand, and Hayes watched the hero hurtle into that wall upon which le Fey had had all of the heroes trapped just a few minutes earlier. Her power was fading however; a part of the wall turned to powder where Skater struck it, and then the whole thing began to rumble ominously before collapsing like it was made of dry sand.

Around the park, the whole of Manhattan was also reeling in the dwindling power of Morgana Le Fey. In the far distance, blocks were switching back to how they had been before, swapping turrets for helipads as the effect of Le Fey's spell wore off. The streets were no longer cobbled, and even the dark swirl in the sky was losing its menace, turning slower than it had at its peak, the lightning within its depths all but spent.

If words were exchanged, Hayes could not hear them – he was too far away and the sounds of battle were too cacophonous, drowning out everything else. But he saw the way that Morgana Le Fey wielded her magic wand like a baseball bat to knock back Ray Cathode and Captain Light, resorting to the most blunt of physical attacks. Then Le Fey fell to her knees, even as Cathode and Light were getting back to their feet, and she dropped her wand, her hands reaching for her head.

"No!" Le Fey screamed. "Leave me! Leave me alone!" She was frantic, seeing something in her head which no one else could see. "Orcades, my sister! Don't make me! No!!! *Nnnoooooooo!!!*"

Astra's yellow-clad form strode out from the trees at the edge of Sheep Meadow then, evidently concentrating all of her incredible powers on Morgana Le Fey as the witch woman fought with the visions that played inside her head. Astra was a telepath who could reach into a person's mindscape and turn their most wicked wishes against them, disabling them with their own wants and fears. Evidently Astra had done just that to Morgana Le Fey.

Hayes watched as Captain Light took up a position before the frantic, shrieking form of Morgana Le Fey and inhaled a deep breath. Then, with one mighty bellow, Captain Light let loose his incredible spectral scream, opening up a rift in time and space like a tear in the cloth of reality. Morgana Le Fey's trembling form was yanked out of this world like she had been plucked up by a vacuum cleaner, dragged through the rift in space where it hung like a stalactite in the air above Sheep Meadow, out and away across the dimensional planes. A moment later, and the window of the rift sealed shut, cutting off Le Fey's scream abruptly as she disappeared behind its closing lid.

As Astra strode to join the other heroes, the air above Central

Park glistened like fireflies. They were not insects, however – they were the burning pages of the spell book which Morgana Le Fey had used to ensnare the heroes, and which had been set alight in her hands.

"Look at it," the Mechanist told his allies as the fluttering ashes wended slowly back down to earth. "In the right light, even evil can look beautiful."

Licking their wounds, the Rangers and their temporary allies, Captain Light and Damocles, agreed with the sentiment. All except for Ray Cathode, that is, who was too busy nursing the burnt fingers he had received when he had set the spell book aflame to voice an opinion.

According to the morning news, Damocles had cunningly dispatched his sentient sword to free his fellow heroes while he had kept Morgana Le Fey and her armies distracted after his arrival. Hayes figured that was probably what had been happening when he saw Le Fey knock Damocles' sword from his hand – it had been some kind of set-up by the masked hero, who had intended to "lose" the self-propelled sword all along. Leave it to a swordsman to know when to feint, Hayes thought with a grim smile, as he nursed a cup of steaming coffee.

He had not been to sleep.

The world had righted itself somewhere in the small hours, after the faerie sorceress had been sent back to her home dimension or wherever it was that Captain Light's spectral scream had imprisoned her when it had opened that rift between worlds. Le Fey's mind was still trapped in the nightmare of visions Astra had plagued her with, so she would not be coming back any time soon.

With the witch gone, her unnerving armies had disappeared too, turning an unseen corner in the midnight shadows like they were walking through a revolving door, until suddenly they were simply no longer there. Even the dragons that had briefly patrolled the skies above Central Park had departed, sent back to another dimension by the combined efforts of Captain Light and the Mechanist wearing a cobbled-together approximation of his armor. The Mechanist stated to an inquisitive reporter on the scene of the clean-up that there was too much risk in leaving such beasts in this dimension.

Hayes took a sip from his mug, but the coffee was still too hot to enjoy.

He had found his car where he had left it, untouched on the grassy verge between lanes, driven home in the small hours, crashed on the couch with a bourbon and some painkillers, and watched news reports until the sun came up at six. Then he had taken more painkillers, put on a pot of coffee, and reacquainted himself with the couch for a couple more hours while the news of last night's attack washed over him again and again, looping every twenty minutes or so.

When everything had started to fall apart and right itself, in that nutty way that costume stuff did, Hayes had stashed the gun back in his pocket, snatched what he could and run back to his car. No one had stopped him. It was 2am and Manhattan was feeling a lot like it was recovering from a hangover.

There was no mention on the news of Hayes and what he had done. There were one or two anecdotes of where New Yorkers had taken on the fae, and one guy with a shock of black hair that looked like he had just stepped out of a wind tunnel took credit for kicking one right in the crotch, but Hayes' efforts with Retro's gun had not warranted a mention.

That gun sat beside him, in the armchair by the couch, given its own seat as if it was a visitor. Hayes glanced over to it now and then, checking it was still there. He had shot Melanie. He had pulled the trigger of that blasted gun and shot her, or something that looked like her for a single instant, a fragment of Melanie in time.

It had shaken him up, what he had seen when he had shot the fae soldier. He understood that the faces of the fae were odd and unreal, that their features did not quite conform to those of a person. Objectively, he understood that it was this quirk that had caused him to see Melanie's face on the third fae he had shot. But that did not make it easier.

The Mechanist popped up on screen in a clip that Hayes had seen cycle round twice already, where the costumed hero gave a quick sound bite of reassurance to the breathless reporter. His usually shiny armor looked like the inside of a pizza oven, aged and burnt and scarred.

Hayes flicked off the television and drank the rest of his coffee in silence, with only the muffled ambience from the street outside as company.

Sometime later, after he had showered, Hayes spent some time sitting on his bed, massaging his left foot. The pain was just a twinge now, like an insect bite every now and then if he twisted his foot a certain way. Like everyone who had ever hurt a part of themselves, Hayes tried twisting the foot to the place where it hurt, assessing the pain.

"So, I shot you," Hayes said to the empty bedroom. The words were matter-of-fact, like he was checking on the weather. "Yeah, I did."

He closed his eyes and saw the fae sprawled in the midnight grass of Central Park, guts hanging out and its face scrunched up in agony; the face that looked like Melanie.

"Was I right to do it," Hayes asked the emptiness, "or was I wrong? I don't know. Didn't make a shred of difference to the outcome of the fight, as far as I can tell. But I'm sorry anyway. I don't even know what it is I'm sorry for, Melanie, but I'm sorry."

Hayes pushed himself up, leaning on his good foot to stand before he made his way back to the en suite. He pushed at the cupboard there to open it against the magnetic spring lock, reached for the over-the-counter painkillers from the shelf. Then he closed the cupboard, the mirror that served as the door spinning the room around deliriously as it swung back in place. Hayes ran the cold faucet, took the painkillers with some water, and stood leaning against the basin, gazing into the depths of the mirror.

Melanie never showed. For the past five weeks she had come to visit him in these moments, sometimes, when he felt lost and aimless, when he had been unsure of what the hell he was doing. She had come and she had said, "Quo, do this" or "Quo, don't do this" or something. And now she was gone. Because he had shot her; shot her memory.

Hayes wandered back into the bedroom, listless and alone. He had known all along that the wife who came to visit him in those dark moments of uncertainty was not real. How could she have been? Melanie was dead, crushed by a helicopter that had been dropped on her from the sky above Sixth Avenue. The world was crazy, full of seemingly impossible things, fae armies invading Central Park and satellite repair systems that somehow gained sentience and tried to destroy Times Square. But dead wives did not come back, not even to dispense advice when you really needed it.

"I loved you," Hayes told the other side of the bed, where Melanie had slept for the too few years they had had together.

Maybe it had taken killing the fae with her face to make him say that.

20

Hayes slept through the rest of the day. He had been up all night and he was bushed.

When he awoke it was dusk, with its special, eerie kind of light seeping through the bedroom window. He looked at the window, watching the carousel of clouds trundle past on the wind, hurrying out of sight before night caught up with them.

Hayes stretched, feeling the aches in his muscles. He had not meant to fall asleep, but exhaustion coupled with the combination of painkillers and bourbon in his system had been enough to finally do for him. He glanced at the screen of his cell phone as he rolled to a sitting position, saw he had missed a call from work. He looked at the clock on his phone, tried to figure out whether Jeff Puchenko would still be in the office, and decided he probably would be. Hayes called him.

"Jeff, it's Jon Hayes."

"Jon boy, you got my messages!" Jeff sounded cheered, as though this was the happiest event of his week.

"I saw you'd called," Hayes confirmed. "Sorry, I was... uh..." He trailed off, suddenly embarrassed by his daytime nap.

"Jon, you know me," Jeff told him as Hayes floundered. "You don't need to explain. If you got yourself another job, *that* you would need to explain. But I just want you back. What say you?"

Hayes thought about his bank balance, and about what Culper

had told him about the cost of costumed tech on the gray market. "I'm thinking that maybe I could come back for a few hours," Hayes said. "Take it slow. See how I fit in."

Jeff Puchenko made an uncertain sound at the other end of the line, and there was a pause. Then he said, "I'd have to clear that with the boss, Jon. I mean, we all want you here and heaven knows we appreciate right where you are coming from just now. But–"

"But?" Hayes prompted.

"Look, just leave it all with me and I'll see what Rourke says and I'll get back to you, okay?" Jeff said, with genuine sincerity.

"Thanks."

"And hey, Jon," Jeff said as Hayes was about to disconnect. "You eating okay? You seeing people?"

"I'm eating just fine," Hayes assured him, "and I, er, caught up with a whole group of folks last night."

"Well, good for you," Jeff told him. Then he hung up.

Hayes made his way to the kitchen, opened the fridge and put together something that approximated a meal from what he could find there. He ate without really tasting, just needing the nutrition to keep him going.

Sitting in the lounge, Hayes thought about that other man who had looked like him. There was a trickster part of his mind that had expected Jeff to tell him that he had been coming into work every day for weeks now, and then maybe ask after the mysterious Bobbi. He had been relieved to find that the guy had his face but not his life, not because it meant he was still himself, but because he would not wish this life on anyone else. He missed Melanie.

The TV waited darkly on the wall, and Hayes stretched for the remote where he had left it on a low table. As he reached for it, cheese grease on his fingers from the pizza that he had reincarnated via microwaves, he saw what the remote was resting on. It looked like an article someone had torn from a newspaper, though its edges had been singed black with fire. Hayes had grabbed it at Sheep Meadow before he had left the scene last night, blown out the flame that was licking at its edge when he caught it, and stuffed it into his pants pocket. It was a page from Morgana Le Fey's spell book.

Hayes wiped the grease on his shirt and then unfolded the singed page. It was not even a page, more like a half or a third of one, torn from that huge book that Le Fey had been holding like a baby.

He had placed it under the TV remote that morning, with an almost irresponsible carelessness. He had been exhausted and not thinking straight, more concerned with his need to stash Retro's gun; the whole incident with the fae with Melanie's features had left him drained.

He examined it now and wondered what it was he was looking at. The paper was old and thick, some kind of parchment produced from animal skin. The words on the page were in Latin and indecipherable to Hayes. He could translate it with a little help from an online translation program, he figured, but what he had here was only a part of the phrases from the page, which meant it was probably useless.

I could sell it, Hayes thought.

Burnt page from Morgana Le Fey's spell book – $200 ONO.

Sure. Or he could keep it and figure out what, if anything, you did with a cropped spell from a magic book from another dimension.

Hayes stood up and went over to the bookcase, where he pulled out the wedding photo album. Still standing, he opened it up at the first page. Hayes felt a twinge of sadness as he saw the picture there – it showed him and Melanie together just moments after they had wed, all smiles and with faces looking to the future. He flattened the salvaged page from Morgana Le Fey's spell book, placed it in between the cover and first page of the album and closed it. Then he slipped the wedding album back in its place on the shelf.

* * *

Hayes watched sitcom reruns until two in the morning, then went back to bed and forced himself to sleep. His foot had stopped hurting by then, and he skipped the painkillers and just let sleep fix whatever it found broken.

The alarm went off at 7am. Hayes had set it the night before, knowing he needed to get back into a routine. He had had about four hours sleep and his body did not want to get started. He took a long, hot shower until his muscles felt massaged back to life, then hit the street for a run.

Hayes ran six miles. He took some of it at a jog, but for the most part he pushed himself, wanting to feel the buzz of lactic acid tearing through his body.

When he got home, he showered again, ate a bowl of dry cereal – he needed to get milk in – and downed enough coffee to make him feel altogether human.

Then, after checking on his car, Hayes hopped on the train into the city.

Hayes went back to Sixth Avenue, to where Melanie had been killed. He stopped on the sidewalk close to where Sixth met with West 24th Street, looking at the new tarmac that had been laid where the crater had once been. It was like nothing had happened, as if the whole thing – the helicopter crash, the lives lost – had all been erased.

On the street, vehicles drove past, oblivious to what had happened here a month and a half ago, their wheels rolling on the smoothed-over grave, courier bikes and delivery vans finding new lanes in the street, new gaps in which to weave and flow, like water finding a way through rock. The sidewalk traffic went by with its usual New York urgency, too, people scurrying from coffee shop to office, office to coffee shop, oblivious to one another and to Hayes as he stood at the edge of the curb and just looked.

Hayes glanced at his watch, sensing the time as much as seeing it. It was 11.11 – on the digital display it was just twin uprights with an empty gutter between them, holding time in place. This was when she had died. This was when the helicopter had struck the ground and killed his wife.

"I love you," Hayes said, whispering the words to the featureless asphalt that held whatever last molecules there were of his wife's body, whatever trace DNA remained.

And then he walked away.

Hayes walked east towards Madison Square Park, then headed north up Fifth, thinking about Melanie and about everything that had happened since she had died. The wail of emergency vehicle sirens came and went and came again, store and car alarms going off now and then in the distance, the sounds of a city in freefall.

Hayes thought about Manhattan and the "mousetrap" – his theory that most everything that happened to the costumes got its start here. He thought about the man who had stepped out in front of his car wearing his face, and the woman with the headscarf and the fifties-style shades who kept witnessing costume events, and the Melanie on the news reports who had not been Melanie at all. And he thought about their wedding day, and of how she had flip-flopped between a church wedding and a civil ceremony and finally opted for the latter. Melanie had been brought up a Catholic, but she had only spoken of that occasionally to Hayes, usually at Christmas or when Easter fell early, when the weather was cool and the church services seemed warm and inviting and homey.

The cross streets were in the high forties when Hayes took any notice of where he was again. He had reached the art deco triumphs of the Rockefeller Center where it spanned several blocks. It was the start of lunch time for the cube farms, and the streets were getting busier again. Cabs played their familiar refrain, like an

orchestra tuning up, honking like geese at every other vehicle or
pedestrian, as if all those others had dared violate their private
road space.

Up ahead, poised to his right across the far side of the street,
Hayes saw the twin marble steeples of St Patrick's Cathedral
peering around the edge of the buildings that had sneakily
sprung up around them in the intervening years like some weird
game of sardines. The cathedral had patiently waited here for
over a century, an oasis of calm in the ever-whirring hubbub
of midtown.

Hayes had no religious proclivities. He had grown up agnostic,
following the lead of his parents, who had got married in church
but only attended for weddings, christenings and funerals. Hayes
had never specifically asked Melanie about her beliefs – all he knew,
she had volunteered. But he knew she had grown up with faith,
and places like this cathedral still held something intangible for her.

Hayes crossed at the intersection and ascended the short flight of
steps to St Patrick's high doors, passing the tourists taking pictures
of themselves before the twin spires and on the steps.

A sense of calmness struck Hayes the moment that he passed
through the doors, as if he had left the merry-go-round that was
New York City behind.

Within, things echoed, and the temperature was cooler, all of
which added to that sense of calm. There was no service being
held at that moment, but the cathedral welcomed visitors and so
Hayes dug into his pocket and dropped a donation through the
slot by the entrance.

A wide aisle stretched before him, framed by wooden pews and,
beyond these, great white columns that lunged up towards the
high ceiling like artificial trees holding the sky aloft. Up ahead,
dominating the space, was the Rose Window, a beautiful, circular
construction of stained glass that filtered light into the vast
cathedral space. Below the window were the numerous pipes of
the organ, arranged in perfectly straight lines as though soldiers
standing to attention.

Hayes walked up the aisle, unsure of what he was doing or why he was here. Was he here looking for some great almighty, something he could understand as his creator? Or was he just here hoping for an apology, either to give one or to receive one, for everything that had happened?

Hayes' footsteps echoed from the hard floor, the noise following him like a shadow.

There were other people here, visitors and tourists. Some were just sitting quietly in the pews, saying prayers to themselves, while others were admiring the statuary that was dotted throughout the nave, the plaques and the names of those who had served here and those who had been a part of the congregation.

Gradually, the sound of his footsteps clip-clopping behind him, Hayes made his way to the front of the church. Melanie was dead. Had he come to ask for forgiveness for that?

Hayes was almost at the altar, where it was framed by the brilliant spotlight of that breathtaking, stained-glass window, when something caught his eye. He turned his head to his right and saw the set of simple shelves standing over to the side of the pews. There were several lines of candles on the shelves, just short stubby things, like tea lights. A box was attached to the shelves with a slot for coins, and Hayes realized it was intended for the donation that went with the prayer one made when lighting a candle, a way to pay for the materials that were used. He recalled how, on the few occasions that he had visited a church with Melanie, she had taken a moment to light a candle and say a prayer in just this manner.

Hayes strode over to the shelves of candles, withdrew a bill from his wallet, folded it, and dropped it through the donation slot. Then he took a candle and lit it with a taper, taking the flame from another candle that was already burning among those lit prayers on the shelves. Hayes did not know much about prayers or praying, but he figured that the candle was for Melanie and that she would know what to do with its flickering light.

The flame swirled and dipped in the breeze like a child playing a game, its brilliant depths seemingly infinite and ever replenishing. Hayes stood there for a while, his eyes losing focus as he watched the flame dance on its wick.

21

Being in the cathedral had made Hayes realize something. Matters of faith, and of hope, and cosmic design all coalesced in his head as he took the E train back to his home in Queens.

There was a pattern to the stained-glass window, just like there was a pattern to the world. And maybe only the great omniscient creator himself knew what that pattern really was, maybe only he could see it.

What Hayes realized, as the train thundered and screeched along the rails like it was being tortured, was that he needed to make his own plan and break into the design. He needed to perceive the pattern in its entirety, become not just a part of it but a force that could completely alter it, change every damn thing that the costumes did. He needed to crack the glass. That was the only way he could figure out what had really happened to Melanie, and finally lay her memory to rest.

He had tried shooting her and he had tried appealing to her through faith. Now he was going to go after Captain Light and finally find out what these conceited costumes actually knew and just who was pulling his strings.

Let's get a gun, Hayes told himself, thinking back to the story Jonas Culper had told him about forties heroine Holly Belle. A grim smile crossed his lips at that thought, but it was all but masked in the shadow cast by his up-drawn hood.

* * *

Back home, Hayes went to his basement and collected Retro's gun from its hiding place in the paint can. By his reckoning it had four shots in it, which would not be enough for what he had in mind.

He flipped the pistol over in his hands, amazed once again at the lightness of such a powerful weapon, and pushed back the catch that revealed the charging point. He could try something – maybe hook it up to a car battery somehow, using jump leads and some crocodile clips, but there was every chance he would blast out the side of his wall in the process. That was simply too dangerous.

So, he needed to get his hands on other tech, either by stealth or by cash. Jonas Culper did it by throwing a shed load of money at the problem, scooping up the so-called props he wanted for his collection through the mighty dollar. Hayes could refinance the car, and maybe get a second mortgage on his house. He could get another job, work two jobs for – what? Years? Years, so he could buy some dinged-up ray gun that had found its way out of a precinct evidence lock-up and didn't have any charge left? No, that was going to be too slow and too uncertain. He needed props that were operational and still had some life left in them, and he needed to get them faster than his cash flow would ever allow.

So, then: *option two*.

Hayes had found Retro by luck, but it had clued him in on something, the thing he called the mouse hole. The mouse hole was Manhattan, that's where the largest concentration of these costumed characters appeared, playing out their schemes and scams and crazy, building-shaking battles. He would go to Manhattan and wait for his mouse to appear.

Mice, Hayes corrected. It couldn't just be one. It needed to be more than that. He needed to get out there and snare these incredible, costumed men and women before they knew what hit them.

Hayes rewrapped Retro's gun in the rag and stashed it back

in the paint can. Catching mice needed traps, and traps needed cheese. The four shots left in Retro's gun were something to keep in reserve, for when he ran up against something that needed that kind of force to slow it down. For now, Hayes was going to take a different hunk of cheese with him, the kind that held fifteen shots of 147 grain parabellum in a butt-loaded clip.

Hayes went back to the map he had started working on a month before, tabulating the frequency of costumed-related incidents. He knew he had to go after the street-level guys; if his experience with the fae warriors had taught him nothing else, it had taught him that.

He was looking at the dozen or so streets south of Central Park through to just beyond its northernmost point, set between the loosely parallel lines of Madison and Tenth. He could stretch the boundaries a little, to accommodate the incident in Washington Square Park which was in line with those parameters but fell further south than Madison Avenue itself, but otherwise he sensed that this area was right. It was a big area, roughly one hundred blocks. Tenth Avenue stretched almost the entire length of Manhattan, and all those cross streets had to accommodate hundreds, if not thousands, of businesses – offices, stores and anything else you could think of.

Knowing that he needed to tighten the area, Hayes brought up the website of the *New York Echo* and ran his eyes over the main stories. There were three costume incidents covered from the preceding twenty-four hours, two of which involved Eternal Flame. Hayes marked the locations on the map with a pen.

Then he went to the *Echo*'s search function and put in the term *Eternal Flame*. A plethora of hits came back. Hayes brought up a handful and noted where they had occurred, adding those locations to his map. He skipped past anything too large or other-worldly – what he was doing was not an exact science here but he did not want to run into another Morgana Le Fey-level incident if he could possibly avoid it.

Another search – *Captain Light* – and six locations became twelve and – *the Hunter* – twelve became twenty, and before long Hayes had a much clearer idea of where he needed to set his trap.

With hindsight, it was obvious: he needed to be on Fifth Avenue, beside the Nexus Range building, headquarters of the Rangers.

22

The next morning, his loaded Glock in the glove box, Hayes drove into the city and found a parking lot in a side street behind Madison Avenue from where he could spy on the Nexus Range. The towering skyscraper stood firm, a monument to justice and to liberty, its four uppermost floors obscured behind the shimmering screen of protective energy.

It was 8am.

Hayes left his car in an open spot on a lower story and walked up the cold, echoing staircase to the roof. Cars already occupied most of the parking spots, and he had been lucky to nab the space he had got.

The top story was open to the air, with a wire fence running all the way around its edge above a hip-high concrete barricade. There was no movement up here, just parked cars that could have been put there five minutes ago or could have been here for twenty years. Hayes walked across the rooftop, eyeing the tower of the Nexus Range where it loomed just a few blocks away.

Manhattan was packed, a tiny island crammed with building stacked upon building, each one vying for a tiny bit of room, each stone laid to get the maximum space it could ring fence for its owners. The Nexus Range was taller than anything around it, those top stories with their slowly rotating force field poking head and shoulders above the surrounding skyline.

173

Hayes looked at the energy field, scanning slowly along its brilliant edge to what parts he could see. The last time he had been here he had been south, back from Central Park and on the opposite side to where the Ranger Jet launched. From this side, conversely, he could see the hangar door, flush to the building's sloped roof but painted fire engine red as if to alert anyone who saw it that an emergency was imminent.

Hayes waited for that emergency.

He sat down on the cool edge of the concrete barricade, where he could watch the Range's upper levels and the tops of the buildings surrounding it. Eight o'clock became nine, and nine ticked its slow, gradual way towards ten. A couple of cars switched spots on the top level behind Hayes, and the sirens of emergency vehicles howled once down on the distant street below, but otherwise there was no activity so far as he noticed.

It was as if he was waiting for a robbery. Hayes wondered if this was what armored van drivers felt every time they went out on a delivery or a pick-up: tense and bored and on edge. He had done his share of waiting in the Navy. A lot of that role *was* waiting, turning up in places just so you could say you'd been there to support the local army or calm a situation purely by your presence. He had done ops that had been wait-wait-wait, what they called "hurry up and wait" in the army, watches synched and fuck-all to do until the minute hand hit pay dirt and wait-wait-wait became go-go-go.

By eleven, Hayes was feeling bored, and by twelve he felt like he was kind of a dumb schmuck for sitting out here all this time. At least it was warm. Nothing happened over at the Range, no jet launch, no costumed call to arms, no alien attack.

By one o'clock, Hayes was conscious of the hunger that seemed to be prowling inside his guts like a caged tiger, and also of how he had lost all sensation to his butt where he had sat in one position too long. He was also aware of something else – someone approaching by the sound of the heavy fire door's swing, where it opened to the stairwell.

"Hey, buddy? Lost your car?"

Hayes turned, wincing as pins and needles played along the top of his right leg like someone was running the flame of a blow torch along it. A white-haired man in an oil-streaked jumpsuit was striding across from the fire door, smiling amiably, a walkie-talkie type radio in his hand.

Hayes nodded to him. "Hey."

"I saw you on the camera," the white-haired man called over as he approached, shouting over the noise of the wind. "You been up here a while. Forget where you parked?"

Hayes shook his head. "No. Just wanted to get some air."

"I tell you, this is a lousy spot for a suicide," the white-haired man said cheerily. "That fence is twelve feet high, and that's on top of the barricade. Last guy who tried that, he slipped on this side, fell straight back down and fractured his ankle right there where you're sitting. Or was it his knee? Something, anyway."

Hayes smiled. "I'm not planning to commit suicide," he assured the man in the overalls.

His alabaster-haired inquisitor made a show of looking Hayes up and down before speaking with the knowing wisdom of the streets. "Well, you ain't a hobo, judging by your clothes. That and you're not out here if you want to keep out of the wind."

"No, I'm parked downstairs," Hayes told him, pulling his car key from his pocket and holding it up before him like it was a security pass. "Really."

"Okay then," the man said, but he had a wary look in his eye. His radio crackled and Hayes heard someone on the other end talking through the static, asking what was happening. The man held up a hand to Hayes as if in apology before turning away and talking quietly into the radio. "Guy says he's parked here," he said. "Just wanted to get some air."

There was a crackled response from the other end, and then the man spoke into the microphone again:

"Yeah, I'll tell him."

He turned back to Hayes with a look of consternation on

his features. "Look, don't take this the wrong way but my boss downstairs is asking if you can move along," he said, "because otherwise he's going to call the cops."

Hayes thought this over for a few seconds, then stood, wincing again as the flare of pins and needles ran down his leg. "You ever just look out there?" Hayes asked, gesturing to the skyline dominated by the subtle glow from the Nexus Range. "Just to take it all in?"

The man with the white hair nodded. "It's a beautiful city," he said. "The higher you go, the more beautiful it gets. When I was a kid, I used to spend hours up on the roof of our apartment building, just looking across the river at all of this like it was a picture. I'd watch the lights come on in the buildings and try to imagine who was over there, switching on those lights." He smiled at the memory, then snorted and shook his head.

"You need a hand finding your car?"

"No," Hayes told him. "C Level, I remember."

The man in the overalls waited while Hayes made his way towards the stairs, taking just a moment to look out on the panorama of skyscrapers that stood like building blocks just beyond the reach of the rooftop. Then he joined Hayes, walking down the hard, concrete stairs with him until they were at the level where Hayes had left his automobile. He left Hayes to go find it, making his way back to the security booth at street level.

Hayes pulled out of the parking lot and drove south via Fifth Avenue, past Washington Square Park. He pulled in at a spot a half block from the firing range he frequented, grabbed some street pizza to satiate that prowling tiger in his stomach, and then headed there. The cashier with too much eye liner and the lip piercing looked at him through narrowed eyes as he bought a spare case of ammo and booked a session on the range. With the mascara pressing its weight down on her lashes, it was as though she was looking at something very distant.

"I know you, right?" she asked Hayes. "You come here a lot."

"I wouldn't say 'a lot'," Hayes corrected, feeling he had had this very same conversation before.

"You need anything else?" Counter girl asked, running the ammo through the till.

"Just some targets," Hayes told her, making his way towards the door that led to the firing range.

Hayes rattled off several dozen shots, hitting head and center mass every single time. Paper targets, even moving ones, were easy to hit. Hayes had been rigorously trained. But using space guns like the thing he had taken from Retro, brawling with fae warriors – these were things no one could teach you; they were things you just learnt on the job.

Bang!

Another hole appeared in his target's head, square between the eyes.

Learning on the job was another part of this whole costume thing that he hadn't considered. How the hell do people like Captain Light and Eternal Flame figure out when to use their powers, let alone how much? If Captain Light overexerted his powerful muscles, a man capable of holding back a Greyhound bus, he could break a normal man in two. When do you learn *not* to do that?

Bang!

How many people get snapped in two before you figure it out?

Bang!

And maybe catching falling helicopters was a one-time deal, and no matter how much time or warning he had had, maybe Captain Light could never have been expected to catch the one that got dropped on Melanie. Captain Light could bench press a Cadillac, but maybe Hayes had been blaming him for not doing something he could never have done.

Bang!

The target on the range fluttered with a rustle of paper as Hayes' bullet drilled a hole clean through its heart.

It was after five by the time Hayes left the firing range. The evening traffic was starting to build as office workers got the jump on getting home. In half an hour, the city's streets would be gridlocked.

Hayes cut across to Madison, then drove north, passing the Nexus Range at a sedate crawl as the lights shuffled each block of traffic one square on like some giant board game. There had been no robberies, no super scientists with out of control machines that needed stopping, no meteor strikes that turned out to be alien cries for help. It had been a quiet day for the Rangers.

Hayes took a right and turned back into the same parking lot he had used earlier that day. He followed the ramps up to the highest level, drove to the edge and pulled over by the concrete barricade that marked the roof's end. It was not a parking spot – this part served as a turning area for the already-full parking spaces to either side. Hayes figured he could back up if someone needed to get access. For now, however, he wanted to watch the tower a little longer, wait things out and see if maybe something kicked off.

He stayed there until after nine, by which time the parking spots to either side had cleared and Hayes' gut had developed that hollow feeling that meant he needed to eat and maybe find a restroom sometime soon. His breath was tasting bad too, where he had not had enough liquids. Ahead of him, framed by the solid edges of his windshield, the Nexus Range stood against the darkening twilight sky, its four floors of force energy lighting the space around it like a beacon, promising the city that all was well, and that it always would be.

Hayes slipped into gear and headed home. He had spent over fifty bucks on parking in a day.

23

Hayes tried the same basic tactic for the next two days with the same inconsequential results. Three days eating nothing but street pizza was enough to make any man reconsider his plan.

He took some time on Saturday to get his hair cut, and, on the Monday, Hayes went back to work. Jeff Puchenko was both ecstatic and harassed to see him. There were cardboard boxes piled up to the ceiling in the little glass-walled office they shared, offset from the packing and distribution area. The boxes lurched against the walls and propped on chairs, with a mismatched pile of returns taking up a chunk of what had been Hayes' desk.

"Miss me?" Hayes asked as he took a look around the office the two men shared.

Jeff sneered. "I miss smoking and I miss my second wife's cooking. You, Jon boy? Not so much. Welcome back, find your seat if you can and see if you can make sense of this manifest," Jeff said, slinging a stapled sheaf of loose papers down on Hayes' chaotic desk. As he did, a stack of boxes slid over and tumbled to the floor, eliciting a curse from his downturned mouth.

Hayes removed the boxes from his chair, stacking them against another pile by the wall until they came up past his knee. Then he sat down, cleared some space on his desk, and starting looking over the pages of documentation he had been handed.

Jeff rubbed his eyes and reached for a cup of coffee that had cooled to room temperature on his desk. "I'll have to get you some paperwork, let Old Man Rourke know you're back," he said, calling across his messy desk to Hayes. "You are back, aren't you?"

"Yeah," Hayes assured him. "But I wanted to talk about my hours."

Jeff sighed heavily. "Jon, I'll be honest with you," he said. "I asked about your changing hours but... well, we have been swimming in it up to here without you, but you're not irreplaceable. Rourke's sympathetic, he lost his wife to cancer last year, you remember? But, if you can't be here, he'll hire someone else."

"I can be here," Hayes told his supervisor. "What I want to do is start earlier, come in at seven, maybe six."

"This one of those work-life balance things?" Jeff asked, frowning. "Free up your afternoons a little?"

Hayes nodded. "Yeah." He did not elaborate on how he intended to spend his afternoons.

Before he had gone back to work, Hayes had looked at the FBI statistics and realized that robberies were more likely to occur in the afternoon. There was no hard-and-fast rule for this, but banks tended to get robbed during working hours – presumably when the vault could be opened by the staff – more frequently in the afternoon and most often on a Friday.

Hayes had no idea why afternoons. He speculated that maybe bank robbers weren't morning people, but he guessed there were other factors too like how street traffic would affect getaway chances. After all, you try robbing a midtown bank at 8am, you hit traffic getting there and your getaway is going to be a crawl until around ten.

The same "afternoon" stats held roughly true for jewelry stores and other high-reward store robberies, and those were the kinds of things that attracted the costumes. Costumes went big and flashy with these things – you never heard of someone like Shocktopus or Reverb mugging an old lady for her purse; it was all big risks/ big rewards stuff.

Old Man Rourke acceded, and so Hayes spent his mornings at the packing company, working through to a little past noon before traipsing across town to that section of the city he had identified between Madison and Sixth, the zone of pronounced costume action – the mouse hole. Not that he saw a lot of action there for almost a month. Instead, Hayes got into a routine, settling in a few cafés whose windows overlooked the banks and department stores on Fifth and Sixth, or peered across to the towering edifice of the Nexus Range. He didn't stay too long in any one of them, an hour or so sometimes, and made sure he switched between cafés on a daily basis so no one got too used to him. He didn't want a repeat of the parking garage incident where the staff had him pegged for a suicide case or a hobo because he was just hanging around.

Hayes took some time, too, to watch the comings and goings at the offices of the *New York Echo*, hoping to catch up with that punk kid photographer, Ben Jermain. The kid was still showing up with photographs of the costumes, mostly Eternal Flame whom Hayes figured he had some kind of publicity deal with. Maybe they were business partners who split the profits on the pics, or maybe Eternal Flame just appreciated the public recognition that the *Echo*'s articles gave him, and Jermain was earning a tidy living from it. Maybe Eternal Flame sought *eternal fame*?

Three weeks into his stake outs, care of a live news story on the radio, Hayes got wind of a Fifth Avenue jewelry store getting hit. He was in a café on Madison at the time, just a couple of blocks away, with the radio broadcast chirruping away to itself behind the counter. Hayes left the coffee shop and hurried over to the jewelry store at a sprint, weaving through pedestrians and crossing an intersection against the light, resulting in a near-miss with a courier bike.

Hayes could hear the ringing of the jewelry store's alarm even before he turned the corner. By the time he reached the scene, there were three heavy duty SWAT trucks and a whole cavalcade of cops and emergency service vehicles cluttering up the street. A policeman in a padded flak jacket held a megaphone to his lips and was barking out commands about how the place was surrounded, when the front of the store seemed to explode outwards.

Hayes and the other people along the street, along with the cops, reared back, covering their faces with their hands.

Thick glass that could stop a bullet burst from its settings in the jeweler's windows, shattering into heavy shards. An instant later, the Spin came through the exit, knocking the reinforced door in its frame as he did, so that it teetered there, held in place by one hinge like the last leaf clinging to a tree in the fall.

The Spin was dressed in black and white strips that encircled his head, body, arms and legs. His arms were outstretched as he spun from the store interior, and they were lined with necklaces and bangles that he had evidently procured from store's display. He also had a briefcase in one hand, and a black pack on his back. His mouth was open – a split within the black stripe there – and he was laughing like the demented maniac he was. The laughter sounded like someone running up and down a glockenspiel.

The police girded themselves as the Spin emerged into the sunlight. Guns were leveled from behind shields and open vehicle doors, and over the protective cover of police car hoods. The Spin saw them as he turned in place, laughing louder as he counted them off.

"Forty-seven guns," he said in a voice that chased up and down the scale with every syllable. "You must know, officers, that you have seriously underestimated me."

As he said this last, the Spin began to pirouette on the spot, arms stretched out before him with those bands and necklaces glinting in the sun like a hundred winking, golden eyes.

"He's spinning!" one of the police officers shouted in warning.

A dozen shots rang out, and members of the public began to run. But it was already too late. The Spin had picked up speed, like some kind of human hurricane, and where he had stood a moment before there was now what looked like a fast-moving funnel of black and white.

Hayes knew about the Spin – he figured probably most people

did. The guy was a high-profile costumed criminal with a homicidal streak. He had one power – his ability to rotate at incredibly high speed and with such ferocity that he could knock through walls, cars and even right through people, gutting them in less than a second, hence the homicidal streak. He could also repel bullets when he was spinning at high speed. To make matters worse, he favored automatic weapons and somehow retained perfect aim even while turning at super speed. How the Spin achieved his high-speed trick was uncertain, but Hayes imagined that there was technology involved somewhere, probably stashed in the hump on back of his costume, because he was otherwise a grade-Z dirt bag, a quality only found in human beings.

Hayes watched from the corner of the street as the Spin knocked into an armored SWAT truck, flipping it up and over as he crossed the street like a hurricane. Cops ran for cover while others lined up new shots, but the bullets were useless against the Spin's unnatural abilities.

Hayes had been looking for just this kind of action. A costumed villain who worked solo and used tech to commit their crimes. His patience had paid off. There was just one thing – he had no idea how to stop someone like the Spin; the man was a psychopath and if three SWAT teams and a precinct of New York's finest couldn't slow him down, Hayes didn't stand a chance. Hayes was grateful that the whirlwind blur that was the Spin was moving in the opposite direction, south down Fifth Avenue. Good riddance.

Cars and vans were flipped over as the Spin traveled down the center line of the street. A squat two-door electric car was flung right across the road and went crashing into a stand selling *I Heart NY* T-shirts and mugs and key fobs.

Then, a block away from where Hayes was watching, a figure in a red body glove seemed to drop directly from a rooftop to land before the Spin. It was Eternal Flame, wisps of fire sparking from his body as he strode across the intersection into the path of the villain. He held his right hand up as he did so in a *halt* gesture, shouted something that Hayes could not hear from so far away.

"It's Infernal Flame!" some squeaky-voiced teen said from just behind Hayes.

"That ain't Infernal Flame!" a friend berated the kid.

"Sure it is! That's his costume!" the kid insisted.

"He's called *Eternal* Flame," the teen's buddy said, "you dope!"

Down the street, Eternal Flame was being knocked sideways by the Spin. He came hurtling up the street towards where Hayes and the SWAT teams were, impacting with the ground with such force that he left a bubbling, melted trail in the asphalt. A rumble of concern and fear burbled from the watching crowd of onlookers, and a few even ran to the hero's aid. But Eternal Flame stood up before anyone could reach him, dusted himself down and leapt into the air, one fist out before him, hurtling over the roofs of the stalled vehicles there.

A moment later, the so-called "furnace of freedom" struck the Spin who was endeavoring to retreat south, tongues of flame running through the whirling tornado as it careened off course. For a few seconds, the two combatants were nothing more than a blur at the intersection, accompanied by the sounds of fists striking flesh, and pavement super-heated to liquid. Then a gunshot, and Eternal Flame reappeared from the whirlwind, racing to the east and out of sight. At the same instant, the Spin went west, crashing into the edge of a building in a shower of masonry dust.

Hayes didn't see what exactly happened next. There was a streak like fire and then everything moved down the block and out of sight. As Hayes watched the two combatants disappear, it hit home how fast he needed to be if he was to get truly involved in this world of masks and powers. There was no time for planning – you either waded in or you got the hell out of the way. And when it came to psychopaths like the Spin, getting the hell out of the way was doubtless the best call.

24

The report on the *Echo* website that evening confirmed that the Spin had been apprehended by Eternal Flame following a battle waged through the streets of downtown. Besides the jewelry store's front, the battle had done some minor structural damage to a building off Fifth Avenue, and shattered two shop windows. There were thankfully no casualties. The report was accompanied by some blurry phone camera footage along with some photographs credited to *B. Jermain*. Hayes recognized Jermain's name and remembered he had wanted to speak to the guy. He added it to his list of priorities.

Seven days passed without incident. Hayes went to work in the mornings then did his round of coffee shops and newsstands as he surreptitiously watched the streets. He found another good location to play lookout – the spacious lobby of the Museum of Modern Art that occupied the block between West 53rd and 54th Streets. The lobby looked out onto Fifth Avenue with panoramic windows that stretched up two stories, giving a great view of everything that happened on the street. Hayes found he could lurk there for hours without being bothered, and if anyone from the staff came over, he would make a face like he was contemplating the grand enormity of modern art in all its many guises and they would leave him alone. There also happened to be a decent hotdog stand on the corner just outside, which meant he could grab some sustenance if things got late while he was waiting for whatever was going to happen to happen. With an ear bud attached to the radio in his phone, he could keep track of the news and hopefully catch any on-the-spot reports about costume activity that happened near by.

Not that anything much happened nearby. He had gone a week since the Spin had attacked that jewelry store, and the only news of costume clashes had been something way out in the East River, where Candiru had suffered a beat down at the hands of Kid Ocean after she had tried to spread a kind of vampire contagion.

There had been other events, of course – rumor had it that the Rangers had engaged in an archeological dig down in Honduras, as well as the usual night-time sightings of heroes like the Hunter and Ghost Bot. But there had been nothing Hayes had witnessed, nothing close enough that he had been able to reach the scene, let alone do anything.

It was a balmy Tuesday at just after 5pm when Hayes spotted photographer Benjamin Jermain exiting the offices of the *New York Echo* on Sixth Avenue. As ever, Jermain was dressed in slacker clothes and had his hair in that constant state of disarray that apparently passed for a style. And, like the last time Hayes had seen him, the photographer was chowing down on a protein bar; given his skinny frame, Hayes speculated that it was just about the only protein intake the guy ever got.

Hayes was pounding sidewalk on West 46th Street when he spotted Jermain, and he followed the lanky photographer as he crossed the street and headed to a bank there. Hayes held back, watching as Jermain worked the ATM before running a frustrated hand through his unruly mop of hair and retrieving his card. Jermain looked over at the *Echo* building and clenched his fist before heading up along the street in the direction of the Rockefeller Center.

Hayes picked up his pace, extending his stride as he deftly weaved through the pedestrian traffic to catch up with the photographer. It took half a block, and then Hayes was directly behind him.

"Excuse me?" Hayes called, taking the last few steps at a jog. "Excuse me?"

Jermain turned round with a look of gormless confusion on his long face.

"Excuse me," Hayes began, "you're–"

"Look, pal," Jermain interrupted with the firmness of an experienced city dweller, "I'm broke, so whatever it is you're selling, I ain't buying. Even if I could."

"I'm not selling anything," Hayes pressed on, thinking quickly. Best to be honest, he figured. "You're Ben Jermain, right? I recognize you from those journalist awards last fall – your photo was in the *Echo*. You remember that evening?"

Jermain slowed his pace just momentarily, a kind of silly smile crossing his face. "Sure. When Grave Max crashed the whole shindig and tried to kill the host–"

"– but got stopped by Eternal Flame," Hayes finished for him. "You took the picture, right?"

Jermain tilted his head with curiosity as he looked at Hayes properly for the first time. "You have a good memory," he said. "What can I do for you, Mister...?"

"Hayes," Hayes said, extending his hand to shake. "I wonder if we could talk about some of your photographs." He tried to make it sound innocent.

Jermain considered this for a moment, then shrugged. "Talk is free," he said. "It had better be. I really am stony broke."

"Then, let me buy you a coffee or," Hayes glanced at his watch, "– too early for beer?"

"I don't drink," Jermain told him as they stood at the light for the crossing. "But a hot coffee sounds good."

As they crossed the street, Jermain smiled and asked Hayes if there was any chance of getting a Danish with the coffee. "I promise not to talk with my mouth full, sir," he added.

* * *

"What I've been trying to work out," Hayes explained as he sat beside Ben Jermain at a high counter looking out the window onto Sixth Avenue, "is how you get those great shots of Eternal Flame."

Tucking into his Danish like a man who hadn't eaten in a week, Jermain didn't even look at Hayes as he answered. "I'm a photographer, that's what I do," he explained between chews. "It's all about the lens and the focus and, you know, catching the right light."

"Yeah," Hayes agreed, "but you get a lot. I mean, you must have taken maybe seventy percent of the photographs of Eternal Flame that have run in the *Echo* over the years."

"It's not that many – is it?" Jermain asked, with a note of uncertainty. "The *Echo* does buy a lot of my snaps. Doesn't pay as well as they should, if you ask my opinion. But you didn't."

Hayes tasted his coffee and thought about how to phrase what he wanted to ask. He had made this mistake once, with the woman in the headscarf and fifties shades, grabbing her with a head full of questions, then sounding full-on insane as he launched into what amounted to an interrogation. At least Benjamin Jermain seemed affable enough – he was a sweet kid, maybe twenty years old, but still with a kind of wide-eyed innocence to his manner, like he came from a rural family or a simpler time. He seemed lonely too, and distracted, like he wanted to be somewhere else.

"I just wondered if maybe you had an in with Eternal Flame," Hayes asked.

"An 'in'?" Jermain replied, bemused.

"An in. A professional relationship maybe, some way to contact him," Hayes elaborated.

Jermain studied Hayes for a moment, eyes fixed on his. "You want to contact Eternal Flame? Are you in some kind of trouble, Mister Hayes?"

"Not me," Hayes assured him. "No, I just want to talk to him.

About... well... the hero biz." *I'm starting to sound like a groupie,* Hayes realized.

"I don't know if it's a business," Jermain told him. "More a kind of calling, from what I can tell. As an observer way outside that circle of people."

"Then, as an outsider," Hayes asked, "how is it you're getting all those pictures? Are you in contact with Eternal Flame? Or does he follow some kind of pattern maybe?"

"You mean, like a... uh... patrol?" Jermain asked. "I guess. When there's danger, he tries to get there and help in any way he can. I just follow. I guess you could say I have a nose for danger, that's all."

"But there's no pattern?" Hayes confirmed. "Not that you know of...?"

"If there is, Eternal Flame never discussed it with me," Jermain said, dropping his napkin on his empty plate and hopping down from the stool. "Good talking to you, sir. Thanks for the Danish."

"You're welcome," Hayes told the photographer, watching him leave. He continued to watch as Jermain crossed the street and got onto a bus that pulled up outside the Rockefeller Plaza.

Well, Hayes thought, *that was all a bust.* Jermain didn't seem to know anything much, he just had a newsman's instincts and the knack of being in the right place at the right time.

Hayes took some consolation from the thought that if there was a knack to it, then maybe he could develop it – *somehow.*

25

Another seven weeks passed with nothing. Hayes would wake up, work out the way he always had, since back before Hell Week in the SEALs training program, when he had first refined his body into a weapon. Then he'd go shower and head to work in the mornings like any other day, clock off just after lunch and travel into that little square of city he thought of as the mouse hole. Then, after six or seven hours of patrolling that "hole", he would grab a bite to eat and head home. Sometimes he would go into the city by car, other times he used public transport.

In a short while, he began to recognize the same faces, and get to know people's routines. He would recognize the couriers making deliveries to the offices, recognize the people who worked in the stores and some of the office workers. The same people living the same lives over and over, with Hayes just watching and waiting, hoping for that one specific change in the routine.

Hayes varied his own routine, different cafés, the MoMA lobby, other spots he found where he could hang out and not be bothered.

But after seven weeks, Hayes had to admit he was losing hope. He had been close to incidents, and would frequently glimpse heroes or bad guys flying past overhead, or the Ranger Jet cutting a path high above the streets. One time, Labnormal commanded something made from what looked like an oil refinery and fairy lights, and Hayes watched it stride across the George Washington Bridge before being hauled back by Captain Light. But reaching any of them seemed to be – well, out of his reach.

Hayes was just leaving a coffee shop on West 18th Street when the hairs went up on the back of his neck. He had glimpsed a guy entering the pawnbrokers two stores down for only a moment before the man had disappeared from view, but some sixth sense kicked in from just the way the stranger carried himself.

The guy was wearing a cowboy hat, but wearing it like a tourist rather than a guy who habitually wore a hat, as if it was a disguise. He had a light mac on which fell to below his knees, covering whatever he wore underneath. Hayes noticed that he wore dark gloves on his hands below the cuffs.

Hayes had only seen him for a second, but the man seemed furtive. He was edgy, and he had hunched forward as he pushed the door open and went inside, as though he did not want to be seen. It was 5.40, twenty minutes off closing time.

Hayes strode swiftly towards the store, conscious of the people and vehicles on the street. Before he reached the store, he detected the woman's scream, albeit muffled by the store's windows and fighting to be heard over the noisy traffic.

The store was double-fronted, a door in the center between long displays of jewelry and computers and pre-loved ornaments. Hayes looked in the store window, peering through the narrow gap between the displays of designer watches and into the store itself, like he was peering through a mail slot. Inside, the guy had removed his coat and hat, revealing an outfit of emerald and black with a hood that covered his face. The outfit looked to be made of some kind of reinforced leather or Kevlar weave, like a motorcyclist's jacket.

The sales assistant behind the counter – dyed blond hair and too much lip gloss – was screaming, hands to her face, full-on panic setting in. Kevlar jacket raised his hand and threw something, and the woman was suddenly shoved back until she adhered to the rear wall covered by what looked like a splatter of paint.

Splatter, Hayes remembered. That's who the guy in the gimp suit was.

Splatter immediately turned his attention to the other figure behind the transaction counter, a business-suited man with a bald head, glasses out of the seventies, and a thick gold chain around his right wrist. The chain glinted, catching the light as he raised his hands in compliance.

Splatter shouted something, pointing at the cash register. Business Suit moved to the register, babbling something that Hayes could not hear. There was sweat on his brow, glistening under the bright lights of the store.

Should Hayes go in? Should he help? It would get him a starring spot on the store's closed-circuit television system and maybe tagged as Splatter's accomplice. Hayes stepped back, pulling his sweatshirt's hood down over his head until it hung just above his eyes.

Inside, Business Suit was filling a holdall with rings, tossing in tray after tray as Splatter leered over him. Then he got another bag and added necklaces, watches and anything else that could be tipped quickly into a bag from behind the display cabinets, all under Splatter's watchful gaze. The other shop assistant – the blonde with too much lip gloss – had fainted, the paint-like splat having affixed her to the wall.

It took less than a minute. As a final act of vandalism, Splatter smashed his fist through a thick glass tabletop. The fist was preceded by what looked like prongs of white paint, hard as hammers, shattering the safety glass into tiny, gravel-like shards.

Then the costume was on the move. Hayes had waited by the store front, without a proper plan, just the intention to bring the villain down. He made his way to the door, balling his hands into fists, figuring he would get the jump on Splatter.

But when he glanced in through the reinforced glass in the door, Hayes saw that Splatter had disappeared, leaving the gutted store along with its two terrified staff members – now with both of them stuck to the wall by those weird paint splats.

He must have used the rear entrance, Hayes realized, glancing up and down the street.

There was an alleyway between stores just beyond the double front of the pawnbrokers. Hayes walked briskly to it, then ducked down it and picked up his pace. The alleyway was narrow, too narrow to even get a bike down, and Hayes had to hunch in to stop his pumping arms knocking the walls. There was moss on those walls, and ancient water stains that were older than he was.

Hayes ran, long strides eating up the distance, heading for the light at the alley's far end.

A moment later he was out of the alleyway. Hayes found himself in a service area. It was dingy and full of overflowing trashcans and broken-down cardboard boxes. Daylight came uncertainly from far above, rendering the whole area in gloomy shadow.

Discarded papers and till receipts tumbled across the floor with Hayes' arrival, like birds flocking. There were barred windows for several premises, along with the back doors to the stores around the block. It lacked the glamour of the store fronts – back here, everything looked tired and hasty, paint slapped on carelessly in poorly matched colors, chipped and peeling and scarred. A dozen or more graffiti tags had been plastered to the red door directly facing the alleyway, street names written in the angular, spider scrawl of kids who could just barely read a sentence yet knew how to misspell their street name. Cigarette butts were piled in old cans by the doors, sucked down to their nubs, their backs broken.

There was no one else in the service area. Hayes glanced right, to the rear of the pawnbrokers. There was a door there, white paint scabbed with blisters, the tag "Fallzz" scrawled in large writing across the center. There was no handle on the door – for security reasons, it had to be a fire door, and so only opened outwards, Hayes realized.

Hayes moved to stand beside the door, its hinges to the far side, placing himself flush to the wall. He bunched his fists, drawing them close to his chest, turning his body enough to face the door without being immediately seen. He would have a fraction of a second to act, that was all. After that, any advantage that the element of surprise gave him would be lost.

He waited, listening, hearing nothing.

Then, *bang!* The door opened with an electronic warning beep, swinging outwards with vigor. Splatter stepped out as the door swung towards the wall to the other side from Hayes, his right hand still on the push bar which opened it, like he was clinging to the safety rail of a fairground ride. He was smiling like some demented Cheshire Cat.

Hayes jabbed out with his right fist, knocking Splatter on the left side of his head before the costume knew what was happening, knocking that grin off his smug face.

Splatter grunted, turning to meet Hayes who was already driving his left fist around in a tight arc to follow up the first blow. His fist hit Splatter hard in his masked face, with a creak of leather and a crack of bone.

From inside the store, someone had tripped the alarm, but the rising sounds of panic were cut off as the heavy fire door slammed closed again.

Splatter looked at Hayes with confusion, almost as though he was offended by what had happened. "Who the hell are–?!"

Hayes struck him again, a swift right hook to the face that drove Splatter stumbling backwards.

Splatter recovered fast. He dropped the bags he had under his left arm and raised both arms up like he was on puppet strings, a cruel sneer appearing below the dark line of his mask. Hayes processed what he was looking at in a fraction of a second, saw that Splatter's costume actually had some kind of bulging constructs around each wrist, which were a part of the dark gauntlets he wore. As Splatter opened his palms, Hayes saw the pipe work webbed over the gauntlets – it was like looking at the back of a water heater.

Hayes ducked at the same moment that the sneering costume

fired his first splatter blast. A white stream of liquid crossed the small service area before striking the far wall with a splat, where it immediately adhered and hardened like glue. The stream of goop reeked with the harsh tang of paint, making Hayes' nose wrinkle in disgust.

"Come on, tough guy," Splatter growled in a New York accent, "let's see you cold cock a guy who fights back!"

The liquid streams from Splatter's gauntlets fired again, and Hayes leapt aside, lifting his feet up as the glue-like substance smeared across the ground.

Still moving, Hayes lashed out again, right fist connecting with Splatter's jaw so that the villain's head was jerked back. But Splatter was tough – he was a brawler who had held his own against Chase on more than one occasion, intelligently employing his glue-like streams to make the road surface impossible for the super-speedster to run on. It told Hayes that he had worked on his hardware, figured out the best way to use it.

As if to prove that, Splatter turned his hands in some way that Hayes was barely aware of, and suddenly the splatter streams congealed on his gauntlets, forming spikes like knuckledusters, only longer and more jagged. Hayes reared back as Splatter swung for him – like having a fist full of knives coming towards you.

How Splatter pulled that trick, Hayes could not imagine. But now was not the time for speculation. It had been two minutes and thirty seconds since Splatter had entered the store to commit the robbery, and the alarm was ringing; before long, cops or costumes would be on the scene to arrest him, which meant they would arrest Hayes for questioning, too.

Hayes danced back out of reach as Splatter's sharp left fist swung for him again, and struck his hip against a trashcan as he ran out of room to retreat. Hayes turned, steadying himself with his hands on the top of the trashcan.

"End of the line for you," Splatter barked, a cruel smile appearing beneath where the mask hid the top half of his face.

Splatter drove his spiky right fist at Hayes' head, but Hayes whipped the lid of the trashcan up at the same moment, using it like a shield to block the blow.

Splatter howled as his spiky gauntlet struck the lid with a loud clang.

Hayes pushed forward without pause, using the lid to drive Splatter back, like a lion tamer with a chair.

Splatter stumbled backwards, tripped over his own feet and collided head first with the wall behind him. Splatter groaned woozily as he slumped to the ground. Still holding the trashcan lid, Hayes drew it up and then slammed it down hard against Splatter's face – once, twice, a third time, each blow ringing with a metal clonk like a bell being struck.

When Hayes drew the trash lid back, he saw the blood streaming down Splatter's face. The crook's nose was broken and there was blood in his mouth, meaning he had either split his gum or bitten his tongue or maybe just lost teeth. Hayes leaned forward, examining the costumed figure on the ground more carefully. Splatter's eyes – visible through the eyeholes of the mask – were closed. Behind the lids, the eyes danced manically as if dreaming.

Hayes switched his grip on the can lid, taking it now by its end like a discus. Then, with a swift up and down action, he drove it hard against the top of Splatter's skull so that the far end struck with another loud endorsement. Splatter slumped lower, all the tension leaving his body as he slipped down the wall which he had been propped against.

Hayes set down the lid of the trashcan, glancing swiftly up and down the alleyways that fed into this service area. It had been at least three minutes since Splatter had started his robbery, maybe closer to four. Hayes did not know how much time he had, but every second added more risk of getting caught.

Splatter was deep in the grip of unconsciousness. When Hayes lifted one of his arms there was no counterforce, it was just dead weight.

Hayes took a moment to study the way the gauntlet connected – remembering the old SEAL adage: *Slow is smooth, smooth is fast.*

Then, he unlocked the three buckles that held the glove in place, two at the far end, midway up the forearm and a third just above the wrist, and pulled it free. He did the same for the gauntlet on the other hand, slipping both gloves into the pocket of his hoodie – as best as he could, since they were not very flexible. Then Hayes got up, as the sounds of sirens wailed closer with the approach of the police.

Hayes took a moment to consider his options – it was a little like standing at an intersection; there were four different routes he could take from the service area, including the way he had come. Then his gaze fell upon the dropped bags which Splatter had been carrying – bags full of stolen jewelry and cash.

Hayes snatched the smaller of the bags and shoved it into his hoodie before zipping it back up. Then he fled the scene, emerging on West 17th Street and then out to Fifth Avenue. He saw a cop car hurtle past on the street, lights flashing and sirens shrieking, but no one thought to stop him, despite the bag he was carrying.

Ten minutes later, Hayes was in the subway system, taking the E train home.

26

The first thing Hayes did when he got home was stash the bag of loot into the trunk of his car. It was 7pm, and his neighbor, Millarini, was just pulling into his drive from a day at the office.

"Hey, Jon," Millarini called as he got out of his car, "you just get back?"

"Yeah," Hayes said, his mind elsewhere. He did not want the stolen loot in the house, not until he knew what to do with it at least, so he pushed it down beside where the back seats met the trunk, wedging it there so it wouldn't roll free.

Millarini was on Hayes' drive by then, looking chipper despite putting in an eight-hour day. Millarini was the same age as Hayes, with slicked back hair and a squint. He wore suits that were always neat and well-tailored. He worked in corporate insurance, or something like that – he had told Hayes all about it once, at great length, and Hayes had come away from the conversation knowing absolutely nothing more than he had gone in with.

"Della says you went back to work," Millarini said as he crept up behind Hayes.

Hayes slammed the trunk closed, testing it to make sure it was locked. "Yeah, couple of months now. It seems to be working out okay."

Millarini nodded and gave him that firm, confidential smile of

man's solidarity to man. "Good for you, Jon. I admire you for…
well, for just hanging in there."

Hayes smiled back. "Just hanging in there is right," he joked.
He wanted to get inside and check on Splatter's gauntlets; he'd
just dropped them down on the table by the door, grabbed his car
keys and come right back outside with the bag of stolen goods. If
Millarini looked up he would be able to see the gauntlets poking
from around the door as it swung gently back. "Anyway, I've
gotta–" Hayes pointed to the house, "–get dinner going."

Millarini nodded, leaning forward as though he could not decide
whether he should pat Hayes on the back or shake his hand. "You
have a good one," he said as Hayes went back inside.

Behind the protection of the closed front door, Hayes snatched
up the gauntlets and made his way through the house. He had
figured on the tense train ride home that the gauntlets needed to
be his priority, that he could worry about the spoils later.

Hayes entered the kitchen, flicked on the lights and placed the
gauntlets onto the kitchen countertop where the light was good.
Then he put on a pot of coffee.

While the percolator was brewing, Hayes took a close look at
the gauntlets. They were identical, apart from the obvious – one
was left and one was right. The sleeve of the gauntlet featured a
series of inside pockets that ringed all the way around its circle.
This pocket contained four pressurized canisters arranged in an
approximate square that would sit around the user's arm above
the wrist, with flexible webbing between the pockets to allow for
ease of movement despite the hard canisters.

The canisters connected to a webbing of narrow, crisscrossed
pipes, none more than about an eighth of an inch in diameter.
The pipes emerged in a line of apertures between the points
where the fingers met the hand, while the thumb had been left
free of piping.

Turning the glove over, Hayes saw that there was circuitry
embedded along the blade of the hand, the line that connects
pinkie finger to wrist. Turning the glove a little way inside out,

Hayes could see more circuitry, and detected a trigger button at the base of the pinkie finger where it could be switched by a stroke of the thumb. There were several other switches in the gloves, and their pattern was not identical to both gloves.

Hayes drank coffee and traced the lines of the miniaturized tech within the gauntlets. They were works of art, almost, beautifully crafted to hold all they required in a small space without being intrusive. Only the canister pockets took up space, a necessary compromise to feed the glue-like substance to the release holes.

Hayes popped one of the canisters free from its housing and slipped it out of the pocket. The canister was about an inch-and-a-half in length and half that in diameter, like hotel mouthwash. It attached to the feed pipes with a rubber seal, locking tightly into place.

Hayes turned the canister over in his hand. It had a small marking written lengthwise in faint, printed writing. When Hayes looked at the print more closely, he could see it was what appeared to be a batch number. Other than that, there were no markings.

Scooping up his coffee, Hayes went to the home office and fired up the computer. He ran a search on the batch code printed on the canister but it elicited no results.

"Black books stuff. Huh," Hayes muttered, staring at the canister. This was secret stuff, hidden from the public. It might be military or could be supplied by a workshop, maybe even someone dealing in pharmaceuticals. Whatever it was, the markings weren't enough to source it. Which meant that, like Retro's gun, he had a limited supply of ammunition for these gauntlets, and no way to replenish it. If that made a difference, he would figure it once he knew what he was going to do with the gloves.

Hayes went back to the kitchen, replaced the canister and slipped on one of the gloves. It was heavy, but the weight was concentrated above the wrist, like he was wearing a heavy cuff or band. *I guess you get used to it*, Hayes figured, *just like a watch*.

He secured the buckle at the wrist, then tried the straps at the top of the gauntlet, struggling a little to get them done one-handed. There was a knack to it, one he could master. For now, he just secured one, to save on the aggravation.

Once the glove was on his left hand, he held his hand up and looked at it, like it was something alien that had grafted itself to his body. He turned his hand around, looking at it from all angles, then swung his arm back and forth to get a better sense of the weight.

Hayes looked around the kitchen, taking in the cooker and the refrigerator and the sink, the everyday appliances that sat under the worktops.

He raised his left hand towards the fridge, figuring it was made of durable metal and had a better than average chance of surviving whatever he threw at it. Better than average was not the same as invincible, of course, but Splatter's gauntlets shot glue, not bullets.

"On three," Hayes murmured holding his arm outstretched, fingers splayed. To an outsider it would have looked as though he was trying to get his hand as far away from himself as possible.

Then, aloud, Hayes counted down slowly from three before he brushed the glove's pinkie trigger with his thumb. And then –

– Nothing happened. No explosion. No burst of adhesive. Nothing.

Hayes looked at the glove on his hand, felt around its seams and edges with his free hand until he detected a stud inside, the size of a rivet in a pair of jeans, just below the canisters. He could not find a way to work it from outside, so he sat down, unbuckled the top strap, and folded the top of the gauntlet down to reveal it. It was a press-stud that linked directly to the circuitry. Like a dead man's switch, the arm had to be resting against it for it to operate, which meant the glove had to be buckled tight.

He buckled up – all three straps this time – and tried again, standing with his arm outstretched and pointed at the fridge.

Whomp!

A blob of white liquid struck the edge of the fridge, like someone had just spat at it. The blob took about a second to harden, the part that had missed the fridge still connected to it and splayed out where it hung in midair over the kitchen trashcan.

"Gonna have to work on my aim," Hayes told himself as he took the two paces across the room to examine where the glob had hardened. The glove had kicked, throwing his aim, and the delivery had been very little, more a globule than an actual splatter. But it worked.

Hayes spent the rest of the evening and long into the night just figuring out what Splatter's gloves did. After experimenting, he discovered that there were two settings.

The first sent an expanding burst of the adhesive substance out, emerging from the main nozzle between middle fingers as a kind of pellet. This pellet would expand like throwing something semi-liquid, until it met with whatever got in its way. It was this burst that stuck people to walls.

The second function utilized all of the nozzles to expel a concentrated burst of the adhesive solution but without the same jet-like propulsion. Because it was not propelled, this burst would drool out close to the hand where it could be snatched, shaped in the brief instant before it hardened, and then utilized. The shaping was important, and took Hayes a few tries to figure correctly. It seemed that, whatever the adhesive was made from, it could be magnetized and, by engaging an electromagnet coil within both gloves, the substance could be molded on the spot, kind of like drawing a pattern in the air, which hardened instantaneously. This was how Splatter had created the hammers to shatter the countertop in the pawnbrokers, and also how he had created the knuckle spikes which he had used in the fight against Hayes. There were other uses too, and with a little ingenuity, Hayes found he could make a tough knife blade of three or four inches. Longer than that and his shaping was not straight enough, and he would end up with something that looked bent like a cutlass and which shattered if he tried to strike anything with it.

These hardened-adhesive creations became a part of the gauntlets, effectively protruding from the nozzles once they had been generated. But there was a kind of "cut-off switch" in the circuitry, which once triggered would cut the electromagnet and cause the knife, spikes or hammer to lose integrity and flake away like dried mud.

The two settings meant that the same ammo could be used to serve very different functions, both as a kind of glue and almost as quick-hardening modeling clay. Both settings were easy to use. Splatter hadn't struck Hayes as a smart guy in their brief meeting, and online footage only reinforced that impression. He was a habitual criminal but certainly no genius. What he had done was to get proficient and imaginative with how he used the adhesive, and Hayes took a little time watching old news footage of the guy in action to get a better grasp on how the gloves worked.

In its liquid form, the adhesive was remarkably strong, more like quick-setting concrete or crazy glue, but the glue dried up and flaked away after a couple of hours on the fridge door, which Hayes figured explained how people got free after a Splatter attack. Whether that was intentional or just a flaw in the concoction, Hayes had no way of knowing. The short version was, if he wanted to stick a friend's beer glass to the table for a gag, the adhesive could bring the yucks; if he wanted to stick a bookshelf in place, he had best be out of the way two hours later when it all came crashing down.

The canisters seemed to hold a plentiful supply of pressurized chemical. Hayes tested the weight of those in the right-hand glove before using that to create his experimental knives and failed cutlass sword. He weighed them again afterward and there was a negligible difference. Not that Hayes could replace them once they ran down, and he could only speculate that Splatter would have armed himself with full canisters before pulling the pawnbroker stick-up.

By the time Hayes was finished experimenting, dawn was an

hour gone, and the world was awake and hustling. Which meant he was already late for work.

A shower.

A change of clothes.

Hayes drove to his workplace in Brooklyn, trying not to think about the fortune in stolen goods he had stashed in the trunk of his 4WD. He had not had time to check on what had happened to Splatter. He hoped the guy had got caught and locked up, but then he started to wonder – if he was locked up – would he talk to the police about the guy who had assaulted and robbed him as he came out of the pawnbrokers' back door? There was a bag of missing stolen goods, which Hayes had taken, and Splatter would need to take the heat off himself about that – ID-ing Hayes would be an ideal way to do that.

The grumpy bellow of a truck's horn startled Hayes from his thoughts, and he hit the brakes on instinct. He was at an intersection in Brooklyn that he didn't recognize, and the honking truck was coming from his right.

"Shit!" Hayes cursed, looking at the traffic light hanging above him. It was red. "Wake up, Quo. Wake up, wake up!" he told himself irritably. It was only Melanie who had ever called him Quo, so the words seemed kind of strange even as he said them. Like he needed her to advise him.

Hayes glanced back in the mirror, checking the street was empty behind him, and backed up six feet until he was behind the line. A delivery truck was ambling behind him a little way down the road, cruising to a slow stop, far enough away that he wouldn't hit it. He checked the mirror again, adjusting its angle to look for Melanie where she had once sat in the back seat after dying, back when he had staked out the Nexus Range in the parking garage that very first time after her cremation. The back seat was empty, just the guilty hint of the bag that was hidden behind it at its edge, out of sight but vivid in Hayes' mind's eye.

Hayes was shaking, adrenalin pounding, his heart drumming against his ribs like it wanted to get free. He took a breath, and looked around, trying to calm himself. There was a car wash a little way down the street, and a double fronted furniture place that specialized in sofas whose patterns would have looked garish in the seventies. Seeing them, Hayes figured that even bad taste could come back into fashion.

The light turned green and Hayes crossed the intersection, switched lanes and made the next right turn, before coming around the block and doubling back on himself. Recrossing the intersection, he followed the street past the garish sofas and the car wash, until he recognized a fast food joint and knew he was close to his workplace.

When he got to work, Hayes pulled in on the forecourt beside the delivery trucks and switched off his engine, taking a few moments just to breathe. Had he almost crashed? He had been driving blindly into traffic for a moment back there. He hadn't slept. He'd fought a costumed villain and had fled the scene of a crime. Maybe he was pushing himself too hard.

27

Work felt like wading through molasses. Hayes' mind wouldn't focus, it kept drifting back to the loot in the back of his car or to the fight in the alleyway with Splatter.

"Want a coffee, Jon?" Jeff Puchenko asked, waking Hayes from his daydream.

"What?" Hayes said, looking up. Jeff was standing before his desk, thumbs tucked in his belt.

"Coffee?"

"Yes," Hayes said.

Jeff filled the percolator that rested atop a filing cabinet, replaced it and waited for it to boil. As it burbled to itself, he looked across the office to where Hayes sat at his desk, muddling slowly through his paperwork. "You look beat," Jeff said. "Like you're coming down with something maybe."

"I'm fine," Hayes told him. "Just tired."

Hayes had done thirty-six-hour shifts in the service, and even occasional forty-eight-hour stints, when an op demanded it. It was exhausting, but you ran on adrenaline and caffeine pills, and caught up on the sleep afterwards. This – being awake all-night operating Splatter's gauntlets – should be nothing. But still, he hadn't had to work through paperwork on no sleep in the SEALs. The figures on the page didn't want to stay in place.

Jeff put a mug down by Hayes' elbow, taking a moment to peer over his shoulder at what he was working on. "Coffee. Drink," he instructed, like he was one of the drill sergeants Hayes had come across in his younger years. "I know you got in late, but clock off on time, go home and catch your breath. We'll manage."

Hayes looked up at him from the dancing figures on the page. "You sure?"

"You've completed two orders this morning when you'd normally do six," Jeff teased. "I'm sure we'll cope without you."

Dedicated, Hayes worked lunch and clocked off a little before two. He kept thinking about that bag of stolen items in his trunk.

"Go home," Jeff told Hayes as he saw him tapping one last order into his screen. "I can finish that. Go on – scoot!"

Hayes was gently pushed aside by Jeff, who assumed his chair and began typing in the order details at what seemed to Hayes like six times his speed. He really was tired.

Slipping his jacket on, Hayes headed to the parking forecourt, passing through the packing area where packers and delivery drivers were figuring out orders to a variety of destinations in New York and New Jersey.

Hayes passed through the opening of a high, rollback door that was tall enough to let a truck back up and be loaded there.

Outside, the sun was peeking sullenly behind gray clouds that had cluttered up the sky. It was warm, but the air felt heavy, like it needed to storm.

As Hayes turned the corner of the forecourt, he saw someone reaching for the trunk of his jeep – the trunk which still contained the stolen goods from the pawnbrokers.

"Hey!" Hayes called, picking up speed, turning his walk into a jog.

The figure by his car – a man in blue slacks and a loose shirt – ignored him, leaning down by the jeep to look where the hatchback door met the frame.

"Hey, get the hell away from there!" Hayes said as he came around the back of his vehicle.

The man glanced up, confused. Hayes was on him in a second. Striding forward, he leaned down and lifted the man by the material of his shirt, bringing him up to his feet and slamming him backwards until he struck the delivery truck parked next to the jeep.

"Hey! What the–?" the man began, bewildered.

Hayes' left hand shot out and grabbed the guy around the throat, pushing him back against the side of the truck. "What were you doing?" he demanded.

"Wha–?" the man responded, his voice strained where Hayes was crushing his throat.

"What were you doing?" Hayes repeated, this time saying each word slower and with more menace, spitting them out between clenched teeth.

The guy did not respond. Caught in the act, he was clearly shocked and scared. Hayes grabbed the front of his shirt with his right hand, pulled him forward a half pace, then shoved him hard against the side of the delivery truck again with a loud clonk.

"Answer me!" Hayes hissed.

"Jon?" the voice came from behind Hayes. "Jon, what's going on here?"

Hayes turned, saw one of the packing crew he knew – a Hispanic guy everyone called Pedro even though it wasn't his name. Pedro went with it for an easy life.

"This asshole was trying to break into my trunk," Hayes explained. *Where the stolen goods are stashed*, he mentally added.

"That ain't no asshole, man," Pedro said. "That's Matt! He started work here, like, three months ago. While you were... you know... off."

Still holding the squirming man called Matt against the side of the truck, Hayes questioned Pedro with just a look. Two other figures had appeared from the doors at the side of the building, picking up their speed as they approached and saw that something was going on.

"Matt's a driver, man," Pedro said. "That's all."

"Then what was he doing in my trunk?" Hayes snarled.

"I… wasn't," Matt hissed, struggling to speak, "… in…"

Pedro stepped into the space between the 4WD and the delivery truck, until he was standing close to Hayes. "Let him go, man," he urged. "Let's all just talk about this, okay?"

Hayes looked at Pedro, a guy he barely knew but knew enough to trust, then back at the mysterious Matt, who was straining against the tight grip around his throat. Hayes released his grip, and Matt sagged, his hands going to his throat as he drew in a deep lungful of air.

"Shit, man," Matt hissed, between wheezing coughs. "Shit. What is wrong with you?"

Hayes glared at the delivery man, body tensed to fight if he needed to. "What were you doing with my car?"

"I wasn't," Matt said, drawing himself up to a standing position. "I wasn't doing nothing, you…" he stuttered.

"I saw you," Hayes said, levelly. "You were reaching under, trying to prize the back door open."

"I dropped my keys," Matt said, looking angry and bemused all at the same time. "I was just…"

The man known as Pedro leaned down, fished around under Hayes' car for a moment with an outstretched arm, and then brought up a set of keys on a fob bearing the packing plant's logo. "These keys?" he asked Matt.

Matt nodded, still holding his neck.

Hayes looked at the man he had just tried to strangle, at a loss for what to say. He didn't quite believe it, but he realized he had jumped to a conclusion here. It was too much to set up between the two of them, and he had worked with Pedro long enough to know how he was, even if he couldn't tell you his real name.

"I'm sorry, Matt," Hayes said sheepishly.

Matt glared at him, wounded. "You almost choked me," he hissed. "What is wrong wit' you?"

Hayes said something about crime in the area, and about

jumping to conclusions and suspecting the worst. It wasn't an apology but it sounded like something at least. Then he opened his car and got into the driver's seat. As he did, he heard Matt and Pedro discussing it as they walked back into the packing building.

"What is it with that guy?" Matt asked. "He a nut-ball?"

"Ex-SEAL," Pedro told him. "You know? The guys who shot Bin Laden."

"And what did *he* do? Forget to signal?"

Hayes pulled out of the parking lot, waved an apology to the two men, and shot out into the road. Traffic was light, but Hayes wasn't in the mood to drive, he needed to stop first and gather himself together; he just had not wanted to do that on the forecourt with everyone watching.

He pulled into a drive-thru and, having missed the lunchtime rush, went straight to the serving window without queuing. He ordered a burger and fries with a soft drink, then pulled in at the restaurant's parking lot and ate them in his car. That stolen loot in his trunk was making him tense. That and the lack of sleep.

What was he doing with the loot anyway? Splatter had stolen it, several hundred bucks in gems and jewelry – perhaps even a couple of grand. Hayes could use that money, plough it into buying requisitioned weapons – "props" – from costumes the same way Jonas Culper did. It could help start him up, get some serious hardware without having to happen upon robberies where he had to cold cock guys in alleyways and fight for his life in apartment buildings. That would be easier. Hayes sneered at the thought: *The American Dream – buying weapons.*

But even to do that, he would need to transfer the stolen jewelry into cash, which he guessed meant using a fence or maybe another pawnbroker. If he went to another pawnbroker, there might be an alert out, identifying marks on something, he could get caught. He didn't know how that stuff worked. And who knew how you found a fence? Either way, Hayes would wind up with maybe an eighth of what the items were worth, maybe less. Those guys weren't dummies – they knew stolen gear when it was hot and they knew that you had to get it out of your hands; so they didn't need to pay top dollar for it.

"Shit," Hayes muttered, scooping up fries from the carton.

None of this was easy. Did he even want to be *that* guy? The guy who sold stolen goods? Beating up on costumes who spent their lives robbing stores and banks was one thing – that was, if not heroic, at least kind of noble. But selling stolen property? There was no nobility in that. That was the kind of shit he and his SEAL buddies had been trying to put a stop to in Colombia and Bolivia, where drug gangs were pushing the addicts into stealing from their own families to feed their cravings.

And what would Melanie have said if she had known he was handling stolen goods? Other people's goods? Other people's lives?

Hayes was just about to pull out of the parking lot when his cell phone went. The screen showed it was Peter Dunn, Hayes' old Navy buddy. He flipped it open and idled in the parking spot.

"Yeah?"

"Now there's a man who sounds like he needs another promotion," Pete began, chuckling at his joke. Then he became more serious. "Did I catch you at a good time, Hayes?"

"Sure, what's up?"

"You ever meet Sundae?" Pete asked. "Tall bastard, served in Team Two out in Somalia and some other hot zones. Called Sundae because he was always cool under pressure."

"I don't remember him," Hayes admitted. The Navy SEALs encompassed over eight thousand people at any one time, it was impossible to know them all.

"Anyhow," Pete continued, "Sundae left the service last year and took a job in security at Rikers. Got himself on special detail, what with his experience – they're crying out for us Navy guys, you know?"

"I'm not after a job, Pete," Hayes said.

"Yeah, I know that, cowboy, just hear me out," Pete said. "I bumped into Sundae last week and he happened to mention the name of one of the specials he's guarding – *the Jade Shade*."

Hayes felt his mouth suddenly go dry at the name, was aware of his heart's pounding against the inside of his ribs. At the same moment, his foot slipped on the accelerator and his engine roared like an angry bear before he quickly shut it off.

On the other end of the phone, Pete was still talking. "I told Sundae about what had happened to your Mel and he said he might be able to do a solid for you, y'know, as a fellow trident wearer."

"I'm listening," Hayes said.

"Sundae got back to me just five minutes ago," Pete said casually, "said if you want to go visit the Shade he can clear the paperwork. Says you'd get two minutes max, because 'the prison governor ain't running no Bedlam freak show thing' – his words, not mine. Apparently, they get a lot of requests from screwballs who think that's exactly what they are running, which is understandable, I guess, what with shit heads like Professor Freakside and Doctor Decay being held there–"

"When?" Hayes asked, cutting off Pete's stream of consciousness babble.

"Let me see what I wrote down here," Pete said, and there was the noise of bristle rubbing against the phone pick-up as he held it between chin and shoulder. "Can you do Monday at 8am?"

Hayes answered without thinking. "Yeah, I'll be there. Where do I need to go?"

"I'll send you Sundae's details by text," Pete said, "let you guys figure it all out. Sound okay?"

"Thanks, Pete," Hayes said. "Thanks for doing this, I mean. You didn't... I didn't expect..."

"Hey, I know, man," Pete told him. "Us Navy guys, we've gotta stick together, right? Look out for each other."

"Yeah, I guess we have," Hayes said.

After he had hung up, Hayes thought again about the stolen

property he had stuffed in the bag in the trunk of his car. Guys like Pete struggled to pay bills, they relied on pawnbrokers and cash lenders to tide them over when times were tough. Maybe Hayes should just return the goods, instead of messing up people's lives by being an opportunist. He could raise that money another way. He'd figure it out.

Hayes hit the mid-afternoon roads, light traffic and slick with the first spots of rain from overhead.

"The Jade Shade," Hayes muttered to himself as he headed for Queens. He hadn't prepared for this – despite all the heartache she had caused, Jade Shade had never featured in his plans. Maybe it was time to change the plan.

28

Hayes booked the Monday off work and spent the weekend reviewing news footage of the Jade Shade in action. He knew her *modus operandi* already – she had what had been described as a living cloak, which wrapped itself around her and granted her incredible super abilities. Those abilities included flight and a kind of enhanced strength which came from the living parts of the cloak rather than through her own body. That was the crucial part, as Hayes understood it – Jade Shade's cloak was made up of not just one creature but a whole ream of them operating on a kind of hive mind, each individual's action functioning to achieve the desires of the group.

How Jade Shade herself – which is to say, the woman who wore the cloak – figured into the hive mind, and what effect she had on its actions, was a subject of fierce debate. Some psychologists argued that the Shade was as much a victim as the people she hurt, her actions guided – and indeed, possessed – by an other-worldly presence which had manifested itself as a cloak. Others believed that the woman was very much in control, and that the cloak only served to enact her deeply rooted homicidal fantasies on as large a canvas as she could find.

The real answer could only come if someone could verify where the cloak itself had manifested. Was it part of a scientific experiment gone awry, or had it happened upon this world and corrupted the woman now known as the Jade Shade in some kind of Faustian pact?

Was Jade Shade a victim? Hayes couldn't guess, but he knew that Pete had done him a good turn here, and that by seeing her he might be able to lay to rest at least one ghost.

Apart from watching news footage, Hayes took time on Friday night, once the dark had descended, to get that bag of stolen goods out of his car. He had still not decided what he was going to do with it, but he knew he could not keep it. It was driving him mad, the way it sat there waiting to be discovered in the back of his jeep. He was on edge about it all the time, and, whenever he tried to relax, the thought of its discovery would come back to him and he'd find himself at the window, checking that no one was breaking into the automobile where it was parked on his driveway.

Under the cover of darkness, Hayes removed the bag, slipping it into a large holdall and zipping that up while it was resting on his tailgate, then marching with the whole thing back to the house. He kept a weather eye out for anyone watching, any late-night dog walkers or *Gladys Kravitz*-type neighbors who had nothing better to do than note the time of day a man was carrying a holdall from his car.

Back in the house, he shoved the holdall with its stolen contents into the cupboard under the kitchen sink, removing a selection of cleaning products that had been stashed there so long that they were thinking of forming a gang to relieve the boredom. After dispensing with any containers that had dried out, Hayes put the remaining cleaning products on the windowsill shelf behind the sink. It wasn't picturesque, but it didn't need to be. It was simply one more problem deferred.

Hayes hit the road at seven on Monday, heading north through Jackson Heights until he reached the bridge that led across to

Rikers Island. Rikers Island had served as a prison for New York State for over a century, with an inmate population that averaged ten thousand, daily. There were a lot of people just waiting for their trial dates here, which meant there was a lot of resentment built up in its walls.

There was a special wing dedicated to the costumes, that particular brand of criminal who used fantastical abilities or weapons to execute their crimes. Hayes had caught up with Sundae via telephone call after speaking to Pete, and had confirmed the time of their meeting and what he needed to bring:

"Two forms of ID, no weapons of any sort, no food."

"Why no food?" Hayes had questioned.

"Some of these costumes use organic matter to bolster their powers," Sundae had informed him bluntly. "You don't want to be the guy who brung the sandwich that killed the governor, do you?"

"True enough."

Hayes crossed the bridge in his 4WD, carrying his cell phone, two forms of ID, no weapons and definitely no sandwich. He had had breakfast before he left home.

The bridge spanned the East River, providing just one single path to and from the island upon which the prison complex was located. The prison was made up of a series of austere stone buildings in gray and red brick, all sharp lines and hard surfaces. It had all the homeliness of a funnel-web spider's nest.

Hayes pulled up to the gates at 7.25, more than thirty minutes early. That was typical for Hayes though, his time-keeping had been superlative since his days in the service. The way he figured it, being early did no one any harm.

And being late gets a helicopter dropped on you, he added bitterly.

What the hell was he doing here? Did he really want to face the bitch who had killed his wife? Did he really have the stones for that? Because he knew that there was a good chance he would just lose it here. He had seen guys in the service get at the insurgents and shit heads who had tried to kill them, and just lose it, showing no restraint, the idea of mercy or humanity alien to them in those hot red moments. Worse too, Hayes had seen men who had got caught up in friendly fire, and the way they had gone for the guy who'd been on the other end of the trigger, the guy whose line of fire they had crossed into. Ostensibly rational guys had turned psycho in those moments, and had had to be pulled away.

Hayes could not afford that. Sundae was doing him a favor here, just the way Pete had said it and set it up. Whatever he found in that cell, just seeing the woman whose actions had killed his wife could not set him off – he had to be sure of that. He had to hold himself together.

Hayes pulled in, shut down his engine, and sat by the gates in his car, hands clenched tight to the wheel until his fingernails pressed crescents into the faux leather. *Holding it together.*

A supply truck approached behind him and passed through the gates, and once it had, someone from prison security came walking out from the door there and tapped on Hayes' side window.

Hayes wound down the window and met the woman's gaze. She was in her thirties, stout and with that no-nonsense look that suggested that she reserved her patience only for things that mattered, like lottery results and parents' evenings.

"May I help you?" she asked in a voice that made it clear she had no help to offer.

"I'm here to see Sundae," Hayes said. "Um… Phil Perks. He's a guard here."

The woman made a sour face, like she was being told something she already knew. "He expecting you, Mister…?"

"Hayes," Hayes said. "Jon. And yes, he's expecting me. He arranged for me to visit a prisoner."

"You got ID?"

"Yeah, let me…" Hayes reached into his glove box and the security guard took a step back and reached for the taser on her belt. She had a gun there too, secured in a pancake holster with a press stud.

"Slow, if you would, Mister Hayes," she said with a warning tone. "No offense to you, but this is a secure unit. We have to expect trouble."

Gently, making no sudden movements, Hayes produced his ID – a driver's license and passport – which the security guard took, telling him to stay parked where he was and adding that people would be watching. She went back to the door in the tall gates and disappeared, closing it behind her.

Hayes waited five minutes until the woman reappeared, along with a tall male guard whom Hayes figured had to be Sundae. Pete had said he was a tall bastard.

"Hayes, that you?" the tall man asked, this time talking through the driver's window.

"Yeah," Hayes said, leaning across and offering his hand. "You must be Sundae."

They shook, and took a few moments to discuss what units they had served in and how life was as a civilian. It was navy guy talk, all reminisce and brotherly respect.

"Park over in B section," Sundae told him, "that's for special visitors, you can't miss it. Then meet me back here and I'll take you inside."

"Thanks," Hayes said, turning his ignition over.

Sundae checked his wristwatch as Hayes slipped into gear. "Hey, you're early," he realized.

"Old habit," Hayes told him before he stepped on the gas.

"I hear that, brother," Sundae said, as he watched Hayes maneuver towards parking area B.

Sundae accompanied Hayes inside, talking about Pete and their South American ops while Hayes had his prints taken and checked and was ultimately cleared for entry.

"Pete says you wanted to see the Shade as some kind of research thing?" Sundae said.

Hayes dipped his head once in agreement. "She was involved

in something I was witness to," he explained, intentionally vague.

"Pete told me she killed your wife," Sundae said with all the subtlety of a grenade through a window.

Hayes took a slow, deep breath before answering. "She dropped a helicopter on Sixth Avenue," he said. "My wife happened to be underneath it when it landed."

Sundae crossed his arms – huge, muscular limbs that looked like he juggled redwoods for fun – and fixed Hayes with a no-nonsense stare. "You want to see the Jade Shade and get some closure, I'm good with that. But you do anything stupid – like goading her or attacking her – and I have to haul you away. And if I haul you away, Jon, they'll lock you up for a long time. Are we absolutely clear?"

"Yeah, that's what I figured," Hayes told him.

"The room is monitored remotely," Sundae explained, "and there's a feed just outside. I'll be watching you the whole time with another guy. You need help, you make it known – don't wait or think you can handle it somehow, because you can't."

"I understand," Hayes said.

Together, Hayes and Sundae walked down the bleak, featureless corridor that led to the cells of the special wing. This was the part of the complex where they kept all the costumed weirdoes, the Professor Freakside and Grave Max types, who wanted to rule the city or rule the world or just kill everyone they came across who didn't see eye-to-eye with them.

It was eerily silent, each cell a blank door with a number and barcode, no sound carrying from within. It made Hayes think of a discrete hotel, the kind where rich old men met with women they ought not to.

Sundae walked to the end of the corridor, to where a monitoring station was located. The monitoring station consisted of a desk in a kind of semi-circle pattern, with five monitoring screens behind it, a chair and a panic button affixed to the wall that was so large and red it looked comical. Another prison guard sat at the desk, wearing a peaked cap, his eyes fixed on the views on the monitors.

"Manny," Sundae said to the guard. "This is Jon Hayes, an old Navy man like me. He's here to see the Jade Shade. Can you bring her up?"

Manny nodded slowly, like he lived his whole life in slo-mo, then toggled something on the desk.

"Come round," Sundae instructed, and Hayes followed him to the side of the desk where he could see the screen displays. There were cells there, in live footage, showing prisoners in overalls. Some were pacing their cells, some slept, some laughed maniacally, and some just sat staring into space. It was these last who were the most unsettling.

"Which one's Shade?" Hayes asked.

Sundae scanned the screens a moment, but Manny was ahead of him and brought up a single image on one of the monitors, leaving the others in split screen mode.

On screen, Hayes could see a cell, fuzzy through the artificial lens of the camera. It looked unremarkable, its walls blank, a single light bulb affixed to the ceiling and held behind wire mesh. Jade Shade sat in the middle, her hands and feet chained and the chain passing into a hollow in the center of the floor. She was kneeling, her head down as though in meditation, dressed in prison coveralls. Her hair was spiky like a teenager's, and her frame was slight. She looked small to Hayes, small and pitiful.

There was a box beside her, with thick metal struts across the sides and top, attached by heavy rivets which held it securely to the floor.

"I can give you two minutes, man," Sundae said. "She's nuts. Hold onto yourself."

"Does she have her cloak?" Hayes asked.

"It's in the locked case inside the cell," Sundae explained. "Their relationship is symbiotic, which means she'd die if they got too far apart. Take the cloak away and she goes into a coma. But don't get any ideas – that case is locked down solid."

Hayes nodded, just barely understanding. This was the world of costumes, all crazy rules and weird quirks.

"Only if you're ready, man," Sundae told Hayes with a reassuring pat on his shoulder.

Hayes nodded, taking in the view on the screen one last time. "I'm ready," he said.

Sundae did something and there was a honk like a truck horn. Then the door to Jade Shade's cell began to slide back on rollers, accompanied by the clunk of bolts being unlocked remotely.

"I have to close the door," Sundae said, "but we'll be right outside, watching it all on screen."

Hayes nodded and stepped into the cell, standing by the door until it had sealed shut behind him with the clunk of magnetically operated bolts.

Inside, the cell was white and featureless. Once the door closed, nothing remained. No Jade Shade. No chains. No box with the cloak. Not even the light bulb behind its cage. It was as though he had stepped into an empty white room – no, not even a room, but a space. An empty, white space.

And the white space went on forever.

"Shade?" Hayes said, speaking to the nothingness, feeling genuine fear creeping through him.

Was this the cloak's doing? The freaky thing was alive and it could change size and density. What was it he had read? – That it was made up of hundreds of life forms, functioning with a hive mind.

"Shade, can you hear me?" Hayes asked again, speaking to the virgin white canvas that was spread before him. "Are you here?"

There was no response, just silence.

Hayes looked down at his wristwatch, saw the digital display there as it ticked over from 8.01 to 8.02. And below this, down there where his feet were standing, he saw that the nothingness continued. The nothingness waited below him like a void, a solid patch of whiteness that had no dimensions, that simply went on and on with no markers and no definition.

The Jade Shade was here. He had seen her on the monitor. He had *seen* her.

Hayes looked up, taking a step forward. It was disconcerting this, walking on nothingness. He sensed there was a floor, he felt it under the soles of his shoes, heard it where he stepped, but he could not see it. The whole room, the whole space, was not there. It had just ceased to be. In that moment when he had walked into the cell, after he had seen it all on the monitor screen which he had no reason to doubt, it had now ceased to exist.

Hayes glanced back, saw the cell door waiting amid nothingness, a single solid feature in featureless space. Upright frame and horizontal casing. It was plain and bland with no handle inside, just the outline of its shape hanging there in the whiteness, not even the evidence of a wall. It looked as if he could walk right around the door.

Jade Shade had to be messing with his mind, that was it. Her or that damn cloak of hers.

Hayes took another step, turned around now and unsure of where he was in the featureless space.

And then he heard that same honk like a truck's horn, followed by the sound of the bolts unlocking. Hayes turned and saw the door pulling back on its slider rail, revealing the corridor outside, the same one through which he had walked. Sundae was standing at the doorway, a way back, hand on the taser he had secured to his belt.

"That's two minutes," Sundae said.

Hayes looked at him, meeting his eyes, but no words would come. Didn't he see it? Didn't Sundae see how there was nothing in the cell? How there was no cell?

"Two minutes," Sundae repeated, a note of impatience to his words.

Hayes walked to the door, glancing back behind him once he was through. The door was already closing, sealing inside whatever it was they thought they had imprisoned here.

"She don't talk much," Sundae said. "You get what you came for?"

Hayes stepped away from Sundae, over to the monitoring station where the guard called Manny was still at his post. "Is she–?" *still in there* – was the rest of his unfinished question, but already Hayes could see that she was, the same as she had been before, meditative pose in the center of the plain-walled room.

Sundae was behind Hayes, placing a hand on his shoulder. "You okay, pal? I can't imagine how upsetting that must have been."

"She wasn't there," Hayes said.

"She's pretty much broken without the cloak," Manny told him, chuckling.

"No, I mean–" Hayes started, then he stopped himself. Sundae and Manny were looking at him kind of weird, like he was talking crazy. "I mean she was real quiet," Hayes finished lamely. "She didn't even move. But you saw it all, on the monitor, right?"

"Every moment," Manny said. He looked disinterested, and reached for a mug of coffee which waited at one side of his desk.

"You need anything else?" Sundae asked.

Hayes shook his head slowly. "I don't… know. I don't think so. Not right now."

As they walked back along the corridor of cells containing a plethora of costumed criminals, Sundae turned to Hayes and there was a look of genuine sorrow in his expression.

"I'm sorry about what happened, man," Sundae said, "with your wife. Pete told me she was one of the good ones. I hope this, today, helped a little."

It had not. It had only brought up more questions in Hayes' mind. Questions he couldn't begin to figure how he was going to answer.

How could a prisoner be both there *and not there?*

PART 4
Rub Out

29

Back home, Hayes sunk down in the armchair and just breathed. He had been shaken all the way home. He could not even remember the journey, he had done the whole thing on some kind of mental autopilot.

How could Jade Shade's cell both contain her and be empty? No, not empty – it was more than that. The cell had failed to exist when he walked through the door.

It was like that thought experiment – *Schrodinger's cat*. Until you open the irradiated box, the cat inside is both alive and dead – that was the essence of Schrodinger's concept, a simple way to explain quantum theory, the idea that possibilities zero in until they settle on one version of reality.

The chaos factor here had to be the cloak. Jade Shade's power came from her cloak, a cluster of living beings not of this world. The cloak gave Shade her powers, feeding off her, too. How had Sundae described it? A symbiotic relationship, where both parties worked together for mutual gain.

If the cloak could grant greater strength, endurance and the power of flight, what else might it do? What was it doing to its wearer's mind, and to the minds of those around it?

Hayes had seen the cloak's container on the monitor that watched Jade Shade's cell, where it was kept so that she could remain close to it to maintain her health. That confirmed that the

227

cloak was in the cell, and so was Shade. Which meant they had to
have been there when he went in.

Or.

Or...?

Hayes wondered what the "or" was. There was another
possibility, that Jade Shade had never been in the cell, and that
somehow the footage on the monitor screen was false. But who
would gain from that? *Cui bono?* Who benefits?

That was the question at the heart of any conspiracy – *who
benefits?* If the Jade Shade was not incarcerated, had *never* been
incarcerated, then where was she and why hadn't she been put
in a cell?

Hayes sighed, the noise loud in the silence of the empty house.
He could not get his head around it, all this stuff with Jade Shade
and the cell. It was costume stuff, and that always had catches and
tricks, like a series of footnotes that made up the minutiae of these
people's lives. What he did know was that Jade Shade was a big
timer, one of those high-powered costumes like Morgana Le Fey
and Doctor Decay, same as the heroes in the echelon of Captain
Light and Eternal Flame. These were people with abilities that far
outstripped a normal man's. And Hayes had decided to go only
after the little guys, the flakes with hypno-discs and pop guns that
melted walls, the street hustlers who inhabited the fringe world of
the also-rans. Guys like Splatter and Retro.

Hayes needed to return his focus to that, the street-level
costumes who robbed banks and pawnbrokers. There were too
many mysteries stacking up, and he was finding it harder and
harder to keep them all in order:

*The repeated faces in the crowds, personified by the woman in the
headscarf and shades.*

*The other Melanie and the other him and Ginnie, their daughter, who
existed in the past in places they had never been.*

*The man with Hayes' face, who lived an entirely different life with a
mysterious loved one called Bobbi.*

The prison cell that possibly did not exist.

It was all bewildering.

Hayes checked his wristwatch and got up, making his way to the kitchen. It was not quite midday; early for lunch but he needed to do something to break his routine, to brush away the circular thoughts about all these mysteries for which he did not have answers. He would hit town in the afternoon and get back to patrolling the mouse hole.

As he ran the faucet in the kitchen, Hayes remembered the bag of stolen loot which he had stashed under the sink. *Shit!* He needed to get rid of that.

It had been five days since he had tackled Splatter and taken the bag. He figured the best thing he could do was to return it. He had been an idiot to snatch it up in the first place – taking a criminal's weapon from him was one thing, but taking this too had been opportunistic and could potentially bring down a whole load of problems he did not need.

After lunch, Hayes took the bag out from under the sink and stashed it in the back of his car again. Then he drove into the city, an easy drive at this time of day when the roads were comparatively clear.

He made good time, and headed for the parking lot behind Madison Avenue, taking a spot a couple of stories up from the street. Hayes got the elevator back down, carrying the bag of loot in a brown paper groceries bag under his arm, his Glock hidden under his hooded sweatshirt in its shoulder rig.

Once he had exited the parking lot, Hayes headed for the nearest mail drop point, over on West 34th. Inside, the place was populated by the lunchtime crowd. Hayes went over to a counter at one side, on which there was a display containing leaflets about tracking your parcel, international tracking and delivery, and the various other services. Hayes took one of the pens from the counter and wrote the address of the pawn shop on the front of the brown paper bag, folding it over on itself so that it fit snuggly around the bag within. Then he went to the counter.

The man behind the counter had enough oil in his hair to grease a pig. He offered Hayes a broad, toothy smile as he took the package, but his eyes looked dead. "Do you know this isn't sealed up?" he asked.

"You have tape here?" Hayes responded.

The guy at the counter said he did, but he looked a little put out about it. "People generally tape their packets before they get here," he explained as he reached for a tape dispenser.

Hayes fixed him with the unemotional look he had perfected in hostile territory back when he was a SEAL. Under its scrutiny, the oil slick behind the counter sealed up the parcel with three long strips of tape.

"What's inside?" he asked as he affixed the first strip.

"A jacket," Hayes said.

"Sounds like something's loose in there," the man opined as he turned the parcel over to seal the other side, shaking the jewelry therein.

"It has a zipper," Hayes told him. "And on the pockets too."

"Got it," oil slick said as he finished taping up the package. Once he was done, he showed Hayes, who nodded, then asked a gamut of questions about value, insurance, and so on.

"Just send it so it gets there," Hayes said.

The assistant weighed the parcel, printed off the postage and Hayes handed over the cash to pay for it.

"You don't have your address on here," the counter assistant pointed out, as he ran the bills through his till.

"You need that?" Hayes asked.

"It's preferable," the man said, like he could not care either way.

Hayes took the package back and wrote something in the top left corner. It was the address of the *Daily Echo* on Fifth Avenue. If, for some reason, the pawnbrokers wanted to come back to him about it, let them chase the *Echo*. The most that would happen is the *Echo* would run another piece about the inefficiencies of the postal services in this city.

* * *

Hayes hit his usual haunts for the rest of the afternoon and into the evening. He drank too much coffee, and watched the grid of streets encompassing Fifth and Sixth and Madison, looking for signs of trouble but seeing none. His mind kept wandering back to the cell on Rikers Island, the cell that was not a cell, and the prisoner who may or may not have been inside.

Hayes realized that his mind had wandered for too long when someone bumped against him the moment he was getting up from his table in a chain coffee shop, and he was suddenly aware that they were slyly reaching for his breast pocket. It was a young guy, skinny, with baggy clothes that showed a lot of label names that doubtless meant more to him than they did to Hayes. Hayes had seen the guy bump someone else maybe an hour before, close to the serving station. Maybe Skinny had been here all that time, or maybe he had just come back.

Hayes let the guy complete his reach – a slick, well practiced maneuver of less than a second – grabbing at the spot in Hayes' unzipped sweatshirt where he guessed Hayes would have his wallet. Instead of a wallet, the kid's fingers met the hard line of the pistol Hayes wore there, and his expression went from concentration to confusion.

Hayes grabbed the skinny guy's wrist at the same instant, pulling the kid forward until his mouth was right next to Skinny's ear. "You know what that is, boy?"

"Whu–? Hey man, I–" the kid began raising his voice like he wanted to create a scene and deflect attention onto Hayes. His voice said, *I'm the victim here, look over here, look at this guy.* People were looking up at the altercation, confused and surprised, not yet knowing how to react.

Still holding Skinny's wrist, Hayes shoved him forward, planting his face against the table which he had just vacated. Holding him firmly, wrist pulled around behind his back, Hayes leaned down and whispered again into Skinny's ear. "That's a Glock-19 and it's loaded with fifteen shiny new bullets. You want to step outside, I'll show you one, up close. *Real* close. You understand me?"

"You-you're crazy, man," Skinny burbled, but he was clearly scared, and his voice came out as little more than a squeak. People in the café were watching, and cell phones had materialized in the hands of several customers as they called for help or took pictures.

"I come 'round here a lot," Hayes told the punk, keeping his voice low. "I see you around here again, trying to take something that isn't yours, I'll put a hole in you. Got it?"

"Yeah… yeah…" Skinny said, straining now where Hayes held him down. "Just… let me up already."

Hayes let go of the kid and stepped back. Skinny got up from the table, glanced back and then bolted for the door. He almost lost his footing as he knocked into a middle-aged couple who were entering, arm-in-arm, before running hell for leather over Sixth Avenue and disappearing down a side street without looking back.

One of the baristas was standing a few feet from Hayes, concerned and unsure. "You okay, man?" he asked, all hipster beard and arts degree.

Hayes smiled grimly. "Yeah," he said. "You noticed a stealing problem in this place?"

The barista looked uncertain. "I don't know," he admitted. "This woman came by earlier saying she thought she'd left her phone maybe…?"

"You won't have that problem anymore," Hayes assured the barista.

With that, Hayes left. He knew, regrettably, that he would not be able to show his face in this coffee shop again – he would be recognized and maybe questioned or something else. The last thing he wanted was to become some kind of local celebrity, or, worse yet, pulled up on an assault charge by some lawyer who put wallet before morals.

Hayes slipped into a department store and lost himself in the men's department and the home electronics for a while, watching the big screens, not looking for anything other than to lose anyone who might have tailed him. He needed to be more careful, he reminded himself, more careful and less impulsive.

He needed to avoid displays like that. Public altercations. Bad enough that he had rashly taken that stolen loot without any idea what he was going to do with it. But to get noticed fighting in a coffee shop, no matter what the provocation, was going to draw attention to himself that Hayes did not want.

It had been an old instinct, of course. Years of drilling for every situation, knowing to keep your eyes open and your weapon close in a hostile environment. When someone came at you, you took them down.

The skinny punk was lucky Hayes hadn't broken his arm.

But if he had, where would Hayes be now? On *Royally Fucked Street*, that's where. Royally Fucked Street with no turn offs for a couple of years with good behavior.

Screw that. Low profile was the way he had to be. Fight the guys who didn't want to be caught. Do it quiet, do it from the shadows. No unnecessary attention; no unnecessary risks. Just like in his SEAL days.

Hayes spent the rest of the afternoon hanging around close to Times Square, a street away from where he usually did surveillance. He returned to his car just after six and headed home early.

That night, Hayes dreamt that he had been caught by the cops for the altercation in the coffee shop and found himself being taken across the road bridge to Rikers. Once he was inside, he was led to a cell just like the one he had seen the Jade Shade being held in.

Hayes tried to explain that he did not belong in this wing of the prison, that this part was for costumes only. But the prison guard would not be reasoned with, he just unlocked the door and instructed Hayes to get inside and serve his time.

In the dream, the cell was brilliantly lit and its walls were blank white. There was no furniture. The only identifying mark it had was a framed picture on the wall. When Hayes looked at the picture, he saw that it showed the inside of another cell, just like the one he was standing in.

In the manner of dreams, Hayes now found himself inside the cell in the picture, and then he found a similar picture on this cell's wall, once again showing the inside of a cell.

When he woke up Hayes figured he had been in five or six different cells, different but the same, each one as blank as the one before.

30

Hayes' weeks passed in solitude. He kept to his routine, working the early shift and then hanging out downtown, hoping to stumble on a costume happening where he could intervene.

He was on the scene when the Wanderer robbed the Sterling Commercial Bank just off Fifth, watched as the costumed criminal stepped out into the street with a haul of cash catching on the breeze around him like birds taking flight. Beneath his top hat, the Wanderer's mask made his face a gray blank, matching the long frock coat he wore over his dark body suit.

Hayes began striding towards the criminal, hoping to catch him unawares, surprised at how much taller he seemed in real life. But at the same moment, the heroine called Skimstone hopped into view with a triple burst of light, a trail of lightning firing from the fastenings of her golden costume.

The Wanderer took Skimstone's appearance as his cue, slipping out of time-space like he was opening a door, and disappearing from view.

Still running, Hayes almost collided with a street lamp before drawing himself up short. Behind him, Skimstone was already fluctuating through reality, crossing from sidewalk to pavement in a double-image blur.

* * *

There were other incidents, too. One time, Hayes had arrived on
the scene a minute too late when a museum exhibit had been
robbed of the celebrated *Goliath Star* diamond by the Mock Maniac.
On another occasion, Hayes had seen the aftermath of a stick up
by Lady Fear at a New York Fashion House, but had hung around
long enough to see Fear get hauled back to the waiting security
guards by the Chase.

Other stuff filtered through on Hayes' news feed. A cadre of
crooks worked together to commit a series of audacious robberies
involving atomic waste and mechanical parts before infiltrating
the power plant and plunging New York into darkness. What their
aim was, the reports were unclear, but the Rangers had ultimately
captured the criminals following a battle with something inhuman
that came crashing out of the power plant's north wall.

Other things happened too, involving Ghost Bot, the Hunter,
Damocles and Captain Light. Hayes kept track of the reports, adding
the sightings to his increasingly overwhelmed map, checking the
news footage at half speed to see if he could find any evidence of
a pattern.

Sometimes Hayes thought he recognized a face in the crowd
on that news footage – the heavyset, dark-skinned guy with gray
hair at his temples, or the woman with the headscarf, or that guy
Hayes had mentally tagged as "Afro Jogger". There were other
faces too, bystanders whom he thought he saw more than once,
each one of them watching these incredible events unfold before
their eyes like they were attendees at a theater show.

Hayes was sitting in the lobby of the Museum of Modern Art on
a Thursday afternoon when a woman caught his attention. She
was dressed in a long, purple coat and slouch hat, like she had just
stepped out of a film noir. She looked incongruous, yet no one else
seemed to pay her the slightest bit of attention.

Hayes watched as she paid the entry fee and then made her
way into the exhibits. She seemed normal enough, but she was

alert and edgy – Hayes could tell that just by the way she carried herself. On a hunch, he followed her.

She was tall, like a catwalk model, and you could tell she had long legs under the coat. The brim of the hat was low over her face, a casual kind of disguise, leaving the high cheekbones and full lips that made up the bottom half of her face clearly on show.

The galleries were sparsely populated, just a half dozen or so people drifting between rooms on a sunny afternoon.

Hayes hung back as the woman in the hat checked out the exhibits on the first floor. She was looking around too much, not at the piles of bricks and the splashes of color that represented whatever mood the artist told you they represented, but at the upper walls and the corners of the rooms. *She's checking for cameras,* Hayes realized.

He followed the mystery woman into the next gallery room, noted as she did the same exact thing – check walls, check corners, hat brim low, looking for cameras.

"Sir?" – the voice came from behind Hayes, right by the door.

Hayes turned, realizing a man was standing just behind him, hands on hips, staring at him. The man was forty, wide as a door, and dressed in a dark blue uniform that evoked the police or naval dress uniform without being either. Security for the museum, Hayes realized. "Sir, could I have a word?" he asked.

"With… me?" Hayes responded.

The man nodded, his expression fixed and serious. "Over here," he said, gesturing to a space just beyond the open doorway, where a corridor split this exhibit room from the next.

Hayes glanced hopelessly back at the gallery room, scanning for the woman in the slouch hat. She was at the far end of the room, passing through the wide doorway there and meeting with another woman.

"Sir?" the security guard urged.

Hayes took a last look at the far doorway, where the two women were discussing. The second was dressed differently to the first, but her clothes seemed intentionally non-descript – another, loose-fitting, long coat that hid her figure down to her knees, revealing only the calf-length boots she wore. She had glasses, ugly, round framed things that looked like they had dropped in from the seventies, and her hair was scraped back in a tight, blond bun. It wasn't a disguise, Hayes figured, not in the traditional sense, it was more like a deflection – a kind of *"hey, don't look at me, I'm boring"* thing. No one was ever *that* boring, Hayes knew.

Hayes tried to keep the women in sight as he followed the security guard into the corridor between exhibits. "Is there a problem?" Hayes asked, glancing momentarily past the guard's shoulder at the far doorway.

"You seemed to be a little rushed, sir," the guard explained. "I was behind you when you came through the gallery room back there and I didn't see you look at a picture once."

Hayes cursed inwardly. He had been so intent on following the suspicious woman in the hat that he had not thought that someone else might find his own behavior equally suspicious. But what could he say? *I was just here following that other woman – ?* Yeah, that wasn't going to cut it.

"I was meant to meet my wife here," Hayes said, thinking quickly. "Melanie. I got here late, missed my train. Figured she was inside."

The security guard weighed the story, looking less than convinced. "You didn't try calling her?"

Hayes shook his head. "Her phone is switched off," he said.

The security guard retained that skeptical look, so Hayes added –

"Melanie respects art. She won't take calls while we're here. Breaks the mood."

The guard nodded at that, beginning to be convinced. Hayes glanced over his shoulder at the doorway where the two women had been talking. They were just leaving, turning away from Hayes in the opposite direction.

"We could put an announcement out," the security guard told Hayes, interrupting his thoughts, "over the system."

"No, no," Hayes insisted. "I'll catch up with her, don't go to any trouble."

"It's really no trouble –" the guard began, but already Hayes was moving past him, back into the gallery room.

Hayes passed through the room in six long strides, trying not to seem too obviously like he was rushing. The women had just slipped out of his view ten seconds ago. He could still catch them.

Hayes passed through into another room, its walls dominated by oversized canvases showing people's faces. They looked like they had been drawn by a five year-old.

The next room was something else, a sculpture that barely registered on Hayes. But the women were not there.

Damn!

Hayes turned on the spot, looking left and right, spying the security man a room away who was still watching him. Hayes acknowledged him with a casual tap to his forehead, then strode towards the nearest throughway corridor, following a sign that pointed to the exit. He had lost the slouch hat woman and her buddy, but maybe he could catch up with them some other way, once they went outside. His instincts said there was something not right here, something about the way the woman was… was what? *Casing the joint?*

Hayes barreled through a glass door that led onto West 53rd Street. It was warm out here, the last rays of afternoon sun enshrining the pavement with its caress, the sound of traffic a constant drone. To the left, Hayes saw the hotdog stand that waited on the corner to Fifth Avenue, twenty yards away. He went to it, long strides and alert to everyone around him, searching for the woman in the hat and her friend.

The dog stand smelled of onions and fried food and grease, appetizing and off-putting all at once. Hayes had eaten from here a number of times when he had been running surveillance at

MoMA or on Fifth, enough that the owner – a short guy with black hair and trim mustache – recognized him.

"Hold the onions, right, chief?" the stallholder asked, making it a statement.

Hayes nodded, smiling uncomfortably. "You see two women pass by here?" he asked, feeling dumb.

The stallholder made a comically sad face. "No. Never. Seriously?"

"One was tall," Hayes explained. "She was wearing a hat with a big brim, like a summer hat, and a purple raincoat." He touched his leg below the knee to show roughly where the coat fell.

The hotdog guy looked unsure, so Hayes continued.

"She was with a friend, also tall, blond hair and glasses," Hayes said. "Her hair was pinned back. They were in the museum together. Did you see them come out this way?"

"Two women," the stallholder said as he lavished mustard and ketchup on the hotdog in a twin attack. "No. Three women, with the purple hat and coat and the blonde – yes. Looked like freaking supermodels, man. I thought maybe one of those lingerie stores was doing a photo shoot or something."

Hayes smiled. "Where?"

The hotdog man pointed to the intersection. "They crossed together, down 53rd towards Madison. Supermodels. Looked like a catwalk show, my man. You know them?"

Hayes shoved a bill in the stallholder's hand, took the dog and hurried in the direction he had pointed. "You have a good eye," he said.

"What can I say? I like tall women," the stallholder said. "Should never have married a chubby pixie." As he spoke, he glanced at the bill Hayes had handed to him, and saw it was a twenty. He called to Hayes about his change, but Hayes was already crossing the street with the light.

Hayes did not know what he was doing. He hurried up East 53rd at a pace that was not quite jogging. The broad sidewalks were busy, but with a little maneuvering Hayes found a clear way through. He ate a bite of the hotdog, then tossed it into a trashcan as he searched the faces for the three women.

They had gone. Maybe they had hailed a cab or had a car waiting. Tall women. Like supermodels. Or *super-costumes*.

Hayes waited in a doorway, watching the pedestrian traffic for a few minutes, hoping he might just catch sight of his targets. But they were gone.

He made his way back to Fifth and the Museum of Modern Art, checking his watch and making a note of the time – 5.20. He was sure something was happening, felt it instinctively. The women – three of them, it seemed – had met here at the MoMA to scope out cameras and exits and all the things that criminals checked out when they were getting ready to make a steal. Three women with catwalk good looks. It reeked of costumes. Hayes just had to make sure he was here when they struck, on site and ready for whatever havoc they unleashed. Easy, right?

31

That Friday, Hayes left work earlier than normal and headed straight for the Museum of Modern Art. He remembered the FBI statistics, how robberies were more likely to occur on Friday afternoons. He had no way to know when the "catwalk models" would strike, so he figured the only thing he could do was to play the odds.

He found a parking lot on West 55th Street, a block away from the Museum. The day rates were extortionate but Hayes wanted to keep his car close today; he had a feeling he might need it.

Hayes stepped out into the full blaze of the midday sun. He found himself surrounded on all sides by edifices of glass and steel and brand names, a thousand different ways to sell and to buy. Heat radiated off the hard surfaces of the sidewalks, roads and buildings, turning the city into a sweat lodge, where the only way out was to go inside a store and buy until your credit line ran out. No credit, no air con.

Hayes trekked over to the MoMA building, carrying a plastic shopping bag containing Splatter's gauntlets, and with his Glock snug in its shoulder rig under his hoodie. The gauntlet bag had a logo printed on the side for a grocery store, totally innocuous. No one would give it – or him – a second glance.

As Hayes reached the corner at Fifth Avenue and West 54th Street, he saw that the friendly hotdog seller was plying his trade in his usual spot at the next corner. There was a lunchtime queue at the stand, and the seller was doing brisk business. Hayes pulled up his hood – he did not want to be seen today, he just needed to be anonymous.

He took a right and headed down West 54th, away from the hotdog stand. There were street vendors here, selling prints and shirts and postcards of the art found inside the museum. It added to the sidewalk traffic, with people stopping to look and make purchases.

Hayes was alert, the way he had been on all those SEALs assignments, a kind of sixth sense kicking in and scanning everyone around him, reaching out to assess body language. It was an inexact science.

He went around the block, neither hurrying nor dawdling, observing the people on the street, stopping occasionally just to watch a cluster of people until they resolved themselves into separate individuals again and proved not to be his quarry. The thing about the women he had seen – assuming he was right, assuming they were costumes – was that they were distinctive. Tall and long limbed with figures like models. Being a costume meant staying in shape.

Hayes circled the block three times, crossing the street and dawdling at store windows opposite the museum every now and then, watching reflections in the glass, just waiting for the thing to happen. He saw no one of interest, no summer hat women with legs like supermodels, no tricked-out crime-mobiles weaving through the traffic, or descending from the air like a flying saucer.

At 4.20 he saw Captain Light cross Fifth Avenue eastbound, high in the air, followed by his train of twinkling stars and accompanied by a whoosh of wind. Then, nothing.

Five o'clock rolled around without incident, and Hayes realized that if the women were going to strike while the museum was still open, it would have to be soon. The FBI stats showed robbers favored hitting while businesses were open, because it avoided having to unlock anything which would slow down the heist. The museum would close at 5.30. Even as Hayes thought this, he realized something else – that hitting a museum at closing time was maybe a smartest time to strike, because it was easier to get lost in the crowds afterwards, all those Joe Schmoes leaving the office at 5.30.

Hayes hung back close to the corner of 53rd and Fifth, where he could observe both the main entrance to the museum and that side entry he had used to exit before. He made a pretense of looking at one of the street stalls, alert to everyone around him.

At 5.25 his patience was rewarded. An inauspicious courier truck pulled up right outside MoMA's main entrance on 53rd, disrupting the flow of traffic. The driver – a baseball cap pulled low over his face – hopped out, and ran to the back, where he opened the twin rear doors. Hayes watched three women clamber down from the back and then stride straight up to the entrance, leaving the driver to close up the doors. The women were tall, with wide-brimmed hats pulled down low over their faces and dressed in raincoats that hid their shapely forms – but even they could not disguise the length of their leggy strides. *This was it.* Hayes knew it.

Hayes left the postcard stall and made to follow the three women as they passed through the entrance of the museum. *And then what?* he thought. *Follow them? Get caught up in the heist, maybe busted along with them? Fuck that noise!*

He switched plans on the fly, changing direction on the sidewalk and letting the women pass into the museum without following. He had intended to accost them, relying on surprise to give him an advantage, but now he saw something better. Instead, he strode towards the delivery truck that had parked at the curbside, much to the frustration of a cab driver behind it who was negotiating the gap between the truck and the far curb with an accompanying director's commentary of expletives.

The truck driver was just closing up the doors. Hayes trotted up behind him and shoved – hard. The driver went tumbling forward and fell into the back of the truck. Hayes stepped up on the metal plate on the back of the truck and sprang inside, following the driver.

The back of the truck was empty, with lines of shelves running along the walls and two open, cage-style bins at the far end, closest to the cab. The driver was sprawled on the floor, his cap fallen from his head. He had dark hair and narrow eyes, with a tattoo running up the side of his neck that was either a badly-drawn rose or an imitation of a weeping wound. "What the actual hell?" he yelped.

Hayes kicked the driver in the side, delivering his boot with bone-crunching force. Something cracked inside the driver's torso, and he blurted out his breath in a rush of exhalation.

Hayes kicked again, this time aiming his strike at the man's gut. Already winded, the man made a choking sound as the blow struck, curling up into a fetal position.

Leaning back, Hayes pulled the remaining open door closed, sealing himself and the driver inside the truck, out of sight of the street. The driver just lay there, moaning quietly to himself.

Hayes dropped down, drew his fist back and socked the driver across the jaw, knocking him unconscious.

He took a moment to check the guy for weapons, finding a little Smith & Wesson tucked into his pants' pocket. Hayes removed that, then hefted the driver up over his shoulder and dropped him down in one of the cage bins that came up to just above Hayes' waist. The driver just flopped inside, folded over himself like a rag doll. He would live.

Hayes scooped up the driver's cap, slipped it over his hood and opened the rear doors once again. Outside, an alarm bell had begun ringing from the museum building, and there were people running along the sidewalk and across the street to get away. Something was happening, there was no question of that.

Hayes closed one of the back doors and pushed the other so that the catch was rested against it without locking. Then he did a quick, three-step run to the driver's cab and hopped inside, placing his plastic, grocery store bag on the seat beside him. The keys were still in the ignition.

He glanced at the museum entrance for a second or two, then tossed the procured Smith & Wesson onto the dashboard shelf and reached into the plastic bag. He pulled loose one of Splatter's gauntlets; the right hand.

Quickly, keeping one eye on the museum entrance, Hayes slipped the glove over his hand and secured the buckles tightly in place.

As he drew tight the wrist buckle, Hayes' attention was drawn to movement up ahead. A side door in the museum building swung open, from one of the emergency fire exits, and three costumed women emerged at a run. Hayes recognized them. Skintight costumes like leotards, not matched but similar, with thigh-high boots and opera gloves, their hair primped where it fell around their masked faces. They were the same women he had seen enter in street disguise. Now they were revealed.

The blonde was called Jettison and she had some kind of force blast which she could deploy against anyone who approached her, driving them back.

The brunette was known as Oasis Black, whose prime ability was to cast vivid illusions through some kind of hologram technology.

The redhead – the one Hayes had first spied entering the museum in slouch hat and Mac – went by the name of Chime, and could send a wave of sonic distortion at an opponent, so powerful it could force a man to his knees.

Together they were known as *Charm Offensive*, and, if Karl Lagerfeld or Coco Chanel had designed costumed villains, they would look like this.

Right now, the three women were sprinting away from the museum's side door, carrying stolen artworks in the holdalls they had over their arms like oversized purses. They were heading up the street, away from Hayes, and looking around as if expecting something: *their ride*, he realized.

A security guard came out of the side door after the three women, the same one who had challenged Hayes just a day earlier, drawing a taser and ordering them to halt. Hayes started the engine as the woman called Oasis Black turned back to face the security guard. He saw the flaming phoenix bird rise from her outstretched hand and swoop towards the security guard, an impossible thing made suddenly real. The security man dropped away, terrified by the illusion that had been fired off towards him. He rolled on the sidewalk, batting at the phoenix, screaming in fear.

Hayes nudged the accelerator and sped along the street towards where the so-called Charm Offensive had emerged. The truck pulled like a bronco, and Hayes suspected that the engine had been tuned up to better function as a getaway vehicle. The costumed women turned, smiling as they saw their ride coming to pick them up. Self conscious, Hayes tugged at the peak of the stolen cap he wore over his hood, hoping the women did not realize something was amiss.

Hayes slammed the brake as he reached the three costumed figures, feeling nervous and dumb all at once.

Chime and Oasis Black ran around to the rear, while the woman known as Jettison leapt into the passenger seat and told him to drive.

Hayes stepped on the gas and pulled out into traffic without looking, ignoring the honk of angry car horns as he crossed the intersection between 53rd and Fifth.

"Hey, slow down, Mac," Jettison said, excited, eyes wide as she stared out of the windshield. "Everything went clockwork smooth in there. We don't want −" she stopped mid-sentence, looking at the man she had assumed was Mac for the first time. "Who on Earth are you?" she asked, raising one opera-gloved hand in readiness to send a blast of force at Hayes.

Hayes struck first, lifting his right hand away from the wheel and triggering the glue-like projectile burst from the main nozzle on Splatter's gauntlet. Jettison was knocked back against the passenger door with the force, a gob of white adhesive splashed across the left side of her face and shoulders, sticking her to the door.

Jettison was outraged as the truck jounced along East 54th Street towards Madison Avenue. Hayes swung a left onto Madison, working the steering wheel one-handed, figuring the five lanes would give him space to maneuver. There was a blare of car horns, as the delivery truck joined the traffic, and the sudden turn threw his passenger back against her door.

Jettison recovered, and began to say something as she tried to fire off a burst of force. "Why, you dirty–"

Whomp!

Hayes fired again, shooting a more-sustained burst of adhesive this time that whipped Jettison's rising hand back against her breasts and locked it there in a splat like paint.

Whomp!

With a quick glance at the road, Hayes sent a third burst of glue at the woman in the passenger seat, covering her mouth and neck.

The truck was tearing down Madison, weaving past other vehicles as Hayes looked for a place to stop. He swung the wheel hard to the right, heard something – or things – rattling around behind him, where the deliveries would normally be contained. Probably his unsuspecting passengers, he guessed.

Hayes took the right turn wide, bumping through a line of bikes parked up by the curb before hauling the wheel around and into the lines of traffic, working it two-handed again.

Muffled voices came from in back of the truck, shouting, along with some hammering against the partition wall behind his head.

The street was a narrow, one-way road, which could only accommodate two lanes of traffic. Cars were parked along the side of the street. Hayes saw someone pull out to his right up ahead, emerging from an underground parking lot beneath a hotel. Hayes pumped his brakes to cut his speed, wrestling with the wheel to turn into the parking lot as the security barrier came down. The truck lurched like it was a punted football as it hurtled down the incline into the parking lot, snapping the descending barrier in two where it struck the top of the cab. Hayes ducked as the bar went flying away in pieces, leaving a cobweb impact strike in its wake across the top fifth of the windshield. Beside him, Jettison screamed against the hard-set glue adhered to her face, but the noise came out only as a kind of grumbling whine from her nostrils.

Coming in too fast, Hayes turned the wheel again and stood on the brakes as the truck skid through the gap between pillars before striking the back of a parked Mercedes and finally coming to a halt.

Hayes pushed the cap from his head and shoved his door open, stepping out of the truck. The Merc's alarm was wailing like a banshee, horn honking and lights flashing on and off, painting a nearby wall in amber bursts like a fireworks display.

He trotted around to the rear of the truck. His bad driving might not have tipped off Chime and Oasis Black – they would likely have initially figured they'd got caught up a police pursuit – but they would surely have found the real driver stashed back there by now.

Hayes approached the back doors cautiously, unable to hear anything much over the sounds of the car alarm.

The double doors swung open before he got there, revealing Chime standing in the doorway with her arms raised. Hayes knew how she operated – she would send some kind of sonic blast from her hands that would knock an opponent down. The moment the doors opened, Hayes became aware of a tickling against his ears over the blare of the alarming car. The noise of the car was enough to screw up the sonic attack for just a fraction of a second.

Right hand raised, Hayes fired a shot of Splatter's adhesive at Chime and watched her double over as it struck her in the belly. It was a clumsy shot, desperate really, but he was a trained marksman and, even with the newness of the weapon in hand, he knew enough to go for center mass.

As Chime sagged to the deck of the truck, Oasis Black emerged from its shadowy depths, her hands posed as if she was an old-time magic act about to reveal something in a burst of flash powder.

Hayes was aiming the gauntlet at her when the illusion hit. It looked like a dog, only with three heads, teeth exposed, slather on its jaws. The analytical part of his mind figured it was Cerberus, guardian of the underworld in Greek myth, and a part of Hayes knew it was make-believe even as he reared back.

Cerberus leapt for Hayes, big as a minivan and with legs as thick as tree trunks. Hayes dropped and scrambled back on instinct, his heart pounding like a steam engine, his legs kicking out like a beached fish where he lay on his back.

It couldn't be real. He knew it couldn't be real. And yet, you come up against this shit, right there, inches from your face, and your mind starts doing loop-the-loops.

Somewhere in the distance, way behind the wall of muscle and sinew that was Cerberus, Hayes could hear a woman's laughter. *Oasis Black.* Had to be.

As Cerberus pinned Hayes to the hard surface of the underground parking lot, poised over him, jaws smeared with drool, Hayes unzipped his hoodie and reached inside, pulling the Glock from the shoulder holster. He didn't aim; he couldn't, all he could see was that hound of hell obscuring his vision and overwhelming all of his senses. So, he just squeezed the trigger.

Bang!

And again –

Bang!

Again –

Bang!

There is a certain sound a body makes when it falls under the impact of a bullet, the way the muscles go lax and the human frame suddenly becomes a dead weight. Hayes heard that sound then, a hard thud against the concrete floor of the underground lot. The sound was accompanied by another noise, a gurgled choke of pain and expelled breath.

Cerberus disappeared, winking out of existence like a light being switched off.

Hayes was on his back, Glock in his right hand, the padding of Splatter's gauntlet making it unwieldy, like he was holding it with thick, snow mittens.

The Mercedes had quit its noisy alarming, though its lights still flashed to a metronomic beat, painting the nearby walls with amber and brilliance.

Hayes took a breath, closing his eyes, just letting reality sink in. He was panicked, he knew. His heart still drummed out a tattoo inside his ribs, and his guts were churning like he'd eaten spoiled meat.

He forced himself up, pushing himself from the ground with his left hand, the Glock still clenched in his right. The back of the delivery truck was ahead of him, doors open wide. There was a woman's body on the ground in front of it, face down, breathing shallowly, back rising and falling. It was Oasis Black.

Hayes stood up, a kind of rolling gait maneuver as if he was on deck during high seas. He could see Chime's legs protruding from the open back doors of the delivery truck like the Wicked Witch of the East, where she had been stuck fast to its deck by the blast from Splatter's glove.

He approached, woozy on his feet, still feeling the aftershocks of the panic attack. He stepped past Oasis Black, eyeing her for a few seconds to see what condition she was in. She was face down, blood slowly pooling by her side, but she was breathing regularly. She would live; maybe.

Hayes stepped up onto the metal back plate of the truck, and dropped back down immediately as he saw the third figure launch at him from the darkened interior. It was the driver, dark hair in disarray, murder in his eyes. He roared like an animal as he came crashing through the opening of the double doors.

Hayes swiveled his whole body, hands together, swinging out with his right elbow and driving it into his assailant's gut. The driver doubled over and fell back as Hayes' blow struck, tumbling back against the truck and almost falling over as his legs clipped the protruding back plate.

The driver recovered in an instant, driven on by rage and adrenalin. He ran at Hayes who had reverted to a standing position, having switched the Glock over to his left hand mid-attack. As the driver swung his fist at Hayes' head, Hayes jabbed forward with his right arm, pumping more of the high-pressure adhesive mixture through the gauntlet and triggering the electromagnet therein. The adhesive emerged as something that approximated a baton, though with a spiked end like an icicle. As the driver came in to strike, Hayes had generated the baton and it was sealed to his hand. Hayes turned it on the man in a brutal two-strike blow to gut and jaw – *wham, wham!*

The driver flopped to the ground, KO'd. It was like he had been hit by a metal bar, which was a pretty close comparison to the strength the adhesive had in this form.

Hayes worked the toggle inside the gauntlet and the baton dropped away, clattering to the ground and disintegrating. He was aware that there were sirens getting louder, out there on the street. He had to get moving.

Hayes clambered into the back of the truck via the footplate, and then crouched down before Chime. She was flat on her back, sprawled between pieces of modern art that had tumbled from the bags with which the three women had escaped MoMA. There was pale goop splashed across Chime's torso and the deck below, sticking her in place and trapping her elbows so that she could not move her hands. Her face was clean, however, and she glared at Hayes from where her head was forced back by the hardened adhesive as if she was wearing a neck brace.

"Who are you?" she said to him, watching him down the length of her nose, unable to move her head. "Do I know you? Are you one of the blasted Rangers?"

Hayes shook his head, ignoring her question. Her arms had been pinned down by the way the adhesive had caught her, but her hands were free. "Tell me, how do your sonics work?" he asked.

"What?!" Chime spat.

Hayes brought the Glock in his left hand around and jabbed its muzzle against Chime's forehead, right between her eyes. "Tell me. Now."

Chime cursed, trying to break free from the adhesive and failing.

Hayes watched her, his eyes never leaving hers. After a moment, she looked back at him, realizing she was not able to get free.

"Tell me," Hayes repeated.

"There's a circuit that runs through both gloves," Chime said. "It taps into a power pack on my belt."

Hayes looked at the woman's waist, but it was hidden by Splatter's adhesive, which meant he could not reach it.

"What about the others? Oasis? Jettison?" Hayes asked. When Chime did not respond, Hayes pushed the gun harder against her head, pressing down with a little force, enough so she would feel it.

"The same, the same," Chime spat. "They work the same way, damn it."

Hayes removed the gun, placing it down beside him. Then he reached for Chime's right arm, and began unpeeling the opera-style glove that she wore there.

"Hey!" Chime shouted. "Get off me, you pervert. What the hell are you doing?"

Hayes smiled within the shadows of his hood. "Disarming you," he said.

A moment later, Hayes had the woman's gloves, both right and left. Then, Glock in hand once more, he stepped out of the truck, listening for the sirens as they got louder. They were close now, maybe on the same street.

Hayes paced across to where Oasis Black lay, her breathing as shallow as a puddle in the Mojave Desert. Working swiftly, he peeled off both of her gloves, and took her belt too, drooping it over his left shoulder. As he stood up, he looked at the costumed criminal with annoyance. "You'd better live," he muttered.

Hayes went back to the cab of the truck, where Jettison was stuck fast to the door, her mouth covered. She was still making a kind of muffled scream which could be heard through her nostrils, like the whining of a dog, and her eyes were wide with terror.

Hayes ignored her, grabbing the grocery store bag that contained Splatter's other gauntlet, and adding the opera gloves and belt to it. Behind him, he heard noises coming from the open entry onto the street, the same one he had used to get in here, and he realized his time here was up.

Hayes slipped his Glock-19 back in its holster and zipped up his sweatshirt. There was no time to remove Splatter's gauntlet from his hand – that was a fiddly operation with the way the buckles were – so he would simply have to hide it. As for Jettison – there was no time left to take her weapons, instead he just left her, stuck to the passenger door and whining like an abandoned dog.

As two cop cars came bumping down the parking entry, Hayes stepped into the elevator that went up into the hotel, having used another glue burst from Splatter's gauntlet to stick the garage attendant who tried to stop him to the wall.

Hayes took the elevator to the third floor, and just wasted some time walking corridors and avoiding people while trying to figure a good way to get out unnoticed. He had been smart not to go direct to street level – there was too much going on there, with cops descending from all sides.

The hotel was expensive, and it showed. The carpets were so thick it was like walking on grass, and the walls featured prints from the Museum of Modern Art as well as photographs of New York that dated back to the 1930s. The fixtures were all mahogany and brass, each one polished to a shine.

Hayes passed by a store room at the end of a corridor, then, on a whim, he went back and tried the handle. The door was unlocked. Hayes stepped inside, pushing the door closed behind him and just leaned back against it in the absolute darkness of the room. The room smelled of cleaning fluids, a kind of acrid citrus fruit smell mixed with ammonia, and he almost choked when the first breath hit his throat. He waited a moment like that, breathing through his nostrils, trying to restore some sense of calmness.

Things had got crazy. He had nailed the museum heist, totally figured it out and wrecked it, stealing costume weapons and leaving the loot for the cops to retrieve. But, hot damn, he had not got out alive yet.

Hayes found the switch for the light, flicked it on to reveal a bare bulb above the door. He was in a tiny room, little bigger than a shower cubicle. There were shelves against one wall on which had been placed bottles of cleaning fluids like they were in a police line up, along with an array of pads and scourers, a dozen different ways to kill germs. There was a mop and two buckets, a trolley the size of a hostess trolley but with an open bag in front which served as a trash receptacle, and a flat surface with a little faucet and a drain.

Hayes let himself sink down to the floor, bringing his knees up against his chest. Then, sitting there in the little closet room, he unpicked the buckles on the gauntlet he wore, and slipped it from his hand.

There was a commotion out in the corridor, and Hayes' heart jumped as a new surge of adrenalin shot through him. He heard voices, raised and urgent in tone, the actual words lost. For a couple of minutes there came knocking at a few doors down the corridor and the occasional sounds of doors opening and the briefest of conversations. And then nothing.

Hayes waited. *They'll check the cleaning closet*, he kept telling himself. *Any minute now, they'll come check it. Any minute.*

But they didn't come. He was safe.

Hayes let an hour pass while he waited in the tiny cleaning closet, hood down, listening to the indistinct sounds of people coming and going from rooms, the running feet of kids arriving back from a shopping trip in the Big Apple. He waited it out, knowing that the very best thing he could do was wait and let the heat die down. The cops would be all over the place for a while, looking at CCTV footage from the parking lot and questioning staff and customers.

But once they found nothing, and with the stolen goods and the criminals all laid out for them like a gift down in the parking area, they would cease the search, or widen it so it left the area. Couple that with the other factor, that any evidence Hayes left would point to Splatter; *Was that guy still loose or had he been caught? –* Hayes could not remember.

It was almost seven when Hayes stepped out of the closet. He had shut off the light thirty minutes earlier, and had just sat in the darkness, listening and waiting, occasionally pressing the stud on his wristwatch which lit the display.

Outside, the corridor was empty. Hayes walked briskly down its length, plastic bag in hand. He peeked out the window at the far end that looked out onto the street. The sun had begun its slow demise behind the tallest skyscrapers in the west, out over Long Island and the East River. There were vehicles on the street below, cars, a silver bus and the ubiquitous yellow cabs that populated New York City.

No cops.

That was the crucial part.

Hayes went over to the elevator and pressed the call button, watching the street again while he waited for the elevator car to arrive. It appeared thirty seconds later with a pleasant and unassuming ding. The doors opened and Hayes stepped aside as an older couple came out, arm-in-arm. The gentleman had a white mustache like the Monopoly man, and he nodded to Hayes as they passed.

The couple headed for their room, talking merrily about their day in the big city. They looked happy together. Decades from now, that should have been him and Melanie, Hayes thought, spending their autumn years together, just living and being. But that was all gone, taken away from both of them by the costumes and whatever it was that compelled them.

He stepped into the elevator car as its doors began to hush closed, holding them back with a brush of his palm. Then he selected the lobby, and the elevator doors closed and it began its descent.

Hayes emerged in the lobby – the first time he had seen it. It was all cream-colored sofas and rugs, glass tables and dazzling chandeliers. He passed the reception desk without looking back, walking through the revolving door where a doorman tipped his hat as he departed.

Hayes headed west, walking back to the parking garage on West 55th Street where he picked up his car. Sure enough, the fees for his eight-hour stay were exorbitant, but he paid cash and "got the hell out of Dodge", as Pete Dunn used to say back in their navy days.

32

"... the stolen artworks were recovered and the criminal gang known as Charm Offensive has been taken into custody," the radio report summarized. "Police have denied early reports that a separate, costumed criminal was involved, sparking rumors of an escalating war between rival criminal factions. More on this in our midnight bulletin in an hour's time."

Hayes turned the volume down as a commercial started. He was in his basement, studying the workings of the weaponized gloves he had taken from Chime and Oasis Black under the glow of the bare bulb. There was a plate of cold pizza beside him, balanced amid the chaos of a fold-out workbench.

Hayes had spent some of the past couple of hours picking apart the gloves along their seams. They were elegant and skintight on the women, which had meant that his big hands could not get into them. He had unpicked the seams of two of the gloves using the tip of a craft knife, working with care, conscious that they contained delicate mechanics.

Once he had the first one open – a purple glove worn by Chime – he could see the webbing of circuitry therein, running from the tips of the fingers right up to the elbow. There was a small but powerful, circular speaker located in the palm, and it was from this that Chime's sonic assault would be unleashed.

Hayes studied the speaker and traced the circuitry, finding an operating switch along the inside flat of the hand, between thumb and index finger. A simple twitch of the thumb would be enough to trigger a sonic burst once the glove was active.

The glove tapped into a wireless power source which was stored in a battery pack in the belt, in Hayes' case using the one he had snagged from Oasis Black. It took Hayes a few tries before he figured out how it worked – the gloves charged when they were in contact with the belt, completing a circuit. Presumably, Charm Offensive charged the gloves by the simple act of standing or walking with their arms brushing their sides, providing enough power to fire off a blast or two at any given moment, the effects of which would allow them to deftly recharge through a further, swift movement of their arms. Like the other costume tech Hayes had snagged, it was decidedly simple and functional in its approach; no sense having a long reload time when you were facing a super-speedster like Chase or the Skater.

Hayes tried a quick test, wrapping the unpicked glove over his hand and then triggering a short burst of sonics. He was aware of the noise, but only faintly, like the buzzing of a fly's wings. However, in front of him, atop a small stack of newspapers he utilized when decorating, the topmost pages began to turn over, as if caught by a strong breeze. "Directional sonics," Hayes muttered. Sound so strong it had a physical effect. "Incredible." Probably best not to stand on the other side of the blast.

Hayes shut down the glove.

The illusion-casting gloves of Oasis Black operated in the same manner, although there were additional triggers arrayed along the upper end of each glove, to presumably provide her with a plethora of different animations to conjure. The base of her gloves, along the bottom of the palm at the heel of the hand, had a strip of diodes arranged in three tight rows, one atop the other. Hayes pondered these for a while, before locating their trigger.

With the glove seam unpicked, Hayes lay the glove on his bench and fired the trigger as he had Chime's, casting a random hologram from the gloves. From behind, Hayes saw the back of a three-dimensional projection which showed a lion with an eagle's head and wings – a griffin, if he recalled his mythology correctly. From this side, it did not seem intimidating, despite the technical brilliance of the projection.

Hayes left the projection running as he slowly stepped around his workbench to check that the diode strip had lit. As he did so, he felt a sudden jab of fear, and the hologram seemed alive and tactile where it had not before.

Hayes swore, putting his hands over his eyes and stumbling back. The sense of fear was real and he could feel the edge of panic taking hold of his mind, his heart thudding against his chest wall.

"It's not real," Hayes told himself, hands still fixed over his eyes. "Damn thing. It's not there. It's not real." He could hardly convince himself, and, when he looked again, the griffin was swiping at him with a clawed foreleg, its sharp beak open wide to reveal a forked tongue as thick as a cobra's body. Hayes wanted to run – it was the fight-or-flight reaction kicking in, that most basic of survival instincts.

He moved back without looking where, squeezing his eyes closed against the griffin's attack like a child afraid of the bogeyman.

Hayes knocked into something with his left knee, and heard a metallic clatter as cans of paint fell in disarray across the basement floor. Then he found the wall with his outstretched left hand, and hugged against it. He opened his eyes just a sliver, his nose pressed against the wall with its patina of mold decorating bricks that felt cool to the touch.

"It's not real," Hayes told himself firmly, looking only at the wall. Then, using the wall as a guide with his right hand trailing along it, he followed the room around, step by slow step, opening his eyes only in momentary glimpses, until he was back behind the workbench. Once he was there, Hayes opened his eyes.

The glove was still projecting the griffin, and from this side it seemed innocuous, nothing more than a special effect in a movie or a video game. His fear was abating – in fact, Hayes was embarrassed by how he had reacted, though he could still feel the turbo-burst of adrenalin racing through his veins. He reached forward and shut down the glove's projector.

The basement seemed different with the glove shut off. The radio was babbling away to itself from the shelf, something Hayes had been entirely unaware of while he was in thrall to the illusion.

He looked at the shut-down glove, turning it over in his hands. The diodes did not project the illusion, that came from the shiny disk located in the center of the palm, the same place as the speaker he had located on Chime's gloves. The disk was black and looked like Perspex, but it had enough flexibility to allow the wearer's hand to bend.

So, what are the diodes for?

Hayes thought about how he had reacted, still feeling off-balance thanks to the illusion's effect. He had an idea about what had happened, but he needed to check on that. He took the glove upstairs into the house along with the pizza plate, slung the plate by the sink and fired up the computer.

It took a few minutes of searching, following an instinct Hayes had, for something he had heard about while with the SEALs. There had been a rumor about a seizure-inducing gun going into production for the army. The gun was designed to essentially trigger an epileptic fit in the person it was fired at, through a combination of light and white noise. Hayes figured that the glove did something similar, combining that with the illusion in a manner which worked a little like hypnosis, and a little like inducing a seizure, convincing the victim that the illusion was real. Nasty stuff, screwing with people's senses, playing with their minds.

Hayes could not find any definite link to the diode strip, but he concluded that was likely its function.

"Note to self," Hayes said wryly to the empty room, "don't look at the glove when it's working."

With that, he returned to the basement, packed up the items he had been working on, and stashed them in a cardboard box on a shelf. He spent a couple more minutes putting the fallen paint cans back in their positions like some surrealist sculpture, the kind of thing he had walked past in the Museum of Modern Art, then called it a night and went to bed.

Hayes went into work the next day, but did not go into the city in the afternoon. Instead he went home and unpicked the other gloves, so that he could get to the circuitry inside.

He spent a few days experimenting with the gloves, looking at ways he could add them to his growing arsenal. They were too small for him to wear, and they created an additional problem in so much as if he was to use Splatter's gauntlets then he could not utilize an additional set of gloves, let alone two.

Hayes sketched out a few ideas, racking his brains to try to lock down a way to rework the circuitry in such a manner that he could access the powerful abilities of sonics and illusion casting. What made it harder was that he had no one he could discuss this with – how do you start that conversation with the hardware store clerk? *"Hi, I'm looking to repurpose some super-weapons from costumed criminals but I need to keep my hands free."* Yeah, that wasn't going to wash.

He would consider the problem in his idle moments at work, looking over the tools that the guys on the packing floor and the delivery drivers used. There was a variety of knives and scissors and tape and trolleys, but nothing that seemed to fit what he needed.

Hayes tried approaching the problem differently. What if he had no hands – how would he work the gloves then? On his feet maybe? But he soon realized that this was a dead end too. He knew vets who had lost their hands and bravely found a workaround that let them live independently, but he just couldn't imagine any of them in the role of a costume. Being a costume required speed as much as tech, and the combination of the two was the sweet spot that meant you might stand a chance going toe-to-toe against someone like Eternal Flame or Skimstone. *Or Captain Light*, Hayes reminded himself – that was the real target here.

He investigated devices used to extend a person's reach, simple grabbing tools that amounted to pincers on sticks operated by a clutched trigger in the grip. But all of them required one hand free to operate, and none of them really replaced a hand, they were more akin to using a couple of sticks on a spring than actual fingers.

Then, Hayes considered, maybe fingers weren't needed. The gloves he had taken from Chime and from Oasis Black functioned on the same principles – an emitter and a charger. Their location over the hand was for convenience – you aimed a gun with your hand and, like a lot of costume tech, these were ultimately nothing more than proxy guns.

So, then.

Hayes thought about other weapons, and whether there was a way to attach the circuitry and the emitters of the gloves to a gun. He could use his Glock with Splatter's gauntlets, but it was not easy. In fact, the way those gauntlets covered his hands it was easier to create weapons, like the baton he had generated from the hardened adhesive with which he had knocked the getaway driver out.

Maybe something similar could work. A baton or a staff of some sort, something that could house the circuitry and the emitters as well as containing the trigger switches. In fact, a staff could also hold the power source, which would save on the need to constantly recharge by touching the belt. *Okay*, Hayes thought, *now we're getting somewhere.*

He went out the next day after work and purchased an extendible metal bar, the kind you could use to hang a shower curtain from. He chose this for two reasons – first, it had potentially six feet in length at full extension; and second, that it had a hollow core which contained the spring. He could utilize that hollow space to hide the circuitry, and with a little drilling and welding he could put the whole thing together in such a way that it became a fixed stick with the mechanics inside and only the triggers and emitters on show. At least, that was the theory.

Hayes had four gloves – two from Oasis Black and two from Chime – and two charging packs from Black's belt. Which meant he had a little extra to experiment with, if his first attempt did not work.

Reports from the city told of a late-night street battle between the police and a new costume called Shark Angel. Shark Angel used a tricked-out motorcycle to perform her audacious robberies, busting into a stockholders' meeting at a tech giant, and later crashing a party held by a billionaire whose portfolio included an arms manufacturer that worked closely with the CIA. Shark Angel's motives were not reported, but her fearsome mask and choice of targets suggested to Hayes that the whole thing was personal, some quest to right a perceived wrong. Hayes was not unaware of the similarity to his own mission, although he was after something bigger than an individual or a conglomerate. He wanted to reach the man behind the curtain, the one who seemed to be controlling all of this costumed activity and somehow coordinating it for their own amusement.

After a week-long campaign of terror, Shark Angel was taken down by the Hunter, and her unconscious form was found bound to her motorcycle outside the Nineteenth Precinct House. The Hunter had already departed by the time arresting officers came to untie Shark Angel and take her into custody.

33

Summer became fall. The days grew shorter and colder and the leaves changed color and dropped.

Hayes continued with his routine: a punishing dawn workout before going to work in the early mornings, then heading into town for what he thought of as mouse hole patrol in the afternoons and into the evenings. With the nights drawing in he found that, conversely, he was staying out longer, drawn to the artificially lit streets as they tried to hold the dark at arm's length.

Catching the Charm Offensive trio had been a learning experience for Hayes. Now he felt he had an insight into how to find costumed criminals and catch them, alert to the signs and the kind of venues they liked to target. He would often go into the city unarmed, and just scope out areas within his grid, widening the search as the weeks turned to months. He saw the Ranger Jet launch from the Nexus Range on a dozen occasions, one time he even saw it twice in consecutive days.

But for all he had learned, Hayes failed to come across any further incidents where he could actually strike and make a difference. He saw several costumed criminals suffer their respective beat downs at the hands of this or that hero, watched as the likes of the Golden Grotesque, Jargonaut and Funeral Pyrate were taken off into custody, licking their wounds.

Captain Light was a background presence in the city, as was

265

Eternal Flame, but it was the street-level heroes – guys like
Damocles and the Hunter – who saw most of the action where
Hayes was circulating. They dealt in simple crimes, really,
straightforward robberies and burglaries and kidnappings, the
kinds of stuff that criminals had been doing for hundreds of years
wearing one disguise or another. Captain Light and the Rangers
dealt in more esoteric fare, Hayes surmised, when the planet or
the time stream or the fragility of reality itself was under threat.
Eternal Flame somehow bridged the two spheres, tackling both
cosmic threats and street level stuff, but he mostly focused on the
street stuff that was too powerful for brawlers like the Hunter.

After two months of nothing, Hayes tried going to the seedier
spots, the 24-hour clubs where the wannabe gangsters hung out
to watch pole dancers paying their kid's way through school.
But, although Hayes thought he recognized a few faces – square
chins seeming oddly naked without their masks above them, or
perhaps the distinctive silhouette of a henchman – nothing came
of it. More significantly, Hayes soon realized that these kinds
of venues made it their job to recognize regular patrons, which
began to draw down attention he did not need. The strippers
could disrobe for the costumes-out-of-costume; Hayes couldn't
make the surveillance work. After twenty days he quit on the idea
and looked for something else.

He tried hanging around outside the clubs, in torrid little back
alleys where breast implanted and tattooed bodies brought their
nicotine habits to feast, destroying their insides after trying so hard
to create a kind of idealized perfection of their exteriors. Perhaps
they thought that the inside could be corrected too, with the right
surgery and the right ink.

The surveillance was – perhaps ironically – a bust. There were
cameras out here and doormen with stern looks and prison tats
who didn't take kindly to an ex-SEAL just hanging around. Hayes
got into an altercation with one doorman who spoke with an accent
and sneeringly asked if he was homeless because that would mean
he could kill him without anyone giving a crap. Hayes broke the

guy's leg with a single, swift kick, then broke his arm as he toppled painfully to his knee.

"You ought to be careful who you threaten," Hayes warned him. "Next time you might meet someone with less patience than me."

The doorman wailed like a baby as Hayes let go of his arm and walked away. But Hayes knew he could not come back. He reached the conclusion that waiting outside clubs was a non-starter.

Over the same period, Hayes worked on his arsenal, exploring ways to utilize his meager stash of costume weapons – those devices that Jonas Culper had called props – without overtaxing their power systems or his supply of ammo. The latter was a critical point for Hayes – he was conscious that he had no way to resupply these devices once they ran down, everything had to be there for him when the time came to strike.

But when will that be? – he kept asking himself. Was he putting his imagined meeting with Captain Light off for a reason other than opportunity – such as fear? Had he become so enamored with his quest that he had lost sight of the goal? Fearing that maybe this was the case, Hayes went back to the wedding album he kept on the bookshelf in the lounge and reminded himself of the woman he had lost and everything that their relationship had meant. He worried if perhaps he would forget Melanie. Already he had lost her spirit, the Melanie who would visit him and talk with him when he was at his lowest, when he did not know which way to turn. That Melanie had been a ghost constructed from his memory, a guardian that only he could see. But now there was just him.

One Sunday morning, with fall turning aside to winter's touch, Hayes spent an hour on the computer looking at clips of costumes in action, examining the crowds the way he had in those early days, looking for Melanie and perhaps for Ginnie and himself;

looking for things that never happened but still got somehow recorded on camera.

After an hour, he went into the bathroom and washed his face. His eyes were red, and he could not say for sure if that was from looking at a flickering screen for too long or if he had been crying.

Hayes put on some sweats, shoved his keys in his pocket and left the house, hitting the sidewalk at a fast jog, running from the demons who snapped at his soul. Whatever he had got wrong, he could outrun it – that had always been his way.

He pushed his body hard, driving himself at a punishing run that ate up the miles with no destination in mind, just leg whipping out in front of leg, foot before foot, the steady beat of his steps on the sidewalk as his only companion.

Hayes had run seven miles, his muscles fired up, his chest taking great lungfuls of cold winter air, when he crossed over a street that brought him past a church named for St Benedict. The church was an old stone building set in its own small grounds, within which stood the headstones of parishioners who had died a century before. A parking lot to the side was heaving with cars as people attended the morning service.

He slowed his pace and entered the grounds on a whim, remembering how Melanie had appreciated the sanctity and traditions of the church even though she described herself as having lapsed. His jog became a walk as he traveled the path to the church doors without thinking. As he approached the doors, two looming wooden structures that arched almost five feet above his head, Hayes heard the words of a service in progress, the steady drone of the priest's voice as he delivered today's sermon.

Hayes gently pushed one of the doors open, and crept inside. Attendance was strong. There were a dozen or so rows of chairs to each side of the broad aisle, and in total these were at least three-fourths full. The chairs were modern and stackable, at odds with the age of the building, its stained-glass and solemn statuary, its gathered dust from countless preceding sermons.

Incense burned, filling the air with a cloying perfume, sweet and musky all at once, like a bite to the nose.

A priest stood in the pulpit up front, speaking with gentle honesty to his flock. He looked to be in his fifties, slight of build and with a full head of hair that was turning iron gray. He seemed not to notice as Hayes entered at the rear of the church, though a few of the congregation turned around to see what the disturbance was, perhaps detecting the momentary blast of cold air when he had opened the door.

Hayes waited in the porch, just inside the doors, where it was dark. The sermon was about kindness, and about the creator's plan in all things, no matter how obtuse it may sometimes seem. Hayes listened, closing his eyes to absorb the words.

… the creator in all things…

The power and the glory…

… forever and ever…

Hayes stepped out as the sermon concluded, dropping a bill into the collection plate at the back of the church.

Outside the air was cold from winter's embrace, but it felt fresh, like everything had been remade while he was inside, cleaned up for his run home.

Hayes hit the road again, beginning the seven-mile trip back to his house in Forest Hills, Queens, thinking about the unfathomable plans of an unknowable creator.

34

Winter was in full swing. Like his neighbors, Hayes had begrudgingly become used to the chore of scraping ice from his windshield each morning, and running the engine to get his car heated up.

New York was revving up for the holidays. The stores were suddenly full of red ribbons and fake snow stencils on the windows, and every display seem to remind a passerby that they needed to spend well and spend often to show that they cared for the people in their lives.

Hayes wondered who the people were that he cared for. His father was in a retirement complex in Laredo, Texas, slowly losing his mind. His mother had been dead nine years from cancer. And Melanie – Melanie was a few specks of DNA under the asphalt of Sixth Avenue, and Ginnie just a figment of imagination, a beautiful thing that never was. There were Melanie's folks, Jack and Jodie, but Hayes had not spoken to Jodie in four months and not to Jack since the funeral.

Jeff Puchenko at his work? The guy had so many kids and exes all over that he dreaded the holidays and every lick of enforced family spirit they tried to engender.

Pete Dunn was an acquaintance. A good one, but an acquaintance all the same. Pete wasn't a guy you gave a present to, unless it was a bottle of scotch and the occasion was to drink a bottle of scotch.

So Hayes walked the streets, watching the happy faces as shoppers marveled at the displays, the efforts of every business to get themselves noticed and remembered and adored. But he didn't see any costumed criminals scoping out the banks or the jewelers or the expensive department stores. Maybe they didn't come out for the holidays. Maybe the costumes left the holidays alone in some strange adherence to the notions of peace and goodwill. Or maybe holiday showdowns between the costumes didn't make for good press.

It was a week after Thanksgiving when it started snowing in New York. It was an indecisive kind of snow, wafting in the air but turning to water the moment it hit the ground, like it couldn't quite muster the energy to settle. It eventually turned to a mean-spirited, icy rain, accompanied by a chill wind that made Hayes' old scars burn. His scars did not like cold weather, and they nagged like toothache every time the temperature plummeted towards zero.

Hayes was just unlocking his car – parked once more on the top story of the parking lot off Madison that overlooked the Nexus Range – when he sensed the change in the atmosphere. The weather had got just that little bit colder, bringing with it an unreal half-light to the clouded sky. Hayes brushed icy flecks from his sweatshirt hood and climbed into the driver's seat, slamming the door to keep the cold at bay.

It was after seven, and the roads would be quieter, at least as much as New York City roads ever got quieter, but the bridges would still be clogged with commuter traffic. Hayes started the engine, checked his mirror and pulled out of the parking spot, heading for the exit ramp.

He reached street level and paid, flicking on the radio as he pulled out into the traffic. He cut across to Park Avenue and then headed north, accompanied by the drivel of a shock jock hosting some phone-in chatter concerning whether the holidays really meant anything anymore.

Hayes was just entering the Queensboro Bridge – a structure of metal lines that looked like some weird, robot skeleton had landed itself in the middle of the East River – when he became aware of the darkness descending from above. The darkness was saucer-shaped and looked to be a couple of miles across. It was dropping through the clouds with a low rumble like a charging elephant.

Tapping the brakes, Hayes looked for a way to turn back, but he was already caught up on the bridge now and would have to cross before he could change direction. The vehicles around him slowed, as everyone rubbernecked, trying to see what was happening out there.

The saucer was dark in color, its surface gray and black like metal, dragging wisps of clouds with it as it loomed into view.

Queensboro Bridge had two levels for traffic. Hayes was on the bottom level, which made clearly seeing the thing that much harder. Hayes saw it only when he peered to the side, in the gaps between the next lane of traffic to his left, and out through the skeletal struts that made up the exterior of the road bridge. It was like he was seeing it in a flicker book, glimpsing this majestic and awe-inspiring thing as it fell from the skies, image by image, frame by frame. Only it was not falling, it was coming down at a controlled pace, one that seemed slow from this far below, even though Hayes knew that was an illusion of perspective, the way a jet aircraft can seem to descend slowly towards the runway when you're on the ground.

As the saucer dropped, the gravitic effect was sufficient to draw the surface of the East River upwards. Displaced river water slammed into the piers along the lower east side. Foamy water rolled over the five lanes of the bridge where Hayes could see, before sinking back down to its original level.

Hayes divided his attention, watching the giant saucer descending through the clouds and keeping an eye on the watery road and the slow-moving traffic. Everyone had slowed down – it was like when fog descended on New York on those cold mornings at the start of winter, when visibility dropped and everyone dropped their speed just a little in deference to it.

The woman on the radio's tone had become more excited, as she relayed initial reports of what could be seen from the station's twenty-third floor studio off Seventh Avenue. Before this, Hayes could not have imagined that the woman could sound more excitable, but it seemed she had a whole other level she was tapping into now, sounding like a commentator in the final furlong of a horse race. It was not manufactured anger in her voice now, but wonder. Wonder and fear.

The saucer had descended to a spot over the eastern side of the city, reaching a standstill where it remained hovering about a half mile above the ground. White smoke wafted from its surface, and then Hayes spotted a moving white light, swiftly accompanied by three more in quick succession. The lights looked like fireworks, bursting out from the underside of the colossal saucer. More lights began ejecting *en masse*, but before Hayes could make sense of them his view was blocked by the side of a refuse truck as it drew beside him in the left lane.

Frustrated, Hayes dawdled forward with the other lines of traffic, listening to the report over the radio. The husky-voiced radio host was already describing the thing as a flying saucer now, and asking the kinds of questions that phone-in hosts ask – *Tell us what you see, tell us what you know, what do you think it means?*

It was getting colder inside the jeep. Hayes reached for the air blower, toggling it to its fiercest setting and rubbing his hands together before the vent on the dash as his line of traffic slowed to a crawl. He wanted to see what was going on out there, find out what that flying saucer was all about, but he was trapped as effectively as if he had been locked in one of those special cells on Rikers Island.

A caller to the radio station was excitedly describing what it was he could see from his window. "Whoa! I just saw something drop from the bottom of that disc thing," he said in a thick Bronx accent.

"What did it look like?" the radio host purred.

"I don't know what," the caller said. "Kinda… wait a minute, there goes another. There's a load of them. I don't believe this!"

"How many?" the host urged. "What do they look like?"

"They're white people," the caller said. "Like… like snowmen or those stormtrooper guys outta *Star Wars*. There's gotta be a hundred of them dropping outta the bottom, Nancy."

"Like the guys in *Star Wars*?" the host asked. "You mean, they're wearing armor?"

The caller said nothing in response, and after a moment the host urged him to speak.

"Whoa!" the caller said, suddenly. "That was a close one."

"What is it? What can you see?"

The refuse truck to Hayes' left finally drew ahead, and he could see beyond the bridge once more. As the radio caller described it, he saw the white-armored figures dropping from the base of the saucer in their dozens, great clusters of them spiraling towards the ground like the parts of a dandelion clock caught on the breeze.

"It's either armor or some kind of natural shell like a turtle's," the radio caller was saying. "Whatever they are, they ain't human, I'll tell ya that!"

Ahead of him, Hayes saw his line of traffic pick up speed. He pressed his foot down on the accelerator at the same moment that something crashed into one of the bridge's towering support struts. Suddenly, the whole bridge seemed to reverberate with a noise like a bell being struck, and Hayes braked. The bridge held, the aftershocks of the strike continuing to resound through the metal structure in a discordant echo of clanging bells.

The car's radio growled out a loud burst of static, and Hayes reached for the knob to shut it off. Whatever was occurring was screwing with the reception, either here at the bridge or on Seventh Avenue where the broadcast originated.

As Hayes switched off the radio, something crossed through the lanes of traffic, left to right across his eye line, about eight cars ahead of him. It was dressed in what appeared to be white armor, and was large as a rhino, but it walked on two legs. Its armor – or carapace, or whatever it was – sparkled like snow, catching the headlights of the cars. Up ahead, an automobile swerved while another struck the side of the walking thing – which knocked it aside with a flick of one powerful limb. Hayes watched as the knocked car flipped over and over on its Y axis before colliding with the front of a truck and coming to a crashing halt, accompanied by the angry yap of car horns.

The armored thing knocked through a railing and disappeared over the far side of the bridge.

Some people pulled to a stop and left their cars, hurrying over to check on the overturned car and its occupant.

Hayes put on his emergency brake, watching out the side window where the flying saucer loomed like some giant cog from a machine.

The driver from the overturned car was pulled to safety, and other vehicles started up again, the traffic flowing slow and wary now like kids playing a game of statues, frightened of being caught in movement.

Hayes passed the scene of the accident, peering to see what had happened. The hatchback was a write-off, its chassis concertinaed and a plume of dark smoke trailing from its hood. The truck it had hit had done better, though its grill was hanging askew, with a nasty-looking dent in the chrome. Both drivers looked disoriented, and the one from the car had blood running down his face, a Morse Code line of red spots dotted across the white collar of his shirt.

Hayes drove past. Drivers were panicking with what they had seen, and the appearance of the vast spaceship – or whatever the heck it was – had encouraged more people to take to the roads to get away. As if you could ever get far enough away from a two-mile-wide spaceship, like there was a safe distance.

He had reached the Queens side of the bridge when he saw the trail of light cross the sky like a shooting star, just below the clouds. Hayes tracked it, but it was lost in an instant, such was the speed with which it was moving. Hayes looked in his side mirror, searching the sky above the cars behind until he caught sight of the streak of light crossing the very edge of the glass. He could not see the figure that preceded it but he recognized the trail of stars that followed, sparkling in the night sky like sparks from an angle grinder. It was Captain Light, flying at high speed as he headed towards the colossal disc that hovered above the river and the city. Hayes wondered if maybe he should be cheering the hero on, but at the same time he saw the chaos on the roads surrounding the Queensboro Bridge, and thought about the way that automobile had been flipped right before him just a couple of minutes before. Hayes could not shake the feeling that Captain Light – and all these other so-called heroes – were in some way creating these problems, drawing down the other costumes, the "bad" costumes, and the space aliens and the other-dimensional tyrants, like they needed the mayhem that they brought to justify their own existence, to keep them in work.

The driver behind Hayes sounded his horn twice, and Hayes picked up speed again, falling into step with the traffic around him as it headed off the bridge. He joined the Queens Boulevard, occasionally using his mirrors to see if he could make sense of what was going on behind him, a half mile above New York. He saw flashes and explosions caroming across the surface of the dark disc that waited in the sky, but there was no way to understand it from this distance – it was just another act in the theater play that encompassed the lives of the costumes.

Figuring there was nothing he could do, and no gain in his staying, Hayes completed the journey to Forest Hills and his home.

35

The rolling news captured the story in real time.

The incursion – that's what a reporter called it, and the name stuck – was confirmed as an extra-terrestrial object entering Earth's atmosphere. It threatened to be the beginning of an alien invasion, with armies led by an alien warlord called Dominax.

Shaky helicopter footage covered the story from different angles on different channels as it played out live. Captain Light flew at full speed into the side of the spaceship where it waited above the East River, smashing through the hull, with an accompanying sonic boom, and a line of twinkling stars scored across the sky in his wake. His spectral scream could open holes in space, so it was no surprise to learn that Light could open a hole in the side of a space-going vessel that had traveled light years to invade our planet.

Most of what happened next occurred inside the spaceship, hidden from view, and for five minutes the human race waited in fearful anticipation. Eventually, there was an explosion somewhere on the rim of the disc-like vessel's hull, and Captain Light emerged looking tired, the white of his uniform marred with grime. Armored warriors – of the same type that Hayes had seen crossing the Queensboro Bridge – burst from the hull with Captain Light, but where he flew majestically in the air to recover, they plummeted, striking the icy East River at terminal velocity, all of it captured in real time, on shaky cam, lit by spotlights from the news and police choppers.

One camera operator spotted something through one of the breaches in the alien ship, and word spread across the networks like a meme. Captain Light was targeting his spectral scream on an alien figure sitting in a kind of hovering chair that looked like an insect made of metal. The figure in the chair was humanoid but he seemed remarkably short; some later estimates had him at just four feet in height. This figure was Warlord Dominax.

Followed by his twinkling trail of flickering stars, Captain Light flew at top speed through the hole in the spaceship's hull. What happened after was lost from view again, leaving reporters and news anchors to speculate as they filled the airwaves, while the shaky feeds from the cameras continued to fill viewers with a sense of remote helplessness and dread.

Something exploded out of one end of the spaceship – the far side to where Captain Light and Dominax had first been seen clashing. The explosion looked like water, but it was a vivid green that reflected the spotlights of the news choppers as it spurted out of the ship. It was as if someone had cut an artery – maybe someone had.

Tense minutes stacked up, one after the other, with only uncertain sounds echoing above New York while the ship waited in darkness. Then, without explanation, the spaceship began to drop from the sky. Not in the way it had before – this was no controlled descent, it was a crash, happening in real time, live on air, with the lives of eight million New Yorkers at stake. If willpower alone could have reversed an event, it would have turned the spaceship back. But it didn't.

Instead, as the spaceship dropped that miniscule final half mile towards the buildings and the streets of the Big Apple, something impossible opened in the air, a gaping maw that expanded to absorb the two-mile-wide disc from space. It was a gateway, the kind of dimension-crossing portal that Captain Light's scream could open when he unleashed it at full intensity, and it was larger than anything anyone had seen him produce before.

One second the ship was there, the world was threatened, lives were about to be lost.

The next, it was over, the ship was gone, the threat had evaporated, the world was saved.

Then, with a disbelieving human race still watching, still trying to comprehend what they had just witnessed on TV sets and inside internet windows in a billion households, a figure fell from high out of the cloudy, night sky. Camera operators zoomed in, finding their focus as that figure fell. It was one lone man in a white costume with gold trim and a cape that had become a shredded rag.

"There's no trail of stars, do you see that?" one of the reporters famously said in those tense seconds as the world let out one single, communal gasp. He was right. Captain Light was not flying, he was falling.

And he fell.

And he fell.

He fell from way up high above New York City until –

Crash!

– he struck the water of the East River with an almighty splash, sending a rising wave out in all directions until it struck the shores of the Upper East Side and Long Island.

Port authorities sent out boats to locate the costumed hero, with divers searching the river. The whole drama played out on the networks, with shameless reporters finding local New Yorkers to interview about how they would feel if it transpired that Captain Light was dead. One network reported that he had died, only to retract the statement a few minutes later, acknowledging that it was unconfirmed. This was ambulance chasing journalism, reveling in the worst-case scenario, tapping into the grief a nation could feel rather than the relief people felt at being saved. It was the old rule, that bad news kept viewers tuned in.

But it didn't keep Hayes tuned in. He shut off the TV at a little before 3am, while the river was still being searched for Captain

Light, knowing that the story would go on to its conclusion whether he watched it live or not.

Hayes slept, but it was a restless kind of sleep. In his dreams, he was trying to get the nursery window open when a disc-shaped spaceship appeared outside. His window was jammed, and all he could do was watch as armored figures landed and ransacked his neighborhood, scuttling off with the Millarinis hoisted over their shoulders before finally busting into his house and coming for him.

Hayes woke up in a sweat, checked his phone and flicked on the television at the end of the bed. It was before seven, and he had crammed in about four hours sleep.

The breakfast news was jubilant, repeating the top story that Captain Light was alive. Footage showed Light being helped onto a port authority boat by a crowd of people sometime in the small hours. He looked exhausted but relieved.

"How does it feel to know you saved the world?" was the first question someone asked as a mic was shoved under his face.

Captain Light seemed to think for a moment before replying. "Like Thursday," he said, with a grin.

It was Wednesday.

Over the subsequent few days, a wealth of footage appeared online showing the so-called incursion and its aftermath. One popular theory had it that Warlord Dominax had invaded during a cold snap because his race was only able to function in low temperatures. There were other theories, slowed down clips of footage that purported to prove this or that conspiracy, faces "discovered" in the way the smoke billowed from the spaceship when it descended, number theories about the date and the time of the spaceship's appearance, and the time it had exited this plane of existence.

It was 9/11 all over again, tons of new footage uploaded from every nobody who had a camera, seeing the same thing happen over and over from different angles, *ad nauseam*, until it seemed to normalize in people's minds.

Hayes found himself sucked into that weird world of online footage for the best part of a day, looking at this still image coupled with that overlay, or some piece of footage that had been slowed down until a hidden something-or-other would be circled and the narrator would say what it could mean.

Most of it was bullshit.

On the Friday, New York's Mayor, one Antonio Castlebridge, announced that the city would be honoring Captain Light at a ceremony to be held shortly, and to which the hero would be invited.

"It would be my honor to present the key to the city to the man who saved us all," Castlebridge said at a press conference, before adding in a jokey manner: "We really oughta give the guy the key to the *planet*, for what he did. He deserves it."

There was some online mockery about whether there really was a key to the city and what it meant to receive it, but the overriding sense was that Captain Light deserved recognition for his part in turning back an invasion by a hostile, other-worldly force.

Hayes quit patrolling the grid of Manhattan streets that he had termed the mouse hole. The time was approaching, he knew. There was no more time to prepare – now it was time to strike.

36

A week passed. Hayes went to work in the daytime, and spent his evenings working on his arsenal in the basement of his Forest Hills house, familiarizing himself with how the stolen weapons functioned until their use was second nature. His biggest concern was ammunition. He had discovered no way to replace that, and even a telephone discussion with Jonas Culper – who had given Hayes his number when Hayes had promised him Retro's gun – provided no illumination. Hayes would have to go into battle with what he had, and hope it was enough.

"Hope" was not a particularly recognized aspect of the SEAL philosophy which Hayes encapsulated. It sat badly with him, and doubt set in as the date of the Captain Light ceremony became finalized and Light confirmed that he would attend.

Maybe Hayes really was crazy, challenging Captain Light for an answer to what had happened to Melanie. Maybe Captain Light was as clueless as he was about who was manipulating the costume scorecard. Maybe there was no scorecard – the appearance of Dominax and a whole alien army was hard to factor into Hayes' calculations. Dominax did not fit the pattern of those other activities – the way costumed criminals would appear, fight their respective hero a couple of times, get incarcerated and then reappear a while later, perhaps wielding a souped-up version of the props they had utilized the first time, a kind of *Villain 2.0*. That was the pattern.

But there were other patterns, or other parts to the pattern. Hayes was sure of that. The fact that Dominax and the alien incursion did not fit into the one he recognized did not mean that the patterns didn't exist. Maybe Dominax was like Morgana Le Fey and all those other other-worldly curiosities. Even Jade Shade's cloak could be considered to fall into that category, couldn't it, if you looked at it in the right way – an alien object that had grafted itself to a human being to wreak havoc across the city. And Jade Shade was normal enough – *she* fit the pattern. Even now she was in a cell, waiting for release when she would likely reappear with a new plan, a new set of victims, a new Melanie broken apart under a new helicopter.

But the cell was not complete, Hayes reminded himself. That was profoundly unsettling. The way the cell had ceased to exist when he had entered it, and the way that the guards, Sundae and Manny, had thought nothing of that, had just seen what they expected to see on the cell's monitor, as if nothing was wrong.

Sometimes not knowing the answer, Hayes realized, *was really because you didn't know the question.*

But Captain Light knew the question. He, or others like him, knew what the world was. They had to – they were its stars.

The ceremony was set for a Saturday afternoon in the middle of December with the shopping season at its height. It would be held in Central Park, beside the Belvedere Castle on the shores of Turtle Pond. Belvedere was a faux-medieval castle created as a folly in the nineteenth century and evocative of a fairy tale location. In reality, it held a gift shop and a weather station, but had stood in for a fairy tale site in numerous wedding photographs for couples who had married in or close to the park. It overlooked a pond that was about the size of a city block, with an artificial island in the middle like a rest home for wildlife.

Hayes checked out preparations on Friday afternoon, when security was already getting tight. Barricades had been erected right around the western edge of Turtle Pond, and there were several portable cabins lined up to host the media who would cover the event. Hayes wondered how much security a guy who could shrug off a 9mm bullet would need. But then he mentally answered his own question – it wasn't 9mm bullets you had to worry about, it was all the other costumes bearing props and grudges.

The observation level of the castle was open and gave good views of the park and the city, but there was no way to access it with the way security was. As Hayes looked up there, he could already see FBI guys checking out the area, all dark winter coats, dark glasses and dark expressions, like they'd been scribbled into existence in just a few quick lines of ink.

Hayes watched the preparations for a while, trying not to be obtrusive, which was not so hard with the number of people who were doing the same. You set up anything in New York, or any other city, and people stop to look, like building a stage is some kind of theater show in itself. The crazy thought occurred to Hayes that maybe all these people wanted to bring Captain Light down for some reason, that they were all here to scope out the area in readiness for their day of reckoning. Maybe he'd come back tomorrow to find a hundred costumed villains all tripping over one another as they tried to reach the Beacon of Light. And maybe Hayes would be the only civilian here, like the guy who brought a knife to a gun fight.

As the chill of the afternoon began to bite, Hayes followed the walking tracks to the café located by the open-air Delacort Theater in the park. The café was playing seasonal music and offering mulled wine along with its usual menu. Hayes purchased a bottle of water and found a window seat where he could watch the world go by, and maybe get an inkling of the ongoing preparations for tomorrow's event. The water was ice cold and it made his teeth ache when he drank it, the coolness burning at the sides of his throat when he swallowed.

Hayes headed back home with the commuter rush. The trains were packed anyway this time of year, and he wanted to take

some time just scanning the faces to see if any of the usual
suspects were out – the woman in the headscarf, the man with
gray at his temples, and all the others he had come to recognize
over the months since Melanie had been killed, maybe even that
other Hayes who got hit by his car. He did not see any of them,
but something in the back of his mind told him they were about,
maybe sitting in the next subway car or walking the streets above
his head.

When he got home, Hayes pulled out the wedding album and
took a moment to find a particular picture of Melanie that had
somehow captured something of her that no other photograph
ever had. In the photo, she was laughing as she spoke to an old
friend, but the friend had been cropped in the framing. There was
a glass of sparkling wine in Melanie's hand. Hayes missed her
laughter. He missed it the way he would miss a limb.

37

Saturday.

Hayes was awake at five – wide awake – and out of bed in just a few seconds. He had always been like this in the old days, when the SEALs were going on an op, entering enemy territory, starting something new. It wasn't restlessness, it was just the desire to seize the day and take it for all it was worth. Because if you didn't, the other guy did, and that "other guy" was invariably the guy who was trying to point *his* gun at *your* head.

Hayes put on a pot of coffee, showered and shaved, then drank coffee until he was wired. He had the TV on while he shaved, listening out from the en suite for any indication that the Captain Light ceremony had been cancelled or postponed. It hadn't. Plans were going ahead, and at three PM Mayor Castlebridge would be in attendance to present Captain Light with the key to the city. And Hayes would be there too.

Down in his basement, Hayes made one final check of his arsenal. A final weapons check was not a ten second job, glancing a gun over and putting it back in its holster. For a SEAL, a weapons check was a ritual, one enacted with love. It took ninety minutes to check every knob and canister, test every piece of soldering.

Once he was done, Hayes headed back up to the kitchen, carrying the weapons with him. He sat at the kitchen table and pushed the Glock-19 into its holster at his shoulder, knowing it was the least of the weapons he had for this scenario.

He rolled up his pants to reveal the second holster he wore, this one around his ankle. Retro's gun was already stashed there, bulky enough that he had chosen loose camo pants that would better hide it. The holster included a button-down strap over the handle of the gun, to ensure it couldn't slip free. Hayes had weighed that decision carefully before making it, concluding that if he required faster access than unlatching the button allowed – if things got that tight – he would have needed to be wearing shorts anyway.

He looked over Splatter's gauntlets one last time, flexing his fingers unconsciously as he stared at them and thought about how they functioned and what they could do. He looked over at the refrigerator where he had fired that first blast from the left gauntlet, saw the mark on the metal finish of the door where he had almost missed the door and had had to scrape out adhesive from the seal using a knife after it had dried.

Then came the staff which Hayes had constructed from the extendable shower rail. It featured trigger buttons at both ends and in the center, wired to function interchangeably depending on how and where he gripped the six-foot-long pole. In combat, sometimes you were forced to change your grip, so Hayes considered it wise to be prepared for any eventuality.

A dial was inlaid about a third of the way along the pole, where the join was located which had originally functioned as the release for the section of the pole which could extend. The dial could be used to select the illusion the pole cast, projecting it from one of the two emitters set in the center of its length. The options allowed Hayes to access the array of illusions which Oasis Black had used in her career as a costumed criminal, and were largely adopted from Greek mythology. The dial worked a little like a vending machine, you selected your request using a combination of the buttons rather than having a huge array to push. It would slow him down a little, but it was a toss up between space and variety.

The diode strip which Hayes had concluded sent out a kind of hypnotic or seizure function resided between the two emitters and would come to life every time Hayes triggered the illusion projector. He just had to remember to keep it pointed away from him, and he had added twin strips of rough bobbles close together on one side of the cylinder so that he could tell which way the pole was facing without looking. The bobbles were hard to discern through Splatter's gauntlets, but they would do. It was another trade-off – he needed the gauntlets as much as the rest of the equipment if he was going to stand a chance against Captain Light.

On the other side of the diode strip, a second emitter had been cannibalized from Chime's gloves and could fire off a sonic blast. The triggers for the sonic blast were located next to the ones for illusion projection.

Sitting at the kitchen table, Hayes took out tape and some plastic wrap, along with a mop. He placed the mop beside the staff – it was shorter by about two feet but that wouldn't matter, this was all about appearances, and camouflage only needed to work long enough for your prey to look past you and onto something else. He tied the staff to the mop, so that the mop's shaggy head protruded beyond the length of the weapon. Then he wrapped the two of them in plastic, using the tape to hold everything together with the mop head sticking up out the top like a soldier peering up over a parapet.

There was one last thing Hayes needed. He left the kitchen, taking the staff and mop combo to the front door and leaving it propped there, rested against the shitty job he had done with the wallpaper those many months ago. Then he turned back and went into the lounge, and walked over to the bookshelf. The wedding album waited there.

Hayes took the wedding album in his hands and turned its

pages, looking again at the picture of the two of them together, just married, eyes set on the future that was waiting for them, the future that had been torn away. Then he looked at the picture of Melanie with the glass of sparkling wine, the laughter it had captured and held in a single image, framed on the page forever.

"I miss you," he told the picture. "Now, let's make it right."

It is right, Quo, the picture seemed to tell him. *You just can't see it yet.*

Hayes closed the wedding album and slipped it under his arm. He wanted to show Captain Light the woman he loved, wanted the hero to see what had been lost when he and the Jade Shade had performed yet another act in the costumes' never-ending cabaret, that day on Sixth Avenue, when dropping a helicopter from the sky had just been another part of the show. He wanted Captain Light to see that there were consequences, so that he would tell him why these things happened and no one ever seemed to give a damn so long as the bad guys got caught. He wanted to confront Captain Light with a death that was not an "event", that was not something that a costume would come back from by recharging their powers inside the sun or by some new experimental procedure that could never be repeated because it could only work on other costumes, or by a hundred other get-out clauses that the costumes seemed to keep up their costumed sleeves, be they good guys or bad.

"Mop" in hand, Hayes left the house. It was time to clean things up.

Traffic was light until Hayes hit the Upper East Side. Once he did, he hit diversions that had been put in place for the day, and everything just snarled up. Hayes didn't stress – he was always early. Right now, he was three hours early and the old SEAL rule stood firm: *Slow is smooth, smooth is fast.*

Hayes pulled in at a spot on the street on East 79th, catching it just as someone was pulling away. It was a tow-away zone, outside of a hotel, where cars had to move on after thirty minutes. Hayes didn't even read the sign. If his car got towed today, it wouldn't matter – getting your car towed was low-risk on an op like this.

He was early. He figured he could kill time, but he didn't want to eat. He hadn't wanted to eat before SEAL ops either, not in those few hours before. He'd preferred to let his body run the adrenalin clean, without interruptions clogging up his system. That's how he thought of it.

The temperature was December cool. Hayes pulled the hood of his sweatshirt up as he climbed out of his car, feeling the chill on his bare hands. At least the gauntlets wouldn't look so odd today, with everyone else bundled up for the winter. Hayes could not bundle up too much – he needed the freedom of movement that the hoodie and the camo pants granted, but he had layers underneath to stave off the worst of the cold.

Hayes walked around the jeep and opened the back, where he pulled out the bound staff and mop. There were people on the street, but no one gave him a second thought – he was just some guy with a new mop; that was all he was. Maybe he was a cleaner, or maybe it was a present for his wife, like some Christmas joke thing – who cared when they had their own lives to live?

Hayes headed into Central Park on foot.

Crowds were gathering. Some people had been here all night, camping out and braving the below zero temperatures in little tents with portable gas stoves, like they were waiting for a department store sale or a music festival.

Cameras were all over. The media was excited. Hayes saw the same teenage girl get interviewed three times by different stations in the space of two minutes, watching as she fluttered between them like a butterfly collecting pollen, enjoying her one-hundred-and-twenty seconds of fame.

Some people had brought flags and banners, and there was a roaring trade in T-shirts and buttons by sellers wandering the park, all the while keeping their eyes open for cops who'd move them on.

Hayes saw a shirt that read, "There's no trail of stars, do you see that?" and another that read "Like Thursday." Everybody knew the slogans and knew what they meant. They meant we had lived.

"You want a shirt?" a red-faced guy asked Hayes as he headed up the busy paths towards Turtle Pond. "A button?"

Hayes waved the guy on, glancing at him for just a moment. The guy was overweight and looked permanently harassed, figuring he would make a killing today on illegal T-shirts.

Closer to the Belvedere Castle, time had been spent dressing up the pathways. Here, the grass was held at bay by low iron fences which came up to below the knee, like the grass was an animal that needed to be kept behind bars. The fences had been sprayed with gold for the occasion, and there was bunting stretched across the walkways in the places where paths met, as if attendees were crossing the starting line of a race.

Hayes looked at his wristwatch. It wasn't even one o'clock yet. He had plenty of time.

Hayes stopped in the shadow of the King Jagiello Monument atop its plinth, across the water from Belvedere Castle. The life-size monument depicted the king on his horse. Jagiello had two swords raised as he headed into the Battle of Grunwald in the year 1410. Jagiello had been victorious, driving back the Teutonic Order, and changing the world.

Hayes stood, reading the simple engraving on the pedestal, which only gave the king's name. That granted Hayes a moment to assess the crowds and to check for spooks, to make sure he had not been noticed or followed.

A family walked past, a blond-haired kid of maybe five years old supremely excited to be seeing Captain Light that afternoon, like it was a visit to some department store Santa Claus.

Hayes found a spot by the trees and crouched down, resting his body as he waited for the time to arrive.

By 2pm, the park was really filling up. There was a break in the clouds enough that a few hopeful rays of sunlight had decided to peer through. Crouched beneath the tree, Hayes took that moment to put on the gauntlets which he had stolen from Splatter. He had got used to the triple buckles now, and cinched them tight in a swift, well-practiced move. With his sleeves pulled down over them, the gloves looked like skiing gloves and no one would give them a second thought.

Hayes slipped the backpack back onto his shoulder, and then made his way around the curving paths towards Belvedere, not rushing, just like he was taking a stroll. A security guy stopped him as he approached and asked to see inside the backpack, while his stony-faced partner looked on, saying nothing. Hayes opened the backpack and showed the spook what was inside.

"What is that?" the spook asked. "A photo book?"

"Yeah," Hayes said. He knew it was best to say as little as possible to FBI guys because if you got chatty they figured you were nervous and started poking at that flaw to see if it would crack.

"May I see it?" the agent asked, a question that clearly only had one answer.

Hayes reached into the backpack and drew out the wedding album. "It's just a photo album," Hayes said. "My wife..."

The agent opened it at a couple of pages at random then closed it again. "She with you?" he asked, suspicious.

"Taking a pee," Hayes said. "She just walked right past you on her way to the restroom."

The agent frowned as if trying to recall. "Yeah, I remember her."

"I bet she'll be queuing a quarter hour yet," Hayes said, casual now that he had the agent fooled.

The agent smiled at that, nodding knowingly. "I hear ya," he said. "Women, huh?"

Hayes passed on without further incident, locating a spot down near the side of the folly castle where it overlooked Turtle Pond. From here he could see the temporary stage that had been set out overlooking the water. It was a raised stage with wooden steps and bunting above, along with a banner that said:

NYC thanks Captain Light

Beyond the stage was the large body of water, roughly a city block in size, which meant the stage could only be approached from the side. Not that that mattered to Captain Light, a man who could fly through the air at will.

The location of the stage commanded good views of the water, and hence people were gathered on the far side to watch proceedings.

There were large speakers to each side of the stage, mounted on high poles so that they stood about eight feet above the stage itself, along with two large television screens set to either side. The screens would relay the whole event to the massed crowd, with close ups on the action on stage, like being at a stadium concert.

There was a sense of excitement in the air. It was like the day peace got announced after a long war. People just wanted to believe the world had been fixed for good; forever. Even now, sailors were probably looking for nurses to kiss in perfectly framed black and white stills that would capture the sense of relief everyone felt.

Hayes suspected he was the only person who could see how broken the world had become.

At 3pm, Captain Light descended from the sky, trailed by a swirl of shimmering stars, bright even in the daylight, and the crowd cheered and screamed in adoration.

At 3.01 Hayes would make his move.

38

"…and it gives me great pleasure to present you, our savior, with the key to New York City," Mayor Castlebridge pronounced as he handed an oversized key made of burnished brass to Captain Light on the stage before the Belvedere Castle.

Castlebridge was a tall man with just a little middle-aged paunch which he hid well with good tailoring, but he looked short standing before Captain Light. Up close, Light was a tower of a man, every muscle defined in the skin-tight white costume he wore, the white cape with golden trim swirling around him in the breeze like it was forever captured in a slow-motion film. It added a grace to his movements, even a movement as simple as reaching for the proffered, oversized key while turning his head and smiling for the cameras.

The crowd was wild, cheering and applauding and shouting and whooping. At least two women shouted "Marry me!" loud enough to be heard over the noise of the public address system, and their pleas were followed by a man's voice requesting the same, accompanied by an uncertain ripple of laughter. Then some joker shouted "Nah, marry my sister!" and the crowd laughed even louder.

In that moment – when the press were lined up to take photos for tomorrow's papers, and the film crews were documenting every action for the evening news – the world seemed ideal, a perfect place where only good things happened, where no one ever got hurt and costumed heroes really did marry the kind of ordinary people you went to school with. Hayes envied that moment, letting it wash over him like a wave on the beach. This was how it had been in the SEALs, that one instant before everything cut loose, when for just a moment the world seemed like it could be a joyful place of peace and happy endings. Perhaps the fairy tale castle behind the stage added to that sense for Hayes, making the whole event seem like it had been found inside the pages of a story book, one where the handsome hero had really saved the day, happily ever after, *the end*.

Then, Hayes stepped out of the crowd at the side of the stage, marching downslope towards the steps that led up to the temporary stage itself, tearing the plastic wrap and the mop from the six-foot long staff and clutching it in his left hand.

A security guard, alert to danger, stepped forward to stop Hayes. "Excuse me, sir," said the guard, "you can't–".

Hayes' right hand whipped forward, delivering a punch to the man's throat. The punch was augmented by a knuckle duster made of instantly hardened adhesive, created in that moment when Hayes had stepped out of the crowd and seen the big bruiser spot him and begin to challenge. Bruiser went down, collapsing to his knees and buckling over, hacking – a mournful sound – as he tried to catch his breath. He would live. The blow was designed to bruise his windpipe into spasm, but he would live through it. Hayes wasn't here to kill anyone.

Other security guards were becoming alert, and someone in the crowd behind Hayes shouted something in surprise.

Hayes brought up the staff, holding it horizontal in a two-handed grip and triggering the illusion projector. A hydra sprang to life from thin air, half as tall as the castle behind, with a multitude of swaying and darting snake heads on long, serpentine necks. The security guards, FBI and anyone else who saw that projected image face-on recoiled in fear, like some perverted version of *the Wave* running through everyone standing before Hayes on his route to the stage. Hayes strode through their ranks as they dropped to the ground or turned away in terror, one guard twice the size of Hayes just throwing himself in the icy body of Turtle Pond to get the hell out of there.

Across the water, the crowd realized that something was happening, but they were not yet sure if this was a genuine attack or if it was part of some act staged for their entertainment.

On the raised platform, Mayor Castlebridge and Captain Light were aware that something was occurring just out of their eye line. The Mayor's voice boomed out –

"What the heck is going on over there?"

– and it echoed across the water, carried via the public address system that had been installed for the event, making the whole statement seem surreal.

Captain Light's white costume flashed into view as Hayes rounded towards the steps of the stage. Light was headed for the steps from the other direction, about to come down them as Hayes paced through the ranks of fallen security men who had been caught up in the throes of sheer terror.

"Stay behind me, Mayor," Captain Light instructed, turning momentarily to make sure the mayor was okay, and handing him the oversized key.

Hayes shut down the projector. He did not want Captain Light incapacitated by fear of an imaginary beast. Hayes wanted him to see him, to see the face of the man whose wife had been killed.

A frown crossed Light's handsome features, and he stopped at the top of the short flight of stairs to the stage. "Who are you?" he asked.

"Hayes," Hayes told him, striding through the field of fallen guards and crowd members like the last survivor on the battlefield.

Captain Light did not move, he simply surveyed the scene from his position at the top of the stairs, like a king of old casting his judgment. "You've hurt people," he said. "If you know anything about me, you must know that I can't allow that to continue."

"You don't know what hurt is," Hayes told him. He was ten

feet from the stage steps now, and he set himself there, ready for what would happen next. What would happen is what always happened with the costumes – they fought, using fists and powers and their own bodies as weapons, until one of them fell. It was the same chorus to every single verse that their confrontations had. Only this time, Hayes would make it different. He shrugged the backpack from his shoulder, drawing out the book that waited inside to show to Captain Light.

Light took that moment to jump him – or, more accurately, to fly at him. The hero launched from the stage, taking to the air from a standing start, just rising up like it was the most natural thing in the world for a human being to do, and powering across the space between himself and Hayes, right fist poised ahead of him, like a human rocket.

Hayes had anticipated this. He had watched dozens of clips of Captain Light in action, analyzing how he preferred to start battles, how he engaged his foes. After a vocal warning, Light almost always used physical force in his first attack, a shove or a punch, to presumably gauge the strength of his opponent and thus assess their threat level.

A flying man coming at you followed by a trail of twinkling stars is no mean thing to face. Hayes let go of the album, shifted his weight subtly, and then, as Captain Light made to intercept, he dropped and fired out a sonic burst from the staff's second emitter.

Captain Light was fast. As a rule, he did not miss. But the way Hayes dropped, along with the physical blow of the sonic attack was enough to shift Light's trajectory by a matter of inches. Instead of hitting Hayes he went sailing over his shoulder and, like a man missing the last step on a stairwell, suddenly became what would be described as wrong-footed had he been on his feet instead of in flight. As it was, Captain Light seemed to speed up and roll, turning his tumbling flight around and landing behind Hayes, among the fallen bodies of the security guards.

Hayes turned, bringing the staff around in both hands for the second defense. Captain Light would be wise to him this time, but that did not matter – there was more to winning a fight than simply knowing an opponent's next move, you had to be able to defend against it.

"Put down your weapon, Hayes," Light said as he stood before the waters of Turtle Pond, his white cape whipping around him with a Renaissance painter's flourish. The crowd across the way was excited and fearful, like they were watching a car crash and couldn't turn away.

Captain Light began to stride towards Hayes then, offering no room for discussion, his expression fixed in heroic determination, fists clenched at his sides.

Hayes worked the toggle on the staff again, and sent another sonic blast in the direction of the hero, this time opening the focusing lens to create a wider burst. The blast would drop a lesser foe, but Captain Light simply stood his ground, letting the sonic blast pass over him and looking like a man walking against a strong wind. "I won't ask again," he said, a confident smile crossing his square-jawed face.

But then the smile withered, as Captain Light suddenly became aware of screaming coming from behind him. The sonic blast that Hayes had sent at him was not just for him. It had struck the surface of Turtle Pond and generated a rising wave which was gathering volume and height as it went hurtling across the huge pond towards the crowd of startled onlookers.

This was another thing that Hayes had learned from all those hours of footage he had watched. Captain Light would shift his priorities if other lives – the lives of innocent bystanders, for instance – were in danger. It was what Light should have done when the Jade Shade dropped the helicopter, but he had been too slow, it had been asking too much. That time, Captain Light had been knocked from the air by the thrown helicopter and had gone spinning away like a discarded rag doll while the chopper continued its deadly descent. This time, Captain Light was immediately in the air – again, a maneuver that, up close, amazed Hayes at how effortless it was. Light sped across the surface of the pond in what looked like one high leap, outpacing the rising wave and turning his head back, mid-flight, to unleash one of his incredible spectral screams.

From this close, the sound of the spectral scream was eerie, an ululation that sounded like a siren call. Hayes watched as the swirling line of the scream burst from Captain Light's open mouth like a laser light of liquid gold with swirling, colorful depths, before striking the base of the wave with a sound like breaking glass. The wave lost integrity in an instant, like a runner whose legs had been cut out from under them, and where it had roared across the pond a moment before, suddenly it was collapsing in on itself. The leading edge of the wave became nothing more than two-inch high ripples that bumped across the water like a kid rolling pastry flatter and flatter, before sloshing up uselessly at the sides, their fury spent.

A cheer rose from the crowd again, while Captain Light pivoted in mid air, the stream of stars that followed in his wake swirling in place like glitter dropped into stirred water.

There was no way to stop a guy who could fly, Hayes realized. But even as he thought that, another thought occurred to him. It was the kind of wild idea that only a maniac – or a Navy SEAL who knew that the way to win a battle was to control all the terrain – would dare to try.

"I think it's time you were taught a lesson, Hayes," Captain Light announced, in a voice that somehow made the words seem reasonable – *"no fighting in the park!"*

"That's good," Hayes told him as Captain Light prepared to launch at him again, "because I'm here to learn – "

Hayes leaned down and flicked the trigger of Retro's gun where it was still holstered at his ankle.

" – and I have a lot of questions!" Hayes finished as the holstered gun blasted a burst of pressurized air and an *Eeeee-owwwww* of Hendrix guitar lick. The effect sent Hayes up off the ground and into the air. An instant later, Hayes collided with a very surprised Captain Light a few feet from the Belvedere Castle shore of Turtle Pond, knocking the hero hard in the flank.

Captain Light was suddenly spinning, no longer in control of his flight path. He went crashing down to earth in the dirt by the stage, in the shadow of the fairy tale castle's turret.

Hayes was less fortunate. His inspired action had knocked Captain Light from his path, but it sent the ex-SEAL hurtling in an uncontrollable trajectory that ended when he struck the surface of Turtle Pond somewhere close to the east shore. The water was shallow, but it was cold – like being thrown inside the freezer compartment of a refrigerator. In the SEALs they used to call temperatures like this "toasty warm", which was a sarcastic way of saying you could live through them and so not to complain.

The holster containing Retro's gun had ripped away with the force of the air blast, taking the gun with it and sending both items plunging into the water. Hayes figured Jonas Culper could pay a diver to find it.

Close by, bystanders at the shore were reacting in different ways. A lot were backing away, generating as much space between themselves and Hayes as they could, like he was one of those crazy, costumed villains Captain Light usually fought. Others stood right up to the railing or just a little way back, aiming camera phones at him, trying to capture the fight for posterity or ViewTube hits. Three guys jumped the railing and came charging towards Hayes, the lead one sloshing into the cold water without a thought. They were big guys, well fed on New York cuisine, and they looked mad as hell.

"Some kinda wise guy, huh?" the lead figure shouted as he waded towards Hayes. His face was red as a tail-light with the flush of anger. "Think you can beat up on our hero?!"

Hayes casually sent a blast of adhesive from his left gauntlet, striking the man full in the chest. The guy dropped back from the impact, collapsing into the water with a splash as the expanding adhesive blob hardened across his chest and face.

The two men behind him slowed their advance just subtly, wary of what they were – literally – wading into now. Hayes tapped a code on the studs of the staff and directed the emitter at the two men and the crowd behind them, casting an illusion of a Charybdis rearing out of the usually placid waters of Turtle Pond. A Charybdis was a ferocious sea creature from Greek Mythology that looked kind of like a worm with a mouth full of dagger-like teeth. The stories had it that it used to swallow up whole ships by creating whirlpools. Hayes' would-be opponents went stumbling back as panic took hold, like sinking ships.

The wedding album! Hayes thought. *Where was the wedding album?* He had dropped it at the start of the fight. It was sitting there on the ground, ten feet away from the side of the stage, close to where Captain Light was picking himself up from his crash landing.

"You have to see," Hayes murmured as he waded out through the water, his eyes fixed on Captain Light.

Turtle Pond was not deep, but there was water, and water was a SEAL's element. As Captain Light looked around, trying to locate Hayes, the ex-SEAL ducked down under the surface, so slick and so sudden that he barely left a ripple.

Then, remaining beneath the surface, Hayes began to swim, moving like a torpedo through the frigid water, a single breath and a movement of his feet enough to power him across its expanse unseen. This was basic training, *BUD/S Week Two* stuff. This was what SEALs did to get warmed up.

On the far side of the pond, Captain Light was looking bewildered. Moments ago, he had been fighting the man in the hood with the weapons staff, the man who called himself Hayes, but now Hayes had disappeared. Did he have some way to turn invisible? Was it a cloaking device, stealth tech? Something otherworldly? Captain Light had faced enemies with all of those ways to make themselves unseen, and he had defeated every last one of them by listening for their breathing or by using rainwater to trace their outline, or by simply creating a cordon with his spectral scream so that they could not approach. But he had lost track of Hayes, lost him for just a few seconds, unsure of where he had landed after they had clashed in mid-air.

Or maybe he wasn't invisible. Maybe Hayes had taken to the skies the same way he had come flying at Captain Light thirty seconds earlier, yet another ability revealed in his arsenal. Or maybe he could teleport.

"Who is he? Who is this... *Hayes*?" Captain Light pondered aloud.

Without warning, the surface of the water broke and Hayes came sprinting out towards Captain Light, his face hidden by the hood, just the gleam in his eyes the only hint of humanity within.

"I'm going to show you what you did," Hayes snarled, swinging the staff like a bat, "and you're going to tell me why!"

Captain Light leapt, one of his famous leap-to-flight take-offs, vaulting over the reach of the swinging staff and hovering in place eight feet above the ground.

But Hayes was fast and prepared. He raised his other hand and blasted, a jagged line materializing from his gauntlet as sharp as a stalactite, lancing out towards Captain Light's square jaw.

Light blocked the lance, knocking it aside with a sweep of his hand. At the same moment, Hayes switched off the electromagnetic current in Splatter's gauntlet and the lance lost integrity and disintegrated, showering Captain Light with flaking adhesive like a snowfall as it turned to dust. For an instant, Captain Light was blinded.

Hayes took that moment to scramble and reach for the wedding album, grabbing it up in his free hand. He opened the album to show to Captain Light hovering above him, where he was brushing away the snowfall-like remains of the flaking adhesive.

"Look!" Hayes snarled. "She's dead because of all of this! Because of what you do!"

Captain Light looked down on the ground and saw the hooded man amidst the carnage he had wrought, the fallen figures of security men and sound check guys and the people of the press; and all the innocent people around the pond who had been caught up in this unexpected attack. Captain Light drew a breath and prepared to fire off a spectral scream that would knock his foe flat on his back.

Hayes had studied footage of Captain Light. Hayes recognized the way the hero drew that breath, and he triggered the sonic emitter on his staff, having theorized it could possibly counter the sound wave, disrupting it just enough for a man to survive.

"Tell me why!" Hayes demanded as he flicked on the sonic emitter. "Tell me what it's all for!"

Captain Light was surprised to find his spectral scream blunted by the sonic attack as sound wave countered sound wave. Blunted, yes, but not completely blocked. He needed to up his game, channel more power into the scream, enough to send his foe somewhere he could do no further harm. The rest could come after that, once Captain Light had figured out a way to stop this madman.

"I have to know why!" Hayes demanded as he held the wedding album out before him like a wanted poster, an accusation to his wife's killer. "Who's behind it all?"

Captain Light unleashed his most powerful spectral scream, the type he had used to stop that spaceship crashing into Manhattan, the type he had used to dispatch Morgana Le Fey back to her home dimension. The scream was a golden streak in the air but it was tinged with all the colors of the spectrum in a furious blaze of dazzling light.

"Who?!" Hayes said again as the spectral scream struck, blasting into the wedding album he held up before him. The spectral scream hit full power at the same time as Hayes demanded his answer. "Show me!"

Inside the album, perhaps forgotten, was the one last prop that Hayes had taken from a costume. It was a single, singed page from the spell book of Morgana Le Fey, snatched from the air by Hayes when he had witnessed her defeat in Sheep Meadow months before. The words he had never translated.

And the spell was a wish.

And the wish

        came

           true.

PART 5
Vanishing Point

39

"You okay, dude?"

The voice came from off to Hayes' left, just over his shoulder. He was on his hands and knees on a wooden floor that smelled of polish, and his head was spinning.

"Um... dude?" That voice again, more insistent this time, and sounding worried.

Hayes turned his head, momentarily dazzled by bright lights. He was on the floor next to an unadorned table. It was one of a line of similar tables that had been arranged together, each one just a little narrower than an office desk, kind of like a school desk. There was a man standing over him, a kid really, a teenager with a mop of lank, greasy hair, and the kind of mustache that you grew when you were seventeen. He peered through his glasses at Hayes, with a look of consternation.

"What?" Hayes asked, confused.

"I think you fell over, dude," the mustached kid said, offering Hayes his hand. He wore a T-shirt with a figure printed on the front, and carried a plastic bag with a red logo on it.

Hayes waved the kid's hand away, and used the table to get to his feet. "Thanks."

"No problem," the kid said. "They said Langdon's back in thirty minutes."

Hayes had no idea who or what Langdon was, so he just nodded, but his head throbbed with the movement.

The kid walked away, and Hayes looked around him properly for the first time. His vision was flickering like an old-fashioned movie projector, the rods and cones firing over and over like he had just looked into a camera flash. He closed his eyes tight for the count of three and tried again, opening them tentatively. His vision seemed restricted, the edges fuzzy, but he could see.

He was in a large hall, kind of like a sports hall, except there were lines of desks and colorful displays everywhere, the ceiling going way up to maybe three or four stories above him. The desk he had fallen beside was at the end of a line of similar desks, some with people sitting at them talking amongst themselves or to other people who were queuing on the far side of the desks, like they were here to buy tickets or food or something. A few people were at their desks eating – sandwiches, sushi and snacks.

Hayes spotted a leather folder propped behind the table where he had fallen, roughly a foot across by a foot-and-a-half. The zipper was open, and so Hayes made to peer inside.

"Hey!" a man's voice called from a couple of desks along. "Hey, leave that."

A rotund man with receding hair and glasses got up from his seat, where he had been eating a sub. "You're not allowed back here, you know!" he said, trying to look fierce. The impression was somewhat ruined by the T-shirt he wore – a stylized illustration of Damocles that had become grossly broadened by the force of his gut against the material.

"Nice shirt," Hayes said as he stepped out from the behind the desk, backing away.

Where the hell was he? A minute ago, he had been on the receiving end of Captain Light's spectral scream while he fired off a counter-wave from the sonic emitter. Now, somehow, he was at some kind of… *show*, he guessed you would call it, and Captain Light was nowhere to be seen.

Conscious that Damocles-gut was watching him, Hayes ran his gaze swiftly over the desk where he had first appeared. It was wipe-down white and there was a little folded paper construction to the side which had been made into a kind of long pyramid on which was written a name – *Manny Langdon*. The name meant nothing to Hayes.

Behind the desk was a temporary partition wall, and Langdon's name was written there too on a printed sheet of paper. That was all there was.

Confused, Hayes turned and almost walked into the back of the Swan.

"Hey!" She turned around, and Hayes saw that she was African American, and that her trademark white hair was a wig, and not even a particularly convincing one.

"Sorry, I didn't see you," Hayes apologized.

"Look but don't touch, yeah?" the "Swan" told him before hurrying away on heels that were way higher than she could comfortably walk in. Her costume showed a lot of skin, more than Hayes wanted to see; maybe more than anyone wanted to see. It was almost like she was a parody.

Hayes peered around, still trying to get his bearings. He was at a kind of intersection, where four aisles of desks met. Across the way, a stall had set up with lines of boxes in front and a wall of magazines behind. The covers of the magazines were interchangeable, characterized by illustrations of costumes doing incredible acts.

Hayes approached, looking at the back wall, recognizing some of the individuals there.

"Fifteen percent discount on the latest issues 'til Sunday," the stallholder said, catching Hayes' eye. He had a tattooed sleeve and his beard looked like a bird could have nested in it.

"What?" Hayes asked.

Bird's-nest-beard indicated a space between the rows of boxes, where magazines had been laid out in piles so that their covers faced towards the ceiling. "Fifteen percent off, convention special," he said, as if the coded words somehow made sense.

Hayes looked at the magazines laid out on the table, his eyes still straining, his head throbbing. There was not a single title he recognized, and what's more they were smaller than the kind of magazines he was used to. But the names were familiar – really familiar. One magazine purported to be devoted to Damocles, others to the Rangers and Eternal Flame and several other costumes. Some he had not heard of.

As his aching eyes scanned over the covers, one in particular caught his attention. It looked to be a souvenir magazine dedicated to the *Key to the City Ceremony* which Hayes had just come from. The magazine was entitled *Captain Light* and its illustrated cover showed an unsettlingly familiar scene – Captain Light and a hooded figure were clashing in mid-air over Turtle Pond, with Belvedere Castle framed in the background. Hayes picked the magazine up, looking more closely, suspecting that the illustration style meant it was some kind of satire.

There were words on the cover in a kind of jagged circle, all in uppercase and reading: *"The key to... death!"*

Hayes opened the magazine. There was an advertisement for a movie he had never heard of on the first page. Opposite the advert was an illustration showing Captain Light descending from the sky to where Mayor Castlebridge waited on the podium at the beginning of the *Key to the City Ceremony* – the same ceremony which Hayes had just come from. Hayes turned the page, saw that the ceremony had been rendered in comic strip form, brilliant colors and poses making the whole event seem dynamic and exciting. It was a comic book, he realized, a pamphlet made up of thirty-or-so pages. Hayes turned those pages quickly, and then –

A sinking feeling gripped Hayes' stomach when he saw the hooded figure on the page, emerging from the crowds at the back of the stage and knocking aside the security men who challenged him. The figure carried a staff, and his face was hidden behind the folds of a dark hooded top. It was Hayes.

"$3.39 with convention discount," Bird's-nest-beard said cheerily, leaning forward to upside-down read the page Hayes was looking at.

Hayes looked up from the magazine, confused.

"Plus tax," the stallholder said as if answering his unspoken question.

Hayes reached for his wallet in a kind of daze, handing over a five-dollar bill. The stallholder produced change, took the souvenir magazine from Hayes' hands and slipped it into a brown paper bag, then handed the bag to Hayes. "Have a good one," he said, before turning away to deal with two kids who were standing to Hayes' left.

"Thanks," Hayes said, wandering away from the stall.

Hayes staggered through the convention center, feeling numb. Everything seemed busy but muted, like there was too much going on for his senses to process. He felt exhausted, as though he hadn't slept in a week. He felt too warm, too. He was dressed for December in Central Park and now he was indoors, and his head was pounding. He pushed back his hood, running a hand through his damp hair.

Finding a table at the cafeteria, Hayes slumped down with a cup of coffee served in a paper cup on which was printed the smiling face of Eternal Flame and a circular logo that read: *Comic Daze Book Convention*.

At the table, Hayes noticed for the first time the way that his pants leg was ripped. *Must have happened when Retro's gun tore away*, he realized. He tucked the torn cuff into his boot and took a taste of the coffee. Splatter's gloves were gone too, he realized now, red marks on the skin around his wrists where they had been – *what?* – torn away? He rubbed at the marks idly, feeling nauseous. He figured the coffee would settle his gut.

As he drank, Hayes drew the *Captain Light* magazine out from the paper bag, returning to the moment where the hooded character – *his* character – appeared.

On page, Captain Light stood before Mayor Castlebridge on the stage, a look of heroic determination on his face. A speech balloon from his mouth exclaimed: "Stay behind me, Mayor."

It was clear that the illustrator was a talented draftsman. His choice of angles and the way he showed Belvedere Castle and its surroundings was both accurate and had the effect of enticing you into the retelling.

In the next image, Captain Light was standing on the steps to the stage, as the hooded figure of Hayes strode towards him with his back to the reader. "Who are you?" Light was asking. He looked heroic, his cape catching on the wind with a Renaissance painter's flourish – it was familiar and yet it seemed exciting and brilliant on the page.

The next shot showed the hooded figure mid-stride amidst the field of fallen guards and crowd members, like the last survivor on the battlefield. "Haze," came the hooded figure's response.

"Haze...?" Hayes whispered, incredulous. The name made sense, on page. His character's face was hidden by the hood, and what could be seen was just a shadowy blur – *a haze*.

Hayes read on, working through the familiar scenes as the story played out on page. The two figures challenged one another, familiar words rendered in bold uppercase letters in white balloons. They fought, clashing in mid-air until Hayes – or Haze, as he was on page – utilized the image projector in his staff to create the Charybdis and drive back any crowd members who tried to take him on. There was no mention of where his weapons had come from – on the page, the staff he used appeared to be some bespoke weapon, like any other that the costumes used, and the air blast from Retro's gun in his ankle holster was used with no reference to Retro, as if it was a weapon from this Haze character's arsenal.

In fact, from what Hayes could see, the Haze character had no back story. He was even described as "a mysterious new foe" in one of the Mayor's speech balloons. Hayes ran a hand over his head, trying to make sense of it all. Somehow whoever was telling the story had got it all wrong – he wasn't the bad guy, he had only gone to ask Captain Light why his wife had died, and what was behind the whole world of costumed fights.

The final pages of the story showed Hayes emerge from the

water of Turtle Pond and raise the wedding album – which looked like a blank book in the illustration – as he demanded answers from Captain Light.

"I have to know why!" the Haze demanded on page. "Who's behind it all?"

It was unclear why this Haze was asking the question. It could have been that he wanted to know who had organized the ceremony to celebrate Captain Light's victory, as if he was some PTSD vet jealous of the recognition this costumed hero was getting. Without context, the "she" he had referred to could have been America, or his mother, or the Virgin Mary.

Hayes turned the pages and saw Captain Light unleash that spectral scream of his in a whirl of colors, building in strength over a series of impressive images.

"Who?!" Haze said in a double page spread as the wedding album along with his whole body was bathed in brilliant light. "Show me!"

Page turn, another sequence of images. Now, a window in the fabric of space was opening around Haze, in the same way Hayes had seen such a window open to ensnare Morgana Le Fey. Hayes read on, dumbfounded, as the "him" on the page – the man in the hood with the hidden face – was yanked into the dimensional window and disappeared, leaving behind only the weapons staff and the ashes of the book he had been holding which had burst into flames.

"He's no danger to anyone now," Captain Light assured the mayor, who was cowering among his security guards on the far side of the stage.

Mayor Castlebridge looked reassured. "Where did he go?" his speech balloon asked.

"I've sent him away," Captain Light replied. "A long, long way from here. Somewhere he won't hurt anyone." As Light spoke these last words, the illustrator had chosen to focus on the weapons staff and the smoking remains of the album that lay in the dirt by Turtle Pond where the dimensional portal had now sealed to nothingness. The juxtaposition of the words and the image lent the scene poignancy, as if all that the man called Haze really was was the bitterness he had left behind.

That was it. There was no indication of where this Haze guy had been sent, the portal had been opened and he had disappeared, after which it had sealed shut.

A caption across the bottom of the page read: "Next month: Danger is... Dagger Dark!"

Hayes turned back to the cover, trying to make sense of it all. There was a circle in the upper left corner, he noticed now, a stylized letter "*O*", around which were the words "*Oblivion Comics*". Beside this was a number and a date. The number was 171 and the date was May.

Turning back to the first page, Hayes noticed there was a list of names there of the people who had written and illustrated the magazine, along with a line in tiny, typed print at the bottom of the page that stated that this was issue 171 and that it was a work of fiction.

Fiction.

His life. Every event at that Key Ceremony, maybe every event leading up to it. All of it just fiction...?

40

Hayes drank his coffee, and spent a few minutes quietly watching the Comic Daze convention people walk past as he let everything sink in. There were plenty of teens and kids, but it was mostly older men. A proportion of people had dressed in homemade costumes of their favorite characters, and some of them looked just like the real thing. Hayes spotted another Swan, two Captain Lights, and a whole gaggle of Rangers who came into the cafeteria for smoothies together. There were bad guys too, a couple of Doctor Answers who had simply put on a suit and carried a tablet computer with a sticker on the back, an impressive Morgana Le Fey with full headdress and a push-up bra doing some heavy lifting, and even a would-be Professor Freakside in full gorilla costume. When he passed, Freakside smelled noticeably of sweat. Hayes almost jumped from his seat when he spotted Retro coming directly toward him, only for the man to veer off at the last minute and reveal a ponytail that the real Retro had never sported. *The real Retro?* Hayes wondered if that even meant anything.

It seemed that almost everyone who wasn't in costume – and that accounted for the vast majority of the attendees – had come wearing T-shirts showing one of the costumes in action, often accompanied by a logo of the character's name or a catchphrase.

Hayes realized something as he watched all those people in their T-shirts and home-made costumes – that each of the costumes, the *real* costumes, was somebody's favorite, even the costumes which Hayes thought of as bad guys. Probably even the Jade Shade.

What the hell had he walked into?

Hayes looked at the opening page of the comic book again and recognized one of the names there. The artist was called Manny Langdon – presumably the same Manny Langdon whose table Hayes had disrupted when he had found himself on the convention center floor after Light's scream had enveloped him. If he could find this Langdon guy, he figured he might have a shot at making sense of everything else.

As he thought about "having a shot", Hayes remembered something. He had dropped the weapons staff and the wedding album, but the comic had not shown his Glock. He could feel its weight under his left armpit, where it resided in the shoulder rig. But he could not check it here, he was too exposed.

Hayes rose from his seat and headed for the nearest rest rooms, staggering a little, unsteady on his feet.

Hayes found a vacant stall and locked himself inside. Once he had, he closed the lid of the toilet and sat down, just taking a few seconds to calm his breathing. His head was whirling and he felt panicky, like those early days of BUD/S training when he was being starved of oxygen during a dive. He needed to calm down.

Fiction. His whole life was fiction.

Hayes unzipped his hoodie and pulled the Glock-19 from its holster, turning it over professionally in his hands. It was still loaded with its full compliment of fifteen shots.

Let's hope the bullets are real, he thought grimly as he slipped the Glock back into its holster.

Hayes exited the rest room and made his way across the convention hall floor. This time he took more notice of his surroundings, conscious that he was staring sometimes where his vision was still troubling him. He had no peripheral vision, that had completely gone. He just had to stay aware. It was like everything was in low light, the colors muted and dull. Like he'd stared into the sun for too long, and now nothing looked bright.

The costume people attracted the eye, but there were a lot more normal folks around, adolescents and adults carrying the same convention bags stuffed with comic books and paraphernalia.

There were a vast number of stalls selling the same basic wares as Bird's-nest-beard guy, comics displayed on their back walls as well as on tables and upright in boxes. Most of the stalls also had comics that looked to be thicker and with more pages, more like books, and some of these were hardcovers with high price tags. Some stalls also sold toys in glossy packaging, and statuettes of characters whom Hayes recognized from news reports, replicated in twelve-inch high miniature, often standing on what looked like the tumbling remains of a wall or chimney. There were other things too, names he did not recognize, whole super teams he had never heard of. It was like there was another world of costumes out there that Hayes had no prior knowledge of.

Hayes got his bearings and found his way back to Langdon's stall, the place where he had first... *"arrived"*, he guessed you would say. The desk was empty, but a sign had been taped to the surface that read "Signing at 4pm" along with a sketch of Captain Light in silhouette rendered in marker pen. Hayes checked his watch, but suspected that what it read might not be right anymore because of how he had come to be here.

There was a queue waiting at the desk beside Langdon's, where a woman with dyed red hair and square framed glasses was drawing a pencil sketch while a girl engaged her in conversation.

"Hey," Hayes said, butting in. "You have the time?" He tapped at his wristwatch.

"Hmm?" the woman with the glasses replied, slightly put out. "It's five to two." She went back to her sketch.

"You know where this... where Manny Langdon is?" Hayes

asked, trying not to sound anxious. You didn't spook civilians, not in the SEALs.

Glasses woman looked up again, while the girl crossed her arms and glared at Hayes. "Con Suite Two," the woman said with the sharp edge of impatience in her tone. "He's on the panel there."

"Thanks," Hayes said. "Sorry if I disturbed you." He wasn't sorry, he just did not want to draw any more attention to himself by being labeled a jerk.

It took Hayes a few minutes to find Convention Suite Two. When he got there, it was marked by a pair of bland double doors in a broad corridor. The corridor was populated by a half dozen convention goers sitting on the floor comparing their hauls of comic books.

There was a laminated schedule tacked to the left-hand door. Hayes scanned it, trying to get an idea of what was happening inside. He found he was leaning against the door for balance. His head was nagging with a headache like sleep deprivation, and the words swam in front of his eyes until he put his hand more firmly against the door. For 2pm the topic of discussion was "Into Oblivion" followed by a list of five names including Manny Langdon.

A minute late, Hayes opened the door a crack and peered within. Inside was an auditorium in low-light with a stage at the front which was lit more brightly, and a projection screen behind. On stage were six chairs – all of them occupied – and a low table to one end. The low table had a pitcher of water and some upturned glasses. A man to the far left was talking into a handheld microphone. He was dressed in a suit jacket over a T-shirt and jeans, and was introducing the other people to the audience.

"... Philip Perks, writer on *The Rangers* and *Captain Light*."

A man with a shaven head and glasses gave a self-conscious wave to a ripple of applause from the audience. He wore a checkered shirt, jeans and baseball boots.

"Next to him," the compère continued, "is his partner in crime on *Captain Light*, artist Manny Langdon."

More applause, as Langdon – a young guy with long hair and sideburns and clothes out of the seventies muttered a "Hey" into the radio mic that was attached to his *Keep on Truckin'* T-shirt.

"And finally, editor Mags Crewe."

A woman at the near end of the group punched the air with a loud "Yeah!" She wore a polka dot dress and an apron out of the fifties, like she'd just come off the set of *I Love Lucy*. Hayes figured she'd say she was wearing it ironically, whatever that meant.

"Our panel," the compère concluded.

As the audience cheered, Hayes slipped into the auditorium and found himself an end seat a couple of rows back from the stage. He wished he had night vision goggles as he went to the seat, the lighting was so low that he nearly tripped on a step up before finally taking it.

What followed was a discussion between the people on stage – who also included a young Asian woman wearing a *Star Wars* T-shirt and cat ears on a hair band, and an older man dressed like a history professor – concerning something called "the Obliverse" and what would be happening there over the next twelve months. It took Hayes a couple of minutes to make sense of the conversation – not just the topics but the way in which the panelists discussed them, which seemed to be casual and frequently mocking, like they were having a joke with the audience.

During those first minutes, Hayes recognized a few names – the Hunter, Eternal Flame, Skimstone – and gradually pieced together what the people on stage were talking about. It seemed that the Obliverse was a fictional universe that derived its name from the *Oblivion Comics* company – the same company whose logo was on the front of the *Captain Light* comic book which Hayes had purchased – and that it encompassed the adventures of a whole host of characters who were familiar to Hayes from news reports. Although all of these characters functioned in the same world, it gradually became evident to Hayes that their individual stories were the creation of many hands – different writers and artists and editors – meaning that the person who wrote stories concerning Captain Light was a different person to the one writing about the Hunter, for instance. In fact, Hunter's stories were being penned by the history professor-looking guy on stage, and he seemed very prickly about involving "his" character in anyone else's stories.

"Hunter's an individual," the professor-type stated in a Southern drawl. "He doesn't belong on anyone's team, because his methods are too extreme. He doesn't play nice."

"Yeah, well maybe the Rangers don't want him!" – that was Philip Perks, the writer of both *The Rangers* and *Captain Light*, and he elicited a good laugh from the audience as he said this.

Hayes listened to the discussion, with the unsettling sense that he was hearing about future events that were really going to happen. For him these stories were real, but for the people here they were something else: entertainment.

After twenty-five minutes, the compère opened the discussion up to questions from the audience. A few hands went up and a guy in his thirties with hair like a brush asked the first question:

"Manny, are you ever going to bring back the Swan?"

On stage, Manny Langdon made a waving gesture and shook his head. "I swear I'm asked this at every con," he said wearily. "I only drew the last two issues, that final beat down with the Prime... Intellect...? Intelligence. Prime Intelligence."

At this point, the lady who had been introduced as Mags Crewe spoke up. "The reality is that the sales figures on *The Swan* were not so great. Everyone at Oblivion Comics loves the character, but she never really caught on, so after eighteen months the decision was made to ax her series."

To ax her series...? Hayes heard the words and realized that they were talking about the Swan's disappearance in his world, the way she had fought bad guys for a while then dropped out of the public eye. People thought she'd quietly retired.

"However," Mags continued, "we're looking at reviving her in a mini series early next year. It will be four issues, and Kelly here is going to be drawing it once she's done with the *Ghost Bot* special."

The Asian woman at the other end of the stage nodded and said something about redesigning the costume for a modern audience.

There were other audience questions, most of them about things Hayes could barely make sense of. Then a skater girl with a nose ring just a couple of seats along from Hayes asked a question that hit Hayes like a punch to the gut:

"Where is Jade Shade and will we be seeing her again any time soon?"

On stage, Perks and Langdon did a little back and forth about who was going to answer. Perks got nominated.

"Jade Shade will be breaking out of prison for the multi-villain story – *The Trial* – that runs through the title next summer," Perks explained with a flippancy that alarmed Hayes. "We'll see her create all kinds of havoc for Steve Lowe and the people he loves now that she knows the Captain's secret identity. It's going to be a lot of fun!

"As for where she is right now," Perks continued, turning to Langdon, "Manny?"

"She's in prison. I'm still working out the ideas for her holding cell on Riker's," Langdon said. "It's going to look super-cool when you see it on the page."

The cell wasn't drawn yet, Hayes realized. The blank cell, where he had gone to visit the Jade Shade on Riker's Island – it was blank because it hadn't been drawn yet, the design had not been finalized. The realization made Hayes want to be sick.

"There's just time for one more question from the audience," the compère said eventually. Hayes found his hand rising, and the compère seemed to zero in on him like a laser sight. "Yes, you, sir, in the third row. Your question?"

"I was wondering," Hayes began slowly, "who the people are in the crowds. The ones who witness these… fights."

"Extras," the professor guy said.

"Yeah," Kelly said. "They're just bystanders. You have these big events going on, you know, alien invasions and bank vaults getting stolen by helicopter and, well, I figure there's people that would watch that. I'd watch that if it was happening down my street!"

"I just draw these shocked faces," Langdon added. "Phil is always asking for more emotion, more drama. I'm like – *dude, seriously, I can only draw so many different people in a crowd.*"

Faces in a crowd, Hayes realized. That's all they were. That's all that Melanie was, and all that Ginnie was. And all that *he* was.

On stage, the compère thanked Hayes for his question and began wrapping things up, thanking the panel and everyone for attending. Hayes watched Langdon and the others for a few moments, trying to make everything fit in his head. Then he got up and headed for the exit with the other attendees.

They were normal people, these writers and artists who came up with these stories about the costumes. Minor celebrities maybe, at least here in this convention hall where everyone came to get their signatures and their sketches and hear or read their words of wisdom. But they didn't look like celebrities, the way Hayes understood the term, they weren't polished and plucked and airbrushed – they were just the same kind of people who worked the stalls out there, the same kind of people who worked the hot dog stand and the souvenir stands outside the Museum of Modern Art. Nobodies, like the shocked faces in the crowds that Manny Langdon drew in his comic book pages.

Hayes stopped at another interchangeable stall selling comic books, studying the selection on show. There had to be close to a hundred different titles, with some characters appearing multiple times in different iterations. Hayes saw one title where Damocles worked solo, and another where he combined forces with a rotating cast of characters including the Mechanist and Missing Link, a different partner on each cover. Those characters had their own books too, as well as appearing together in a comic book called *The Rangers*, presumably the book Phil Perks wrote.

Hayes flicked through several titles, recognizing parts of

New York, and the vibrantly costumed characters who made mayhem in its streets. Then he spotted a title with a familiar image on its cover – it showed Eternal Flame struggling against Dread-0 in the neon canyons of Times Square, just like that time months ago when Hayes had lost his Glock. The comic was about six times the volume of the regular titles and was priced higher. "What is this?" he asked the stallholder, a cutesy blonde with a bored look and fifteen ear studs.

"Trade edition," the blonde said with eyes half asleep.

Hayes turned the book over in his hand. "What does that mean?"

The blonde looked at Hayes like he had beamed down from another planet, then pointed to some blurb on the back cover. Unlike the other comics Hayes had looked at, this one did not feature an advertisement on the back but rather a bold image of Eternal Flame alongside some text. "It collects issues 106 to 111," the blonde said. "We have the new collection, too…" she reached across the counter and picked up another *Eternal Flame* book of the same dimensions, but with a different image on the cover. She turned the book over and ran her eyes swiftly over the text there. "This one's 112 to 117."

"When you say it collects them…?" Hayes said, making it a question.

"Reprints," the blonde told him. "I'm with you, man, I just download everything, y'know? But some people like the physical editions."

Hayes took the other book from the stallholder. "This brings me up to date?" he asked.

"Pretty much," the blonde said. "They're on 119 now, so these are a couple of issues behind. I think the next collection is out in June or something."

Hayes fished out his wallet and asked how much the books were before purchasing them both. Before he left the stall, another question occurred to him which he voiced in a way he hoped sounded knowledgeable. "Do you have any *Swan* comics?"

Blondie laughed. "The Swan? Seriously? That comic was dreck!"

"I heard it got cancelled," Hayes said.

"Yeah, like four years ago or something," the stallholder said, chuckling. "Don't tell me you actually liked it."

"Well, no," Hayes said. "I thought I saw her once, but it wasn't me."

The blonde looked at Hayes with confusion. "Wasn't... what?"

"Doesn't matter," Hayes said. "So, four years ago you said, since it got canned."

"Something like that. Maybe five."

"Thanks."

Hayes walked away from the stall, wondering about the Swan. The news footage he had found of himself and Melanie and Ginnie watching her in the aftermath of that fight in the Bronx had come from about fourteen months before he had first found it, almost two years now. But the comic had been cancelled *four or five* years ago, according to the blonde at the stall, which meant there had to be something screwy with how time worked in this world in relation to the stories. That made no sense.

Unsure of where else to go, Hayes returned to the cafeteria in the convention center. On the way, he spotted a curtained area which promised "Cosplay Repairs". Hayes did not know what "Cosplay Repairs" meant, but as he passed, he could see people in home-made outfits having cloaks and gauntlets sewn up where a seam had come loose. He figured it was some kind of tailoring service, and wandered into the marked-out area.

"Hi. Can I help you?" a bright-eyed man in his twenties asked Hayes. The man was skinny and pale, and he wore a skin-tight black top and drainpipe pants that only emphasized his slender frame. His hair was black as a crow's feathers.

Hayes pointed to the torn leg of his pants. "My leg got caught," he said vaguely.

Skinny tilted his head apologetically. "You're not really in costume," he began, then smiled," but it's quiet, so I can patch it up, I guess."

"Just give me a needle and thread and I'll do it," Hayes told him. You learnt a lot of survival techniques in the SEALs, and they weren't all holding your breath while planting a charge underwater.

Skinny found Hayes a needle strong enough to pierce the material of his camo pants, and threaded it with dark thread that matched the pants. Hayes took a seat in the Repairs area and, still wearing the pants, began to work on the torn leg, with his foot resting on his knee.

"Pick up anything good?" Skinny asked, indicating the bag of comics on the vacant seat beside Hayes.

Hayes focused on his repair. "Comics," he said, dismissively.

Skinny smiled. "You a collector? I love the alternative titles. *Wet Blanket* is just awesome!"

The words triggered a memory in Hayes, and he looked up at Skinny as the guy extolled the virtues of this Wet Blanket's adventures in great detail. He had never heard of Wet Blanket, and the stories sounded dour and ordinary, nothing like what the costumes did.

"Do you know a guy called Jonas Culper?" Hayes asked, interrupting his chatty companion.

"Jonas...?" Skinny shook his head. "I don't think so. Does he draw?"

"He's a collector," Hayes stated.

Skinny laughed and indicated the convention hall with a sweep of one hand. "Ninety percent of the people here are collectors," he said. "Maybe your Jonas friend is here too."

Hayes was not quite following. "These people collect...?" he enticed.

"Comics," Skinny explained. "That and toys and those little tiny figurines, and – well – you name it, right?"

"You ever hear of anyone who collected costume props?" Hayes asked, recalling the terminology that the millionaire collector had used.

Skinny looked at Hayes uncertainly. "Like movie stuff?"

"No, like... um, say Rattenfanger's rat pipe got picked up," Hayes said, "something like that?"

Skinny shot Hayes an odd look and then began to chuckle. "You! Seriously, you totally had me," he said, blushing. "Rattenfanger's rat pipe! That's too rich."

Skinny stood up to help someone else who had entered the cosplay area dressed as Hunter, and Hayes went back to his repair.

The more time Hayes spent here, the more uncertain he felt. He needed to get some air.

41

Hayes located an exit from the convention center and, much to his surprise, found himself in the familiar surroundings of Seventh Avenue outside Madison Square Garden. It was warm, like spring, and he was maybe a half mile from where Melanie had died.

The sky above was clouded a silvery gray as the afternoon faded.

Hayes stopped on the sidewalk outside the convention center and breathed deeply, taking in his surroundings. He felt like he was going to drop, and he leaned heavily against a rail there and concentrated on trying not to fall. His eyes still ached and his head pounded, like he was suffering from a migraine.

The street was busy with afternoon traffic, the usual New York mélange of yellow cabs swapping places with delivery trucks and private cars as if they were playing some colossal game of Tetris. It didn't just look familiar, it smelled familiar too, the way New York always smelled, that faint underlying odor of exhaust mixed with street food.

Stumbling out of the path of pedestrians, Hayes found a nook by the convention building and tried to still his racing mind. Everything he knew was a fiction. At least, that's how it seemed. Somehow, that blast from Captain Light had opened a rift in reality and sent him here, to a world where Captain Light and the other costumes existed only within the brightly colored pages of comic magazines. That was weird enough, but seeing the way that he was portrayed – or Haze, as he had been called – within that one comic book as just another costumed villain had been utterly disorientating. Hayes considered that, trying to work out why he had been so unsettled. Was it the thought that his whole life had become a part of someone else's entertainment, like he was an actor on stage playing a part? Or was it something else, the way that he had unwittingly become the villain in someone else's story? Because he had not intended to be a villain. He had wanted only to find a way to ground Captain Light long enough to find out who was behind the great scheme of costume battles, who set the unseen fight card.

Set the fight card *and* decided who would win, Hayes told himself, as he thought it through. Now he had found who was behind all of this, who was orchestrating the constant stream of costumed battles that loomed large in the news. It was people like Langdon and Perks, and that editor Mags Crewe and the Kelly woman and the professor-type guy, probably others. Like the storytellers and balladeers of old, these people were bringing the stories to life for other people's entertainment.

And in the entertainment world, Hayes was a bad guy.

"Shit," Hayes muttered. A father with two kids in matching Damocles shirts glared at him as they passed on the sidewalk.

Hayes pushed off from the wall and fell, sinking to the ground as his legs gave out. Dad with the twin Damocles fans glanced back and said something to his kids about "the drunken man" before hurrying away.

Hayes' head felt tight, like the skin was contracting, and his sense of balance was about where it had been when he had done his first *High Altitude, Low Opening* jump above some overgrown corner of Bolivia.

He pushed himself up on one knee and held the wall to his right, breathing slowly through his nose. *Calm down*, he told himself.

Gradually, the sounds and smells of the city reasserted themselves the way he knew them, and Hayes felt like he could stand again. He pulled himself up, took several more deep breaths, then walked back to the convention center entrance, passing through one of the vast sets of doors. When he reached the lobby, a twenty-something woman with dyed streaks in her hair and a tablet computer in her hand walked over to him and smiled.

"May I see your entry pass?" she asked, bright eyed and friendly.

Hayes' mind raced. "I just left here five minutes ago," he said. "Stepped out for some air."

"I'm so, so sorry," the woman told him as if she was pleading, "but no pass, no re-entry. If you booked online I can take you over to registration and they may be able to issue another pass. How many days were you here for?" As she spoke, she was already tapping something into her tablet screen.

Hayes looked at her and at the lobby area with its steady flow of fans and costume wearers. "You know what – this was my last day," he explained apologetically. "I've seen enough, no point worrying about the pass. I'll get going and grab an early dinner."

"All right, if you're sure that's okay," the woman said. "I'm really sorry." She stretched out the word *really* like it had a too many Ls in it. It seemed like she genuinely wanted to help Hayes find his mythical convention pass.

"I'll be fine," Hayes assured her as he turned and headed back for the street.

So, what now? Hayes wondered. He was sitting on a bench in the concourse of Pennsylvania Station, just along the block from the convention center. The concourse was a huge space, busy with commuters, and framed with brightly-lit stores.

Hayes reset his watch by the clock on the wall, noting it was coming up to 5.30pm. The commuter rush was building, turning the whole station into movement like a rushing river. The movement was good, it meant that no one stopped long enough to bother Hayes.

He sat watching the crowds for a few minutes, feeling overwhelmed, feeling scared. There was so much going on, so many moving parts to what he could see, people going in all directions, store displays beaming brightly, conversations firing back and forth from a hundred people on a hundred phones, tapping and chatting and updating their feeds, unknowingly turning their own lives into entertainment with every status update. He felt like a dancer caught up in a spin, needing to spot so that he wouldn't keel over.

Hayes reached into the bag of stuff he had bought and drew out one of the trade collections of the *Eternal Flame* comic book. It was the one with Dread-0 on the cover. He hunched over it on the bench, flicking through the pages until he located the story from the cover. It showed the very battle that Hayes had witnessed in Times Square between Dread-0 and Eternal Flame, brilliant colors and poses bringing the whole clash to life. There was Dread-0 swallowing up a bus as it blurted: "I am Dread-0! I shall repair all!" In the next frames, Eternal Flame was spying the scene from the air, before diving down to face the monstrous mechanism.

A speech balloon hovered above Eternal Flame as he landed, reading: "Meal time's over, Dread-0!"

"I am Dread-0," Dread-0 responded. "I must repair!"

Hayes mouthed the words that he remembered came next as he turned the page: "Then repair this…"

Eternal Flame was standing to one side of a double-page illustration, his hands joined together and firing a blast of brilliant energy at Dread-0! "Then repair this!" his speech balloon read.

Hayes smiled uncomfortably at his own recognition of events. Fictional events from a fictional world.

He had come in mid-story, so turned back several pages until he found the start. The story began with that photographer Hayes had spoken to, Benjamin Jermain, arriving in a yellow cab at a press conference along with the blonde reporter who dressed like she was going to band camp. Jermain was flustered, expressing his desire not to let his boss down again or he wouldn't be able to pay his rent. The reporter – who, according to a narrative caption, had the unlikely name of Gemma Stone – was less than sympathetic, repeatedly calling Jermain a loser.

Inside, it seemed, the press conference was already in progress. An Albert Einstein-a-like was extolling the benefits of the "Digital Repair Enabling and Access Device (number zero) – or Dread-0," as he called it, in keeping Earth's artificial satellites operational long past their initial lifespan.

Hayes turned the page, saw another scientist working behind the scenes. This man had a hatchet face and referred to something called SCAR, a handy footnote for which helpfully explained that the acronym stood for the *Scientific Commune for Advanced Research*. It seemed the SCAR guy was in the act of sabotaging Dread-0, and a page later the tiny mechanical unit, which was about the size of a trash can at this point, burst from its housing and crashed through the wall of the building, much to the surprise of the audience of press people.

That same page, Ben Jermain swiftly ditched Gemma Stone and slipped into an empty lab where he removed his press pass – turn page – before transforming his whole body into the glowing form of Eternal Flame.

"Ben Jermain is... Eternal Flame?!" Hayes muttered, incredulous.

It was crazy. He had spoken to the guy, bought him coffee. Ben Jermain was some slacker kid who lived in a one-room apartment in Harlem where he could barely pay the rent. But so, too, was this guy on the page.

Hayes leafed through several pages that seemed to deal with an unrelated aspect of the story about a young girl in a wheelchair. Then the story of Dread-0 picked up again as the mechanical construction reached the center of New York. Dread-0 was larger by now, and panel after panel showed it swallowing up metal objects to add to its mass. By page ten of the story, it was charging outside the offices of the *Daily Echo*, smashing the newsstand there into shrapnel.

Hayes felt a chill run down his spine. The story was playing out the exact way he remembered it, just like the *Key to the City*

Ceremony with Captain Light. There was the mail truck being cut in half by the insatiable Dread-0, and then it barreled ahead towards Times Square and the pages where Hayes had begun reading. Hayes turned back, studying the sheared mail truck scene more closely. He could not see himself there, not distinctly. Instead, the monstrous Dread-0 thundered towards the reader as the mail truck was ripped apart and its driver leapt aside.

But there was a figure on page, hooded like him, and glimpsed only in the shadows of the buildings. In the static image of the comic book panel, the indistinct figure seemed to be running behind Dread-0, towards the mailman. But what happened after never made it on page, that moment when Hayes had saved the mailman and lost his Glock. In reality the whole event had taken just a few brief seconds; on page it seemed to have fallen down the gaps between the panels, while the reader's focus remained on Dread-0's path of destruction.

Hayes turned from the comic and rubbed his eyes, massaging his temples. The events on the page looked almost real to him, more so than the happenings that were occurring around him in the station concourse. In comparison, the concourse events were like viewing something through smeared glass, and yet somehow too detailed and too busy to properly take in.

As Hayes watched, his mind drifting, he became conscious of a number of people carrying plastic bags with the red logo of the Comic Daze convention on them. It was after six, and the con was turning out, Hayes realized.

Hayes did not know anything about fan conventions, but he figured there were schedules and that they came to an end each evening so that the convention center could be set up again for the next day. Slipping the *Eternal Flame* book back into his bag, Hayes got to his feet, breathing deep against the wave of nausea that came with the movement. Then, slowly, he headed out of the station.

* * *

When he hit the street, Hayes came face to face with a veritable army of convention goers. Some were dressed in costume or the remains of costumes that had been partially swapped for street clothes – a cloak here, golden boots there, that kind of thing. Most looked normal.

He moved through the crowds, heading back along West 31st Street to Madison Square Garden's entrance on Seventh. He had come here by challenging Captain Light with the intent of finding out who was manipulating everything and why. Now he knew who, so he wanted to find out why. Why did these Philip Perks and Manny Langdons and all the others who created these scenarios put people like Hayes through such heartbreak? Why had Melanie had to die?

Hayes weaved through the approaching crowds like he was swimming against the current, a Navy SEAL swimming against the tide.

Streams of people were still coming out of the convention center, talking excitedly about what they had done and seen and bought, about the heroes they had seen there – both real and imaginary.

Hayes used a lights change to cross, and planted himself opposite the convention center doors on the far side of the street, where he could watch them. He stood with his shoulder pressed against the frame of a fire door, tamping down the waves of nausea that kept rising within him.

There were fans, hundreds and hundreds of them. Hayes scanned every face, looking for the telltale sign of the woman with the scarf and shades, or the guy with graying temples, or himself or Melanie or Ginnie. Hayes had always been good with faces. Every face was different. Every face was unique. And not one was a face he knew from all those hours of watching news footage on ViewTube.

Eventually, the torrent of people became a trickle, as the last of the conventioneers made their way to their hotels or headed home. Among them were a few staff members, including the woman who had spoken to Hayes in the lobby when he had tried to gain reentry. Hayes ducked his head, subtly covering his face, but she did not see him all the way across the wide avenue.

He waited forty-five minutes after the flood, and there were still a few people dripping from the doors as the sun set. There were people arriving now too, cleaning staff come to tidy things up for the next day's events. Finally, Manny Langdon came striding down the steps talking animatedly with Philip Perks. Langdon had the big leather folder swinging from his left hand. They were among a group of a half dozen people who also included the polka dot dress editor, Mags Crewe, and the college professor-type who wrote the *Hunter* comic book. Hayes watched as a few fans hurried over to them with comic books to sign, the last stragglers of the day. Langdon seemed gracious as he scrawled his name on a fan's convention booklet.

Hayes watched the group, conscious of the weight of the Glock in its shoulder holster, wondering what it was he was going to do. The words came back from the sermon he had heard that Sunday in Queens, in the church named for St Benedict:

… the creator in all things…

The power and the glory…

… forever and ever…

He was looking now at the creator in all things, a few ordinary men whose omniscient tools were keyboards and pencils and pens. The power and the glory was theirs to bestow, theirs to enjoy. Forever and ever.

The group turned down Seventh into West 33rd Street, and Hayes followed, determined now to find the truth. He suspected that things were going to get ugly, but then, truth was ugly too. The ugliest.

42

The group of comics creators settled in a nearby bar that served buffalo wings and fries, and had three different shows playing on TVs located on the walls.

Hayes followed them and ordered a soft drink when he caught the attention of the waitress. His stomach was rumbling, too – how long had it been since he had eaten? – but he did not eat before an op, that had always been his way. He would keep going on whatever fuel he had stored in his muscles, driven on by the need inside, until he had seen things through to the end.

His vision was messy, the edges fuzzed like he was looking down a tube, and his balance felt off. Maybe those were the effects of not eating, Hayes thought, but still he decided not to eat yet. Not until the mission was complete.

Hayes found a seat at a side table designed for two, from where he could watch the comic book group as they ordered food and chatted, laughing and exchanging work and ideas. Langdon produced pages of original artwork from the leather folder he carried with him, as did another guy at the table who had a similar folder. The pages went around the table of eight, treated with a kind of awed reverence.

The *Hunter* guy was a lot like his character, Hayes noticed with knowing irony, older than the others and keeping everyone else at arm's length because of it. *How much of what a writer writes reveals who they are?* Hayes wondered. Had Captain Light let Melanie die because Phil Perks and Manny Langdon wanted her dead?

Food came, and more beers. Hayes got a refill on his drink, watching the television screens on the wall, watching the group as they ate. The *Hunter* guy drank like prohibition had just been revoked.

After close to an hour, one of the women got up from her seat and made for the restroom, and editor Mags Crewe joined her. Some guy that Hayes did not know went next and when he came back to the table he grabbed his bag and left with one of the women, saying something about having a train to catch.

Hayes watched for another hour, keeping tabs on the routines of who left the table and when. There was a pattern in all things, Hayes knew, even the seemingly random schedule of who went when to the restroom.

Finally, confident he had the patterns down, Hayes left his table and headed for the men's restroom alone, carrying with him the bag of comic books that he had purchased at the convention.

There was another guy in the restroom. Hayes entered just as he finished up and headed out. Hayes checked the stalls, confirming that each one was empty. Then he waited by the three basins that lined one wall, checking that he could watch the door in the mirror there, and propped the bag of comics upright where the counter met the wall.

Hayes looked at himself in the mirror. He looked tired, and the lights on the mirror seemed faded to him, like the bulbs were of low wattage or perhaps about to fail. Hayes was still feeling woozy, and he clung to the solidity of the marble counter like a shipwrecked man clinging to a hunk of driftwood.

The door swung open less than a minute after, accompanied by the hubbub noise from the bar. Hayes was on edge. He watched, eyes flicking up to the mirror to see the man enter. It was nobody, no one he knew anyway.

The stranger did his business, washed his hands with a minimal effort, belched and headed for the door. He had acknowledged Hayes with a nod, but had not said anything, and if he found it strange that Hayes was ostensibly washing his hands the whole time, he did not comment.

The next person to enter was Philip Perks, and he was followed ten seconds later by Manny Langdon.

"Some day, huh?" Langdon said as he took up a position at the urinal where Perks stood.

Perks nodded, but did not look up. "Way too much beer," he bemoaned as he urinated.

Hayes stepped away from the basin, and moved silently until his back was to the exit door. He pushed his foot against it, holding it shut with his heel, preventing anyone else from coming in.

Langdon finished first, then made his way to the line of basins, followed by Perks a few seconds later. Hayes stepped away from the door and, in two easy strides, was behind Perks, shoving him aside.

"What the–?" Perks began, as he almost doubled over the counter top. Hayes had judged his attack carefully, putting enough force into it to surprise Perks but not to really hurt him. Hurt could come later.

Langdon was turning in surprise, his reactions slowed by alcohol. He looked surprised and scared and like he was going to start laughing. "What's going on, man?" he burbled.

Hayes glared at him. "Who am I?"

Langdon wouldn't meet his eyes. "Phil, you okay?"

Perks groaned. "Yeah," he said.

"Answer my question," Hayes growled, taking a step forward. "Who am I?"

Langdon shook his head uncertainly. "I don't know, man."

"Look," Perks mumbled, rising from where he had struck the basin counter, "if it's money you want–"

"I don't want money," Hayes said. "I want to know why you killed my wife."

"What the what...?! I don't know what you're talking about," Perks said. "Manny?"

"I didn't kill anyone, buddy," Manny Langdon said. "Seriously. Seriously. I think you have us confused with someone else."

Hayes pulled down the zipper of his sweatshirt enough to remove his Glock from its holster.

"Whoa, time out," Perks said, backing away into the corner of the restroom beside where Langdon stood.

Langdon had gone as pale as the paper he drew on.

"Tell me who I am," Hayes said, raising the gun until it covered the two men.

"I don't know," Perks and Langdon squeaked in frightened unison.

Hayes caught a glimpse of himself in the mirror at that moment, and realized his error. He reached behind him with his free hand and pulled up the hood of his sweatshirt until his face was almost hidden in the shadow of the hood. "Yes, you do," he said, his eyes glinting from beneath the dark folds of the hood.

Langdon was beginning to realize, though he clearly had not processed what his eyes were trying to tell him yet. Perks looked bemused, like he was dealing with a madman; perhaps he was.

"You call me Haze," Hayes said.

"Shit," Langdon said, shaking his head. "This is... shit, it's unreal."

Perks stepped forward, showing more bravery than Hayes had given him credit for as he put himself in the line of fire before his collaborator. "Look, this is some impressive method cosplay you have going on here," he said, "and you totally, totally got us. Are we cool now?"

Hayes fixed Perks with a no-nonsense look, and gestured with the gun. "Tell me why she had to die," he said.

Emboldened by alcohol and his suspicion that Hayes was pulling some kind of costumed prank, Perks spoke up again. "Who had to die? I don't follow. Do you, Manny?"

"I don't even get what's happening," Langdon admitted. "This guy is shitting us, right?"

Hayes looked at the fear and confusion in the men's faces and realized he had approached this all wrong. He had known they were just civilians, ordinary people, and yet he had approached them in the same manner he had approached Splatter and Charm Offensive and even Captain Light, like they were costumes who would use weapons and powers and super-tricks to try to do him over. Slowly, his eyes never leaving the two men, Hayes lowered the pistol.

"That's good, friend," Perks encouraged. "Let's just put that little prop away."

Hayes did not put the gun away. He simply held it loosely in his hand at his side as he spoke to Perks and Langdon.

"You are the creators," Hayes began, "of a comic book concerning Captain Light."

"Well, we didn't actually 'create' him," Perks corrected. "That was two guys back in the sixties."

"But you tell his stories," Hayes confirmed, a tinge of uncertainty suddenly crossing his thoughts, "don't you?"

"Yes," Perks said, and Langdon nodded, clearly terrified.

"Then you know me," Hayes said. The two comic book creators said nothing. "I'm the person you call Haze."

"You can't be," Langdon said, finally finding his voice. "Sure, you look like my drawing maybe but Haze wasn't, like, based on you."

"Then where did he come from?" Hayes asked, his tone commanding.

At that moment, the door to the restroom swung open and a guy in a sports jacket with leather patches at the elbows came in to use one of the stalls. Hayes effortlessly palmed the Glock, hiding it against his side so that it could not be seen. The two comic book men watched, uncertain what to do now.

"Do you want to finish this discussion somewhere a little less…" Perks looked around, "restroomy?"

Hayes nodded once. "Where do you suggest?"

"We're both staying at the Merryard up the street," Perks

suggested. "It's a block away. You want to maybe go there? Without your little friend," and he indicated the palmed Glock with an incline of his head.

"Without my little friend," Hayes agreed with a nod. "When? Now?"

"No time like the present, big guy," Perks said with more enthusiasm than he felt.

Hayes reached across the basins and grabbed the bag of comics he had purchased. He figured he might need them before he got everything straight.

Perks was as good as his word. He and Langdon made their excuses from the table of their cohorts, threw in a few bills to cover the food and the drinks, then met with Hayes outside the bar after about ten minutes. Langdon had the flat leather case with him which Hayes had noticed earlier, and he pointed to it.

"What do you keep in there?" he asked.

"Oh, it's just some pages for my dealer," Langdon said.

"Your dealer?" Hayes said uncertainly. "You mean drugs?"

"No, man," Langdon said very rapidly. "Art, man. My art dealer. I sell pages sometimes, brings in a little extra income after the issue's gone to press."

"Lucky you," Perks groused as the trio walked down West 33rd Street. "No one ever wants to buy old scripts."

"Why would they?" Langdon teased him. "You could print off ten more the moment you sold them, man."

The two men seemed more at ease now that they were out of the confines of the restroom and that Hayes had put away his gun. Sometimes, Hayes reminded himself, trust is better than intimidation for getting information. With these guys right now, he probably had mostly intimidation, but at least they were talking, even if it was hard to make sense of all that they said.

The mismatched group walked a block to the Merryard Hotel, where both Perks and Langdon had rented rooms.

"I guess you might as well come up," Perks said to Hayes as they called for the elevator.

"I'm on five," Langdon said, brows furrowed.

"No, let's go to me on twelve," Perks told him, pressing the floor button. "Better view."

They rose through the building until they reached the twelfth story.

Hayes looked out the window at the "better view" from the twelfth-floor room. He found the feeling to be disconcerting. This high up he could see nighttime New York spread out before him, but the familiar Nexus Range with its illuminating beacon of force which should be lighting up the sky was missing.

"How do you people know you're safe?" Hayes asked, without really thinking.

"What?" Philip Perks asked. He was pouring from a can of diet soda he had purchased from a machine in the hallway.

Hayes tapped the glass of the window. "There's no beacon," he said, "no Nexus Range."

Manny Langdon was sitting on a chair propped against the far wall by the bathroom door, with his portfolio resting against the wall beside him. He laughed. "That's Phil's gig," he said. "I don't illustrate the Rangers."

"But you… write their stories," Hayes said, addressing Perks.

"Yeah," Perks confirmed, "for the past three years. You remember when Morgana Le Fey changed New York into a kind of fifth century fiefdom? That was me."

"I shot some elves," Hayes said, nodding to himself.

Perks looked at Hayes with concern, trying to assess him, as though he could read the man's thoughts from a balloon that floated unseen above his head. "Don't take this wrong, my friend, but you are possibly the scariest man I have ever encountered."

"They were foot-soldiers," Hayes said. "One looked like my wife."

Langdon nervously ran a hand through his long hair. "I don't think I read that issue," he said.

"They're just stories," Hayes said, "aren't they? Everything I know – just fables."

"Stories," Perks agreed. "If I've understood what you've told us. You're the Haze and somehow you came out of a comic book and landed here, in New York."

"At the Comic Daze Book Convention," Hayes clarified.

Langdon laughed uncomfortably. "This is whacko," he said. "How did you get here? From a comic? What, you stepped out of some origami thing and–"

"Captain Light sent me here," Hayes said. "Don't ask me how it happened, I set a counter-wave in motion against his spectral scream and I demanded to know who was behind everything because I wanted to be shown that." Hayes reached into the bag of comics he had brought with him, drawing out the issue of *Captain Light* entitled "The Key to… Death". He handed it to Perks, and Langdon got up from his seat and came over to see.

"I remember this, yeah," Langdon said.

Perks opened the comic, skimming over the pages. He made a double take as he looked at the hooded figure of Hayes in the room and compared it to the Haze on page. "It could be him, all right," he muttered, speaking to himself. He reached the final pages. "And Cap opens a dimensional gateway with his spectral scream and – whammo – *you're* shoved through."

"I'm shoved through," Hayes agreed.

"What's he holding, Manny?" Perks asked. "You remember drawing this?"

"That book?" Langdon said. "It's his keepsake. I have the art for these pages with me."

"Let's take a look," Perks said, intrigued now.

"I can tell you what it was," Hayes reminded them both. "It's my wedding album."

"That's right. You said you were married," Langdon said. Then he looked at Perks with evident confusion. "He's married, right?"

Perks looked similarly confused. "The back story on Haze was intentionally hazy," he said. "That was the whole premise. Hazy guy, no real features, he could be anyone under that hood."

"My name is Hayes," Hayes said.

"Yeah," Perks said, "we know that."

"No, not Haze – *Hayes*," Hayes said, and spelled it out: "H-A-Y-E-S. Jon Hayes."

"And you're married," Perks said.

"Any kids?" Langdon asked.

"Yes... no," Hayes said. "Our daughter never got born. My wife was pregnant when she died."

"Shit, that's rough, man," Langdon said, producing the relevant pages of artwork from his folder. He had the final three pages from the Captain Light issue, ready to sell on to his art dealer contact. They were stark black ink on white, the color waiting to be added later to separate computer files.

"Where did you send me," Hayes asked, "when this dimensional gateway opened?"

Perks looked around the room uncomfortably. "We didn't really send you anywhere," he said. "When Captain Light defeats a bad guy – I'm sorry, but you are –"

Hayes nodded in acknowledgement.

"– well, we put that character on ice, as it were," Perks explained. "They get stuck in prison or sent to another dimension for a while, and if the readers like them then we bring that character back. No one ever really dies or disappears in these stories. The same bad guys have been fighting Captain Light for, like, fifty years now."

"And me?" Hayes asked.

"Well, you're new," Perks explained. "We like to mix things up. You can't have Cap fighting with Jade Shade every issue, it would just get stale."

"Then what's my back story?" Hayes asked, finally beginning to understand.

"You don't have one yet," Perks said. "You're a mystery. We like doing that, it gives us something to reveal later when a character

comes back. No point showing all your cards right away, right? I'm
sorry, I shouldn't have said that. This is your life."

"I have a life," Hayes told him, "and a story, and motivations.
Just like all these other people in these pages." He upended the
bag of comics, and the two volumes of *Eternal Flame* dropped onto
the plush carpeted floor of the hotel suite.

"You don't even have a face, man," Langdon said, shaking
his head. "Shadows in a hood, that's all you were drawn to be.
Shadows in a hood."

Hayes turned to look at his reflection in the darkness of the
window, overlaid on the view of a New York that had never known
the Rangers. Sure enough, his face was nothing but shadows in a
hood, just the way Langdon had described.

43

"Who are the people who die?" Hayes asked, still looking at his hooded reflection in the hotel room's window.

"What, like Eternal Flame?" Perks asked. "Um… I didn't write that story."

"I think maybe Jake Rusch did that one," Langdon added, trying to be helpful.

"Not Eternal Flame," Hayes said grimly. "My wife. Melanie. Who are the people in the crowds? Who are the people who die? How do you choose them?"

"They're just faces," Langdon answered.

Perks was shaking his head, and Hayes watched the movement in the window's reflection. "You don't want to hear this, Jon," the writer said, "but they're only there to add drama, raise the stakes. Make it real. You know?"

"So, to you," Hayes said, turning to face the two men, "she was nobody."

Both men looked uncomfortable. Langdon finally said: "I would have drawn her as well as I could."

Perks nodded in support. "How is it that she died?" he asked Hayes.

"Sixth Avenue. Jade Shade dropped a helicopter on her," Hayes said.

"I remember drawing that," Langdon said. "Shade threw the chopper at Captain Light and it missed and hit the street."

"It didn't miss," Perks said with certainty. "Captain Light would have stopped it if it had missed him. It hit him, knocked him out of the sky before it fell. The news crew died, which all led into that story we did where the press try to make out Cap is negligent and it all goes to trial. You remember?"

"Yeah," Langdon said, "and the prosecuting lawyer was Griff Zephyr."

"AKA the Red Griffin," Perks added.

Hayes was shaking his head. "I missed all of that," he said.

"I'm sorry, man," Langdon said. "If what you're saying is true… if you really believe you're this Haze guy from our comic, then whatever we did was nothing personal. It's just a story."

Hayes glared at Langdon down the fuzzy tunnel of his vision. "I'm not a story," he said.

Perks put down the glass he had been drinking from. "I think what Jon here says is true," he said. "It sounds crazy, but it makes perfect logical sense in the Obliverse, with comic book logic. Captain Light opened a dimensional portal which sent Jon here to our world, which would count as another dimension. That's not how I wrote it – we never really said where you went, Jon – but there's gotta be some crazy super-science reason in his world that made it happen."

Hayes shook his head as he tried to make sense of it all. His eyes were tired and the tunnel he felt like he was looking through was closing in, creating a curtain of darkness at the edges of his vision. "What is super-science?" he asked.

"It's what you guys in the Obliverse think of as science," Perks explained. "Like, for example, Jade Shade's cloak – it's a sentient alien creature that somehow bonded with her psyche, right?"

"That's what they say," Hayes confirmed.

"You see, that's just BS," Perks told him. "It's 'super-science', comic books are full of it, and so are movies and TV shows. It's that kind of hand-waving that sounds cool but isn't really science at all, because it doesn't work, you couldn't recreate it in a lab."

"What if you had another alien cloak?" Hayes asked.

"The alien cloak doesn't exist," Perks said. "That's the point. None of this stuff exists. It's all made up. And, if you think about it, if it did really exist, even in your world by your rules, everyone should have super-powers by now. Because there's not just one guy using an innovation like the wheel or a cell phone, sooner or later everyone gets the technology. But these unique super-powers only ever seem to happen to one guy."

"Or one woman," Langdon added.

Hayes couldn't make sense of it. To him, his world made perfect sense, followed clear rules, everything fitted together. There were no holes in the logic, even when someone like Morgana Le Fey or Dominax invaded the planet they did it in a way that seemed to be intelligible. At least, it did to him.

"Have you heard of Holly Belle?" Hayes asked, wondering if Perks and Langdon knew the same history as he did.

"Holly Belle," Perks mused, and a smile crossed his lips. "*Uncle Sam's Fightin' Glamor Gal!* Oh yeah, I spent a whole summer when I was eleven trying to track down her old comics."

"Is she real?" Hayes asked.

Perks shook his head. "She's a comic character, just like… well, you, I guess."

"Then what happened to her?" Hayes asked. "In my world she died."

"*Holly Belle* comics sold like gangbusters in the war," Perks began, "World War Two, I mean. But times change, markets change. By the fifties those patriotic heroes were looking tired, and the whole hero boom was played out for a while, so they revamped her title as a romance comic."

"What does that mean?" Hayes asked, shaking his head.

"It means she wasn't a costumed hero anymore," Perks explained. "Now she was just a civilian, falling in love with her little gang of friends around her who all worked at the same movie studio. The comic was cancelled in, I dunno, 1950-something. Then in *The Number Men* a few years ago, they brought her back in a flashback where it was revealed she got killed while she was still crime-fighting. Shot. It was heartbreaking. I convinced my wife that we set an extra place for her at dinner after I'd read that issue."

"But you said her stories became a romance comic," Hayes queried.

"The Number Men story ignored that," Perks told him. "It's called retroactive continuity, no one reading today would have read those comics, pretty much, so sometimes it's easier to simply ignore them. So Holly Belle died in 1961, but we only found out three years ago."

"Then you can retroactively save my wife," Hayes deduced, beginning to comprehend.

"No," Perks said slowly. "We'd need a reason – a story reason – to do that."

Hayes looked around the room, holding his hands out. "*This* is the story," he said.

Langdon looked at Perks but the writer was shaking his head. "She was just a bystander," he said. "We did the Red Griffin story. That was the helicopter story. Your wife wasn't in it."

Hayes nodded solemnly. "I think I understand," he said. "I'm trying to." You could petition your creator to change the world for you, but he didn't have to do it. And maybe if he did, then the whole world would fall apart.

Hayes was about to say something further, but suddenly he felt himself losing his balance. He staggered forward, trying to reach the bed for support, but keeled over before he could get there. He dropped to the floor with a thud.

"What the hell?" Langdon said, taking a step back from where Hayes had fallen.

Perks called for Hayes, but the man did not answer.

"He dead?" Langdon asked.

"No, he either fell asleep or he's blacked out," Perks stated, rising from his seat. He went over to check on Hayes, confirming what he thought – "Unconscious."

"We should call a cop," said Langdon. "He has a gun. He threatened us."

Perks looked uncertain, like he was thinking about something else. "We let him in voluntarily," he mused.

"Under duress!" Langdon insisted, but then he saw that look on his creative partner's face. "You actually believe him, don't you? I thought you were humoring him, but don't tell me that you actually believe this bullshit about his being Haze come fresh out of our effing comic? That's impossible."

"At first, I was – humoring him, that is," Perks said. "But you have to admit he presents a fascinating possibility."

"Man, you sound like Mister Spock," Langdon said, with a curse.

Deep in thought, Perks looked back to Hayes on the floor by the bed. "If it is true, what he says, then I don't think he's stable here," Perks speculated. "That's why he's blacked out."

Hayes began to stir. He groaned unintelligibly and tried to sit up, but he seemed to be having trouble with his coordination.

Kneeling at his side, Perks spoke to him gently. "It's okay, don't rush yourself. You fell."

"I've been doing that a lot," Hayes said with an embarrassed smile, "ever since I got here." He pushed himself up and, with Perks' help, sat on the floor with his back leaning against the bed, his legs sprawled out before him.

As Perks helped their guest, Langdon excused himself and disappeared into the bathroom.

"You're not made for our world," Perks told Hayes. "Your world is two-dimensional."

Hayes shook his head, groaned at the nausea it triggered, and stopped doing that. "My world is as real as yours. Brighter, more vibrant maybe, but the same."

"You notice any differences?" Perks asked.

"Details," Hayes said. "Like sometimes the focus is too sharp, and... it's hard to explain it. It's just not quite right."

"I think we need to get you back, or you'll die," Perks told him.

"Because I'm just a story," Hayes said with a note of challenge to his tone.

"Because this isn't your world," Perks said.

Langdon reappeared from the bathroom, putting his cell phone back into his pocket. "Hey," he said, calling Perks over.

Perks glanced at Hayes then got up and crossed the room to where Langdon was standing. "What is it?" he asked.

"Hotel security are on their way," Langdon told Perks in a whisper.

Perks glared at him, shaking his head. "We don't need them," he hissed.

"Yeah, we do," Langdon told him quietly. "This guy could go nuts at any time. Any time."

Slumped by the bed, Hayes heard the men mumbling behind him. "You talking about me?" he asked.

Perks shot a glare at Langdon before returning to where Hayes could see him. "Jon, my friend, we need to get you home. We don't have much time."

"Why would I want to go back?" Hayes asked. "Melanie's dead and, with all your infinite power, you won't bring her back for me."

"I just tell stories," Perks said gently. "I don't save lives."

"But you could," Hayes insisted.

Perks shook his head. "Go home," he told Hayes. "You still have stories waiting for you."

From somewhere beneath the hood, Hayes met Perks' gaze. "Will they be good stories?" he asked.

"No," Perks told him. "Not for you. But I think you know that."

Hayes bowed his heavy, hooded head. "I think that I do," he said with resignation.

There came a knock at the door at that moment, and Langdon strode across the room towards it. From the far side of the door came a man's voice. "Someone here called hotel security?" he asked through the door.

Perks hissed across the room to Langdon where he was in the abbreviated corridor, reaching to open the door. "We don't need them," he said.

Langdon looked like he wanted to argue, bit down on the words, and made a gesture with his hands as though to say, "to hell with it". Then he opened the door.

The hushed voice of the security man came from the corridor.

"Reception got a call, room 1218," he said. "May I help you with something, sir?"

Langdon said nothing for about five seconds, then finally shook his head. "False alarm," he said, wearily.

The security man held the door. "Perhaps you'd like me to check the room, sir?" he said in a way that made it not so much a question as an order.

Perks looked up, calling to Langdon. "Sure, let him in," he said, and he reached forward and pulled Hayes' hood back from his face before rising to his feet.

As the security guard came in, Perks introduced himself and explained that this was actually his room. "My friend there fell over and Manny here panicked." He looked at Langdon. "He's a worrier."

"I'm just cautious," Langdon explained as if trying to save face.

The security man, a big bruiser in a too-tight shirt and a tie whose narrow width made his chest seem all the wider, nodded uncertainly. "Uh huh. And you're sure everything is all right here?" he asked, looking down at Hayes where the ex-SEAL was sprawled by the bed.

"Yeah, we're fine," Perks insisted.

The security man did not seem convinced. He took a couple of steps closer to Hayes and peered at him. "And you, sir? Are you okay?"

Hayes smiled and nodded. "Cramp," he said. "It's an old injury I got in the service, plays up sometimes."

This seemed to satisfy the hotel security man, and, after a cursory check of the windows and bathroom, finally he left.

"That is one big, big man," Langdon said, laughing uncomfortably.

Perks went back to where Hayes was sitting, looking him in the face. Hayes looked pale. "Manny," he called, "you have your pens with you, right?"

"Always," Langdon responded. Immediately, he was at his portfolio case, the one that Hayes had somehow fallen out of, reaching for the side pocket where he kept pencils, an eraser, a

ruler and several grades of marker pen. He popped them onto
the chair and reached for a large, ledger-sized pad of blank paper.
"What do you have in mind, Phil?"

"I think our friend Haze here," Perks said, looking at Hayes,
"crossed dimensions but got pulled back and reabsorbed by his
own world."

Langdon took up a spot on the chair, leaning the pad on its
arm. "This is going to be scrappy," he said apologetically, pencil in
hand, "but I can tidy it up at ink stage, okay? So, how do I show
'reabsorbed into his own world'?"

Perks thought, watching as Hayes lay there, his head wavering
as though it had become too heavy for his neck. "Sequential panels,
beginning in the exact same spot where issue 171 ended when the
portal closed," he said. "It's – what issue are we on? 177? Let's say
it's three months later. It's midnight, and the moon is high in the
sky. Central Park is empty, trees silhouetted against the darkened
sky, Belvedere Castle painted white by streaks of moonlight."

Langdon began to draw, starting with the faint construction
lines that would inform the illustration.

"The rift reopens, but it's sickly now," Perks continued, "like it's
become infected."

Langdon worked on the breakdowns for the page, firming up
the sequence, adding the frames.

"And then Haze," Perks said, pulling Hayes' hood back up over
his head, "hood up, comes tumbling out of the rift between worlds,
crashing to the grass by Belvedere Castle."

Langdon worked quickly, putting the basic shapes together to
show Haze tumbling from the hole in space.

"Where he falls, he's left a trail in space, a trail of nothingness,"
Perks said, glancing up at Langdon.

Langdon took out his eraser and rubbed out the background
immediately behind Haze's falling form on the page, leaving a
blank white line amidst his nighttime rendition of Central Park.

Perks looked back at Hayes, and saw the man was indistinct now,
his hooded face a blur – *a haze* – the way it had been represented

in the comic. "Haze is sprawled on the ground, fetal position, like he's just been born, only he's an adult.

"And then let's pull back from the scene so we see cops closing in as they check on the reopening of the rift –"

Langdon sketched the figures into place, working fast, adding scribbles of detail and shadows that seemed to bring the whole thing to life.

Perks watched Hayes become increasingly indistinct before his very eyes, watched as a miracle took place. "Then let's pull way back even further," he said, like his mouth was working on autopilot, "so that we see New York's skyline where it looms at the edge of Central Park."

Langdon brought out his ruler again, and worked swiftly to create three-point perspective for the buildings, marking the vanishing point that made the image trick the eye into believing it was real.

"And there's Captain Light, flying in from off panel, heading down at speed to investigate what's happening," Perks said. "Whoosh!"

Langdon had been working on the page for twenty minutes now. It was sketchy and the shadows had not been spotted yet, but it was looking like what Perks had described.

On the floor of the hotel room, beside the bed, a patch of carpet lay, empty apart from the sense that someone was still there, someone fading into the ether.

Perks looked at the last trace of Hayes as he faded away from the real world. "And then..." he said.

EPILOGUE

Hayes crashed down on the damp grass in the shadow of Belvedere Castle in Central Park, beneath a moonlit night sky. The grass smelled of green, the fragrance of vegetation. He was exhausted, his whole body aching where he had landed hard against the ground, like he had just been born again. He could hear sirens wailing in the distance, and there were urgent voices issuing commands as they got nearer.

"Stay where you are, sir," someone barked through the augmentation of a megaphone.

Hayes was aware of running feet now, and the sirens were getting closer and sounding more urgent the way multiple sirens always sound more urgent. It sounded like the whole of New York's finest were out in force tonight, descending on this very spot in the middle of Central Park.

"Don't move a muscle!" megaphone voice shouted from somewhere.

Hayes ignored the voice, pushing himself unsteadily up from the ground by hands and knees.

He could see the fairytale towers of Belvedere Castle up ahead, looming over him, painted in broad white streaks where the moonlight hit them.

"Hold your fire," someone was saying from over to the right. "Wait... wait..."

Hayes looked that way and saw a gaggle of police officers

clambering down the slope beside the castle, guns poised in their grips. They shuffled like a child's toy caterpillar, as if they were all joined together, rocking back and forth to get anywhere at all.

"Hands in the air," someone shouted from Hayes' left, and the command was repeated by another voice, and then the megaphone behind him, like a campfire song.

Then a woman's voice said something that carried right across Turtle Pond. "Hey, isn't that the Haze?"

"Hell yeah," her colleague confirmed. "That crazy psycho! What on Earth is he doing here?"

Surrounded on all sides, Hayes began to raise his empty hands, glancing right and left. It was then that he heard the sound of the air splitting, and a dazzling light flashed in the sky above him as though someone was letting off fireworks. He looked up, tilting his head to see the familiar trail of stars that sparkled in the air in Captain Light's wake.

The hero landed a dozen paces ahead of Hayes an instant later, placing himself between Hayes and the approaching police officers, his star trail burning to nothingness in the air above them like a cloud of firebugs.

"So, you finally got free, did you, Haze?" Captain Light said, hands on hips.

Hayes met Captain Light's stare with his own, his eyes glinting as he peered from the shadowy depths of his hood. "Looks like," he said.

"Tell me," Captain Light said with a flash of that genuine smile of his, "do you want this to go down easy, or do you want it to go down hard? It's your choice."

Hayes smiled too, within the masking shadows of the hood. "You know what –" he muttered, "let's give the people a show for their money!"

And then Hayes began to run at Captain Light, reaching into his sweatshirt and pulling loose the Glock from its holster.

Light was faster of course. He disarmed Hayes in just a few moves – but they were good moves, and Hayes knew that they must have made strong poses on the comic book page. It didn't matter that he lost, not when the show was so good.

And afterwards, Hayes was sedated. When he awoke, he was in a cell on Rikers Island, under strict psychiatric watch, pumped full of drugs to make him docile and keep a hold on his rage.

But Hayes knew now. Knew that he was the bad guy. And that, in stories like Captain Light's, bad guys lost.

Sometimes villains could redeem themselves. But not him, not today. Not for a while anyhow.

He figured that the cell probably looked normal from the outside, a reinforced door with a keycard reader like a hotel room. There was a covered hatch in the door, with a metal flap which came down to create a kind of shelf on which meals could be placed, and through which people could observe Hayes if they wanted. He didn't care. For them the cell was made of four walls and looked clean and modern, or maybe it looked sickly and unkempt like his supposed state of mind. To him, though, it had spaces in it that had not been filled in yet, spaces where the artist – maybe Langdon, maybe someone else who would take up Haze's story for their own comic, and pit him against a different hero for a month or two – had not yet finished the design. Maybe when an artist did, Hayes would find an escape tunnel right here, scraped into the wall, hidden behind a vent cover or a dodgy floor tile, or behind a poster he would never have noticed before that day.

Until then, Hayes would wait. Wait and plan, studying the patterns again, searching for the clues and the ways to reach out to the people who controlled everyone's lives.

It wasn't every moment of their lives that were being documented, Hayes understood now. Only those moments that had drama, those times when aliens invaded or banks got robbed, or when helicopters got thrown at heroes and flattened innocent bystanders like Melanie. Hayes would exist between those moments, plotting his revenge between panels, hidden away in the flutter of the turning pages. Waiting for revenge.

ANGRY ROBOT

We are Angry Robot

angryrobotbooks.com

Science Fiction, Fantasy and WTF?!

@angryrobotbooks

We are Angry Robot

angryrobotbooks.com

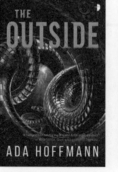

Science Fiction, Fantasy and WTF?!

@angryrobotbooks 🅾🐦 f

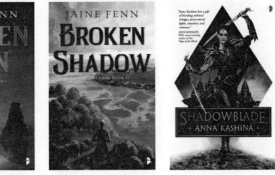

ABOUT THE AUTHOR

RIK HOSKIN is an award-winning author of novels, comic books, animation, video games, and audio plays. He won the Dragon Award for Best Graphic Novel for *White Sand I* in collaboration with Brandon Sanderson, and has also written comic books for Star Wars, Superman, Doctor Who, and many others. He has written almost 30 books, the majority under the pen name James Axler.